Georgia Stories

Also Edited by Ben Forkner

MODERN IRISH SHORT STORIES

A NEW BOOK OF
DUBLINERS

LOUISIANA STORIES

Also Edited by Ben Forkner and Patrick Samway, S.J.:

A MODERN SOUTHERN READER:
Major Stories, Drama, Poetry, Essays,
Interviews and Reminiscences
from the Twentieth-Century South
(Peachtree)

A NEW READER OF THE OLD SOUTH:
Major Stories, Tales, Slave Narratives,
Diaries, Essays, Travelogues,
Poetry and Songs: 1820–1920
(Peachtree)

STORIES OF THE MODERN SOUTH

STORIES OF THE OLD SOUTH

Georgia Stories

Major Georgia Short Fiction of the
Nineteenth and Twentieth Centuries

Edited with an Introduction by
Ben Forkner

PEACHTREE PUBLISHERS, LTD.
Atlanta

Published by
PEACHTREE PUBLISHERS, LTD.
494 Armour Circle, NE
Atlanta, Georgia 30324

Manufactured in the United States of America

Design by Candace J. Magee
Text composition by William P. Eiselstein

Library of Congress Cataloging-In-Publication Data

Forkner, Ben.
    Georgia Stories: Major Georgia Short Fiction of the Nineteenth
    and Twentieth Centuries / edited by Ben Forkner.
       p. cm.
    ISBN 1-56145-066-9 : $21.95. -- ISBN 1-56145-067-7 (pbk.) : $10.95.
    1. Short stories, American--Georgia. 2. Georgia--Fiction.
I. Forkner, Ben.
PS558.G4G43 1992
813'.01089758--dc20

For my mother

Contents

ACKNOWLEDGMENTS

First of all, a deep debt of love and gratitude to my immediate family: my grandfather, Judge Flem C. Dame, gentle Georgia scholar and hard-fighting friend of the poor; my grandmother, Lillian Hughes Dame, the little girl in white on the cover, author of *Sweetwater: Recollections of a Georgia Childhood*, and a brimming source of countless south Georgia stories; my mother, Olive Dame Peterson, the barefoot girl from Homerville to whom this book is lovingly dedicated; my stepfather, Pete Peterson; my brother John; my Uncle Brother; my Aunt Catharine and her two sons, Tommy and Charles (to me more brothers than cousins); my wife Nadine, who as usual read every line with an unerring eye; and my son Benjamin, who was always willing to practice his fastball when I got tired of sitting at the desk. Next a prolonged bow of reverence and recognition for a number of good friends who have never failed me in my requests for help: Patrick Samway; Barbara and Weldon Thornton; Patricia and John Paine; and Jerry Kennedy. A special word of thanks to my two editors at Peachtree, Laurie Edwards and Emily Wright; their literary skills and good nature have improved the book, and have made the working out of its problems a pleasure. Finally, I would like to thank my Uncle Tom Forkner of Atlanta, whose generous gift at the right time helped me defray a large share of the expenses required in putting together this collection.

INTRODUCTION

I MIGHT AS WELL CONFESS from the outset that along with all the other reasons for making this collection, I am probably obeying a sort of aboriginal cultural reflex. Both my mother and father, and their families, were native Georgians, and though I was born and raised in suburban Florida, I was never allowed to completely shake the sensation of having been displaced from a more authentic source. In my grandparents' stories of small-town rural Georgia, life was harder and heartier. There was more pain, but also more resistance to pain. The threats of sudden violence were constant: disease, accidents, wild animals, treacherous strangers. Death came in the form of lockjaw, cottonmouth moccasins, rabid dogs, and midnight murder. But apparently these could be overcome, given good friends, a steady faith, and a close family. Otherwise, of course, there would have been no one left to tell about it. Their lives contained more than hardship and suffering. In fact, they were rather well off and even prosperous compared to many of their neighbors. But in every way their Georgia was more fundamental than my Florida, closer to the earth and the seasons, and to the sad human history of the Old South.

Yet the talk of the past had far more humor than sadness, and the outstanding characters, always a bit larger than life, were remembered for strong stubborn qualities, outrageous or noble, ugly or fine. An independent spirit was the most notable quality a human being could possess, and since this was never quite enough, it helped if he also had a bitter biblical sense of his own unimportance and a good democratic dose of humorous self-mockery to sweeten the swallow. If for some reason he lacked the latter, members of the community could usually find a way of providing it for him, free of charge.

Posturing and deliberate deceit were publicly condemned, but an individual standing up alone on principle, no matter how eccentric, was not only tolerated but admired. The sudden flaring out of a fierce hidden will in an otherwise wholly familiar and predictable small world characterized most of the stories. They were the ones that could not be forgotten. As I remember them they were mainly momentary incidents intensified into a static photographic clarity; whatever complex pattern there may have been behind the image was suppressed in favor of the solitary vivid portrait. A small barefoot girl sitting on her front porch with her mother saw a Model T come by with two men in the front seat, and a woman in the back. Her mother told her: "There goes Sheriff Lee taking Miss Cora Sweat to Milledgeville." By Milledgeville she meant, of course, the state insane asylum. An hour later the Model T came back again in the opposite direction, this time with the woman driving and the two men in the back.

On another day the same girl was looking out the living-room window at one of her father's favorite bird-dogs in the front yard. This gentle dog all at once began to crazily whirl around in circles, his face terrorized by what was happening to him, a fit of madness striking secretly from within. Suddenly he stopped, turned, looked the girl straight in the eye, and leaped at her, crashing through the window into the house. Without faltering he ran up the stairs, jumped through another closed window, and fell with the broken glass flashing in the sun onto the porch roof below.

At times the shock of an independent gesture could be fixed in a single word. The girl's father took her to a cemetery, isolated like many rural cemeteries in the middle of a stand of old shade trees in a field. The father pointed to the two tombstones where his wife's grandparents were buried. The girl knew they had been savagely killed by tramps wielding axes. The tombstone had been put there by her grandfather and his brothers. Against every known dictate of community convention they had rejected the usual standardized epitaphs and had inscribed one word under the names on both stones: MURDERED. They had made sure that at least one foulness would not be disguised before God or man.

When I listened to all this then, as a boy in suburban Florida, I may have been displaced, but in thinking back about it now, I cannot pretend to have been wholly dispossessed, since most of the family discussions eventually circled back home to Homerville, in Clinch County, where many of my relatives continued to live, and since most of the voices I heard every day around the dinner table had been permanently tuned to all manner of shrewd and singing south Georgia modulations.

Thus, after twenty years in France, when I found myself turning to stories and novels set in Georgia, I could easily explain to myself that deeper regions than the intellect were being stirred. Had the fascination stopped at mere genealogical nostalgia, however—a risk that even non-Georgians, or for that matter, non-Southerners, are often helpless to avoid—I would have a poor claim and a poorer excuse for putting together this collection. Even an incurable anthologist would have to admit that. But together with all my rather uncertain attachments of the blood, I could also count on a long-standing professional interest in the short story, and in the whole question of Southern literature. I did not have to rely on my memories of the dinner table to convince myself that many of the qualities I admired most in the modern Southern short story—the piercing individual portraits, the forceful combination of earthy ironic intelligence and moral independence—were very often found in the best Georgia writers, and that these same writers had happened to write some of the most original and powerful short stories of the modern South.

Certainly no one needs a first-hand or even second-hand knowledge of Georgia to admire Flannery O'Connor, or any of the other well-known twentieth-century figures included in *Georgia Stories*. They are read, praised, and translated all over the world. Not too long ago I made a quick visit to a local bookshop in my current hometown of Angers and found all of Flannery O'Connor and most of Carson McCullers, Erskine Caldwell, Alice Walker, and Mary Hood translated into French and readily available. Enough for an entire Georgia shelf. Jean Toomer's violent, visionary Georgia stories in *Cane*, lyrical, searching, alive in every line, were missing, but Toomer was the only conspicuous absence. At any rate, translated or not, the dozen modern Georgia writers included here, beginning with Toomer and Caldwell in the twenties and thirties, on through O'Connor and McCullers in mid-century, and ending with the newest generation of Mary Hood and Greg Johnson, should require no special pleading to justify placing some of their best stories side by side in a single representative collection.

There may be some surprise, however, in learning that there is a special Georgia skill in the short story that reaches beyond the twentieth century back to the very beginnings of a distinctly Southern literature. It's this sense of a demonstrable literary tradition that has been the guiding principle behind most of my selections, and that, I hope, will strike the reader as one of the persuasive and attractive features of the book as a whole. None of the early Georgia writers, with the possible exception of Joel Chandler Harris, are as well known as their modern counterparts, for understandable reasons. It is difficult to read through the many volumes of William Tappan Thompson, Richard Malcolm Johnston, Charles Henry Smith, or Will Harben, without concluding that their overall literary achievement, taking them one by one, has been modest, at best. They had a tendency to repeat themselves in story after story. When their original inspiration failed they did not stop writing, but all too comfortably relaxed into a mood of bemused front-porch reminiscence and nodding late-afternoon humor that possessed far more good intentions than wit. One of the paradoxes of literary history, however, and one of the satisfactions of the anthologist, lies in the realization that a writer whose life work may not be indispensable in general can sometimes be discovered to have written one or two pieces that are entirely worthy when considered by themselves. For anyone even remotely interested in Georgia, the South, or the history of American literature, I can think of few more striking portraits of the rural Old South to recommend than those that can be found in Thompson's "The Duel," Johnston's "Investigations Concerning Mr. Jonas Lively," Smith's "Uncle Tom Barker," or Harben's "The Heresy of Abner Calihan." Taken together, in succession, the individual stories in *Georgia Stories* by these otherwise minor nineteenth-century writers are, at least to my mind, proof of the paradox, and proof as well of a native Georgia literary culture that was vigorous and vivid and enduring at a time when the great mass of Southern fiction, with few exceptions, had precious little to praise or preserve.

There are two early Georgia writers of short stories who stand out powerfully from all the rest, and in each case their first book of stories struck pioneering new directions in Southern fiction. It cannot be emphasized too strongly that the appearance of Augustus Baldwin Longstreet's *Georgia Scenes* in 1835 and Joel Chandler Harris's *Uncle Remus: His Songs and Sayings* in 1880 had a profound influence on the other Georgia writers. These two books gave them the best possible demonstration that the source of their strength would derive not from the language of literature, certainly not from the weary, ritualistic phrase-making and false refinements of popular fiction, everywhere much the same, but from the local language of the land, "racy of the soil," and from the largely unexplored folk culture of the rural South. Despite Longstreet's satirical thrusts, and despite his moral distance from the rough manners and raw ripe speech of the half-frontier society he describes, he was the first to approach the authentic character of the lower-class Southern whites with any degree of familiarity and appreciation. And Harris, of course, placed every other Georgia writer in his debt by introducing the first real black voice in Southern literature, not just as a comic or pathetic diversion from standard English, but as the revealing human expression of a fertile imagination and a deep, determined inner life.

Actually, Longstreet, Harris, and the early Georgia short story writers in general owed their vitality to a number of forces, not the least of which, if I may be permitted a bit of reckless rhapsodizing on a favorite subject, might possibly have sprung from the nature of the short story itself. There are all kinds of short stories, of course, capable of treating a rich diversity of themes in many different modes, but they all tend to concentrate on a single emphatic incident in the life of a single character. In Longstreet's time this is perhaps the only link between his own humorous sketches in Georgia newspapers and the great symbolic parables of Nathaniel Hawthorne or the wild demonic tragedies and gothic farces of Edgar Allan Poe, but it is a link worth remembering. Longstreet and most of the other Southern humorists who followed him did not consider themselves professional writers.

They were lawyers, doctors, and newpaper men who were content to entertain their readers with amusing portraits of the odd characters they had come across while riding the circuit, visiting a sick slave in a remote swamp, or attending a political barbecue. But this haphazard joining together of an observant reporter's eye for the vivid detail with the demanding solitary vision of the short story had the effect of gradually creating a rather powerful image of individual solidity that was extremely rare in the early Southern novel. Not all Southern stories pretended to be accurate, detailed accounts of the visible world, but even so the natural effect of concentrated focus seemed to require some sort of accepted commitment to sensual reality. William Gilmore Simms, for example, not always much of a committed realist himself, was capable of complaining that Poe had been "grievously" indifferent to the actual vegetation and landscape on Sullivan's Island in South Carolina in one of Poe's few Southern short stories, "The Gold Bug."

Even the enormous amount of boasting, exaggeration, and outrageous tall-tale invention that entertained readers of the Southern humorist stories could be defended, with a certain perverted empirical logic, as a rather realistic account of actual frontier speech. Realism, however, is perhaps not the best term to use; there were collective social realities in the nineteenth-century South that were to become not only inescapable, but sovereign. And here is a predicament that hatched another. In an age of powerful public ideologies and nationalistic demands, the novel, or any other literary work that pretended to speak for the whole society, was bound to shy away from merely private truths. This was precisely the case in the great mass of Southern novels written during the nineteenth century. Their fascination with the sweeping historical panorama and the grand public gesture almost always resulted in losing the actual man standing on his patch of earth to the impersonal political myth. Herein lies one of the therapeutic virtues of the short story, as an antidote to the excesses of public-spirited novelistic abandon. And having gone this far, I might as well plunge heedlessly on and argue that the short story must tend, by necessity, towards the anti-mythical, the anti-heroic, and the anti-historical. Because of its restrictions of scope and focus, it cannot pretend to offer much more than the single limited human creature all at once.

Would I be prepared then to argue that the short story all by itself saved the early Southern writers from the relentless romanticism they invariably succumbed to in the long narrative, and helped generate the only legitimate tradition of Southern realism in the Old South? Probably not, but how else to account for the almost palpable impression of individual reality that comes through in many Southern stories of the nineteenth century, but almost never in the novel? Few readers, even with the best will in the world, are able to conjure up enough suspension of disbelief to finish the novels of Thomas Nelson Page in Virginia or, closer to our subject, those of Longstreet and Harris in Georgia. But each one of these writers wrote short stories that somehow convey an unmistakable resonance of truth from beginning to end. At any rate, whether or not the effort was entirely deliberate, a number of Southern writers, beginning with Longstreet and his *Georgia Scenes*, gradually felt their way into the short story's natural magnetic pull away from exclusively social or public considerations toward a more private, personal, even eccentric vision of reality. And though I doubt at this point I need to proclaim my own preferences, that is the vision I have always found the most compelling, not only in these Georgia stories, but, with only a few exceptions, in the entire body of Southern fiction.

Having read through all these remarkable claims for the short story, no reader should expect me to say much in favor of the vast, capacious Georgia romance, a postbellum genre that did not begin with *Gone With the Wind* in 1936, but goes back to the now happily forgotten best seller *St. Elmo*, published by Augusta Jane Evans in 1866. Actually, I have no unusual objections to either of these two books, or others like them. I do know that the serious straining after mythic grandeur in these big Georgia books could not help but sacrifice the compressed energy and irreverent acceptance of human nature I admire in the short stories. But the literary aims and underlying esthetic convictions of the two forms are so radically opposed that comparisons are hardly worth making. It is of some interest, however, to note what happens when even a hint of plantation society invades the imagination of certain Southern writers. As the responsible standard bearers of Southern hierarchy, caste, and political leadership, the planters were constantly being called on, almost by the spirit of the times itself, to glorify their own importance, and the popular novelist all too willingly offered his or her services as literary magnifying glass. The fictional planter eventually made such a powerful impact on the public imagination that even today it is difficult to look back on the Old South regime without resorting to all those fixed stereotypes of the dashing dueling cavalier woodsman or the well-read country squire entertaining his friends with generous helpings of bourbon and Latin poetry. This is a shame, because there is certainly more truth than fiction in the notion that the Southern plantation created an independent and perhaps even unique class of gentleman farmer, and I for one would happily trade all the overwritten romances for one full-bodied realistic novel that combined the honest wit and self-knowledge of William J. Grayson's *Autobiography* with the attention to day-to-day detail found in Theodore Rosengarten's recent edition of Thomas B. Chaplin's plantation journal, *Tombee: Portrait of a Cotton Planter.*

Anyway, for what it matters, I am willing to admit that *Gone With the Wind* does contain at least a half-dozen sharply defined vignettes of Georgia scenes not entirely swallowed up by romantic intrigue and Scarlett's endless undramatic accommodations to historical fate. And I am willing to admit as well that Margaret Mitchell possessed a respectable knowledge of middle Georgia's newly formed antebellum community, up and down the social scale, and a historian's talent for pinning down a type. *St. Elmo* is another kettle of fish, or beached whale. Its enormous success in the nineteenth century is difficult to understand today, but apparently had something to do with the principle of combining the encyclopedia with the sermon. Today, *St. Elmo's* sheer physical bulk seems to be its only concession to the real world, although its main character, the orphan Edna Earle, does demonstrate an independence of female character that I like to think has something to do with Evans's Georgia birthright. Remember what Sherman wrote to his wife from Savannah in 1864: "There are many fine families in this city, but when I ask for old and familiar names, it marks the sad havoc of war—the Goodwins, Teffts, Cuylers, Habershams, Laws, etc., etc., all gone or in poverty, and yet the girls remain, bright and haughty and proud as ever."

As Sherman's sober list of lost families suggests, there is definitely something in the tragic rise and fall of the Confederate South that calls for the great unfolding epic novel, but thus far no single work of fiction has ever approached the genuine tragic dimension achieved by another Georgia book, *The Children of Pride*, the immense collection of letters exchanged between 1860 and 1868 by the Reverend Charles Colcock Jones and the various members of his family in and around Liberty County, Georgia, and edited by Robert Manson Myers in 1972. Otherwise, need I insist, with very few exceptions, the best fiction of the Civil War has been short, and more ironic than tragic: Mark Twain's "History of a Campaign That Failed," a few of Ambrose Bierce's cynical tales, Grace King's "Bayou l'Ombre," Stephen Crane's *The Red Badge of Courage*, Thomas Wolfe's "Chicamauga," William Faulkner's "Mountain Victory" and the stories in *The Unvanquished*, and perhaps even Flannery O'Connor's "Late Encounter with the Enemy."

Unfortunately, the most recent serious Georgia romance, by the French Catholic writer Julien Green, threatens in its final form to dwarf both *Gone With the Wind* and *St. Elmo* combined. In many ways, Green's unfinished work fits more securely in the old elegiac tradition of Southern plantation fiction than either *Gone With the Wind* or *St. Elmo*, concerned as he is, almost exclusively, with the various romantic agitations and high-toned social ceremonies revolving around a wealthy planter family near Savannah. Green's grandfather was a well-known figure in antebellum Savannah, but Green's own long life as a

Paris-born Southern exile has deprived him of any first-hand experience of Georgia realities. He is a highly sophisticated French stylist,
but I, for one, heartily regret that he has not read deeply enough in the
down-to-earth tradition of Georgia short stories. After having recently
published The Distant Lands and The Stars of the South, he has announced
that he is ready to begin the third volume of his massive trilogy in
French, to be called, in its finished form, Dixie. Green is in good health,
and I wish him well, but he turned ninety-one this year. Perhaps Georgia
Stories has arrived just in time.

Given his age and his restricted transatlantic vision, Green probably should not be too severely taken to task for ignoring Georgia's
literary history. As I suggested earlier, even among those readers who
know and admire the best modern Georgia writers, there are few, I
suspect, who would think it necessary to go further back than Caldwell
or Toomer to begin a good representative collection. The widespread
brilliance of Southern fiction in this century may also be part of the
problem. We are so familiar with the names of Faulkner, Wolfe,
Glasgow, Porter, Welty, Taylor, Warren, O'Connor, Price, and Percy,
having burst into print all over the South with masterpiece after
masterpiece, that it would be difficult to choose one region over
another as worthy of special attention. A better case could certainly be
made for a more general anthology aimed at demonstrating the
strange power of a common Southern identity, even in the broken
twentieth century, capable of uniting writers as far removed from each
other as South Carolina and Arkansas. Once we begin to look backward, however, as so many of the early modern Southerners did
themselves, the situation changes, and Georgia begins to stand out,
almost, but not quite, alone, as an original literary source for much of
what is most vital and vigorous in twentieth-century Southern fiction.

Georgia's peculiar relationship to the older coastal settlements
in Virginia and South Carolina played a large role in the process. It
seems to me that it has not always been recognized that the two most
enduring historical forces behind the modern revival can be traced to
two well-defined subregions of the Old South, lower Louisiana and
middle Georgia. In both cases, native writers from these two areas
used striking examples of local evidence to challenge and deepen the
image of a collective South, and they did so almost invariably in the
relatively new and incisive form of the short story.

The Louisiana writers, in many respects, were closer to the
twentieth century, not only in time but also in their critical preoccupation with the meaning of Southern identity shaped by slavery and
history. Their great themes were the failure of public discourse and the
tragic fall of the Southern aristocracy after the Civil War. In the
passionate confusion of defeat and destruction, however, it was

difficult to address these themes openly and directly. They were helped by Louisiana's still-remembered history as a separate country. Given Louisiana's recent past as a French colony, writers such as George Washington Cable and Grace King, both based in their native city of New Orleans, could look to the lingering remnants of a conservative Creole society, having declined steadily since it was sold by Napoleon into the United States in 1803, almost wholly out of phase with the modern world, yet desperately clinging to a strict sense of caste and an inflexible code of cultural superiority. Cable, especially, deliberately concentrated on the proud lost cause of the old Creole families in order to dramatize the larger but comparable plight of the entire postbellum South.

Historical considerations enter into the Georgia story as well, but reflect different circumstances and a different mood. Writing in the decades before the War, Judge Longstreet and his followers humorously described their own youthful experiences in a rapidly changing, unstable world on the edge of the frontier, but they did so out of a loyal belief in the future of a Southern community that had not yet fulfilled its potential strength. Their satiric portraits and rowdy humor derived from a self-confidence that encouraged free speech and the probing of weakness wherever they found it. Even when they preached a bit, as Longstreet did, they wrote primarily as entertainers, not as evangelists, and each one of them would have spurned the throne of public wise man. But nevertheless their rough journalistic sketches fully satisfied at least one of the main requirements any culture worth its salt should demand of its artists: the possession of an honest eye and ear. What the modern reader remembers when he turns to these early stories is that the South was comic before it was tragic, and that a vigilant comic spirit has been, especially in the twentieth century, one of the genuine humanizing gifts of Southern fiction. Longstreet's stories also applied to a broader range of experience than the later Louisiana writing. Only a small minority of Southerners could identify with Cable's French-speaking Catholics of southern Louisiana, and those who could, in the older plantation settlements of the Virginia tidewater and the low country of South Carolina and coastal Georgia, would have resisted the similarities. On the other hand, there must have been few inhabitants even near Richmond or Charleston or Savannah who could not recognize in the uninhibited speech and outrageous acts of Judge Longstreet's rural inhabitants and small-town characters scenes from their own backyards.

What they could recognize, however, the staider citizens might have preferred ignoring, and this brings me to the important question of Georgia's role as a sort of defiant member, from the beginning of its history, of what came to be called the Great South. Georgia was the last of the original colonies, and in the Old South replaced North Carolina as the popular counterculture of genteel Virginia and South Carolina. In fact, a large majority of early Georgians had moved there directly from North Carolina. In many respects the highly fluid Georgia society did not fit neatly into the clear-cut social categories of the old established plantation regime and the wild Southern frontier. Actually, Georgia, the largest state east of the Mississippi River, contained both categories simultaneously, and continued to do so throughout the entire century. In and around Savannah, on the coveted sea islands, up and down the coast, and reaching up the Savannah River, were some of the wealthiest plantations in the South, and there are many ancestral homes not destroyed by Sherman still standing today—not to mention old Savannah itself, with its walled gardens and oak-lined squares—to attest to at least the high architectural quality of Georgia's patrician culture. But not too far from Savannah, and very close to Longstreet's Augusta, the frontier did exist, a vertical line moving rapidly westward as new immigrants flooded in after the Revolutionary War and as the native Indians were pushed from river to river, with one sorry land cession after another, until finally, in the shameful New Echota Treaty of 1835 and subsequent "trail of tears" removal of 1838, they were forced out of Georgia altogether.

But there was a third category in Georgia too, found primarily in middle Georgia, the large area of land stretching out from the Savannah River toward the Chattahoochee, whose geographical center, as Joel Chandler Harris proudly claimed, came within a map's thumbprint of his own hometown of Eatonton. In this part of Georgia too there were plantations, some large and prosperous, especially after the spread of cotton began to dominate Southern agriculture in the first decades of the nineteenth century. Most of the landowners, however, had stepped into their adult lives propelled far more by hope and ambition than by inherited wealth or family distinction, and middle Georgia by the time Longstreet published his first stories was a land rich in cheaply obtained soil and promise that consisted for the most part of modest farms, scattered hamlets, and small towns and county seats just beginning to breathe the air of social ceremony and settled respectability. And here is where the Georgia short story and Southern literature begin.

When Augustus Baldwin Longstreet was born, in 1790, his birthplace of Augusta contained a little over a thousand citizens. Even though it grew rapidly, reaching over six thousand in 1800, Longstreet's boyhood memories were those of a village becoming a town, a place where the relatively free and easy mixture of different types—brawling backwoodsmen, family-proud Virginia exiles, enterprising merchants lured west from the eastern cities, idealistic New England schoolteachers, hustling horse traders, and hapless drifters from nameless origins—could all be observed, especially on a Saturday afternoon, elbow to elbow with the more representative Georgia population of cotton planter, cracker farmer, and the occasional slave with a pass, walking along busy Broad Street with its hundred stores and shops, or standing around the courthouse shooting the breeze. Later, when Longstreet became a lawyer and rode the middle circuit, when he married and moved to his wife's hometown of Greensboro (much smaller than Augusta), and when he eventually was elected judge in 1821 and was responsible for holding court in the seven rural counties of the Ocmulgee District, he was able to study the far-from-plain folk of small-town Georgia in greater detail and on a wider scale.

From the moment Longstreet began publishing his stories in Georgia newspapers in 1834, their great success, then and later, can be attributed to the sheer comic originality of his low-life portraits and rural dialect. When *Georgia Scenes* was first published in 1835, Edgar Allan Poe announced in a famous review that he had seldom laughed as immoderately over a book. Aside from Longstreet's obvious gifts as an original humorist, however, one of his innovations lay in the recognition, based on long experience as lawyer and judge, that the compact Southern town was a ready-made theater or public tribunal full of dramatic possibility. Two of his best-known stories, "The Horse-Swap" and "The Fight," are good examples. They both present powerful struggles between two opponents who are encouraged and judged by a crowd of onlookers in the street. Although Longstreet insists primarily on the comic nature of these contests, one a hard-fought verbal duel full of bluff and cunning and the other brutally physical, there is the serious suggestion in these and many of his other stories that the middle Georgia country town offered a popular arena of communal justice that helped emphasize the wide-open democratic character of Georgia itself.

The trouble with some of his stories, at least from a modern perspective, is that the Judge could not help making sure his own judgment was abundantly clear. All too often he takes the unnecessary pains of adding little cautionary asides lest his own position be misunderstood. Actually, he may not have known exactly where he did stand as he looked back on a half-civilized world he half-regretted. There is far more exuberance than cruelty in his portraits, and at any rate, he always reserves his sharpest criticism, in true middle Georgia style, not for the vulgar defects of the lower classes, but for the absurd mannerisms of the falsely refined. For Longstreet there is no contempt worse than the contempt of man's natural lot.

I somehow doubt, however, if Longstreet's contemporaries, North or South, paid that much attention to his moral positions, even when he spelled them out in no uncertain terms and awkwardly tacked them on to the end of the stories. His readers were probably far more amused by his free and easy style, and by the way he craftily overplayed the outside image of the Georgian as a regional type. This was a deliberate strategy on his part, and another powerful influence on later Georgia writers. Georgians had long been the target of neighborly jests on the part of those aristocratic twins of the Old South, Virginia and South Carolina, and usually answered them in kind. For the Georgians, the Virginians were haughty and humorless, and for the Virginians the Georgians were brash and underbred. A good example of the early Georgian version of the self-exalted Virginian can be found in the portrait of Major Ferguson Bangs in William Tappan Thompson's "The Duel," the second story in *Georgia Stories*. Thompson had worked for a time on Longstreet's newspaper, the *State Rights Sentinel*, and was an enthusiastic admirer of *Georgia Scenes*. As one of the most successful disciples of Longstreet's brand of humor, he must have pleased his mentor enormously with his account of how blustery Major Bangs found himself humbled into a hard corner for which he had only his careless tongue and drunken conceit to blame.

Georgia's reputation as a barbaric refuge for the uneducated, the uncouth, and very likely the unreformable, could be traced all the way back to Oglethorpe's initial scheme of founding Georgia as a philanthropic colony for debtors and other unfortunates unable to find work in England. It did not matter that only a handful of the original colonists fit that description; the legend had too much negative appeal for it to be challenged on the basis of mere historical fact. The proximity of the frontier and the large expanses of thinly populated territory only accentuated the prejudice. Most of the rival mockery among the Southern states was good-humored, in the spirit of Thompson's "The Duel," but it could, on occasion, turn harsh. Daniel Hundley, a Southern intellectual spellbound by the chivalric ideal of the Virginia gentleman, wrote in his *Social Relations in Our Southern States*, published in 1860, that unlike the aristocratic Virginian, the self-made Georgian was ruled by raw personal ambition alone: "In Georgia they grow to enormous sizes, reaching six feet and a half. Muscular, heavy-jawed, beetle-browed, and possessed of indomitable energy, they are well calculated to command respect almost anywhere, did one only have it in his nature to forget that SELF is the only god they worship, and MONEY the only incence that ever ascends as a sweet-smelling savor to the nostrils of their idol."

There is no evidence Longstreet ever read Hundley, but had he done so he would have certainly rejoiced in the ripe opportunity to humorously exaggerate the exaggeration. Hundley's caricature was a sour variation on the old Virginia joke that the typical Georgia tradesman was a shifty frontier rogue always looking for new ways to turn a profit, and it reflected just the kind of superior attitude that Longstreet and early Georgians in general loved to turn on its head, by the simple but extremely effective method of pretending to justify its wildest accusations. A good case in point can be found in a newspaper article written by a Georgia journalist in *The Macon Telegraph* a few years before Longstreet began writing and a full generation before Hundley. Its playful catalogue of local business activities makes Hundley's description seem pale and unworthy when compared to the real amplitude of scheming Georgia genius:

> As warm weather comes on, and the bilious and bullying season approaches, the demand increases for Lee's pills and pocket pistols, and goggles and gun powder, black patches and dirk knives grow in demand. Sundry of the *beau monde* have mounted green spectacles, and a rise is expected in sword canes and epsoms. The superior courts in the different circuits are also in session, and a good deal of lawing and liquoring is going on, as well as fighting and physicking. Attorneys and physicians, it is presumed, have their hands full. We like to see all trades prosper, and in a bil-ious season, those of the lawyers and doctors are not the least useful. One unravels a tangled case, the other cases up a shattered limb—one dives into the bowels of a statute, the other into the state of the bowels. This bleeds a patient in the arm for the sake of his health, the other bleeds him in the pocket for the health of his estate. Gamboge and gambling are seen in the back rooms, and ginger bread jacks and judges in the public squares. Duns and dirk knives grow saucy during court week, and mayors and bailiffs feel ticklish. *Enemas* and endorsements are sought for by some, cocktails and characters sued for by others. Half-pints and hickories are flourished in these times, and teething and gouging tolerated—all for the honor of liberty and the encouragement of business.

Longstreet, as a newspaperman himself, was quite capable of this kind of editorial jocularity, but in his best stories he was more careful than other early Southern writers not to take the exaggeration so far that all dramatic conviction was lost. He was perfectly willing, not just in the name of broad good humor, but in the name of honest realism as well, to expose the failures and faults of his fellow Georgians. But most of the time he manages to avoid the brazen definitive type by portraying each character as a distinct individual specimen. More often than not he establishes a hierarchy of characterization even when he is dealing with only one level or class of society. On the other hand, Francis Robinson, another Georgia humorist and, like William Thompson, a great admirer and disciple of Longstreet, almost always limits himself to the extreme case.

Robinson is represented in *Georgia Stories* by his little-known sketch "Lije Benadix." As a fantastic example of the most benighted kind of poor-white greed, Robinson's Lije is hard to forget, but he exists almost entirely for the sake of the anecdote. By the end of the story the swollen flesh of Lije has achieved an undeniable presence, an absolute presence, but Robinson never tries to prod it into revealing the least sign of dramatic life. This is perhaps one difference between the tall tale and the short story, a difference easy enough to grasp when we compare Robinson's story with Longstreet's "The Fight." In "The Fight" every single character belongs to the same common small-town lower class, even the profoundly ineffective local sage, "Squire" Loggins, otherwise known as Uncle Tommy. The moral gap between Ransy Sniffle, however, who "in his earlier days, had fed copiously upon red clay and blackberries," and the two fighters, Billy Stallings and Bob Durham, is considerable. Ransy is an inspired coward, but a coward to his innermost bone. Stallings and Durham are coarse and crude and tough as nails, but at the same time they are men of honor capable of mutual respect once the blood is shed and the battle is done.

Of all the debts the various writers in *Georgia Stories* owe to Longstreet, going beyond his pioneering realism and his unholy celebration of the Southern small town, the most far-reaching must certainly be his discovery that the whole range of rural Southern dialect, with its salt and savor and sting, its vivid metaphor and ballad-ringing rhythms, was a remarkable, unexploited natural resource. Longstreet and his immediate followers relied on the dialect primarily for comic effect, but Longstreet, especially, possessed a keen ear for the actual sounds of the Southern voice, and just as important, a contagious delight in accurately recording what he heard. The accuracy and the delight have continued to be key signatures of the Georgia writer, from Joel Chandler Harris on down to Flannery O'Connor and others. Longstreet does not go as far as O'Connor does in probing the negative power of language to harbor deep-seated habits of bigotry and bonehead certitude no matter how striking or comic the idiom, but like O'Connor he is capable of revealing an almost Joycean desire for absolute veracity in putting on the page the exact words of a conversation he has overheard, for the simple musical pleasure of the act and with the knowledge that the literary artist has nothing more to add. When O'Connor repeatedly argued in her essays and letters that Southern speech remained, even late in the twentieth century, a rich blessing of creative vitality no serious writer in the South could afford to ignore, there was one old Georgia ghost she was bound to please.

Longstreet had a reputation as a storyteller before he became a writer, and by all contemporary accounts he was a gifted mimic. But I wonder if his literary fascination with all the rank raving boasts and howling invective he heard around him in his youth and subsequently placed in his fiction, all the fire and fever and kick and color a lowly, unschooled verbal wit could freely roar out in the open air without risking his social status, all the hell-bent extravagance of phrase allowed the poor in pocket, was a revenge of sorts on his own highly visible public position and the moral constraints it imposed. I would not want to overstate the contrast. Like many other Southern professionals with university degrees, Longstreet could slip from one level of discourse to another with an ease that could confound an outsider. He admits as much, with characteristic apologies, at the end of his preface to *Georgia Scenes*. But as his career moved progressively up the rising cline of social respectability, the private occasions of jesting with his male friends in tavern or inn or on the open road would have steadily decreased. They had already become more or less memories of his youth when he published *Georgia Scenes* at the age of forty-five. This may help explain too why he did not publish anything else of a permanent literary interest; a handful of anti-abolitionist tracts and the moralistic temperance novel *Master William Mitten* are best forgotten. All those demanding roles as distinguished community spokesman finally tamed the maverick humorist.

As a minister, for example, Longstreet disappointed listeners who came to hear, if not the famous wit, at least a strong pagan measure of the thunder and lightning demanded in traditional Southern preaching. One old slave, when asked one Sunday if he liked what he had heard, suggested something about the dry, legalistic style of Longstreet's sermons when he complained: "Mars Gustus can't preach, he just gets up and laws it." Despite the reservations he may have come to feel when speaking in his own voice, however, Longstreet maintained a faith in his ability to speak in everybody else's that almost defies belief. At the beginning of the Civil War, seventy years old and president of South Carolina College, he formally volunteered his services to Robert E. Lee by stating that it would be the easiest thing in the world for him to destroy most of the Yankee fleet lying off the South Carolina coast if only Lee would give him permission. Knowing that slaves had been secretly rowing out to the ships at night to sell goods, Longstreet announced that all he had to do to get on board with enough dynamite to do the job was to disguise himself as a slave and take a few of his university students with him disguised the same way. The students could row; he planned to do all the talking himself. Not surprisingly, General Lee courteously but firmly refused.

I have insisted more on Longstreet than the other individual writers in *Georgia Stories* because he is not as well known as he should be, and because his importance in nineteenth-century Southern literature cannot be overemphasized. His influence was felt by every major Southern humorist of the period, from George Washington Harris in Tennessee to Thomas Bangs Thorpe in Louisiana to Johnson Jones Hooper in Alabama and, through them, to Mark Twain and *Huckleberry Finn*. His sketches, though unpretentious and unpolished, had a healthy liberating effect on the language of Southern literature that went far beyond his own modest aims. In his day, Longstreet's stories were often called subliterary, but *extraliterary* would have been the more proper term. W. B. Yeats once remarked that anyone could learn to construct a story, but if a writer did not possess the gift of an abundant, resonant, laughing, living speech, his art would never last. Whatever his limitations as a wholly convincing craftsman, Longstreet deserves to be read and remembered for his boisterous voices, and for having launched a movement that revolutionized the possibilities of literary English in permanent ways. As far as the better Georgia writers of the century were concerned, his was the paternal spirit that their own work was meant to please. The one other Georgia writer of the Old South who matched Longstreet in originality, and who eventually surpassed him in skill and influence, was Joel Chandler Harris, and Harris never lost an opportunity to acknowledge the legacy.

Harris was born in the small town of Eatonton, in 1848, a time when the development of schools and churches and civic stability had banished the rougher elements of the Georgia frontier further west. Eatonton was the county seat of Putnam County, one of the seven counties in middle Georgia that Longstreet himself had ridden as a circuit judge a generation earlier. There would have been vestiges of Longstreet's wilder world in the nearby hamlets and river camps, and in every older man and woman's memory, but Harris always recalled his boyhood in Eatonton as a nostalgic paradise of slow-moving rhythms and communal harmony, all the more surprising when we know he was born in circumstances that had all the painful potential of a Victorian melodrama. He was an illegitimate son of a father he never knew, and his unmarried and deserted mother had to toil as a seamstress to make a bare living for herself and her only child. But the townspeople of Eatonton took care of their own. His mother was provided with a small house, and with regular work. As a boy playing on the streets with his friends, Harris was at home everywhere he went.

Most readers of Southern fiction know the rest of the story, how little Joe Harris at the age of thirteen was given a job as a printer's devil to help Joseph Addison Turner, the owner of the Turnwold plantation near Eatonton, publish his weekly journal, *The Countryman*, during the Civil War. At Turnwold Harris learned the newspaper trade from the bottom up; he made his first tentative efforts at writing under Turner's benevolent eye; he lived and worked and hunted with the slaves whose stories and folklore he eagerly absorbed and never forgot; he witnessed the ruin of the plantation system and the ripped-out roots of the old assumptions; and he watched and considered the dramatic impact the shattered South's new estate would eventually make on each one of its citizens, black and white. After the war and the end of his apprenticeship with Turner, Harris went on to a successful career in journalism that took him from one Georgia town to another, from Macon to Forsyth to Savannah, and that finally reached its peak when he was invited to join the staff of editor Henry Grady's *Atlanta Constitution* in 1876. That same year he began writing his Uncle Remus column, and in 1880 published his first and still best-known book, *Uncle Remus: His Songs and His Sayings*. By the time of his death in 1908, he had written well over thirty volumes of stories, novels, and children's books, and had been read and acclaimed by everyone from the local newsboy to Theodore Roosevelt and Rudyard Kipling.

Harris knew many of the early Georgia humorists individually, and liked to present himself as a "cornfield journalist" belonging firmly within the tradition that Longstreet had established. He gained his initial reputation, in fact, as a columnist on the newspaper in Savannah, the *Morning News*, that William Tappan Thompson had founded in 1850. Thompson himself had worked on Longstreet's Augusta newspaper, the *State Rights Sentinel*, so there was a direct personal link between Longstreet and Harris, even though Harris never actually met the Judge. The work of each of the humorists played a role in Harris's development. Thompson's genial cracker spokesman, Major Jones of Pineville, helped Harris shape his own version of the type when he began writing, much later on, his Billy Sanders stories. He considered Richard Malcolm Johnston's *Dukesborough Tales* the most faithful and best-written chronicle of the old-time middle Georgia community, and he admired Charles Henry Smith's ironic, good-natured "Bill Arp" letters as sharp and sensible reflections of the common man in the depressed times after the Civil War. I think it well to remember too that Harris's extreme care in representing the life and language of the Georgia black is best understood as the logical extension of the sympathetic realism shown by the humorists in their portraits of the lowly Southern white.

Harris's position as one of the founders of modern Southern fiction is obvious, though he is not always given the credit he deserves.

Black dialect had been attempted in serious literature with varying degrees of success before Harris, and by his time too there already existed a long list of novels, slave narratives, and miscellaneous writing, in which black men and women played prominent roles. But no other writer of his day had his absolute gift for imitating the exact tones and full poetic range of black speech, and no other writer had more insight into their private imaginative life. It is no exaggeration to say that Harris almost by himself finally forced Southern letters to recognize at least two truths that had been scrupulously avoided in the past: first of all, that in the South, the black and white communities are halves of the same reality, even if that reality be at times cruelly divided; and second, that the singular nature of Southern culture can be grasped only by realizing the extent to which it has been the gradual creation of two races.

His own contribution to that culture is most readily appreciated in his Uncle Remus stories. Full of trickery and feuding and outlandish high-handed gall, especially when Brer Rabbit is on the scene, these tales have to be read out loud to be fully savored; with all their verbal exuberance, bravado, slander, and creative sass, they are the comic black counterpart of the white humorist tradition. They were, of course, the same animal tales Harris had heard as a boy from the slaves at Turnwold. Since they had been transmitted orally, and continued to be passed down in Southern black communities well into the twentieth century, it can't be said that he rescued them singlehandedly from oblivion. But his literary versions—or what he called with a modest bow toward professional folklorists, his variants—have never been improved upon, and Zora Neale Hurston, who knew what she was talking about, and who was delighted to discover the dancing tracks of Brer Rabbit in her folklore excursions into northern Florida, praised Harris often for his combination of authenticity and dramatic flair. Harris realized too what many whites might have been reluctant to admit, that the clamorous surface entertainment of the tales only barely conceals a deeper dimension of racial consciousness. In his introduction to *Uncle Remus: His Songs and His Sayings*, he pointed out that it would take no great scientific effort to show why the black "selects as his hero the weakest and most harmless of all animals, and brings him out victorious in contests with the bear, the wolf, and the fox."

Harris characteristically minimized his own importance in writing down the Uncle Remus stories; he always insisted that he had simply tried to record as faithfully as possible what he had remembered from his boyhood. But the character of Uncle Remus was Harris's own creation, and Uncle Remus's complacent or at least uncomplaining attitude toward the Southern regime that had enslaved him has raised questions in many modern minds about Harris's willingness to challenge racial stereotypes as thoroughly as they deserved. Uncle Remus does seem to conform a bit too easily to the postbellum image of the devoted old retainer who looks back longingly to the peaceful days before the war when life on the plantation was slower-paced, and more predictable.

The problem cannot be solved in a paragraph. There are contradictions and divisions in Harris's work, and it is true he sometimes allows the sentimental impulse of the Victorian age and his own passionate hatred of progressive slogans and modern remedies to override his disturbing perceptions of racial injustice. But he never blindly glorified the Old South, and was consistently on the side of the downtrodden and the suffering when it came to choosing his heroes. And unlike most Southern writers of his time he was sensitive, to some degree because of his own socially ambiguous background, to the complex struggle between public roles and private experience in every human being, including the former slave. Harris recognized that the Southern black had been forced to hide and often compeletely abandon all signs of an independent forceful personality. In its place he had created an elaborate public ritual that could shift from shuffling stupidity to childlike clowning to emphatic formality with little trouble; his survival after the Civil War no longer could be said to entirely depend on these shifts, but his comfort did, and Harris had the good sense to know that the Georgia black was as shrewd and as pragmatic as the plain white cracker of the Georgia hills when it came to taking care of himself. Harris must have appreciated the fact that another native Georgian, Sidney Lanier, in his 1880 essay "The New South," singled out Uncle Remus as having expressed better than anyone else the stubborn empiricism of the small Southern farmer.

There are other elements that raise Uncle Remus well above the level of the conventional black caricature that Harris more than once publicly condemned. If at times Uncle Remus cannot help slipping into the role of only a slightly more human version of the minstrelized black that had become a stock fixture of popular theater from New York to New Orleans, he constantly undercuts that role by offering at the same time the provocative spectacle of a benevolent, grandfatherly black man leading a young ignorant white boy into the instructive mysteries of a hidden world. Harris is thinking back to his own education at Turnwold, but the highly ironic reversal of the usual paternalistic Southern relationship is far too obvious to be entirely unintentional, and at least one contemporary Southern admirer, Mark Twain, proved in *Huckleberry Finn* four years later that he had not been blind to the message.

Harris will probably always be most popular for his Uncle Remus stories, but many of his more personal portraits of native Georgia life and manners bring him closer to the preoccupations of modern Southern fiction than any other local colorist in the nineteenth century, with the possible exception of George Washington Cable, Grace King, and Kate Chopin in Louisiana. In much of his best work, all of it in the short story, his concern with the outsider and the victim led him toward a level of stark dramatic realism that few Southern writers of his day were ready to contemplate. This is especially evident in the story included here, "Free Joe and the Rest of the World," a Georgian pastoral tragedy that anticipates the brutal conflict of human choice and racial fate explored in such modern Southern works as Faulkner's *Go Down, Moses* and Ernest Gaines's *Bloodline*. "Free Joe" was based on Harris's memories of a free black he had known as a boy in Eatonton. It demonstrates among other things that he was quite capable of confronting the negative underside of the same small-town Georgia world he often celebrated in his novels and reminiscences. Among the other stories in the first half of *Georgia Stories*, only Will Harben's harsh description of suffocating moral hypocrisy in his north Georgia portrait, "The Heresy of Abner Calihan," emanates the same grim mood of sober despair. Both these stories point ahead to the sometimes savage, sometimes pathetic modern rural disasters of Erskine Caldwell, Carson McCullers, and Flannery O'Connor. Unfortunately, there is no single collection in print of Harris's non–Uncle Remus stories, and readers interested in judging his scope and skill in such stories as "Mingo: A Sketch of Life in Middle Georgia," "At Teague Poteet's," "Blue Dave," and "Where's Duncan?" will have to search for them in libraries and old book shops, or scattered around in various anthologies.

With Harris, the Georgia short story established itself as a vital and independent tradition with a past and a future, and its future brings me back to where I began, with the succession of short masterpieces Georgians have been writing in almost every decade since the beginning of the twentieth century. Many of these can be found in *Georgia Stories*. Any anthology that includes "Blood-Burning Moon," "The Ballad of the Sad Cafe," and "Revelation" should not have to defend its existence, at least not on esthetic grounds. But the anthologist could, I suppose, be legitimately asked to decide if Toomer, McCullers, O'Connor, and other modern Georgia writers, in their own minds, considered themselves strongly defined by Georgia perimeters. Like other questions I have raised, it may not be possible to answer to everyone's satisfaction. My own belief, naturally, is that these stories, even some of the most recent, by Harry Crews, Alice Walker, and Mary Hood, reverberate with some surprising collective affinities when read together. These would include a radical realism;

a strange old-fashioned faith in human talk, lies and all, as a source of truth; a dramatic preoccupation with the elemental extremes of the rural poor; and a belief that hard humor is still an effective means of defeating the devil and his demons. I do not want to imply that any of these modern Georgia writers would have wanted in the past, or would want now, to be entirely bound by regional considerations alone, whether that region be called Georgia, the South, or the United States. But I do think they all would admit that their private insights into the human condition have been powerfully sharpened by their local vision, and that their stories speak out of a shared Georgia culture even when, or especially when, they have felt free to call into question some of the peculiar forces that made it what it is.

Flannery O'Connor herself, whom no one can accuse of the slightest suggestion of heraldic pride or sentimentality when it comes to regional allegiances, often spoke of her attachment to Georgia as as essential factor in her fiction. On one level it was a simple matter of having been given a richly fertilized field to cultivate: "To call yourself a Georgia writer is certainly to declare a limitation, but one which, like all limitations, is a gateway to reality. It is a great blessing, perhaps the greatest blessing a writer can have, to find at home what others have to go elsewhere seeking." On another level, the reality she speaks of was inner as well as outer, and involved a habit of tough-minded moral independence she felt was one of the gifts of having been raised in a Southern state, and a defiant one at that. When she and other Southern writers were attacked for their so-called obsession with the grotesque, O'Connor countered with the old Georgia trick of turning an outsider's insult into an insider's weapon: "Whenever I'm asked why Southern writers particularly have a penchant for writing about freaks, I say it is because we are still able to recognize one."

As a Catholic in a Protestant society, and as an unmarried woman severely handicapped by a killing disease, O'Connor had more than one way of proclaiming her uniqueness in the general order of the literary world. But whenever she was given the occasion, she insisted that the mysteries and manners of everyday life in Georgia lay at the bottom of everything she wrote. Unless they were accepted and understood, the fundamental meaning of her work was lost. She often railed at some of the fiendish misreadings her stories were given because an obvious local sensibility had been ignored. When the grandmother in her well-known story "A Good Man Is Hard to Find" was called an evil woman, a flat-out witch, by a teacher who complained that his Southern students had resisted his interpretation, she responded that they were right and he was wrong: the grandmother had serious defects, but the students "all had grandmothers or great-aunts just like her at home, and they knew, from personal experience, that the old lady lacked comprehension, but that she had a good heart." Anticipating a similar attack on Mrs. Turpin in "Revelation," O'Connor defended the complexity of her character in terms any pragmatic Georgia farmer would have understood at once. Ruby Turpin was as corrupt as self-righteousness could make her, but it took a "big woman to shout at the Lord across a hogpen."

Actually, if we begin to look for patterns, O'Connor's career reveals more than one odd resemblance with the lives and work of the early Georgia writers. Though born in Savannah, she lived and wrote for most of her life in Milledgeville, only a short ride from Harris's Eatonton, and located solidly in the heart of middle Georgia. She did write two short novels, but the short story was the literary form she favored, and a half-derisive comic voice her dominant narrative mode. Her letters are alive on every page with an infectious enthusiasm for local Georgia speech, full of brilliant scraps of conversation that can be considered almost by themselves as minor works of art. She loved to take hold and wring out the secret poisonous life of an offhand remark or a sudden exchange, especially when it hid an unintended irony or a corrosive contempt for logic. Though she denied having a musical ear, she was as gifted a literary mimic as Harris or the other Georgia humorists, and like them she could not help laughing at her own work. I deny anyone to try reading through her spontaneous accounts of her mother's farm and hired help in The Habit of Being, surely one of the greatest collections of correspondence by an American author, without laughing out loud, and without coming away with an increased respect for her knowledge of the spoken word, down to the syllable. Then there is her lack of interest in the well-off and well-educated, and her deep instinctive sympathy for the deprived lower class. This too brings her directly into the tradition, although, as usual, the moral reasons she gives for her priorities place her in a category all by herself: "I am very much afraid that to the fiction writer the fact that we shall always have the poor with us is a source of satisfaction, for it means, essentially, that he will always be able to find someone like himself. His concern with poverty is with a poverty fundamental to man. I believe that the basic experience of everyone is the experience of human limitation."

With O'Connor, the temptation is strong to keep quoting, especially when she writes about her own work, and especially, as far as I am concerned here, when the steady mounting up of her particular remarks on local life and lore begins to suggest an identification with Georgia that verges on the mystical. O'Connor had no interest at all in Georgia as any sort of abstract political or historical entity, and she often expressed an absolute scorn for Georgia as a sentimental or sacred myth. But why is it that at times she reminds me of fiery-eyed little Alexander Stephens sitting in his federal prison cell after the Civil War and writing in his diary that Georgia was his only country? In this her life seems to reflect a remarkably modern version of the ancient human impulse to be spiritually bound to a physical place, and her short stories a remarkably modern expression of the individual artist's need to declare a cultural homeland. But O'Connor's presence as a central figure in *Georgia Stories*, along with Longstreet and Harris, was assured from the beginning, and it might be more helpful at this point to stop speculating on what she may have felt, and try to explain, at least briefly, some of my overall concerns as I selected the other writers and stories to be included.

My aim was simple: once I had decided to organize the book around Longstreet, Harris, and O'Connor, I set out to choose the best, most representative stories I could find from each successive generation. This explains the chronological order of the stories, and the reason why the twentieth century has been more or less equally divided between the major writers of the early decades and what I consider the most original contemporary writers. I had little trouble selecting the stories from the nineteenth century. Longstreet and Harris each wrote enough good stories to make a deliberate choice necessary, but I can think of no story or writer I have left out for mere reasons of space. The twentieth century raised somewhat different problems. There were far more stories to choose from, and more writers I would have liked to include had the design of the collection been less oriented toward a historical demonstration. Though I had no overriding esthetic thesis to prove, and no single kind of story to promote, I wanted to make absolutely sure that each story would be judged first of all as an independent, fully realized work of art. Otherwise the whole argument of a valid literary tradition would have little meaning, and the entire collection would have lost its purpose.

One question that might bother some readers did not, I must admit, cause me much loss of sleep, and this was the question of native birth. For me the impact of the story itself was the absolute test, thus the presence of several writers who were not born in Georgia, such as Thompson in the nineteenth century, Matschat at the beginning of the twentieth, and McCluskey in the present, but who all succeeded, by a sort of voluntary imaginative naturalization, to join themselves permanently to Georgia's literary culture. Jean Toomer is perhaps the most striking example in *Georgia Stories*, and *Cane* one of the great original poetic books to come out of Georgia in modern times. Toomer lived for only a few months in Georgia, but he had been drawn there by blood, not by simple curiosity. According to the short autobiographical piece he wrote in 1922, a little while before *Cane* was published, that brief, intense stay was enough; he looked back on it as the creative baptism that changed his life:

> My family is from the South. My mother's father, P. B. S.
> Pinchback, born in Macon, Georgia, left home as a boy
> and worked on the Mississippi River steamers....My own
> father likewise came from middle Georgia....A visit to
> Georgia last fall was the starting point of almost every-
> thing of worth that I have done. I heard folk-songs come
> from the lips of Negro peasants. I saw the rich dusk
> beauty that I had heard many false accents about, and of
> which till then, I was somewhat skeptical. And a deep
> part of my nature, a part that I had repressed, sprang
> suddenly to life and responded to them.

Toomer's reference to the folk-songs he heard in Sparta brings me
to a final comment on *Georgia Stories*. At least as long as I have been
reading Georgia fiction, I have been listening to its music, all manner
of blues and gospel singers, the old north Georgia jump-and-holler
string bands, a modern master of the guitar such as Norman Blake.
There is an astonishing musical richness to choose from, going all the
way back to the original edition of the *Sacred Harp* hymnal put together
by two Georgia Baptist singing school teachers in 1844. When I first
began thinking about compiling a collection, and when I first began to
measure the importance of the Georgia short story, the music was
much in my mind. Any individual art that is able to speak fully out of
a local living culture, and yet strike chords of human recognition and
esthetic pleasure far beyond regional borders, is no small thing and
deserves to be acclaimed, especially in a day in which television,
theme parks, and suburban sprawl have cheapened our sense of
cultural judgment to the vanishing point. Fortunately, there have
been some effective counter-movements against the general decay,
such as the wonderful *Foxfire* volumes begun in 1967 by Elliot
Wigginton's high school students in Clayton, Georgia. Every square
inch of lived-on earth has a right to praise what it has helped create,
including its literature, provided it has a genuine literature to praise.
My own firm belief is that Georgia writers in the short story have
produced an unusual number of original voices in an outspoken
independent tradition that somehow, against the odds, continues to
kick and curse and sing and thrive. If in any way the various short fiction
in *Georgia Stories* helps bring other readers, in Georgia and out, to the
same conviction, I'll be satisfied.

BEN FORKNER
ANGERS, FRANCE

The Fight

Augustus Baldwin Longstreet

IN THE YOUNGER DAYS OF THE REPUBLIC there lived in the county of ——
two men, who were admitted on all hands to be the very *best men* in the
county; which, in the Georgia vocabulary, means they could flog any
other two men in the county. Each, through many a hard-fought battle,
had acquired the mastery of his own battalion; but they lived on
opposite sides of the Courthouse, and in different battalions: consequently, they were but seldom thrown together. When they met,
however, they were always very friendly; indeed, at their first interview,
they seemed to conceive a wonderful attachment to each other, which
rather increased than diminished as they became better acquainted;
so that, but for the circumstance which I am about to mention, the
question, which had been a thousand times asked, "Which is the best
man, Billy Stallions (Stallings) or Bob Durham?" would probably never
have been answered.

Billy ruled the upper battalion, and Bob the lower. The former
measured six feet and an inch in his stockings, and, without a single
pound of cumbrous flesh about him, weighed a hundred and eighty.
The latter was an inch shorter than his rival, and ten pounds lighter;
but he was much the most active of the two. In running and jumping
he had but few equals in the county; and in wrestling, not one. In other
respects they were nearly equal. Both were admirable specimens of
human nature in its finest form. Billy's victories had generally been
achieved by the tremendous power of his blows, one of which had
often proved decisive of his battles; Bob's, by his adroitness in
bringing his adversary to the ground. This advantage he had never
failed to gain at the onset, and, when gained, he never failed to
improve it to the defeat of his adversary. These points of difference
have involved the reader in a doubt as to the probable issue of a
contest between them. It was not so, however, with the two battalions.

Neither had the least difficulty in determining the point by the most natural and irresistible deductions *a priori*; and though, by the same course of reasoning, they arrived at directly opposite conclusions, neither felt its confidence in the least shaken by this circumstance. The upper battalion swore "that Billy only wanted one lick at him to knock his heart, liver, and lights out of him; and if he got two at him, he'd knock him into a cocked hat." The lower battalion retorted, "that he wouldn't have time to double his fist before Bob would put his head where his feet ought to be; and that, by the time he hit the ground, the meat would fly off his face so quick, that people would think it was shook off by the fall." These disputes often led to the *argumentum ad hominem*, but with such equality of success on both sides as to leave the main question just where they found it. They usually ended, however, in the common way, with a bet; and many a quart of old Jamaica (whiskey had not then supplanted rum) were staked upon the issue. Still, greatly to the annoyance of the curious, Billy and Bob continued to be good friends.

Now there happened to reside in the county just alluded to a little fellow by the name of Ransy Sniffle: a sprout of Richmond, who, in his earlier days, had fed copiously upon red clay and blackberries. This diet had given to Ransy a complexion that a corpse would have disdained to own, and an abdominal rotundity that was quite unprepossessing. Long spells of the fever and ague, too, in Ransy's youth, had conspired with clay and blackberries to throw him quite out of the order of nature. His shoulders were fleshless and elevated; his head large and flat; his neck slim and translucent; and his arms, hands, fingers, and feet were lengthened out of all proportion to the rest of his frame. His joints were large and his limbs small; and as for flesh, he could not, with propriety, be said to have any. Those parts which nature usually supplies with the most of this article—the calves of the legs, for example—presented in him the appearance of so many well-drawn blisters. His height was just five feet nothing; and his average weight in blackberry season, ninety-five. I have been thus particular in describing him, for the purpose of showing what a great matter a little fire sometimes kindleth. There was nothing on this earth which delighted Ransy so much as a fight. He never seemed fairly alive except when he was witnessing, fomenting, or talking about a fight. Then, indeed, his deep-sunken gray eyes assumed something of a living fire, and his tongue acquired a volubility that bordered upon eloquence. Ransy had been kept for more than a year in the most torturing suspense as to the comparative manhood of Billy Stallings and Bob Durham. He had resorted to all his usual expedients to bring them in collision, and had entirely failed. He had faithfully reported to Bob all that had been said by the people in the upper battalion "agin him," and "he was sure Billy Stallings started it. He heard Billy say himself to Jim Brown, that he could whip him *or any other man in his battalion;*" and this he told to Bob, adding, "Dod darn his soul, if he was a little bigger, if he'd let any man *put upon* his battalion in such a way." Bob replied, "If he (Stallings) thought so, he'd better come and try it." This Ransy carried to Billy, and delivered it with a spirit becoming his own dignity and the character of his battalion, and with a colouring well calculated to give it effect. These, and many other schemes which Ransy laid for the gratification of his curiosity, entirely failed of their object. Billy and Bob continued friends, and Ransy had begun to lapse into the most tantalizing and hopeless despair, when a circumstance occurred which led to a settlement of the long-disputed question.

It is said that a hundred gamecocks will live in perfect harmony together if you do not put a hen with them; and so it would have been with Billy and Bob, had there been no women in the world. But there were women in the world, and from them each of our heroes had taken to himself a wife. The good ladies were no strangers to the prowess of their husbands, and, strange as it may seem, they presumed a little upon it.

The two battalions had met at the Courthouse upon a regimental parade. The two champions were there, and their wives had accompanied them. Neither knew the other's lady, nor were the ladies known to each other. The exercises of the day were just over, when Mrs. Stallings and Mrs. Durham stepped simultaneously into the store of Zephaniah Atwater, from "down east."

"Have you any Turkey-red?" said Mrs. S.

"Have you any curtain calico?" said Mrs. D. at the same moment.

"Yes, ladies," said Mr. Atwater, "I have both."

"Then help me first," said Mrs. D., "for I'm in a hurry."

"I'm in as great a hurry as she is," said Mrs. S., "and I'll thank you to help me first."

"And, pray, who are you, madam?" continued the other.

"Your betters, madam," was the reply.

At this moment Billy Stallings stepped in. "Come," said he, "Nancy, let's be going; it's getting late."

"I'd a been gone half an hour ago," she replied, "if it hadn't a' been for that impudent huzzy."

"Who do you call an impudent huzzy, you nasty, good-for-nothing, snaggle-toothed gaub of fat, you?" returned Mrs. D.

"Look here, woman," said Billy, "have you got a husband here? If you have, I'll *lick* him till he learns to teach you better manners, you *sassy* heifer you." At this moment something was seen to rush out of the store as if ten thousand hornets were stinging it; crying, "Take care— let me go—don't hold me—where's Bob Durham?" It was Ransy

Sniffle, who had been listening in breathless delight to all that had passed.

"Yonder's Bob, setting on the Courthouse steps," cried one. "What's the matter?"

"Don't talk to me!" said Ransy. "Bob Durham, you'd better go long yonder, and take care of your wife. They're playing h—l with her there, in Zeph Atwater's store. Dod etarnally darn my soul, if any man was to talk to my wife as Bill Stallions is talking to yours, if I wouldn't drive blue blazes through him in less than no time."

Bob sprang to the store in a minute, followed by a hundred friends; for the bully of a county never wants friends.

"Bill Stallions," said Bob, as he entered, "what have you been saying to my wife?"

"Is that your wife?" inquired Billy, obviously much surprised and a little disconcerted.

"Yes, she is, and no man shall abuse her, I don't care who he is."

"Well," rejoined Billy, "it an't worth while to go over it; I've said enough for a fight: and, if you'll step out, we'll settle it!"

"Billy," said Bob, "are you for a fair fight?"

"I am," said Billy. "I've heard much of your manhood, and I believe I'm a better man than you are. If you will go into a ring with me, we can soon settle the dispute."

"Choose your friends," said Bob; "make your ring, and I'll be in with mine as soon as you will."

They both stepped out, and began to strip very deliberately, each battalion gathering round its champion, except Ransy, who kept himself busy in a most honest endeavour to hear and see all that transpired in both groups at the same time. He ran from one to the other in quick succession; peeped here and listened there; talked to this one, then to that one, and then to himself; squatted under one's legs and another's arms; and, in the short interval between stripping and stepping into the ring, managed to get himself trod on by half of both battalions. But Ransy was not the only one interested upon this occasion; the most intense interest prevailed everywhere. Many were the conjectures, doubts, oaths, and imprecations uttered while the parties were preparing for the combat. All the knowing ones were consulted as to the issue, and they all agreed, to a man, in one of two opinions: either that Bob would flog Billy, or Billy would flog Bob. We must be permitted, however, to dwell for a moment upon the opinion of Squire Thomas Loggins; a man who, it was said, had never failed to predict the issue of a fight in all his life. Indeed, so unerring had he always proved in this regard, that it would have been counted the most obstinate infidelity to doubt for a moment after he had delivered himself. Squire Loggins was a man who said but little, but that little was always delivered with the most imposing solemnity of look and cadence. He always wore the aspect of profound thought, and you could not look at him without coming to the conclusion that he was elaborating truth from its most intricate combinations.

"Uncle Tommy," said Sam Reynolds, "you can tell us all about it if you will; how will the fight go?"

The question immediately drew an anxious group around the squire. He raised his teeth slowly from the head of his walking cane, on which they had been resting; pressed his lips closely and thoughtfully together; threw down his eyebrows, dropped his chin, raised his eyes to an angle of twenty-three degrees, paused about half a minute, and replied, "Sammy, watch Robert Durham close in the beginning of the fight; take care of William Stallions in the middle of it; and see who has the wind at the end." As he uttered the last member of the sentence, he looked slyly at Bob's friends, and winked very significantly; whereupon they rushed, with one accord, to tell Bob what Uncle Tommy had said. As they retired, the squire turned to Billy's friends, and said, with a smile, "Them boys think I mean that Bob will whip."

Here the other party kindled into joy, and hastened to inform Billy how Bob's friends had deceived themselves as to Uncle Tommy's opinion. In the mean time, the principals and seconds were busily employed in preparing themselves for the combat. The plan of attack and defence, the manner of improving the various turns of the conflict, "the best mode of saving wind," &c., &c., were all discussed and settled. At length Billy announced himself ready, and his crowd were seen moving to the centre of the Courthouse Square; he and his five seconds in the rear. At the same time, Bob's party moved to the same point, and in the same order. The ring was now formed, and for a moment the silence of death reigned through both battalions. It was soon interrupted, however, by the cry of "Clear the way!" from Billy's seconds; when the ring opened in the centre of the upper battalion (for the order of march had arranged the centre of the two battalions on opposite sides of the circle), and Billy stepped into the ring from the east, followed by his friends. He was stripped to the trousers, and exhibited an arm, breast, and shoulders of the most tremendous portent. His step was firm, daring, and martial; and as he bore his fine form a little in advance of his friends, an involuntary burst of triumph broke from his side of the ring; and, at the same moment, an uncontrollable thrill of awe ran along the whole curve of the lower battalion.

"Look at him!" was heard from his friends; "just look at him."

"Ben, how much you ask to stand before that man two seconds?"

"Pshaw, don't talk about it! Just thinkin' about it's broke three o' my ribs a'ready!"

5

"What's Bob Durham going to do when Billy lets that arm loose upon him?"

"God bless your soul, he'll think thunder and lightning a mint julep to it."

"Oh, look here, men, go take Bill Stallions out o' that ring, and bring in Phil Johnson's stud horse, so that Durham may have some chance! I don't want to see the man killed right away."

These and many other like expressions, interspersed thickly with oaths of the most modern coinage, were coming from all points of the upper battalion, while Bob was adjusting the girth of his pantaloons, which walking had discovered not to be exactly right. It was just fixed to his mind, his foes becoming a little noisy, and his friends a little uneasy at his delay, when Billy called out, with a smile of some meaning, "Where's the bully of the lower battalion? I'm getting tired of waiting."

"Here he is," said Bob, lighting, as it seemed, from the clouds into the ring, for he had actually bounded clear of the head of Ransy Sniffle into the circle. His descent was quite as imposing as Billy's entry, and excited the same feelings, but in opposite bosoms.

Voices of exultation now rose on his side.

"Where did he come from?"

"Why," said one of his seconds (all having just entered), "we were girting him up, about a hundred yards out yonder, when he heard Billy ask for the bully; and he fetched a leap over the Courthouse, and went out of sight; but I told them to come on, they'd find him here."

Here the lower battalion burst into a peal of laughter, mingled with a look of admiration, which seemed to denote their entire belief of what they had heard.

"Boys, widen the ring, so as to give him room to jump."

"Oh, my little flying wild-cat, hold him if you can! and, when you get him fast, hold lightning next."

"Ned, what do you think he's made of?"

"Steel springs and chicken-hawk, God bless you!"

"Gentlemen," said one of Bob's seconds, "I understand it is to be a fair fight; catch as catch can, rough and tumble: no man touch till one or the other halloos."

"That's the rule," was the reply from the other side.

"Are you ready?"

"We are ready."

"Then blaze away, my game cocks!"

At the word, Bob dashed at his antagonist at full speed; and Bill squared himself to receive him with one of his most fatal blows. Making his calculation, from Bob's velocity, of the time when he would come within striking distance, he let drive with tremendous force. But

Bob's onset was obviously planned to avoid this blow; for, contrary to all expectations, he stopped short just out of arm's reach, and, before Billy could recover his balance, Bob had him "all under-hold." The next second, sure enough, "found Billy's head where his feet ought to be." How it was done no one could tell; but, as if by supernatural power, both Billy's feet were thrown full half his own height in the air, and he came down with a force that seemed to shake the earth. As he struck the ground, commingled shouts, screams, and yells burst from the lower battalion, loud enough to be heard for miles. "Hurra, my little hornet!" "Save him!" "Feed him!" "Give him the Durham physic till his stomach turns!" Billy was no sooner down than Bob was on him, and lending him awful blows about the face and breast. Billy made two efforts to rise by main strength, but failed. "Lord bless you, man, don't try to get up! *Lay* still and take it! you *bleege* to have it!"

Billy now turned his face suddenly to the ground, and rose upon his hands and knees. Bob jerked up both his hands and threw him on his face. He again recovered his late position, of which Bob endeavoured to deprive him as before; but, missing one arm, he failed, and Billy rose. But he had scarcely resumed his feet before they flew up as before, and he came again to the ground. "No fight, gentlemen!" cried Bob's friends; "the man can't stand up! Bouncing feet are bad things to fight in." His fall, however, was this time comparatively light; for, having thrown his right arm round Bob's neck, he carried his head down with him. This grasp, which was obstinately maintained, prevented Bob from getting on him, and they lay head to head, seeming, for a time, to do nothing. Presently they rose, as if by mutual consent; and, as they rose, a shout burst from both battalions. "Oh, my lark!" cried the east, "has he foxed you? Do you begin to feel him! He's only beginning to fight; he ain't got warm yet."

"Look yonder!" cried the west; "didn't I tell you so! He hit the ground so hard it jarred his nose off. Now ain't he a pretty man as he stands? He shall have my sister Sal just for his pretty looks. I want to get in the breed of them sort o' men, to drive ugly out of my kinfolks."

I looked, and saw that Bob had entirely lost his left ear, and a large piece from his left cheek. His right eye was a little discoloured, and the blood flowed profusely from his wounds.

Bill presented a hideous spectacle. About a third of his nose, at the lower extremity, was bit off, and his face so swelled and bruised that it was difficult to discover in it anything of the human visage, much more the fine features which he carried into the ring.

They were up only long enough for me to make the foregoing discoveries, when down they went again, precisely as before. They no sooner touched the ground than Bill relinquished his hold upon Bob's neck. In this he seemed to all to have forfeited the only advantage

7

which put him upon an equality with his adversary. But the movement was soon explained. Bill wanted this arm for other purposes than defence; and he had made arrangements whereby he knew that he could make it answer these purposes; for, when they rose again, he had the middle finger of Bob's left hand in his mouth. He was now secure from Bob's annoying trips; and he began to lend his adversary tremendous blows, every one of which was hailed by a shout from his friends. "Bullets!" "Hoss-kicking!" "Thunder!" "That'll do for his face; now feel his short ribs, Billy!"

I now considered the contest settled. I deemed it impossible for any human being to withstand for five seconds the loss of blood which issued from Bob's ear, cheek, nose, and finger, accompanied with such blows as he was receiving. Still he maintained the conflict, and gave blow for blow with considerable effect. But the blows of each became slower and weaker after the first three or four; and it became obvious that Bill wanted the room which Bob's finger occupied for breathing. He would therefore, probably, in a short time, have let it go, had not Bob anticipated his politeness by jerking away his hand, and making him a present of the finger. He now seized Bill again, and brought him to his knees, but he recovered. He again brought him to his knees, and he again recovered. A third effort, however, brought him down, and Bob on top of him. These efforts seemed to exhaust the little remaining strength of both; and they lay, Bill undermost and Bob across his breast, motionless, and panting for breath. After a short pause, Bob gathered his hand full of dirt and sand, and was in the act of grinding it in his adversary's eyes, when Bill cried "ENOUGH!" Language cannot describe the scene that followed; the shouts, oaths, frantic gestures, taunts, replies, and little fights, and therefore I shall not attempt it. The champions were borne off by their seconds and washed; when many a bleeding wound and ugly bruise was discovered on each which no eye had seen before.

Many had gathered round Bob, and were in various ways congratulating and applauding him, when a voice from the centre of the circle cried out, "Boys, hush and listen to me!" It proceeded from Squire Loggins, who had made his way to Bob's side, and had gathered his face up into one of its most flattering and intelligible expressions. All were obedient to the squire's command. "Gentlemen," continued he, with a most knowing smile, "is—Sammy—Reynolds—in—this—company—of—gentlemen?"

"Yes," said Sam, "here I am."

"Sammy," said the squire, winking to the company, and drawing the head of his cane to his mouth with an arch smile as he closed, "I—wish—you—to tell—cousin—Bobby—and—these—gentlemen here present—what—your—Uncle—Tommy—said—before—the—fight—began?"

"Oh! get away, Uncle Tom," said Sam, smiling (the squire winked), "you don't know nothing about *fighting*." (The squire winked again.) "All you know about it is how it'll begin, how it'll go on, how it'll end; that's all. Cousin Bob, when you going to fight again, just go to the old man, and let him tell you all about it. If he can't, don't ask nobody else nothing about it, I tell you."

The squire's foresight was complimented in many ways by the bystanders; and he retired, advising "the boys to be at peace, as fighting was a bad business."

Durham and Stallings kept their beds for several weeks, and did not meet again for two months. When they met, Billy stepped up to Bob and offered his hand, saying, "Bobby, you've *licked* me a fair fight; but you wouldn't have done it if I hadn't been in the wrong. I oughtn't to have treated your wife as I did; and I felt so through the whole fight; and it sort o' cowed me."

"Well, Billy," said Bob, "let's be friends. Once in the fight, when you had my finger in your mouth, and was pealing me in the face and breast, I was going to halloo; but I thought of Betsy, and knew the house would be too hot for me if I got whipped when fighting for her, after always whipping when I fought for myself."

"Now that's what I always love to see," said a by-stander. "It's true I brought about the fight, but I wouldn't have done it if it hadn't o' been on account of *Miss* (Mrs.) Durham. But dod etarnally darn my soul, if I ever could stand by and see any woman put upon, much less *Miss* Durham. If Bobby hadn't been there, I'd o' took it up myself, be darned if I wouldn't, even if I'd o' got whipped for it. But we're all friends now." The reader need hardly be told that this was Ransy Sniffle.

Thanks to the Christian religion, to schools, colleges, and benevolent associations, such scenes of barbarism and cruelty as that which I have been just describing are now of rare occurrence, though they may still be occasionally met with in some of the new counties. Wherever they prevail, they are a disgrace to that community. The peace-officers who countenance them deserve a place in the Penitentiary.

Augustus Baldwin Longstreet (1790-1870)

Longstreet was born in Augusta, Georgia. Aside from several pro-secessionist essays and pamphlets and a novel, MASTER WILLIAM MITTEN (1864), Longstreet's major work is his collection of stories and reminiscences, GEORGIA SCENES: *Characters, Incidents, &c, in the First Half Century of the Republic* (1835). "The Fight" is taken from GEORGIA SCENES.

The Duel

William Tappan Thompson

IT WAS ON A RAINY SEPTEMBER EVENING in the fall of 18—, that a group of men were seated round the cheerful bar-room fire of the Planters' Hotel. Among them were several from the country, who were detained in town by the inclemency of the weather, but the majority of the company was composed of citizens of Pineville. Uncle Hearty, who generally presided on such occasions, was present, and Sammy Stonestreet was there, to drink his share of the rum, and to indicate to the rest the laughing places in such stories as had become rather stale, or in which the humour was not easily detected by less experienced jokers.

The evening was well-nigh spent—notwithstanding the company evinced no inclination to disperse, while they freely mixed in conversation, and entertained each other with stories and anecdotes that ever and anon elicited loud bursts of laughter; the usual precursor of which was a shrill squeal from Sammy, who beat the floor with his cotton-stalk, by way of accompaniment. Sometimes Uncle Hearty only evinced his risibility by a sort of asthmatic wheeze in the throat, but when he rose above that, and broke forth into one of his good, old-fashioned, side-shaking laughs, the balance of the company needed no better assurance that there was indeed something to laugh at, and unanimously joined in the chorus.

In the midst of this scene of social hilarity the street door was opened, and a tall, dark-complexioned man entered, and without ceremony seated himself in a conspicuous part of the room. He was at once recognised as no less a personage than Major Ferguson Bangs, and the customary salutation of "good evening, Major Bangs," was uttered by several at the same time. The person thus addressed made no reply; but, crossing his legs and cocking his hat with a most impudent inclination to one side of his head, contracted his thick, black brow, and, after gazing insolently round the room, fixed his fierce gaze upon the fire, and remained silent.

"Never mind, gentle*men*," said Sammy, "the major's got his high-heeled boots on to-night. Go on 'bout Gun Bustin gittin' into the waspses nest."

After the momentary interruption occasioned by the intrusion, the story of Gun Bustin and the wasps' nest was resumed, and Major Bangs left to indulge in his revery of thought, uninterrupted by any further address. As the speaker proceeded with his story, the major smiled a very incredulous smile, occasionally uttering a loud "ahem!"—and in the midst of the general laugh that followed its conclusion, he was heard to mutter something that had a "d—n" in it. But no notice was taken, by the company, either of the clearing of his throat or the muttering. At length the major's patience seemed to have become wearied, and he determined to adopt some surer means of attracting attention. Accordingly, he turned abruptly round in his seat, and fixing his gaze steadfastly upon one who was relating an anecdote in which himself was a prominent actor, waited until the speaker drew to a close, when, as the laugh died away, he exclaimed, aloud—"Doubts arising, sir!"

The major was no stranger to the speaker, and the remark was permitted to pass without notice.

But Major Ferguson Bangs was not to be foiled in his attempt to provoke a quarrel. He became more and more insolent, and seized upon every opportunity to interrupt and insult the speakers, by whistling upon a high key, and uttering such exclamations as—"Bah!"—"whew!"—"that'll do for the marines," and the like.

At length a few whispers were passed between some three or four of the party, and a well-known wag commenced an anecdote. Major Bangs directed his attention immediately to the speaker. As the latter concluded, the major bent upon him a look of most ineffable sarcasm, and exclaimed—"Bah!"

"I'd like to know what you mean by that insinewation, Major Bangs?" demanded Ned Jones.

"Doubts arising, sir!" exclaimed the major, with an oath.

"Doubt who, sir?"

"Doubts arising, sir!" reiterated the major in a fierce voice, as he gave his chair a whirl from under him and rose to his feet. "That's what I mean, sir! Take it up if you dare, sir! Do you know Major Ferguson Bangs, sir? Take care, young man, how you play with the forked lightning! Whew!" and he gave his teeth a grind that was distinctly heard in every part of the room.

"I only axed what you meant, major—I don't want to git into no fuss," replied Ned, apparently half terrified out of his wits.

"Fuss!—bah! you asked what I meant. I've told you, sir. You can pocket it, sir—but don't know me the next time you see me. Do you understand, sir? None but gentlemen are permitted to know Major Bangs, sir."

Then pacing to and fro, the entire length of the room, the major complacently observed the effect of his blustering speech upon the crowd, and casting a searching look at the young man whom he had so rudely insulted, and who was now engaged in earnest consultation with several friends, in one corner of the room, he exclaimed in a haughty tone—

"I despise a slink!"

"Who do you call a slink?" demanded Jones.

"Every dog knows his own name when he hears it, sir," replied the major.

"But look here, mister, I'll let you know I aint no dog—and I aint gwine to put up with no more of your insolence, nether!"

"Insolence, sir! Thunder and furies, do you know who you are talking to, sir?"

"Yes, I'm talkin' to Major Bumblusterbus from Virginia, what got his horse's tail shaved at the Big Spring Barbecue, when he was so drunk he didn't know which end to put the bridle on. That's who I'm talkin' to; and if he don't sing small, the fust thing he'll know he'll git the worst lickin' he ever had in his life, rite here in this room."

As the speaker concluded he stripped off his coat and placed it in the hands of Sammy Stonestreet, who was now dancing about in an ecstasy of delight at the prospect of approaching hostilities, while Uncle Hearty was loud in his expostulations with the crowd.

"Now, boys—come major," said he, turning from one party to the other as he spoke, "do stop it now—whar's the use of kickin' up a rumpus this here time o'night—look here now—listen to your Uncle Hearty, and take his advice—he's older than you all is—come now, Neddy—come, major, let's all take a drink and drap it."

By this time—whether from the influence of Uncle Hearty's harangue, or some other cause, we will not pretend to say—the fiery major had become quite docile, while the other party only grew more and more hostile, until it required some three or four to hold him off.

"Whar is he?" shouted Jones; "jest let me light on him, if you want to see how slick Georgia kin top out old Virginy. Whoopee! I's the boy kin tame your forket lightnin's! I'm the kuja Dick! the big buck of the water! the Georgia stag! Whoopee!—don't hold me!"

"Oh, yes, sir, you've got your friends round you now, and you can talk big, sir. Major Bangs can be found when he's got his friends with him, sir, but he don't fight everybody, sir, nor in a bar-room, sir."

He was now joined by three or four of the party, who professed themselves his friends, and who advised him to challenge Ned Jones, which, they urged, would be much the most genteel way of settling the difficulty.

"Oh, he's beneath my notice," said the major—"I'll not dirty my fingers with him."

"That will never do, major," remarked Bill Peters—"they'll have it all over town before to-morrow morning, that Major Ferguson Bangs was backed out by Ned Jones, a man who everybody knows is the greatest coward that ever lived."

"Think I ought to call him out, eh, Peters?"

"To be sure I do; but I'm afraid there'll be no such thing as getting honourable satisfaction out of him—for I do believe he would quit the state before he'd fight."

"Well, sir, I'm of your opinion, sir,—I'll challenge him to-morrow."

"Now's the time to cut his comb, major."

"Challenge him right here, now?"

"Yes, and you'll see how he'll drop his feathers."

"Well, Peters, write out a challenge, and I'll blow him to the d—l, sir. How dare he call me Major Bumblusterbus,—a man belonging to one of the best Virginia families, sir—Bumblusterbus! That word will be the death of him, sir. Come, let's take some liquor, and then we'll fix the challenge."

Accordingly, Major Bangs, with those who claimed to be of his party, and our friend, Sammy Stonestreet—who drank on this occasion as a neutral—stepped up to the bar, and, having drank "success," pen, ink, and paper were called for, and a challenge drawn in due form, which was borne by Peters to the adverse party. The challenge was promptly accepted, seconds and friends appointed, and the hour fixed for the meeting, which was to take place on the following day, at ten o'clock in the morning, in an old field at a little distance from the town.

"Did he look scared?" asked the major of his second.

"That he did,—he turned pale as a sheet," replied Peters.

"Has he a family, Peters?"

"No."

"Well, that's fortunate, sir. I suppose he knows I'm a dead shot— a perfect liner, sir—cut the cross nine times in ten, on the word. But come, let's take some more liquor."

Uncle Hearty announced that it was "bed-time for all honest people," and, after exhorting "the boys" to go home and take a good nap, and try to get up in a better humour in the morning, that worthy old gentleman took his departure. Soon after the party broke up—the more peaceable members to seek their beds, while the major and his friends went in search of pistols, bullet-moulds, powder, and other necessary equipments, in the collection and preparation of which the balance of the night was spent.

Early on the following morning, Major Bangs was seen blustering through the streets of Pineville, with a pair of large duelling pistols under his arm, wrapped in a red silk handkerchief. His friends had managed to keep up the excitement by frequent libations during the night, and he was now "full of *valour* and distempering draughts."

"Do you think he'll show himself on the ground?" asked the major of his second,—"have you seen him this morning, sir?"

"No, indeed—the sun did not catch Ned Jones in the county, *this* morning, if he had time to get over the line before it rose."

"Do you think he has cut out, sure enough?"

"No doubt of it, major."

"Well, sir, I will have to post him as a coward, you know. But I'd rather do that than take his life, sir, and you know I'm a dead shot."

"To be sure you are, major, and a gentleman of honour."

"Of the Virginia stamp, Peters."

"Right," said Peters—"let's take some liquor."

Notwithstanding the strict injunction of secrecy, Sammy Stonestreet had spread the intelligence of the approaching duel over the whole town, and, long before the appointed hour, the best portion of the male population were on their way to the place of meeting, to witness the combat. As it drew near the time, the major and his friends repaired to the ground, where, greatly to his surprise, he beheld his antagonist quietly seated upon a log, awaiting his arrival. As Major Bangs observed Jones and his friends busied in preparing their arms, notwithstanding his inner man was well fortified with some half-dozen glasses of brandy and water, there was a sudden change in the expression of his countenance, and he turned to his friend and remarked—

"Why, Peters, there he sits, cool as a cucumber!"

"Sure enough!" replied Peters, with well-affected surprise. "Well, major, it will save us the trouble of posting him, you know!"

The major was, just at this crisis, afflicted with a difficulty in swallowing, and before he had time to reply, one from the adverse party called out—

"Gentlemen, are you ready to lay off the ground?"

"Why, it aint time for that yet, is it, Peters?" asked the major in a tremulous undertone.

"Yes, sir, we on the part of Major Bangs, are ready," replied Peters, without answering the major's interrogatory.

"Peters," said the major, grasping him hard by the arm, and whispering in his ear—"let Dr. Jones step it off—he's got the longest legs—and tell him to straddle his best, for you see I'm death on a long shot."

The process of pacing off the ground was now performed with due formality. The pegs were driven, and the articles between the belligerent parties read. The principals were then called upon to cast lots for the choice of position. The major trembled like an aspen leaf, and his lips were colourless. The cool deliberation of his antagonist increased his own trepidation, and, like Bob Acres, he began to feel his valour "ooze out at the ends of his fingers."

"I'm told," said Peters, approaching with a loaded pistol, "that Jones is a dead shot on the third or fourth word—so, major, your best chance is to draw a quick bead."

"The h—ll he is!" gasped Bangs. "Why didn't you tell me that before, Peters?" continued he in a husky voice; "have you got any liquor?"

A bottle was produced, and the major made a heavy draw upon its contents.

"I'm not afraid to die, Peters," said he, as he handed back the bottle, and his filling eyes rolled wildly in their sockets, as if he were about to give up the ghost without a fire. "I aint afraid to die, but somehow I feel sort o' curious. But it's not because I'm afraid, Peters. There are some little matters that ought to be fixed first, and I'd like to live till my time comes. But," he continued, grasping his second by the hand, and vainly endeavouring to make a show of resolution—"you know Major Bangs, Peters——"

"To be sure. I know him to be a brave man, and a man of honour, who would rather die than be disgraced on the field by——"

"Right, Peters, right—toss up for choice."

Up went the dollar, and as it whirled in the air, the major called out—"Heads!"

"Heads it is!" exclaimed Peters. "The choice is ours, major."

There was little or no choice in the ground, so that the major found it a very difficult matter to decide. By the aid of his second he was at length enabled to make a selection, and, staggering to one of the pegs, took his position. Jones was on the ground in an instant—the seconds took their respective places, and the individual who had been appointed to give the word demanded—

"Are you ready, gentlemen?"

"Yes," answered Jones.

"No! stop!" yelled the major, scarce able to keep his feet.

"What's the matter?" asked Peters, approaching.

"Do you think Jones wouldn't make it up, Peters?" whispered the major.

"What, major! We, the challenging party, propose a compromise! That would never do, you know. There's no chance of an honourable adjustment of the matter now, unless they make the proposition to us.

Remember, your *honour* is at stake, Major Bangs, your sacred honour."

This appeal was sufficient, though it was very evident that the major, like many others who have found themselves in a similar *honourable* position, would much rather have ventured his honour at stake than his foot at that peg.

"Right, Peters—tell 'em to go ahead," said he, concentrating his energies into one desperate effort to stand erect.

"Are you ready, gentlemen?"

"Yes," was the answer from both parties.

"Fire! (bang) one, two, three, (bang) four, five—stop!"

Both pistols were discharged—Major Bangs's between the words "fire" and "one." After the discharge of his pistol he could no longer stand, but fell forward on both knees. A proposition was then made, at his request, for a reconciliation. But Jones was inexorable, swore that Bangs had attempted to dodge his fire, and that he would not leave the field until blood had been drawn.

"Load up again, boys," said he, in a voice loud enough to be heard by Bangs, "I'll tap his demijon for him this time, now mind if I don't."

"If I had a thought he was such a blood-thirsty devil, I'd never challenged him," muttered the major. "I see it plain enough—I'm a dead man, Peters. The muzzle of his pistol is as large as the mouth of a Dutch oven, and he loads with buck-shot."

"Oh, no, major."

"I'm sure of it, Peters, for I heard 'em whiz about my head like a swarm of bumble-bees. But pass the bottle here, Peters, and I'll die like a man of honour."

Just at this juncture Jones's second advanced and desired to speak with Peters. The major, strong in the belief that a proposition for a reconciliation was at hand, drew himself up, and assumed a most valorous bearing—all the chivalric sentiment of his soul was pumped up for the occasion, and for a moment he stood the impersonation of resolute defiance. After a brief consultation, Peters approached the major, remarking—

"Jones proposes, major, that as one shot has passed between you without effect, and as he is satisfied——"

"So am I," interrupted the major—"I'm perfectly willing—"

"But hear me out, major. He says he's satisfied that the distance is too great, and proposes to reduce it one-half."

"I'll see him d—d first!" exclaimed the disappointed major, all his feathers and his hopes falling at once. "The bloody-minded devil wants to git my head in the muzzle of his pistol."

The pistols were again loaded, and the parties took their respective positions. All the major's trepidation had returned. As he took the pistol in his trembling hand, he stared wildly into the face of his second, muttering in a low, husky voice:

"Farewell, Peters—I'm a case."

"Tut, tut, major, keep a stiff upper lip, and you'll bring him this time."

On the next fire, Jones fell to the ground with a deep groan! There was a rush to the spot—his breast was covered with blood!

"Oh, my God!" exclaimed Bangs, "I've killed him! Run, Peters, and call all the doctors in town!—run, for Heaven's sake, run! Oh, my Lord, what have I done! The devil will get my soul for this!—I told 'em I was a dead shot.—Why didn't somebody stop the duel?" And away he dashed into town, as fast as he could run, exclaiming—"I've killed him!—I've killed him!—I told 'em I was a dead shot!"

An odd specimen of human nature was Major Ferguson Bangs. A Virginian by birth, he had, some years previous to the date of our sketch, found his way to Georgia in the capacity of a negro trader, and settled near Pineville. The major was a successful planter, but, though he possessed many broad acres, and joined fences with several wealthy neighbours, he had failed in all his attempts to join hearts and hands with some one of their lovely daughters; a circumstance to which some were disposed to attribute certain eccentricities of character in which he was at times wont to indulge. When sober, there was not a more sensible or better disposed person to be found than the proud Virginia major; but with him the old adage which says—"When wine is in, wit is out," was most strikingly verified. Under the influence of liquor he became a very fool, and, strange as it may seem, sought, on all such occasions, to sustain the character—for which of all others he was least qualified—of a fighting man. He was tall, athletic, and masculine in features, with a haughty curling lip; but with all these attributes of a bully, fight was not in his nature; nor could all the stimulus his system was able to bear infuse sufficient of the combative principle within him to render him a hero. The major was singularly conscientious, and, perhaps, his greatest weakness was a firm belief in the supernatural. Drunk or sober he lived in dread of ghosts and apparitions, and those who knew him best were of opinion that, coward as he was, he feared man less than he did the devil.

The reader has already come to the conclusion that the duel was a sham affair, and that the pistols were loaded with powder only. Such was the fact, though Major Bangs, important as was the part sustained by him in the performance, had been left entirely ignorant of the trick, and while the balance of the *dramatis personæ* were enjoying the farce they enacted, he was "doing" tragedy in good earnest.

Poor major! not only had he experienced what it is to be shot at and missed, but now he felt the mark of Cain as indelibly fixed upon his brow as if it had been branded there with a piece of red-hot brimstone, by the very old gentleman himself. He had honourable friends, too, who stuck by him, determined to make the most of the occasion. They drank his health at his own expense, and bragged of his prowess, by which means they managed to keep his imagination up to fever heat, during the balance of the day. Indeed, between the influence of liquor and the pathetic accounts which they related to him of Jones's dying agonies, he had become, towards evening, almost frantic.

About dark, a message was brought to him from Jones. It was an urgent request that he would visit him before he died, and receive from him his pardon and forgiveness.

"No, no, gentlemen; I cannot bear to look at the man I have murdered!" exclaimed the major.

"But, he says he aint got but a few minutes to live, no how, and he wants you to come and see him, so he wont die with no grudge agin anybody," said one.

"Did he say so, boys?"

"Yes, major, and you better go and make it up with him, and then you'll be apt to sleep better, you know."

"Sleep!" exclaimed the major, glaring his eyes wildly open, with a vacant stare—"sleep!—no, these eyes will never sleep again, sir—these eyes—"

"Oh, pshaw, major, come along and don't snap 'em so."

"Yes, come, major," said his second, who joined to persuade him.

"Is that you, Peters? Will you stand by Major Bangs, Peters? Well, come, boys—but I'd rather see the devil. Does he look bad, boys? for I can't look at him if he does."

"Oh, no, he looks pretty well, considerin' he's got a ounce ball right through his guzzler vein—"

"That all comes of being a line shot," interrupted the major, with an involuntary shudder.

"But you must shake hands and make it all up with him before he dies, and then you'll feel better. Besides, major, you know you killed him in an honourable way."

"D—n the honourable way!—it all counts the same—and the devil will make a blizzard of my soul for it."

Taking the arms of two of the company, the major walked over to the "long room" to take a parting look at his unfortunate antagonist. Jones lay in a bed with his head bolstered up until he sat almost erect. His face was well smeared with flour, and bloody cloths were profusely scattered about the room. As the major came quaking to the door, it was flung wide open, and the ghastly spectacle burst suddenly upon him. Shivering with horror, he shrunk aghast, and with mouth distended and eyeballs starting from their inflamed sockets, stood for a moment as if transfixed to the spot, while large drops of perspiration started to his brow. His foot was braced against the threshold, and all the force that could be applied to his broad shoulders was not sufficient to urge him into the room. At length Jones beckoned him feebly with his hand. The major flinched. Jones said in a low voice—

"I'm—ah, oh!—I'm gwine, major!—ah, to—oh!—oh-o-o-o—!"

"Let me go, boys!" shouted Bangs—"let me go!" and with one desperate effort he shook them off, and fled from the house. Had he remained a moment longer, he would have discovered the trick that had been put upon him; for Jones, unable longer to restrain his mirth, sprang from the bed and joined in the laugh.

It had now grown late, and Major Bangs was permitted to seek his lodgings without further interruption. His room was upon the ground floor of an out-house belonging to the hotel—in it there were several beds, but on this occasion he chanced to be the only tenant. Filled with horrible imaginings and gloomy fears, he sought his bed. He was in no mood to be over nice, and as his boots obstinately refused to be drawn, he allowed them to remain—his hat and stock, being articles of minor importance, were also permitted to occupy their respective places. Thus half undressed, he threw himself upon his bed, and endeavoured to find in the arms of Morpheus a refuge from the upbraidings of a guilty conscience. But

> "Instead of poppies, willows
> Waved o'er his couch."

The horrid spectacle of the dying Jones was constantly before him, and when he closed his eyes to shut out the fearful vision, horned devils with long fiery tails danced and frisked around him, with red-hot tridents in their claws, as if ready to pitch him into that unknown country, of which, in his youth, he had been taught to entertain a very unfavourable opinion. It commenced to rain, but the pattering upon the roof was no opiate to him, and the lightning only afforded him horrid glimpses of demons and devils as they skulked into the corners of the room. The storm became more violent—the lightning blazed in upon his face, and the thunder shook the foundations of the old building, while a rumbling sound seemed to come up from the bowels of the earth, as if it were about to open to receive him. He heard the tramp of feet in his room, and

> "He felt his hair
> Twine like a knot of snakes around his face,"

as he beheld, by the fitful glare of the lightning, the old king devil of all approaching his bed. He would have prayed, shouted, fled, any thing, but his very soul was frozen within him, and he sank powerless upon his pillow. The demon approached, and, placing his cloven foot upon the bed-side, leaned over and gazed down upon him with his eyes of fire. The major's lips moved, but he had not breath for a word—he smelt the brimstone and saw the demon's horns. He remembered his grandmother's charm for evil spirits—and he *thought* "in the name of the Lord, what do you want of me?" but the demon only shook its head. In the desperate extremity of his fear the major grasped forward with both hands. By chance he seized the horns—the next moment he was upon the floor struggling with his satanic visitor—a moment after, he was fleeing through the street, shouting and screaming, on his way to the tavern.

Some five or six village gossips were seated round the bar-room fire, when Major Bangs made his *entrée* in the eccentric costume we have described.

"Why, what upon yeath's the matter with the major?" exclaimed Uncle Hearty, rising from his seat.

The major shook in every joint—his teeth rattled and his eyes glared wildly about the room.

"Why, major, what under heavens ails you?" inquired two or three in the same breath.

"I'm right from h—ll!" gasped the major. "I had him by the horns!—I told 'em it would be so—keep him off, wont you, gentle-men—where's Peters?"

"Pore feller!" remarked uncle Hearty—"he's lost his senses. The boys has been projectin' with him agin."

He was wet and cold, and it was quite evident that his physical strength was fast sinking under the terrible excitement of his mind. Humanity suggested that something should be done to check the raging fever of his brain, or dangerous consequences might ensue. Accordingly, he was conducted to a bed and his comfort carefully provided for.

About noon on the following day the major made his appearance in the bar-room, and desired to see the landlord. His face was haggard and pale, his eyes blood-shotten and heavy, and his countenance still bore the traces of the dreadful fright he had experienced. He seemed to have a confused recollection of the incidents of the past day, but on no subject was his memory clear and distinct, except in reference to his encounter with the devil. That circumstance had made an indelible impression on his mind, which his friends found great difficulty in removing—nor is he to this day clearly satisfied that there was not some infernal agency in the matter.

He was duly informed of all the particulars of the duel—how he had been drunk, insulting everybody he met, and how that a few mischievous fellows had made him the hero of a sham duel.

"But, captain," said he, "the devil?—I saw him, sir, last night, as sure as I stand here, sir."

"You saw my old Billy-goat," replied the landlord. "You went to bed in the 'long room,' and left both doors open, and when the rain came on, Billy sought shelter in your apartment."

"Oh, but I smelled the brimstone, sir, as plain as could be."

"You smelled Billy's beard, major, which is quite high flavoured, and might be taken for brimstone by a man who would go to bed in his hat and boots."

"Then you think it really was him I had the tussle with, eh?"

"To be sure it was—he is the only horned gentleman on my premises, I trust."

"Well," replied the major, after a moment's reflection, "I've made a pretty considerable fool of myself, sir, that's a fact. Have my horse brought out, sir, and if ever you catch Major Ferguson Bangs in another such scrape, sir, may the devil get him sure enough, sir."

Major Bangs did not show himself in Pineville for a long time after this event, and when he did visit town again, he had but one quarrel, and that was with the first man who asked him to drink. He was never known to be drunk after the day of The Duel.

William Tappan Thompson (1812-1882)

Thompson, whose father was from Virginia and whose mother was from Ireland, was born in Ravenna, Ohio. He moved to Georgia in 1834 and lived for many years in Savannah. Among his collections are Major Jones's Courtship (1843, 1844, 1872), Chronicles of Pineville (1845), and Major Jones's Sketches of Travel (1848). "The Duel" is taken from Major Jones's Courtship.

Lije Benadix

THE MAN WHO ATE AT ONE TIME TWO PECKS OF PLUMS AND CHERRIES, "SEED, SKINS AND ALL—TOOK A WHOLE LOT OF 'DOCTOR'S TRUCK,' AND LIVED THROUGH ALL!"

Francis Robinson

IN THE YEAR 18— there vegetated a specimen of the *genus homo*, in the county of K—— in the glorious old junior State of the original thirteen, about whom we propose to say a few words, and as a description of his *tout ensemble*, manners, etc. will the better elucidate our tale, we will proceed to give our readers a pen and ink sketch of our friend and hero, Mr. *Lije Benadix*. He was, we suppose, some forty years of age—married, and, as a natural consequence, his table was surrounded with many "olive branches." To feed all these mouths, required from Lije, pretty hard scratching; though the principal *feeder* seemed to be Lije himself. He was, withal, incorrigibly *lazy*—now with plenty to satisfy the appetite—again without a dust of meal in his larder. In fruit season, he could manage to get his fill of fruits; and when plums and cherries became ripe in May, then Lije, cormorant-like, would gulph them down in large quantities, bolting them *en masse!* It is fair to presume that with his lazy habits, enormous appetite and a generous diet, Lije would have soon become a second Falstaff, but as he did not have the good fortune to possess the last named very important accompaniment, he was gaunt as a grey hound, his skin yellow and wrinkled, features shrunken and extremities diminutive! Upon the whole, an observer would at once pronounce him to be a man unused to a diet sufficiently healthy and nutritive: for upon *ordinary* occasions, with his "copperas mixed" clothes hanging upon him as upon a drying line, the conclusion would also be pretty certainly arrived at, that Lije was either "drying" up, preparatory to flying away, or had his garments made amply large for *extra-ordinary* occasions too. As often as he became possessed of a bushel of meal, in pay for "splitting rails," (the only species of work of any kind he seemed to fancy,) he would lie at home, and himself and family would cook and eat continuously until the last "hoe cake was baked" and eaten; then, perhaps, he would stir around for another job of work. Sometimes the opportunity was afforded him to "provision his ship," as for instance when called to the county seat during the session of the Superior Court. On these occasions "landlord, cook and waiters" suffered; for his usual allowance, to give a specimen, *was thirteen cups of coffee* and other provisions in the same proportion. Once he ventured to call for the *"fourteenth"* cup, when his host could stand it no longer, and ordered him peremptorily to leave the house, telling him he was welcome to what he had eaten.

"Why Landlord, do let a fellow finish eatin—I aint nigh done yit!" protested Lije.

"Get out of my house, I tell you; for I'd as soon undertake to feed a caravan of animals, with a circus thrown in!"

And poor Lije, *still hungry*, as he protested, and ready to pay for all he eat, was obliged to *vamoose*.

At one time Lije became possessed, by some means, of a large turkey, which he took to a neighboring county seat during the session of the Court there.—This bird he *sold* to the hotel keeper, and as we shall see, also *sold* the purchaser. Lije received, in cash, one dollar, and was to have his dinner in the bargain! The fowl was duly spitted, *secundem artem*, and our host congratulated himself upon this accession to his ordinary supplied table, and thus being able to give his boarders a treat. In the meantime, Lije hung around the hotel, noticing from time to time, the clock, and peering into the dining room to make his observations. Just before the dinner hour he slipped into the dining hall, called a waiter, told him he was in a hurry to go home, and as his master had promised him his dinner, he wanted some of the "Old Gobler." It was set before him, and he attacked it bravely. Not a long while after Court adjourned, and the landlord took occasion to announce a fine fat turkey for dinner, setting all who heard him on the *qui vive*. As soon as the bell rung all rushed to the table; anxious eyes wandered up and down it—while every one called for *turkey*! The landlord, hearing a report of "there's none, massa, lef," pricked up his ears and called out,

"Waiter! what does this mean? Where's that turkey?"

"Him eat up, sir, all but de bone!"

"The d—l! who done it, you rascal? Tell me, or I'll break every bone in your skin!"

"Dat man you bot um from, sir, I spec, for he come a little while ago and tell me you promise 'im his dinner—he was in hurry—and wanted de *turkey*! Dat all I know 'bout um, massa."

"Bring me the dish, sir!"

The dish was brought, and upon it reposed as nice a skeleton as one would wish to see; not a particle left upon the bones that was eatable. At this "visible explanation," the whole table was set in a roar, and the joke being so good a one, each one good-humoredly forgot his disappointment and made the most of the "common doins'" before them.

   With these specimens of "Lije's" prowess in the eating line, we shall again introduce him to you in another, as the cap-stone of all. There poor Lije lies, stretched on his back, swollen to three times his natural size and laboring under not only indigestion, but the most desperare state of constipation, perhaps, ever attempted to be removed by the medical faculty. It was in the midst of plum and cherry time, and in default of more digestible food, Lije had supplied his larder with a quantity, and had attacked them with his usual voracity and disregard of consequences. Hence his situation; for, like the Anaconda, who upon bolting his occasional meal becomes inert, so Lije had gorged himself until he had become helpless. Contrary to his expectations, his digestive apparatus was insuffcient to accomplish the Herculean task thus imposed, and he was placed thereby, completely *hors du combat*, exhibiting a kind of inanimate existence, only. At this particular stage of his case he called in a physician, who, after exerting his skill for some time, gave him up, with the conviction that there was not yet made known in the Pharmacopiæ of Medicine any *emetic* or *purgative* sufficiently powerful to be brought to bear successfully upon the truly appalling case under his care. He, therefore, retreated from the field, leaving poor Lije in the hands of his Creator and to his own natural powers, satisfied that all human means having failed, nothing short of a miraculous intervention would ever restore poor Lije to active life and to the helpless and dependant family around him. His condition was noised abroad and many of Lije's neighbors had called to see him, and among them was a *"Yerb Dokter,"* as he called himself, named *Lobelia*, with the prefix, of course, of "Dockter." This professional gentleman had, however, no idea of trying his skill, not he! but proposed that a messenger should be sent some fifteen miles to an adjoining county to procure the services of a practitioner of extensive practice and long experience in medicine; who, by the way, was well known in that region, his practice even extending there usually. As Dr. Lobelia made the proposition, he was selected as the messenger to Dr. W——, and there might have been seen the very unusual sight of a "yerb" doctor's going for an allopathic physician! However, we must charitably suppose that Dr. L—— was actuated by sympathy for suffering humanity, and for once laid aside all his professional prejudice and antipathy so notoriously known to exist between the one and the other. He found Dr. W—— worn down with fatigue and unable to return with him that evening, but received the prescription of a dose of *calomel* and the promise of a visit next morning. Now, it is very well known that a mad-dog has no greater antipathy to water than has a "yerb" doctor to *calomel*, the medicine prescribed; and Dr. Lobelia took occasion to express his disbelief in its use, and a want of confidence in it any way!

"Give it to him, sir, as I direct," said Dr. W——, "and it will do him as much *good* as if *you* had every confidence in it!"

Dr. L—— returned to Lije's that evening, but remaining in the "same opinion still" in regard to the calomel, did *not* administer the dose as directed.

The next morning (Monday) by 10 A.M. Dr. W. arrived at the place. There he found a large number of Lije's neighbors, men and women, collected in the house and about the yard, discussing his case pro and con; for it had excited the curiosity of every one, besides interesting many who had kind feelings for him and his family. Dr. W. entered the house, a small, contracted affair, built of round logs and covered with oak boards. In *the* room, for we believe the house contained but a single apartment, on a bed Lije was stretched on his back, an uninterested witness of all that might be said and done. The doctor approached his bedside and made the inquiry,

"How do you feel to-day, Mr. Benadix?"

"V-e-r-y p-o-o-r-l-y, d-o-c-t-o-r," replied Lije.

The doctor then proceeded to examine him, and found his symptoms to be these: "pulse slow and rather feeble, without fever, skin rather cooler than natural, vomiting about every half hour, ejecting a half pint of a morbid secretion accumulated between the intervals of vomiting, abdomen enormously distended and as tight as a drum-head, and tongue but slightly coated." After this examination of the case was concluded he asked,

"Well, Mr. Benadix, how many plums and cherries have you eaten?"

"Not—very—many—doctor!" replied Lije, in a slow and drawling tone of voice.

"Yes, you did," spoke up his wife quickly, "you eat nearly or quite two pecks, and you eat hulls, stones and all—you did."

"Ah! indeed," remarked Dr. W., "it is very strange that a man of your age, Mr. Benadix, should eat such a quantity of plums and cherries, stones and all!—Now, sir, if you had been an old turkey gobler, you might, with some show of reason, have ate those articles, because, then you would have had a *gizzard* with which to have *ground up* such an indigestible mass!"

His wife hearing this and thinking it necessary that "the truth, the whole truth" of the affair should be made known to the doctor, again spoke up and said,

"Yes, an' you eat a pan full of honey-comb on top of 'em, too—you did."

"I-n-d-e-e-d!" remarked the doctor, somewhat tartly, "if you had only ate the pan full of *rich soil* instead of the *honey-comb*, you might very soon have had an orchard and nursery very convenient!"

The doctor was somewhat vexed at the unprecedented imprudence of his patient, and in anticipation of the trouble he would have in consequence; but having received all the information he could, he at once determined to attempt to relieve him if possible. Before leaving home, he had provided himself with all the emetic and purgative medicines, from the simplest to the most powerful known; and, on his way, passing a store, procured a pound or so of tobacco (for enemas) as a *corps de reserve*. He asked and obtained the gratuitous service of a gentleman present as assistant; and to work they both went; commencing with purgatives, they gave him during the day, Castor Oil, Salts and Senna, Salts and Magnesia, Jalap and C. Tartar, Rhubarb and Aloes, Gamboge and Scammony, and Calomel to no purpose, for the stomach would not retain any of them longer than from a half to one hour. *Croton Oil* and a very strong *infusion of Tobacco*, were reserved until towards evening. Continually embarrassed by the ejection of the medicines, but determining not to be backed out, as fast as one dose was ejected another was given, with little regard to quantity, varying the matter occasionally by a simple *enema*. After the day was well nigh spent, and the patient being, (as he very frequently and invariably would say, when asked how he felt) *"about as usual,"* the doctor determined to "charge the enemy" with the "advance guard" of his "reserve forces" in the shape of *Croton Oil*—informing his assistant before he did so, "that it was a powerful drug, and if it could be retained in the stomach one hour he would be hopeful of giving his patient relief, and he would be able to tell in that time what it was capable of accomplishing." So Lije swallowed *two drops*! and the doctor, watch in hand, sat by his bedside to count the moments as they flew, asking his patient at intervals how he felt, and receiving the same unsatisfactory answer of *"about as usual."*

"Do you not feel any effect from the last medicine you have taken?" asked the doctor, Lije being unaware of its name or quality.

"It—burnt—my—throat—a—little!" answered Lije.

The hour passed—an additional half hour—no effect was produced by the Croton Oil—the patient seeming to be *"about as usual!"* Finding the enemy so well fortified, the doctor informed his assistant "that the potent and all powerful 'reserve' must now be resorted to—that tobacco enemas must be used—that the remedy seldom failed to overcome the most obstinate constipation; that at the same time it produced such a relaxation of the system as to give one the appearance of being about to die, and that he (the assistant) must not get alarmed if this should prove to be the fact in Lije's case!" The tobacco had been infused for six hours, and was necessarily very strong; but upon using the *enema* even longer than usual in such cases,

27

the disheartening result was the same as with all the other remedies. For Lije remained still *"about as usual!"* Baffled at all points, the doctor rested awhile from his labors, only, however, to continue the onset with renewed vigor! The sun was now nearly set, and the doctor, before leaving for home, put up a large number of powders, consisting wholly of calomel, about three grains in each, with directions for one to be administered every three hours, day and night, until he saw the case again on the following Wednesday. Before taking his departure, the doctor went to the bedside of his patient to bid him "good-bye," and to speak a few words of hope and encouragement. As he turned towards the door and before reaching it, Lije drawled out the question of

"D-o-c-t-o-r, w-h-a-t s-h-a-l-l I e-a-t?"

Now this was a little more than human nature could put up with, and the doctor turned towards him instinctively and replied,

"Eat! Eat, the d—l! Get what's in you out first, then it will be time enough for you to eat more, sir!" and left him.

Wednesday came and found the doctor, according to promise, at Lije's bed-side, who, he found, upon making inquiry, *"about as usual"*— no better and no worse. He had regularly taken the powders day and night. They were continued, and in addition about the same routine was pursued as on the Monday previous; and after a day's labor with the same result, sundown again finding Lije "about as usual," a large supply of the powders were then made and the same directions given. On this visit the doctor found several of the neighbors at the house, and they were very inquisitive as to the situation of the patient as well as to the kind of "physic" given him. To all the questions put, the doctor cheerfully responded, and was very much amused at the commentaries made. Those who swore at all, swore "he would die in the fix he was in any how, and that if the disease did not *kill* him, the doctor would with all that *calomel!*" Said they: "Why dod-rot it, he'll be salivated so badly, all his teeth will *drap* out and his jaws be eat off, so ef he does git over it, he never kin eat nothin'. He'd e'nymost be dead, for if Lije loves ennything at all, it's eatin."

"Oh! there's no danger," replied the doctor, "the secretions are all suspended, and he cannot be salivated in the situation he is now in!"

"Dun know so well about that nuther, for Dr. Lobelia sez there's many a man's leg bones full of *quick-silver!*"

"Pooh! pooh! what nonsense—all stuff!" answered the doctor, as he turned away to prepare for his departure.

But they continued the discussion, and one might hear an exclamation occasionally of, "Poor fellow! ef the plums don't kill him, the *doctor* and his *calomy* will!" Upon the doctor asking Lije again how he felt, he gave the invariable reply of *"about as usual."* He left him, and did not repeat his visits, though he heard from time to time how his patient was progressing. The calomel powders were continued regularly up to the *following Saturday evening.*

Four weeks after exactly, the doctor, being on a professional visit in the same region of country, observed in the road ahead of him, not very far from a mill and near the stream upon which it was situated, a thin, tall, gaunt man, who at the distance was not a familiar form to him. The man bore some resemblance to "Lije," but the portly aldermanic rotundity he possessed when lying on his back a few weeks before had all disappeared, and instead, he had become shrivelled and shrunken, lank and lean as usual. On a nearer approach, however, the doctor at once recognized his old patient, and accosted him with,

"How are you, to-day, Mr. Benadix?"

"A-b-o-u-t a-s u-s-u-a-l, d-o-c-t-o-r," replied Lije.

"I am very glad, indeed, sir, to see you about, Mr. Benadix, for at one time, we all thought you were not long for this world, sir! I presume after all our labor and pains, the medicine was effective and relieved you at last, sir?" continued the doctor.

"O, *yes, doctor, it commenced about sundown on Saturday evening arter you was thar, and it 'taint done till yit!"* answered Lije, as the doctor, unable to contain himself, he was so full of laughter, made off. His resurrected patient lived many years after, and though he still retained the same "love of eatin'," he was careful not to try again the powers of his *digestive* apparatus by bolting such another lot of plums and cherries, "seeds, hulls and all!"

Francis James Robinson (c.1820-c.1870)

Little is known of Robinson's life. He was a country doctor and county clerk who lived in Oglethorpe County, Georgia, for most of his life. His sole book is KUPS OF KAUPHY: *A Georgia Book, in Warp and Woof, Containing Tales, Incidents, &c, of the "Empire State of the South"* (1853). "Lije Benadix" is taken from KUPS OF KAUPHY.

Investigations Concerning Mr. Jonas Lively

Richard Malcolm Johnston

"I well believe
Thou wilt not utter what thou dost not know,
And so far will I trust thee."—*Shakspere.*

"Man is but half without woman."—*Bailey.*

CHAPTER I

ALTHOUGH MR. BILL WILLIAMS had moved into Dukesborough, this
exaltation did not interfere with the cordial relations established
between him and myself at the Lorriby school. He used to come out
occasionally on visits to his mother, and seldom returned without
calling at our house. This occurred most usually upon the Sundays
when the monthly meetings were held in the church at Dukesborough.
On such days he and I usually rode home together, I upon my pony and
he upon a large brown mare which his mother had sent to him in the
forenoon.

Ever since those remote times, I have associated in my memory
Mr. Bill with that mare, and one or another of her many colts.
According to the best of my recollection, she was for years and years
never without a colt. Her normal condition seemed to be always to be
followed by a colt. Sometimes it was a horse-colt and sometimes a
mule; for the planters in those times raised at home nearly all their
domestic animals. What a lively little fellow this colt always was; and
what an anxious parent was old Molly Sparks, as Mr. Bill called the
dam! How that colt would run about and get mixed up with the horses
in the grove around the church; and how the old mare would whicker
all during the service! I knew that whicker among a hundred. Mr. Bill
used always to tie her to a swinging limb; for her anxiety would
sometimes cause her to break the frail bridle which usually confined
her, and run all about the grounds in pursuit of her truant offspring.
Mr. Bill used also to sit where he could see her in order to be ready for
all difficulties. I have often been amused to notice how he would be
annoyed by her cries and prancings and how he would pretend to be

listening intently to the sermon when his whole attention I knew to be on old Molly and the colt. Seldom was there a Sunday that he did not have to leave the church in order to catch old Molly and tie her up again. This was a catastrophe he was ever dreading, because he really disliked to disturb the service; and he had the consideration, when he rose to go, to place his handkerchief to his face, that the congregation might suppose that his nose was bleeding.

While we would be riding home, the conduct of that colt, if anything, would be worse than at the church. His fond parent would exert every effort to keep him by her side, but he would get mixed up with the horses more than before. Twenty times would he be lost. Sometimes he would be at an immense distance behind; then he would pretend, as it seemed, to be anxiously looking for his mother, and would run violently against every horse, whether under the saddle or in harness. Old Molly would wheel around and try to get back, her whickers ever resounding far and wide. When the colt would have enough of this frolic, or some one of the home-returning horsemen would give him a cut with his riding-switch, he would get out upon the side of the road, run at full speed past his dam, and get similarly mixed up with the horses in front. If he ever got where she was he would appear to be extravagantly gratified, and would make an immediate and violent effort to have himself suckled. Failing in this, he would let fly his hind-legs at her, and dash off again at full speed in whatever direction his head happened to be turned. Mr. Bill would often say that, of all the fools he ever saw, old Molly and her colt were the biggest. As for my part, the anxiety of the parent seemed to me natural in the circumstances; but I must confess, that in the matter of the quality usually called discretion, while the young of most animals have little of it usually, I have frequently thought that of all others the one who had the least amount was the colt.

I did not intend to speak of such a trifling matter, but was led to it unwarily by the association of ideas. Mr. Bill often accepted our invitations to dinner upon these Sundays, or he would walk over in the afternoon. Although he liked much the society of my parents, yet he was fondest of being with me singly. With all his fondness for talking, there was some constraint upon him, especially in the presence of my father, for whom he had the profoundest respect. So, somehow or other, Mr. Bill and I would get away to ourselves, when he could display his full powers in that line. This was easily practicable, as never or seldom did such a day pass without our having other guests to dinner from among those neighbors who resided at a greater distance from the village than we did. Our table on these Sundays was always extended to two or three times its usual length. My parents, though they were religious, thought there was no harm in detaining some of these neighbors to dinner and during the remainder of the day.

Mr. Bill had evidently realized his expectations of the pleasures and advantages of town life. It seemed to me that he was greatly improved by it. He had evidently laid aside some of his ancient awkwardness and hesitation of manner. He talked more at his ease. Then he gave a more careful and fashionable turn to his hair, and, I thought, combed and brushed it oftener than he had been wont. His trousers, too, were better pulled up, and his shirt-collar was now never or seldom without the necessary button. I was therefore somewhat surprised to hear my father remark more than once that he did not think that town life was exactly the best thing for Mr. Bill, and that he would not be surprised if he would not have done better to keep at home with his mother. But Mr. Bill grew more and more fond of Dukesborough, and he used to relate to me some of the remarkable things that occurred there. About every one of the hundred inhabitants of the place and those who visited it, he knew everything that by any possibility could be ascertained. He used to contend that it was a merchant's business to know everybody, and especially those who tried to conceal their affairs from universal observation. He had not been very long in Dukesborough before he could answer almost any question you could put to him about any of his fellow-citizens.

With one exception.

This was Mr. Jonas Lively.

He was too hard a case for Mr. Bill. Neither he nor any other person, not even Mrs. Hodge, seemed to know much about him. The late Mr. Hodge probably knew more than anybody else; but, if he did, he did not tell it, and now he was dead and gone, and Mr. Lively was left comparatively unknown to the world.

Where Mr. Lively had come from originally people did not know for certain, although he had been heard occasionally to use expressions which induced the belief that he might have been a native of the State of North Carolina. It was ascertained that he had done business for some years in Augusta, and some said that he yet owned a little property there. This much was certain, that he went there or somewhere else once every winter, and, after remaining about a month, returned, as was supposed, with two new vests and pairs of trousers. At the time that I began to take an interest in him in sympathy with Mr. Bill, he had been residing at Dukesborough for about three years; not exactly at Dukesborough either, but something less that a mile outside, where he boarded with the Hodges, occupying a small building in one corner of the yard, which they called "the Office," and in which, before he came, the family used to take their meals. He might have had his chamber in the main house where the others stayed, but for one thing; for besides the two main rooms there were a couple of low-roofed shed-rooms in front, one of which was occupied by Susan Temple, a very poor relation of Mr. Hodge. There were no children, and Mr. Lively might have had the other shed-room across the piazza, but for the fact that it was devoted to another purpose. Mr. Hodge—

But one at a time. Let me stick to Mr. Lively for the present, and tell what little was known about him.

Mr. Lively was about fifty-one or -two years of age. Mr. Bill used to insist that he would never see fifty-five again, and that he would not be surprised if he was sixty. I have no idea but that this was an over-estimate. The truth is that, as I have often remarked, young men like Mr. Bill are prone to assign too great an age to elderly men, especially when, like Mr. Lively, they are unmarried. But let that go.

Mr. Lively was quite stout in body, but of moderate-sized legs. He had a brown complexion, brown hair, and black eyebrows. His eyes were a mild green, with some tinge of red in the whites. His nose was Roman, or would have been if it had been longer; for just as it began to hook and to become Roman it stopped short, as if upon reflection it thought it wrong to ape ancient and especially foreign manners. He always wore a long black frock-coat, either gray or black trousers and vest, and a very stout, low-crowned furred hat. He carried a hickory walking-stick with a hooked handle.

He never seemed to have any regular business. True, he was known sometimes to buy a bale of cotton, or it might be two or three, and afterward have them hauled to Augusta by some neighbor's wagon, when the latter would be carrying his own to market. Then he occasionally bought a poor horse out of a wagon, and kept it at the Hodges' for a couple of months, and got him fat and sold him again at a smart profit. He was a capital doctor of horses, and was suspected of being somewhat proud of his skill in that line, as he would cheerfully render his services when called upon, and always refused any compensation. But when he traded, he traded. If he bought, he put down squarely into the seller's hands; if he sold, the money had to be put squarely into his. Such transactions were rare, however; he certainly made but little in that way. But then he spent less. Besides five dollars a month for board and lodging, and furnishing his own room, if he was out any more nobody knew what it was for.

He was a remarkably silent man. Although he came into Dukesborough often, he had but little to say to anybody and stayed but a short time. The remainder of the day he spent at home, partly in walking about the place and partly in reading while sitting in his chamber, or on the piazza between the two little shed-rooms in the front part of the house. He seldom went to church; yet upon Sundays he read the Bible and other religious books almost the livelong day.

In the lifetime of Mr. Hodge he was supposed to know consider-

34

able about Mr. Lively. The latter certainly used to talk with him with more freedom than with any other person. Mrs. Hodge, a tallish, slenderish lady, never was able to get much out of Mr. Lively, notwithstanding that she was a woman who was remarkably fond of obtaining as much information as possible about other persons. She used to give it as her opinion that there was nothing *in* Mr. Lively, and in his absence she talked and laughed freely at his odd ways and looks. But her husband at such times would mildly rebuke her. After he died the opinion became general that no person was likely to succeed him in Mr. Lively's confidence, and there was a good deal of dissatisfaction upon the subject.

Mr. Bill Williams felt this dissatisfaction to an uncommon degree. Being now a citizen of Dukesborough, he felt himself bound to be thoroughly identified with all its interests. Any man that thus kept himself apart from society, and refused to allow everybody to know all about himself and his business, was, in his opinion, a suspicious character, and ought to be watched. What seemed to concern him more than anything else, was a question frequently mooted as to whether Mr. Lively's hair was his own or a wig. Such a thing as the latter had never been seen in the town, and therefore the citizens were not familiar with it; but doubts were raised from the peculiar way in which Mr. Lively's hung from his head, and Mr. Bill wanted to see them settled—not that this would have fully satisfied him, but he would have felt something better. He desired to know all about Mr. Lively, it is true; yet, if he had been allowed to investigate him fully, he certainly would have begun with his head. "The fact of it is," he maintained, "that it ain't right. It ain't right to the Dukesborough people, and it ain't right to the transhent people. Transhent people comes here goin' through, and stops all night at Spouter's tavern. They asts about the place and the people; and who knows but what some of 'em mout wish to buy prop'ty and come and settle here? In cose, I in ginerly does most o' the talkin' to sich folks, and lets 'em know about the place and the people. I don't like to be obleeged to tell 'em that we has one suspicious character in the neighborhood, and which he is so suspicious that he don't never pull off his hat, and that people don't know whether the very har on his head is hisn or not. I tell you it ain't right. I made up my mind the first good chance I git to ast Mr. Lively a few civil questions about hisself."

It was not very long after this before an opportunity was presented to him for this purpose. Mr. Lively walked into the store one morning when there was no other person there except him, and inquired for some drugs to give to a sick horse. Mr. Bill carefully but slowly made up the bundle, when the following dialogue took place.

"I'm monstous glad to see you, Mr. Lively; you don't come into the store so monstous powerful ofting. I wish I could see you here more freckwent. Not as I'm so mighty powerful anxious to sell goods, though that's my business, and in course I feels better when trade's brisk; but I jes' natchelly would like to see you. You may not know it, Mr. Lively, but I don't expect you've got a better friend in this here town than what I am."

Mr. Bill somehow couldn't find exactly where the twine was; he looked about for it in several places, especially where it was quite unlikely that it should be. Mr. Lively was silent.

"I has thought," continued Mr. Bill, after finding his twine, "that I would like to talk with you sometimes. The people is always a inquirin' of me where you come from and all sich, and what business you used to follow, jes' like they thought you and me was intimate friends— which I am as good a friend as you've got in the whole town, and which I s'pose you're a friend of mine. I tells 'em you're a monstous fine man in my opinion, and I spose I does know you about as well as anybody else about here. But yit we hain't had no long continyed convisation like I thought we mout have some time, when it mout be convenant, and we mout talk all about old North Calliner whar you come from, and which my father he come from thar too, but which he is now dead and goned. Law! how he did love to talk about that old country! and how he did love the people that come from thar! If my father was here, which now he is dead and goned, he wouldn't let you rest wheresomever he mout see you for talkin' about old North Calliner and them old people over thar."

Mr. Bill handed the parcel to Mr. Lively with as winning a look as it was possible for him to bestow. Mr. Lively seemed slightly interested.

"And your father was from North Carolina?"

"Certinly," answered Mr. Bill, with glee; "right from Tar River. I've heern him and mammy say so nigh and in and about a thousand times, I do believe." And Mr. Bill advanced from behind the counter, came up to Mr. Lively, and looked kindly and neighborly upon him.

"Do you ever think about going there yourself?" inquired the latter.

Mr. Bill did that very thing over and ofting. From a leetle bit of a boy he had thought how he would like to go thar and see them old people. If he lived, he would go thar some day to that very old place, and see them old people.

From the way he spoke, it seemed that his ideas were that the North Carolinians all resided in one particular locality, and that they were all elderly persons. But this was possibly intended as a snare to catch Mr. Lively, by paying, in this indirect manner, respect to his advanced age.

"Oh!" exclaimed Mr. Lively, while he stored away the parcel in his capacious pocket, "you ought to go there, by all means. If you *should* ever go there, you will find as good people as you ever saw in your life. They are a peaceable people, those North Carolinians, and industrious. You hardly ever see a man there that has not got some sort of business; and then, as a general thing, people there attend to their own business, and don't bother themselves about other people's."

Mr. Lively then turned and walked slowly to the door. As he reached it, he turned again and said:

"Oh, yes, Mr. Williams, you ought to go there and see that people once before you die; it would do you good. Good-day, Mr. Williams."

After Mr. Lively had gotten out of the store and taken a few steps, Mr. Bill went to the door, looked at him in silence for a moment or two, and then made the following soliloquy:

"Got no more manners than a hound. I ast him a civil question, and see what I got! But never mind, I'll find out somethin' about you yit. Now, ain't thar a picter of a man! Well you k'yars a walkin'-stick: them legs needs all the help they can git in totin' the balance of *you* about. And jes' look at that har: I jes' know it ain't all hisn. But never do you mind."

After this, Mr. Bill seemed to regard it as a point of honor to find Mr. Lively out. Hitherto he had owed it to the public mainly; now there was a debt due to himself. He had propounded to that person a civil question, and, instead of getting a civil answer, had been as good as laughed at. Mr. Lively might go for the present, but he should be up with him in time.

It was, perhaps, fortunate for Mr. Bill's designs, as well as for the purposes of this narrative, that he was slightly akin to Mrs. Hodge, whom he occasionally visited. However, we have seen that this lady had known heretofore about as little of her guest as other people, and that, at least in the lifetime of Mr. Hodge, her opinion was that there was nothing in him. True, since Mr. Hodge's death she had been more guarded in her expressions. Mrs. Hodge probably reflected that now she was a lone woman in the world, except Susan Temple, who was next to nothing, she ought to be particular. Mr. Bill had sounded his cousin Malviny (as he called her) heretofore, and, of course, could get nothing more than she had to impart. He might give up some things, but they were not of the kind we are considering. He informed me one day that on one subject he had made up his mind to take the responsibility. This expression reminded me of our last day with the Lorribys, and I hesitated whether the fullest reliance could be placed upon such a threat. But I said nothing.

"That thing," he continued, "are the circumsance of his har: which it is my opinion that it ain't all hisn: which I has never seed a wig, but has heern of 'em; and which it is my opinion that that har is a imposition on the public, and also on Cousin Malviny Hodge, and he

37

a-livin' in her very house—leastways in the office. I mout be mistaken; ef so, I beg his pardon: though he have not got the manners of a hound, no, not even to anser a civil question. Still, I wouldn't wish to hurt a har of his head; no, not even ef it war not all hisn. Yit the public have a right to know, and—I wants to know myself. And I'm gittin' tired of sich foolin' and bamboozlin', so to speak; and the fact is, that Mr. Lively have *got* to 'splain hisself on the circumsance o' that har."

The next time I met him, he was delighted with some recent and important information. I shall let him speak for himself.

Chapter II

Mr. Bill came over to our house one Sunday. I knew from his looks upon entering that he had something to communicate. As soon as dinner was over, and he could decently do so, he proposed to me a walk. My father was much amused at the intimacy between us, and I sometimes noted a smile upon his face when we started out together upon one of our afternoon strolls. As I was rather small for nine, and Mr. Bill rather large for nineteen years old, I suppose it was somewhat ludicrous to observe such a couple sustaining to each other the relation of equality. Mr. Bill treated me as fully his equal, and I had come to feel as much ease in his society as if he had been of my own age. By his residence in town he had acquired some sprightliness of manner and conversation which made him more interesting to me than formerly. This sprightliness was manifested by his forbearing to call me squire persistently, and varying my name with that ease and freedom which town-people learn so soon to employ. This was interesting to me.

When we had gotten out of the yard and into the grove, Mr. Bill began:

"Oh, my friend, friend of my boyhood's sunny hour, I've been nigh and in about a-dyin' to see you, especially sence night afore last—sence I caught old Jonah."

"Have you caught him, Mr. Bill?"

"Caught him! Treed him! Not ezactly treed him neither; but runned him to his holler. I told you I was goin' to do it."

Seeing that I did not clearly understand, he smiled with delight at the felicitous manner in which he had begun his narrative. We proceeded a little farther to a place where a huge oak tree had protruded its roots from the ground. There we sat, and he resumed:

"Yes, sir, I runned him right into his holler. And now, squire, I'm goin' to tell you a big secret; and you are mighty nigh the onliest man, Phillmon Pearch, that I've told it, becase, you see, the circumsances is sich that it won't do to tell too many people nohow; for Mr. Lively he's a curis sort o' man, I'm afeard. And then you know, Philip, you and me has been thick and jes' like brothers, and I'll tell to you what I wouldn't tell to no monstous powerful chance o' people nohow. And ef it was to git out, people, and specially other people, mout say that I didn't—ah—do ezactly right. And then thar's Cousin Malviny Hodge. Somehow Cousin Malviny she ain't—somehow she ain't ezactly like she used to be in Daniel Hodge's lifetime. Wimming is right curis things, squire, specially arfter thar husbands dies. I never should a b'lieved it of her arfter what I've heern her say and go on about that old feller. But wimming's wimming; and they ar going to be so always. But that's neither here nor thar: you mustn't let on that I said a word about him."

I felt flattered by this the first confidential communication I had ever received, and promised secrecy.

"Well, you see, Squire Phil, I ast Mr. Lively as far and civil question as one gentleman could ast another gentleman, becase I thought that people had a right and was liable to know *somethin'* about a man who live in the neighborhood, and been a-livin' thar for the last three year and never yit told a human anything about hisself, exceptin' it mout be to Daniel Hodge, which he's now dead and goned, and not even Cousin Malviny don't know. Least-ways didn't. I don't know what she mout know now. O wimming, wimming! They won't do, Philip. But let 'em go. I ast Mr. Lively a civil question. One day when he come in the sto' I ast him as polite and civil as I knowed how about gittin' a little bit acquainted along with him, and which I told him I was friendly, and also all about my father comin' from North Calliner, thinkin' maybe, as he came from thar too, he mout have a sorter friendly feelin' to me in a likewise way, ef he didn't keer about bein' so monstous powerful friendly to the people in ginerl, which the most of 'em, you know, like your folks, they mostly come from old Firginny. You see I sorter slyly baited my hook with old North Calliner. But nary bite did I git—no, nary nibble. The old fellow look at me mighty interestin' while I war a-goin' on about the old country, and arfter I got through he smiled calm as a summer evenin' like—so to speak—and then I thought we was goin' to have a good time. Instid o' that, he ast me ef I war ever expectin' to ever go thar, and then said that I ought to go thar by all means and see them old people; and then he sorter hinted agin me for astin' about him bein' from thar becase he was mighty partickler to say that them old people in ginerly was mighty fond o' tendin' to their own business and lettin' t'other people's alone. Which I don't have to be kicked downstairs befo' I can take a hint. And so I draps the subject; which in fact I was obleeged to drap it, becase no sooner he said it he went right straight immejantly outen the sto'. But, thinks I to myself, says I, I'll head you yit, Mr. Lively. I'll find out sumthin' about you, ef it be only whether that head o' har is yourn or not."

"Is it a wig?" I asked.

"Phillimon," said Mr. Bill, in a tone intended to be considered as remonstrative against all improper haste—"Philiminimon Pearch, when a man is goin' to tell you a interestin' circumsance about a highly interestin' character, so to speak, you mustn't ast him about the last part befo' he git thoo the first part. If you does, the first part mout not have a far chance to be interestive, and both parts mout, so to speak, git mixed up and confused together. Did you ever read Alonzer and Melissy, Phil?"

I had not.

"Thar it is, you see. Ef you had a read Alonzer and Melissy you would not a ast the question you did. In that novyul they holds back the best for the last, and ef you knowed what it was all goin' to be, you wouldn't a read the balance o' the book; and which the man he knowed you wouldn't and that made him hold it back. And which I war readin' that same book one day, and Angeline Spouter she told me that nary one of 'em wa'n't goin' to git killed, and that they got married at the last, and then I jest wouldn't read the book no longer."

I was sorry that I had asked the question.

"No, Philmon, give every part a far chance to be interestin'. I give Jonas Lively a far chance; but the de-ficulty war he wouldn't give me one, and I tuck it. I'm goin' to take up Mr. Lively all over. He's a book, sir—a far book. I'll come to his har in time."

Mr. Bill readjusted himself between the roots of the old oak so as to lie in comfort in a position where he could look me fully in the face.

"You see, squire," he continued, "Cousin Malviny Hodge, she is sort o' kin to me, and we always calls one another *cousin*. The families has always been friendly and claimed kin, but I don't b'lieve they ever could tell whar it started, but it war on cousin Malviny's side, leastways John Simmonses, her first husband, who his father he also come from North Calliner. I used to go out thar sometimes and stay all night; but I hain't done sich a thing since Mr. Lively have been thar. One thing, you know, becase he sleeps in the office, and the onliest other place for a man to sleep at thar is the t'other shed-room on the t'other side o' the pe-azer from Susan Temple's room, and which about three year ago they made a kind of a sto' outen that. The very idee of callin' that a sto'! It makes Mr. Bland laugh every time I talk about cousin Malviny's sto'! I jes' brings up the subject sometimes jest to see Mr. Bland laugh and go on. Mr. Bland, you know, Philip, is the leadin' head pardner, and one of the funniest men you ever see. Mr. Jones is a monstous clever man, but he is not a funny man like Mr. Bland, not nigh."

This compliment of Mr. Bill to his employer I considered proper enough, although I could have wished that he had made fewer remarks which appeared to me to be so far outside of the subject. But I knew that he lived in town, and I think I had a sort of notion that such persons had superior rights as well as superior privileges to mere country people. Still I was extremely anxious on the wig question. Mr. Bill had told me strange things about wigs. He assured me that they were scalped from dead men's heads, and I did not like to think about them at night.

"But," continued he, "as I was a-sayin', they ain't been no convenant place for a man to sleep thar since they had the sto', as they calls it, exceptin' a feller was to sleep with Mr. Lively; and I should say that would be about as oncomfortable and ontimely sleepin' as anybody ever want anywhar to anybody's house and stayed all night. And which I've no idee that Mr. Lively hisself would think it war reasonable that anybody mout be expected to sleep with him, nor him to sleep with any other man person. When a old bachelor, Philmon, git in the habit o' sleepin' by hisself for about fifty year, I s'pose he sorter git out o' the way of sleepin' with varus people, so to speak, and—ah—he ruther not sleep with other people, and which—ah—well, the fact is, by that time he ain't fitten *too* sleep with anybody. I tell you, Phlimmon Pearch, befo' I would sleep with Jonas Lively, specially arfter knowin' him like I do, I'd set up all night and nod in a cheer—dinged ef I wouldn't!"

Mr. Bill could not have looked more serious and resolute if he had been expecting on the night of that day an invitation from Mr. Lively to share his couch.

"Hadn't been for that," he went on, "I should a been thar sooner than I did. But arfter he seem so willin' and anxious for me to go to North Calliner, I thinks I to myself I'll go out to Cousin Malviny's, and maybe she'll ast me to stay all night, and then she can fix a place for me jes for one night; I sposen she would make a pallet down on the flo' in the hall-room. So Friday evenin' I got leaf from Mr. Jones to go away from the sto' one night. He sleep thar too, you know, and they warn't no danger in my goin' away for jes one night. So Friday evenin' I went out, I did, to supper, and I sorter hinted around that if they was to invite me I mout stay all night, ef providin' that it war entirely convenant; specially as I wanted a little country ar arfter bein' cooped up so long in town—much as I loved town I had not got out o' all consate for country livin' and country ar, and so forth."

He knew all about how to bamboozle cousin Malviny, and country folks generally.

"Cousin Malviny were monstous glad to see me, she say; and I tell you, squire, Cousin Malviny are right jolly lately. She look better and younger'n any time I seen her since she married Hodge ten year ago. O wimming, wimming! But that's neither here nor thar; you can't alter 'em, and let 'em go. Cousin Malviny said her house war small but it war stretchy. I laughed, I did, and said I would let it stretch itself one time for my accommidation. Then Cousin Malviny she laughed, she did, and looked at Mr. Lively, and Mr. Lively he come mighty nigh laughin' hisself. As it war, he look like I war monstous welcome to stay ef I felt like it. As for Susan Temple, she look serious. But that gurl always do look serious somehow. I think they sorter puts on that gurl. She do all the work about the house, and always look to me like she thought she have no friends.

"Well, be it so. I stays; and we has a little talk, all of us together arfter supper; that is, me and Cousin Malviny and Mr. Lively. Which I told you he had no manners. But never mind that now; give every part a far chance to be interestin'. We has a talk together, and which Mr. Lively are in ginerly a better man to talk to than I thought, leastways at his own home. That is, it's Cousin Malviny's home in cose. Mr. Lively and me talk freely. He ast me freely any question he mout please. Our convisation war mostly in his astin' o' me questions, and me a-answerin' 'em. He seem to look like he thought I did not keer about astin' *him* any more: but which he did see me once lookin' mighty keen at his head o' har. And what do you sposen he done then? He look at me with a kind of a interestin' smile, and said I ought by all means to go some time and see old North Calliner. And somehow, squire, to save my life I couldn't think o' nothin' to answer back to him. I knowed he had caught me, and I tried to quit lookin' at his old head. The fact of it is, ef Mr. Lively say old North Calliner to me many more times, I shall git out o' all consate of the place and all of them old people over thar. Cousin Malviny she sorter smile. She look up to the old man more'n she used to. But you can't alter 'em, and 'tain't worth while to try. But I, thinks I to myself, old fellow, when I come here I owed you ONE; now I owe you TWO. You may go 'long.

"Well, arfter awhile, bedtime hit come, and Mr. Lively he went on out to the office; which, lo and behold! I found that Susan had made down a pallet in Cousin Malviny's room, and I war to take Susan's room. I sorter hated that, and didn't have no sich expectation that the poor gurl she have to sleep on the flo' on my account; and I told Cousin Malviny so, and which I could sleep on a pallet myself in the hall-room. But Cousin Malviny wouldn't hear to it. Susan didn't say yea nor nay. They puts on that gurl, shore's you ar born. But that ain't none o' my business, and so I goes in to the little shed-room. And arfter all I war right glad o' that arrangement, because it give me a better chance for what I wanted to do, and was determed *to* do ef I could. I war bent on findin' out, ef I could find out, ef that head o' har which Mr. Lively had on his head war hisn. That's what I went out thar for. I had ast him a civil question, and he had give me a oncivil answer, and I war bent on it now more'n ever, becase I couldn't even look at his head without gittin' the same oncivil answer and bein' told that I ought to go and see

North Calliner and all them old people thar, which I'm beginnin' not to keer whether I ever sees 'em or not, and wish daddy he never come from thar. But I runned him to his holler."

Mr. Bill then rose from the ground. What he had to say now seemed to require to be told in a standing attitude.

CHAPTER III

"And now, Philip, O Philerimon, my honest friend, and companion of the youthful hour, I'm comin' to the interestin' part; I'm a-gainin' on it fast. That man's a book—a far book. If I war goin' to write one, I should write it on Jonas Lively and the awful skenes, so to speak, o' that blessed and ontimely night. But in cose you know, Philipmon, I don't expect to write no book, becase I hain't the edycation nor the time. But now, lo and behold! it war a foggy evenin' and 'specially at Cousin Malviny's, whar you knows they lives close onto the creek. Well, no sooner I got to my room than I slyly slips out onto the pe-azer, and out into the yard, and walks quiet and easy as I kin to the backside o' the office, whar thar war a winder. I war determed to get thar befo' the old fellar blowed out his candle and got to bed. I had seed befo' night that a little piece war broke out o' the winder. I didn't like ezactly to be a-peepin' in on the old man, and I should a felt sorter bad ef he had a caught me. But you see, squire, he didn't leave me no chance. I had ast him a civil question; it war his fault and not mine. My skeerts is cler."

It was pleasant to see my friend thus able to rid himself of responsibility in a matter in which it was rather plain that blame must attach somewhere.

"So I crope up thar, I did, and found that he had let down the curtin. But I tuk a pin and drawed the curtin up to the hole in the glass, and then tuk my penknife and slit a little hole in the curtin, so I could go one eye on him. I couldn't go but one eye; but I see a plenty with that—a plenty for one time. In the first place, Phlim, thar ain't a man in the whole town of Dukesborough exceptin' me that know Mr. Lively is a smoker. I don't b'lieve that Cousin Malviny know it. As soon as I got my eye in the room I see him onlock his trunk, which it war by the head o' his bed, and take out a little tin box, which it have the littlest padlock that ever I see; and then he onlock it with a key accordin', and he tuk out the onliest lookin' pipe! I do b'lieve it war made out o' crockery. It war long, and shaped like a pitcher; and it had a kiver, and the kiver it war yaller and have little holes, it 'pear like, like a pepper-box; and which it have also a crooked stem made out o' somethin' black; and ef it warn't chained to his pipe by a little chain, I'm the biggest liar in and about Dukesborough! Well, sir, he take out his pipe, and then he take outen the trunk another little box, and which it have tobarker in it, all cut up and ready for smokin'. Well, sir, he fill up that pipe, and which I think it hilt nigh and in and about my hand full of tobarker, and then of all the smokes which I ever see a mortal smoke, that war the most tremenjus and ontimeliest! It is perfecly certin that that man never smoke but that one time in the twenty-four hours. I tell you he war *hongry* for his smoke; and when he smoke, he smoke. And the way he do blow! I could farly hear him whistle as he shoot out the smoke. He don't seem to take no consolation in his smokin', as fur as I could see, becase sich everlastin' blowin' made him look like he war monstous tired at the last. Sich vilence can't last, and he got through mighty soon. But he have to get through quick for another reason; and which I ar now goin' to tell you what that other reason is—that is, providin', squire, you keers about hearin' it."

Notwithstanding some capital doubts upon the legality of the means by which Mr. Bill had obtained his information, yet I was sufficiently interested to hear further, and I so intimated.

"Yes, I thought," Mr. Bill continued with a smile, "that maybe you mout wish to hear some more about his carrins on." But the account thereafter was so circumstantial and prolonged that I feel that I should abridge it. Suffice to say that among other discoveries he made was the fact that Mr. Lively, as suspected, did indeed wear a wig. He concluded his narrative of his nocturnal adventures thus:

"By this time I war toler'ble cool, and I crope back to the house and went to bed. And I thinks I to myself, Mr. Lively, you are one of 'em. You ar a book, Mr. Lively—a far book. We ar even now, Mr. Lively; and which I laid thar a long time a-meditatin' on this interestin' and ontimely case. I ast myself, Ar this the lot o' them which has no wife and gits old in them conditions, and has no har on the top o' thar head? Is it sich in all the circumsances of sich a awful and ontimely sitovation? Ef so, fair be it from William Williams!"

Mr. Bill delivered this reflection with becoming seriousness. Indeed, he looked a little sad, but whether in contemplation of possible bachelorhood or possible baldness I cannot say.

"The next mornin' we was all up good and soon. When we went to breakfast I felt sorter mean when I look at the old man, and a little sort o' skeerd to boot. But he look like he have got a good night's rest, and I have owed him somethin', becase I have ast him a civil question and got a oncivil answer; and so I thinks I, Mr. Lively, you and me's about even—only I mout have a leetle advantage. When I told 'em all good-bye, I told the old man that I'm a-thinkin' more serous than ever I'll go to old North Calliner one o' these days and see them old people; and which I tell you he look at me mighty hard. But what struck me war to see how Cousin Malviny look up to him. But wimming's wimming, Philiminon. You can't alter 'em, and it ain't worth while to try."

CHAPTER IV

Mrs. Melvina Hodge being destined for a more distinguished part in the Lively Investigations than may have been supposed, I should mention a few of her antecedents. Some years back she was Miss Melvina Perkins, or rather Miss Malviny Perkins, as she preferred to be called. She had been married first to a Mr. Simmons, who, as we have heard Mr. Bill Williams say, was related to his family. Five or six years afterward Mr. Simmons died. However ardently this gentleman may have been beloved in his lifetime, the grief which his departure produced did not seem to be incurable. It yielded to Time, the comforter, and in about another year her name was again changed, and she became Mrs. Malviny Hodge.

Persons familiar with her history used to remark upon the different appearances which this lady exhibited according as she was or was not in the married estate. As Miss Perkins and as the widow Simmons, she was neat in her person and cheerful in her spirits to a degree that might be called quite gay; whereas, in the married relation she was often spoken of as negligent both in her dress and her housekeeping, and was generally regarded as being hard to please, especially by him whose business it was and whose pleasure it ought to have been to please her the most. Mr. Daniel Hodge had frequently noticed her with her first husband, and apparently had not seen very much to admire. The truth was, he had rather pitied Simmons, or thought he had. But when, about three or four months after the latter's death, he happened to meet his widow, he noted such remarkable changes that he concluded he must have grossly misjudged her. A nearer acquaintance, in which she grew more and more affable, sprightly and generally taking in her ways, tended to raise a suspicion in his mind that, so far as his previous judgment of her was concerned, it was about as good as if during all that time he had been a fool. Mrs. Malviny Simmons had a way of arranging a white cape around her neck and shoulders, which, with her black frock, had a fine effect upon Mr. Hodge. This is a great art. I have noticed it all my life; and, old man as I am, even now I sometimes feel that I am not insensible to the charm of such a contrast in dressing among women, who, having been in great affliction for losses, have grown to indulge some desire to repair them in ways that are innocent.

This new appreciation of Mrs. Simmons increased with a rapidity that astonished Mr. Hodge; the more because he had frequently said that, if he ever should marry, it certainly would not be to a widow. But we all know what such talk as that amounts to. In the case of Mr. Hodge, it was not long before he began to consider with himself whether the best thing he could do for himself might not be to hint his admiration of that white cape and black frock in such a way as might lead to other conversation after awhile; for he had a house of his own, a hundred acres of land, and three or four negroes; and he was about thirty years old. I say he began to consider; he had not fully made up his mind. True, he needed a housekeeper. But he remembered that the housekeeping at Simmons's in his lifetime was not as it ought to have been. His memory on this point, however, became less and less distinct; and, when he thought upon it at all, he was getting into the habit of laying all the blame upon Simmons. To be sure, Simmons was in his grave, and it wouldn't look right to *talk* much about his defects, either of character or general domestic management. Mr. Hodge was a prudent man about such matters generally, and always wished to do as he would be done by. But he could but reflect that Simmons, though a good-enough fellow in his way, was not only rather a poor manager, but not the sort of a man to inspire a woman, especially such a one as Mrs. Malviny Simmons now evidently appeared to be, to exert her full powers, whether in housekeeping or anything else. In thinking upon the case, Mr. Hodge believed that justice should be done to the living as well as the dead, and that in the married life much depended upon the man. This view of the case gradually grew to be very satisfactory, and even right sweet to take. Not that he would think of doing injustice to Simmons, even in his grave; but facts were facts, and justice was justice, and it was now certainly too late to think about altering the former in the case of Simmons. So poor Simmons had to lie where he was, and be held to responsibilities that probably he had not anticipated.

Mr. Hodge began to consider. He felt that there was no harm in merely speculating upon such things. He knew himself to be prudent, and generally accurate in his judgments. But it was his boast, and always had been, that whenever he was convinced that he was wrong he would give it up like a man. This had actually occurred; not very often, it is true, but sometimes; and he had given it up in such a way as to confirm him more and more in the assurance that he was a person who, though little liable to delusion, was remarkably free from prejudice and obstinacy. Probably the most notable instance of such freedom that his life had hitherto afforded was the readiness with which he gave up the erroneous opinions he had previously formed of Mrs. Malviny Simmons, and put the blame of what seemed her shortcomings where it belonged.

He was thus considering the possibility of what he might propose to do some of these days, when Mrs. Simmons might reasonably be expected, young as she was, to be taking other views of life besides those which contemplated merely the past. He knew that there was plenty of time for the exercise of mature deliberation. But somehow it happened that he began to meet the lady much more frequently than heretofore. Mr. Simmons having left his wife in very limited circumstance, she resided alternately with one and another of her own and his relations. These people, though kind, yet seemed all to be more than willing that Mr. Hodge should have the benefit of any amount of her society. The consequence was that, having such opportunities, he was enabled the sooner to bring all his thoughts to a head; not that he contemplated immediate action, but was becoming more and more fond of musing upon possibilities. But one day he had looked upon the white cape and the black frock until he was led to express himself in terms that implied admiration. It was intended merely as a hint of what might come some of these days. One word brought on another. It would be impossible to describe how Mrs. Malviny Simmons looked and how she talked. Mr. Hodge was not a man of many words, and it gratified him when she assisted and accelerated his thoughts, and even almost put into his mouth the very words which, though not intending such a thing just then, he had been considering that he might employ some of these days. Things went on with such rapidity that, before Mr. Hodge knew what he was about, he had the cape in his arms, and was assured that it and the person it belonged to were his now and forever, "yea, if it might be for a thousand year."

Surely, thought Mr. Hodge, no man since the days of Adam in the garden had ever made so tremendous an impression upon a woman. He had not dreamed that such as that was in him. However, we don't know ourselves, he reflected; and there *is* a difference in men just as in everything else.

One week from that day Mr. Hodge succeeded to Mr. Simmons, and Mrs. Malviny went to keep house for Mr. Hodge. There was little in the married life of Mr. and Mrs. Hodge that would be very interesting to relate. I before intimated that the lady was most interesting in those seasons when she was unmarried. The beginning was splendid, but the splendor was evanescent. Mr. Hodge was surprised to notice how soon his wife relapsed into the old ways and old looks. He never should have expected to see that woman down at the heels. But the laying aside the black frock and putting on colors seemed to have had a depressing influence upon her tastes. As for the housekeeping, Mr. Hodge had to admit to himself that plain as things were when old Aunt Dilcy, his negro woman, attended to them, they were not as well ordered now. Then he found that, in spite of his conscious superiority to her former husband, he had apparently no greater success in his efforts to please. At this he gradually began to feel somewhat disgusted. He never had thought much about Simmons in his lifetime; now his mind would frequently revert to him, and he began to suspect that Simmons was a cleverer man than he had credit for. It seemed strange and somewhat pitiful generally that he should have died so young.

But he knew as well as anybody that matters could not be altered now, and he determined to do the best he could. He worked away at his farm, and in spite of difficulties made and laid up a little something every year. No children were born of the marriage; but he did not complain. They had been married several years when, the parents of Susan Temple having died and left her with nothing, the relatives generally thought that Mr. Hodge, who was as near akin to her as any, and who had no children of his own, ought to give her a home. Susan was just grown up, and, though plain, was a very industrious girl. Mr. Hodge suggested to his wife that as the business of housekeeping seemed rather troublesome they might take Susan for that business, giving her board and clothes as compensation. At first, Mrs. Hodge came out violently against it. Such, however, had long been her habit of treating all new propositions of her husband. He was, therefore, not surprised; and indeed was not seriously disappointed, as he was acting mostly for the purpose of satisfying his conscience regarding his orphaned relative. He said nothing more upon the subject then; indeed, he had been ever a man of but few words, and since his marriage he had grown more so. Words, he found, were not always the things to employ when he wanted her to do even necessary offices. After all his previous disclaimers to that end, he was suspected by more persons than one of having some obstinacy; and it seemed to grow with the lapse of time. He kept his pocketbook in his pocket, and his own fingers opened and shut it. Mrs. Hodge often maintained to his face that he was hard-headed as a mule and too stingy to live. He appeared to her most obstinate when she would labor in vain to lead him into discussions upon the justice of her causes of complaint against him generally. One day she did a thing which Mr. Hodge had been once as far from foreseeing as any man who ever married another's widow. Mr. Simmons, with all his imperfections, was a man who would sometimes allow to his wife the satisfaction of leading him into a little domestic quarrel, and to make it interesting would give, or try to give, back as good as he got, so to speak.

However, to return to Mrs. Hodge. One day, when Mr. Hodge was about finishing his dinner, his wife, who had finished hers some time before, having but a poor appetite on that occasion, was complaining in general terms of her own hard lot. He ate away and said nothing. Once he did look up toward her as he reached his hand to break another piece of bread; and as he contemplated his wife's head for a moment, he thought to himself if she would give it a good combing the probability was that she would feel better. But he said nothing. The lady did expect from his looks that he was going for one time to join in the striving which had hitherto been altogether on one side. Finding herself disappointed, she brought forth a sigh quite audible, and evidently hinted a more tender regret for the late Mr. Simmons than she had exhibited even in the first period of her affliction for his loss. She did not exactly *name* Mr. Simmons, but she spoke of what a blessing it was for people to have people to love 'em and be good to 'em; and that some people *used* to have 'em, but they was dead and goned now; and people didn't have 'em in these days—no, not even to talk to 'em. And then she gently declined her head, gave a melancholy sniff with her nose, and looked into her plate as if it were a grave and she were hopelessly endeavoring to hold conversation with its occupant. Mr. Hodge was on his last mouthful. He stopped chewing for a moment and looked at his wife; then he gave a swallow, and thus answered:

"Oh! you speakin' about Simmons. Yes, Simmons war a right good feller; pity he died so young. Ef Simmons had not a died so young, some people might a been better off."

And then he rose, put on his hat, and walked to Dukesborough and back. When he returned, Mrs. Hodge seemed in better humor than she had been for weeks and weeks.

CHAPTER V

On the night immediately succeeding this little misunderstanding, Mr. and Mrs. Hodge happened to meet upon a subject on which they agreed. It would be difficult to say in whose mind the idea first occurred of having a little bit of a store in one of the little shed-rooms. It was so convenient, in the first place. Their house was within only a few steps of the road, on the top of the first hill just this side of the creek; and the little shed-rooms were in front, with little windows opening toward the road. On the night aforesaid Mr. Hodge and his wife seemed disposed to be chatty. Mr. Hodge was gratified that the allusions to his predecessor had so soothing an effect. They talked awhile about their having no children, and both agreed that it seemed to be the lot of some families not to have them. And then it occurred to them that it was a pity that the two little shed-rooms could not be put to some use. True, they had been keeping a signboard which promised "Entertainment for man and horse"; but the stand was too near Dukesborough. Besides, Mrs. Hodge had sometimes had her feelings hurt by occasional side-remarks of what few guests they did have, about the height of the charge, which, though reasonable enough generally speaking, seemed exorbitant when compared with the supper, the bed, and the breakfast.

On the night aforesaid, however, it seemed a fortunate accident that the conversation gradually drifted about Dukesborough, its rapid growth, and the probability that in time it would grow to be an important place. Already people were coming to the stores from six or seven miles around; and it was believed that the storekeepers, especially Bland & Jones, were making great profits. Threats had been made that unless they would fall in their charges they might hear of opposition. While talking together upon these things, Mr. and Mrs. Hodge seemed almost simultaneously to think that it might be well, in all the circumstances, to convert one of the little shed-rooms into a little store. The more they turned this idea over, the more it seemed good, especially to Mrs. Hodge. She was for going into it immediately. Mr. Hodge thought he wanted a little more time for reflection. He did have a few hundred dollars which he had accumulated by honest work and good economy; but he was without mercantile experience, and people had told him that merchants sometimes break like other people. Besides, he should not think it prudent to neglect his farm, and that required most of his attention. But Mrs. Hodge suggested that she could attend to the store her own self. She could do it, she knew she could. He could go on and attend to the farm, and spend what time he could spare from that in the store. Mrs. Hodge reasoned that her husband had sometimes complained that she invested too heavily even in the purchase of necessary articles; and here was an opportunity of getting all such things at home and not have to pay out one cent for them, except, of course, what little was paid out for them in the beginning, and that would be lost sight of in the general profits of the concern.

Mr. Hodge reflected.

What about the housekeeping?

Mrs. Hodge in her turn reflected.

Where was Susan Temple?

There now! If ever one question was well answered by propounding another, it was in this case. Mr. Hodge admitted this to himself. It was a matter he had himself once proposed. The truth was, the house ought to be kept by somebody; and Susan, though a plain girl, was known to be neat, orderly, and industrious. Mr. Hodge thought to himself, that, as his wife's talent did not seem to be in housekeeping, it might not be wrong to let it make a small effort in the mercantile line. And so they agreed.

This was all right. Susan was so thankful for a home that she did her best, and any sensible and honest person would have been obliged to see and admit that the housekeeping improved. Everything was kept clean and nice. Mrs. Hodge, however, thought that if she gave Susan too much credit for this change it might spoil her. It was the way with all such people, she thought. So she took all the credit to herself, and would occasionally remind Susan of what would have become of her if they had not taken her and put clothes upon her back. Susan ought to be very thankful, more so than she seemed to be, in fact, that she had not been left to the cold charities of an unfeeling world. To make things under this head perfectly safe, she sometimes insisted that Susan ought to be ashamed of herself for not doing more than she did, considering what was done for her. Susan, doing everything as it was, would seem to look about as if to find something else to do. Not being able to find it, she would get very much confused, and seem to conclude that she must be a very incompetent person.

But the store. Mr. Hodge went all the way to Augusta. Mrs. Hodge would have liked to go too; but it was thought not necessary for both to go. So Mr. Hodge went alone, and laid in his stock. A hundred dollars well laid out would buy something in those times. Such a sum goes a precious little way these days. He brought home with him some pieces of calico and skeins of silk, a few hats, a smart box of shoes, nails, a barrel of molasses, and one of sugar; some coffee in a keg, two or three jars of candy, mostly peppermint; some papers of cinnamon, a reasonable number of red pocket-handkerchiefs, any quantity of hooks and eyes, buttons, pins, needles, and gimlets; a good supply of tobacco and snuff, and one side-saddle. Mrs. Hodge had urged and rather insisted upon the last article. Mr. Hodge hesitated, and seemed to think it not a perfectly safe investment; but he yielded. In addition to this stock Susan made ginger-cakes and spruce-beer. These sat on a shelf outside the window, except in rainy weather. Mr. Bill Williams once brought me one of these cakes, and I thought it was as good as I ever ate.

Mr. Hodge, being a man somewhat adroit in the use of tools, made his own counter and desk and shelves. It was a great time, when the goods arrived. It was after dark, but there was no going to bed until those goods were opened and set in their places. And oh, how particular they were in handling! Susan must positively be more partic'lar, and quit being' so keerless, because them things cost money. Susan got to be so particular that she even handled the tobacco-box and the coffee-keg as if they were all cut-glass containing most costly liquors. When she took the pieces of calico one by one into her hands and put them on the shelves, you would have thought every one was a very young baby that she was lifting from the cradle and laying upon its mother's breast. When the box of shoes was opened, Susan declared that they actilly *smelt* sweet, that they smelt the sweetest of anything in the sto' exceptin' o' the cinnamon. Mrs. Hodge's feelings were too deep to allow very many words; but she let Susan go on. Much as Mrs. Hodge admired everything, she was most deeply affected by the side-saddle. The seat had a heart quilted into

51

it of red stuff. This was so becoming that Mrs. Hodge declared, and made Susan admit, that it was the loveliest picter that ever was loed and beholded. She said that that picter wer the picter of her own heart, and which it had been on a new side-saddle for she didn't know how long. But still—Mrs. Hodge didn't say any more about it then. She merely kept caressing the heart softly with her hand until Mr. Hodge placed it on a small board-horse which he had made for the purpose, and set it in a corner.

When all was finished it was the unanimous opinion that nobody could have had any reason to expect that that shed-room could have been made to look like it did then. If that store wasn't carefully locked and bolted that night! Susan, who lodged in the other shed-room, lay awake for hours; but, as for her part, she owned it was mostly about the shoes and the cinnamon.

There was some talk about the store in the neighborhood for awhile. Some were for it and some against it. The Dukesborough merchants were all of the latter party. Mr. Bland asked, if Hodge wanted to set up in opposition, why didn't he come into town like a man? It didn't look fair to be having a store away out there an be a-farming at the same time. But when he heard what the stock consisted in, he pretended to laugh, and said that it would never come to anything. Still, some people said that Mr. Bland fell a little in tobacco and shoes.

A person in going along the road, and looking upon this store, might have imagined that, apart from the cakes and spruce-beer, it had been established mainly for the purpose of supplying country people with such little things as they would be likely to forget while in town. Indeed, after the novelty had passed away, it gradually relapsed into such a state of things. It was seldom that a customer stopped while on his way into town. Mrs. Hodge's hopes and reliance were mainly on the outward-bound. When any of these would call, she was wont to meet them with an expression of countenance which seemed to ask, "Well, what is it that you have forgotten to-day?" Like other merchants, Mrs. Hodge, who gradually became the principal person in the concern, studied the chances and possibilities of trade; and her husband, at her suggestion, laid in his stock in the fall principally of such articles as a person might be expected to overlook while making purchases of other more important things. He added largely to his stock of pins, and went very extensively upon combs, buttons, and flax thread.

The side-saddle seemed hard to get off. But Mrs. Hodge at the very start, on learning the cost, had declared that it was entirely too cheap; she asked for the pricing of that herself, and she thought she was warranted in putting it at a high figure. She had offers for it. The heart in the seat had attracted several ladies, and once it was within a half-dollar of going. But Mrs. Hodge, so far from falling, intimated an intention, upon reflection, of rising, and that drove the customer away.

Upon the whole, things went on right well. Mrs. Hodge certainly improved in spirits; but of course she never could attain to that state of contentment which her husband could have wished, and which at first he did fondly anticipate. In the matter of dressing herself she looked up a little, and there was about her person not unfrequently the odor of mingled cinnamon and peppermint. And it must be remarked that the displeasure that it seemed inevitable for her to indulge at intervals was now divided between Mr. Hodge and Susan Temple, with the greater share to the latter. Susan did not reflect nigh as often as she ought what it was to her to have a home and clothes upon her back. The girl knew she ought to do it, and was everlastingly trying to do it, and filled herself with reproaches for her own ingratitude.

In one of his trips to Augusta Mr. Hodge brought back with him Mr. Lively. He had made his acquaintance some time before, and had mentioned the fact that the gentleman had talked about coming to take board with them, and even went so far as to propose, in such an event, to pay as much as five dollars a month. This sounded well. Mrs. Hodge had an idea that the having a boarder might make the house come to be regarded more as a public place; so she said that, as for herself, she was willing. Mr. Lively came. When he did come, she thought he was certainly the queerest person that she had ever seen. She looked at his hair and then at his nose and legs, and then at his hair again, from which he never removed his hat, not even at meals. But he was a boarder, she knew, and was entitled to privileges. She tried to pick him; but Mr. Lively was a man of some experience and would not be picked. Being satisfied that it was best for him to know at once that she was a person of consideration, she berated Susan the very first night of his arrival for her carelessness and general worth-lessness.

Messrs. Hodge and Lively got along together very well. The latter, like the former, was a man of few words; and as time lapsed they seemed to have something of a friendship for each other. On the contrary, Mrs. Hodge had less and less regard for her boarder according as he and her husband seemed to like each other the more, and she was often heard to say that in her opinion there was nothing in Mr. Lively. Whatever estimate Mr. Lively placed upon her, he never told to anybody; but he went along and acted as if Mrs. Hodge and whatever might be her thoughts about him were not at all in his way. As time passed, Mr. Hodge would often sit with Mr. Lively and talk with him with some freedom of his business and other matters. Small as his business was comparatively, he was careful of his papers, and always kept them locked up in his desk.

On one of his return trips from Augusta, Mr. Hodge spent a little more time than usual at his desk in looking over his papers and one thing and another; but when he came out he seemed to be very well satisfied. The next day he was taken sick. Little was thought of it at first; but in a day or two he took on a fever, which looked as if his time was coming. He himself did not seem to be aware of the state of the case until it was too late to leave any special directions about anything. At the last he did rouse himself a little, looked very hard at Mr. Lively, and muttered a few unintelligible words about "my desk," and Mr. Lively's being "mighty particular," and such things. But at last he had to give it up, and then Mr. Hodge carried his succession of Mr. Simmons to extremes.

Chapter VI

So now here was Mrs. Malviny a widow for the second time. The deceased was mourned becomingly by all the household. Even Mr. Lively was seen to brush away a tear or two at the funeral; but Mrs. Hodge and Susan did most of the actual crying, and they cried heartily. Both felt that Mr. Hodge's continued absence from that house was obliged to make a difference.

The question now was, What must be done? Mr. Lively seemed to think that Mr. Hodge must have left a will, so he and Mrs. Hodge in a day or two went together and looked carefully over the papers; and, although Mr. Lively followed Mr. Hodge's last confused directions, nothing could be found. Mrs. Hodge had nothing to do but to heir the property; and, as there were no debts, it was considered not worth while to get out letters of administration. Seeing that she was obliged to take the responsibility of all this business, she submitted, and was very meek, remarking that now she was nothing but a lone woman in the world, the wide, wide world, property was no great thing in her mind. But she thought she could be kind to Susan Temple. Of course, Susan was nothing to her, and it was an expense to feed her and put clothes on her back; still, she might stay there on the same terms as before. People should never say that she had the heart to turn off a poor orphan on the cold charities of the world. Susan was very thankful, perfectly overcome with gratitude, indeed, and continued to do everything; and, like Alexander the Great, would almost weep that there was nothing more to do. As for Mr. Lively, he somehow had got used to the place and didn't feel like going away at his time of life to seek a new home. Mrs. Hodge also disliked the idea of turning away one that had been so good a friend of the family; and indeed, with all the business upon her hands, it did look like that one who was nobody but a poor lone woman in the world should have some friend near enough to go to sometimes for advice, instead of being everlastingly running to a lawyer, and they a-charging all that a poor lone woman could make. Mr. Lively seemed gratified, and thus matters settled down; but all seemed to miss poor Mr. Hodge.

And now many years had elapsed since Mrs. Hodge had been a widow before. She reflected upon it, and was thankful that she could bear up under this repeated infliction as well as she did, and that she was as strong and active as any person who was a mere lone woman in the world could be expected to be. The amount of business now upon her hands would require as much strength and activity as could be commanded. Her looking-glass had somehow got broken some time since, all but one little piece in the corner of the frame. Mrs. Hodge gave what was left to Susan, remarking that as for herself she had very little use for such things. Some time afterward, however, she reflected that even the lonely and desolate should go neatly, and that it always did require more pains to dress in black. Even Susan admitted this to be true, and she fully justified her Aunt Malviny in the purchase of a new looking-glass and a new frock.

Weeks passed, and then some months. Mrs. Hodge's strength and activity grew so that she began to feel as if they might be as good as ever. Mr. Bill Williams and others, including Mr. Lively, had heard her say that, although she knew it must be so, yet she did not feel any older than she did when she married Mr. Hodge. It was plain to see that she was not willing to be considered one day older than she really was; and that if she had to grow old she intended to do so by degrees. Her face certainly looked somewhat thinner than it did in those former years; but in a short time even it began to participate in the general recovery, and to have a peachiness which occasionally extended over the whole jaw. Remarks *had* been made about that peachiness, the various directions it took, and the varying amount of surface it overspread at different times. She heard of some of these remarks once; they made her very mad, and she said that the color of her cheeks was nobody else's business.

The rest of her was satisfactory. She had always been a very good figure of a woman, and even now, from her neck down, she was apparently round as a butter-ball. And how spry she was in her walk! I do think that when she was walking rapidly, at her usual gait, and had to pass any unpleasant obstruction, she could lift her skirts as adroitly as any lady I ever knew. And then she rode a horse remarkably well, for now she had laid aside the old side-saddle and took the one with the heart in the seat.

This restoration of her youth seemed to do away with the melancholy in which her married life had been too prone to indulge. She even became again gay. I do not mean wild; there was not a particle of what might be called wildness about Mrs. Hodge. But apparently she had made up her mind not to yield herself up to useless regrets for what could not be helped, to do the best she could as long as she was in the world, and to stay in it as long as she could. When persons come to these conclusions they can afford to be cheerful, and sometimes even a little gay. She had lost one husband. Many a woman does the same and then gives up; and, although some of them reconsider and take back, yet others give up for good. Mrs. Hodge had put herself right on this point in the beginning. She refused to give up at Mr. Simmons's departure; and then, when another man who was at least as good, and even better, presented himself, she had nothing to take back, and we saw how it all ended. People said, as they always do, that it was heartless; but this gave her no concern. And, if it had, there was Mr. Hodge to help her to bear it. This experience was of value to her in this second bereavement. The course she had pursued in that first extremity was so judicious and turned out so well, that the fact is, she began to ask herself what she might do provided another person of the opposite sex should make a remark similar to that which Mr. Hodge had made, and which had so momentous consequences.

But now, here was the difference. Men are more slow to make remarks of that sort to ladies of forty or there about who have already had two husbands, than to those of five-and-twenty who have had but one. Mrs. Hodge noticed this, and it made the peachiness of her cheeks increase at times to such a degree that it extended up to her very eyes. Yet the more she thought upon the probability that another person might succeed to the position which Mr. Simmons first, and Mr. Hodge afterward, had vacated, the more she believed that an extraordinary amount of happiness might result in such case to all parties. She thought to herself that she had experience, and with sensible persons that was worth at least as much as youth.

I have often heard it remarked, and indeed my own observation, I rather think, affirms, that when a lady who has been married, especially one who has been married more than once, is making up her mind to do so again, she makes it up with some rapidity. Knowing that she did not have as much time as before, she began to cast about, and her ears were open to pertinent remarks which any single gentleman might be disposed to make. But both widowers and bachelors were scarce; and what few there were either were young or had their thoughts upon younger ladies, or possibly did not understand the nature of Mrs. Hodge's feelings.

At first she had not thought much about Mr. Lively. True, he stayed there and looked somewhat after out-door business, and even advised occasionally about the store. For Mrs. Hodge still thought it best to keep up the latter, though upon a scale somewhat more limited than before; and, in the multitude of the business matters now devolved upon her, she could not give her undivided attention as before to this single one. Susan Temple, therefore, who had been anxious, as we have seen, to find additional work, looked after the store, and Mr. Lively gave a helping hand sometimes. Useful as he was, he had not been thought of at first except as a mere boarder and friend of the family. Besides his general want of attractiveness, Mrs. Hodge knew too much about him. I am satisfied that a too long and intimate acquaintance between two persons of opposite sexes is not favorable to marriage connections. You seldom know a girl to marry her next-door neighbor's son. A notable instance, I admit, was that of Pyramus and Thisbe. They did made the effort to marry each other, and probably would have succeeded but for a very hasty and fatally erroneous conclusion of the gentleman touching a matter of fact. But even taking this to be a true history and not a mere fable, I have been inclined frequently, while contemplating this peculiar case, to maintain that the strong attachment of these young persons to each other, residing as they did in contiguous houses, was owing mainly to the fact that their respective families assiduously kept them apart, and thus they were able to court each other only through a hole in the dividing wall. But such cases are very uncommon, even in extraordinary circumstances. My opinion is that, as a general thing, persons who desire to marry well, and have no great things to go upon (if I may be allowed to use such an expression), do best by striking out at some distance from home.

I repeat that, besides his general want of attractiveness, Mrs. Hodge knew too much about Mr. Lively to be capable of entertaining a very hasty and violent thought of raising him to the succession of the couple of gentlemen who had gone before. For two long years and more they had lived in the same house, and long before this period Mrs. Hodge had contended that she already knew all about Mr. Lively that was worth knowing. Except in the matter of his hair, it would have been difficult to say in what both she and Mr. Lively had failed to find each other out in all this time. We never knew much of his opinion respecting her, but we know that hers respecting him fell far short of extreme admiration.

But time was moving on, and, in spite of Mrs. Hodge's own youthful gayety and activity, she had learned to give up some of that ardent appreciation which, in her younger days, she had set upon mere external appearances. It had come to be generally understood that Mr. Lively had property somewhere or other to the amount of several thousand dollars. He was neither young nor handsome. But

Mrs. Hodge reasoned with herself. She remembered that she had had already two young and rather good-looking husbands; and even if she had been younger herself, she could not be expected to go on at this rate and marry an unlimited number of such men. So, to be plain with herself, she thought she ought to be satisfied with what she had already enjoyed of these blessings; and, to be yet plainer, she thought she might go further and fare worse. It has always been a matter of remark with me what an amount of prudence some women can exert under the cover of unlimited frivolity. But I have no idea of pursuing this thought any further now.

Such was the state of things at the period when I first introduced Mr. Lively to the reader. Mr. Bill Williams had noticed, as he thought, that his cousin Malviny was beginning to look up to him.

Nobody knew Mr. Lively's views, either of Mrs. Hodge or of the general subject of marriage. He had never been heard to say whether he would or would not marry in certain or in any contingencies. But, if he intended ever to marry, it was high time he was thinking about making arrangements. This was all that people had to say about it. When Mrs. Hodge began to collect her scattered thoughts, they converged upon him with the strength and rapidity usual in such cases. She had no doubt that this would be an easy conquest. Indeed, her shrewd mind had guessed that this was what Mr. Lively had been staying there for all this while, since the death of Mr. Hodge. But she charged him in her mind with being rather slow to take a hint, after having several times pointedly driven Susan out of the room, and with her looks invited him to tell what she knew must be on his mind. At first he seemed slow to notice all this, and other things. A little bit of a something nice would be sitting by his place every morning. This was for the most part some small fish, a string of which Mrs. Hodge would frequently purchase from a negro or poor white boy who had caught them the night before from the creek. These would usually just be enough for Mr. Lively. Mrs. Hodge and Susan would never accept of any, and the former thought that Mr. Lively ought not to have misunderstood the glance and the smile with which she would decline. Sometimes there would be also beside his plate a little sprig of something or other, mostly cedar. But he would forget to take it up and fix it in his buttonhole. Women do not like for such favors and attentions to pass unregarded. Mrs. Hodge began to be vexed, and speak sharply to Mr. Lively and Susan alternately about her opinions of both. She would say to Mr. Lively that in her opinion Susan was the most good-for-nothing hussy that anybody was ever troubled with; and she told Susan more than once that Jonas Lively was the blindest old fool that ever lived, and that he didn't have sense enough to ask for what everybody could see that he wanted.

Mr. Lively, never or seldom having been the object of any woman's pursuit, was slow to understand Mrs. Hodge. The truth was, he had become warmly attached to the place, and he was very anxious to stay there and make it his home. At first he did not clearly see Mrs. Hodge's plans. But there are some things which even the dullest understandings may be forced to take in after awhile. By degrees he began to open his eyes, to look around him, and to appear to be pleased. The single attachment of such a woman as Mrs. Malviny Hodge ought not to be a thing that could be rudely cast aside by such a man as Jonas Lively. When, therefore, she began to press matters a little, he showed very plainly that he was *not* a fool. And she did begin to press matters. She had even gone to expense. She sat down one night and counted up what she had spent upon him in strings of fish and other luxuries, and found that it amounted to eight dollars and something. Extravagant as this was, she determined to go further, especially as her instincts had taught her that there were at last some signs of intelligence and reciprocation. Mr. Lively had lately gone upon his yearly trip to Augusta, and had returned earlier than usual with some improvement in his dress. This was an excellent sign. Besides, he was growing more communicative with his hostess, and occasionally had a kind word even for Susan. Things began to look well generally, and as if that was one undivided family, or ought to be and would be.

Chapter VII

The cordial relations in the household became more decided after a little incident that occurred one morning before breakfast. Mrs. Hodge had not yet risen from her couch; she had always contended that too early rising was not good for the complexion. Susan, who had other things to think about besides complexion, always rose betimes and went to her work. On this morning, at about sunrise, she was sweeping the store and readjusting things there generally. Susan was an inveterate sweeper; she had made a little broom of turkey-quills, and was brushing out the desk with it. One of the quills, being a little sharpened at the end by constant use, had intruded itself into a crack and forced out the corner of a paper which had been lodged there. She drew the whole out, and seeing that it was one of Mr. Lively's letters, as it was addressed to him, at once handed it to that gentleman, who happened to be standing by the window outside and had just remarked what a fine morning it was. Mr. Lively took the letter, wondering how he could have been so careless as to leave it there. He opened it, looked at the beginning for a moment, and then at the end; then remarking that it was all right, and that he was much obliged to Susan, he went to his office. At breakfast, Mr. Lively said that he believed he would ride to the court-house that day, as he had not been there in some time, but that he would surely return at night. Mrs. Hodge merely remarked that she *had* given orders for a chicken-pie for dinner; but to-morrow would do as well, she supposed. Oh yes, certainly; or Mrs. Hodge and Susan might have it all to themselves. Oh no, no! they could all have it to-morrow.

That night, when he returned and came to supper, there was a sight for the eyes of a man who had ridden twenty miles and gone without his dinner, except a couple of biscuits which Mrs. Hodge had put with her own hands into his coat-pocket in the morning. On that supper-table were not only fried eggs, but two sorts of fish, perch and horny-heads. Mr. Lively had an appetite, and these dishes looked and smelt exactly right. Uncle Moses, Aunt Dilcy's husband, had been made to quit his work for the afternoon for the express purpose of having those fish for supper. Mrs. Hodge looked at them and at Mr. Lively. She said nothing, but there was expression in her countenance.

"Ah, indeed?" inquired Mr. Lively, as he took his seat.

"Yes, indeed," answered Mrs. Hodge.

Even Susan looked gratified; she had fried them every one. In spite of his intense satisfaction, Mr. Lively was a little pained that the ladies should compel him to eat more than as an honest man he considered his proper share. He insisted and insisted, not only that Mrs. Hodge, but that Susan, should take some; and at last he declared that, if they didn't, he would stop eating himself. He maintained that people oughtn't to try to kill a person that liked them as well as he did the present company, by trying to make him eat himself to death, and that, as for his part, he wasn't going to do it, because he felt more like living on in this little world now than he had ever done. Being thus pressed, Mrs. Hodge compromised. She agreed that she would take an egg and a horny-head, or maybe two horny-heads; but she declared that she wouldn't tech a pearch: they was for Mr. Lively, and him alone. Susan had to come in that far also; Mr. Lively insisted upon it. She tried to get off with one very small little bit of a horny-head; but it was no go. Mr Lively maintained that there was enough perch for all, and he made them both come squarely up.

Oh, it was all so nice! Mr. Lively was quite chatty for him. His visit to the county town, the ride, and the supper had all enlivened him up smartly; but, after all, he didn't see that the county town had any very great advantage of Dukesborough. Dukesborough was coming along; there was no doubt about that. As for himself, he would rather live where he was living now than at the county town, or indeed any other place he knew of; he hoped to end his days right where he was. It would have been too indelicate for Mr. Lively to look at Mrs. Hodge after these words, and so he looked at Susan. Both the ladies looked down;

but it was all *so* pleasant.

By the time supper was over, as it had been delayed for Mr. Lively's return, it was getting to be his bedtime; but it didn't look right to be hurrying off after such a supper as that. Besides, of late he had been in the habit of lingering in the house a little longer of evenings than formerly—no great deal, but a little. On this occasion it might have been foreseen that he was not going to rush right away from that society.

"Well," said he, when he and Mrs. Hodge had taken their seats before the fireplace, and Susan was clearing away the things—"well, they *ware* fine! I pity them that they don't live on any sort of water-course. Fish air blessings, certain, even when they air small. Indeed, the little ones air about the best, I believe; because they air as a general thing always fried brown, and then a person don't have to be always stopping to pull out the bones. Those we had for supper ware fried *ex-zactly* right."

Mrs. Hodge was a woman who liked appreciation even in small things. "I'm glad you think so, Mr. Lively. I told Susan to be very particler about 'em, because I thought you loved to have 'em brown."

"Yes," said Mr. Lively, with some emphasis; "always when they air small and you don't have to stop to pull out the bones."

"Yes, you may well say *bones,*" replied Mrs. Hodge—"fish-bones in particler. Fish-bones is troublesome, and even dangous sometimes. My grandfather had an aunt that got one in her throat outen one o' them big fish they used to have in them times, and it come nigh of killin' of her at the first offstart; and it never did git out that anybody ever heerd of. And she used to have a heap of pains for forty years arfter, and she said she knowed it was that fish-bone, and that it run up and down all over her; and even when she was on her dyin' bed with the rheumatism, and I don't know how old she war then, she declared that it was nothin' but that fish-bone that was a-killin' of her."

"My! my! your grandfather's aunt!" exclaimed Mr. Lively, and he could not have looked more concerned if it had been his own grandfather's aunt, instead of Mrs. Hodge's, who had come to such a tragical end. But he reflected, perhaps, that for some time past that relative had been relieved of her sufferings, and then he looked toward the table where Susan was rapidly clearing away the things.

"Be in a hurry there, Susan," said Mrs. Hodge, in a mild but admonitory tone.

"Yes; fish and such-like's blessin's; but yit—" Mrs. Hodge couldn't quite make it out.

Susan hurried matters, I tell you.

"Oh yes, indeed!" suggested Mr. Lively.

"Yes," Mrs. Hodge admitted; "but still fishes and—livin' on watercourses, and—everything o' that kind's not the onliest things in this world."

"Oh no, indeed!" hastily replied Mr. Lively. "But still—I suppose, indeed I think—of course thair must be—and—" But at that moment he seemed too embarrassed to think of what else there was in the world.

"Yes, indeed." Mrs. Hodge, having thus recovered, could proceed a little further: "Fishes and such-like's blessin's, I know; I don't deny it. Of cose it is to them that loves 'em, and to them I s'pose it's very well to live on watercourses. Yit them and everything else is not all to *every* person."

"Oh no, no! by no means." He would not wish to be so understood.

"Not all," continued Mrs. Hodge; "particler that a person might wish in a vain and unglorious world. No, fair be it to them that has loved and lost, and loved and lost again, and might love again once more, and that forever and eternally!"

Pen cannot describe the touching solemnity with which these words were uttered. Mr. Lively was extremely embarrassed. He had not intended to go very far that night; matters were so recent. He looked very much puzzled, and seemed to be trying to make out how an innocent remark about watercourses could have led them away so far into dry land.

"Susan," he called out confusedly, and looked around. But Susan had cleared off everything and gone to bed.

Mrs. Hodge waited a moment to see if he intended to avail himself of the good opportunity of saying anything specially confidential; but he was too confused to get it out. So she thought she would venture a remark about the weather that might reassure him.

"It's right cool these nights, Mr. Lively."

This made him almost jump out of his chair. He had been remarking only a day before how warm it was for the season, and according to his feelings there had been no change since that time. He answered as well as he could.

"No, I don't—yes—it's right cool—that is, it's *tolerable* cool. I suppose—that is, I expect it *will* be *quite* cool after awhile. A—yes—I think a good rain—and a pretty strong wind from the northwest now—would—ah, help—and ah—"

"Yes, indeed," assisted Mrs. Hodge, "and it's about time that people war getting ready for winter. Thar isn't anything like people's bein' ready to keep theirselves warm and comfortable in the cold, cold winter."

Mrs. Hodge shrugged her shoulders as if winter was just at the door, and then she hugged herself up nice and tight.

"Yes, oh yes," answered Mr. Lively, somewhat circularly; "we all don't know. But still comforts—yes—of course—and especially in the winter-time."

Mrs. Hodge looked down, her hands played with a corner of her pocket-handkerchief, and she thought that she blushed. Mr. Lively, concluding possibly that he had carried matters far enough for one evening, rose up and broke away. When he was gone she said to herself: "The slowest, the very slowest man-person I ever laid eyes on!"

Although matters did not advance with the rapidity that might have been expected, yet it was very plain to Mrs. Hodge, and even to Susan, that Mr. Lively saw and appreciated the whole situation. Mrs. Hodge knew that he was a steady and rather a slow man, but persistent in his purposes, and somewhat peculiar in his ways of compassing them. He could neither be driven nor too violently pulled. His growing cheerfulness and the new interest he took in everything about the premises showed that his expectation was to make that his permanent home. He even went so far one day as to say that the house needed repairs, and that it must have them before very long. Mrs. Hodge and Susan looked at each other, and both smiled. Susan, poor thing—for of late her aunt had grown to be somewhat more kind and considerate of her feelings—seemed to be gratified about as much as anybody. Thus it is that a new and very strong feeling toward one dear object disposes us sometimes to feel kindly toward all.

It was delightful to see how pleasant and affable Mr. Lively could be; slow as he might be, he was perfectly affable and pleasant. Mrs. Hodge would have been pleased to see him more ardent; but she knew that was not his way, and she tried to feel satisfied.

Matters grew more and more interesting every day. All parties were perfectly sociable. Improvements were constantly going on in Mr. Lively's dress. A great box came for him one day from Augusta, and the next Sunday Mr. Lively came out in a new cloth suit. Both Mrs. Hodge and Susan declared at breakfast that he looked ten years younger; that pleased him highly. It seemed that thoughts upon marriage had suggested to him the notion of going back to his youth and living his life over again. But how would you suppose Mrs. Hodge looked when, after breakfast, he brought in a long paper bundle, laid it on the table, and then took out and handed to her one of the finest black silk dress-patterns that had ever appeared in that neighborhood?—and not only so, but buttons, hooks-and-eyes, thread, lining, and binding! Nor had that kind-hearted man forgotten Susan, for he handed her at the same time a very nice white muslin pattern and one of calico. "Oh, my goodness gracious *me*, Mr. Lively!" exclaimed Mrs. Hodge; "I knew it; but—but—still I—I didn't—expect it." Susan was overpowered too, but she couldn't express herself like her Aunt Malviny. But she took the pattern, and blushed all the way round to the back of her neck. It was her first present.

And now those frocks had to be made up right away. Mr. Lively required that in the tone of a master, and he intimated that there were other things in that same box. Mr. Bill Williams was not so far wrong when he said that man was a book.

People now began to talk. Already Mr. Bill had hinted to several persons how his cousin Malviny appeared to look up to Mr. Lively. This started inquiry, and the new clothes and youthful looks convinced everybody that it was so. Mrs. Hodge began to be joked; and, without saying yea or nay, laughed and went on. Susan was approached; but Susan was a girl, she said, that didn't meddle with other people's business, and that if people wouldn't ask her any questions they wouldn't get any lies—a form of denial which in old times was considered almost as an affirmative. So here they had it.

Matters had come to this stand when Mr. Lively determined to make a decisive move.

Chapter VIII

It so happened that my parents had made a visit, taking me with them, to my father's sister, who resided about a hundred miles distant. We were gone about a couple of weeks, and returned on a Saturday night. I wished that the next day might have been the one for the monthly meeting in Dukesborough, as I was anxious, among other reasons, to see Mr. Bill, and inquire about the parties on Rocky Creek. The next afternoon I was walking alone in the grove, and was surprised and pleased to see him coming up the road toward me.

"Why, Philip, my dear friend, you've got back, have you? I'm so glad to see you. Mammy said you was all to git back last night, and I thought I'd jes' walk over this evenin' like, and see if you had come shore enough. And here you are! In cose, you've heerd the news?"

"No; we got back last night, and have seen no person but the negroes. What news?"

"About the old man Jonis. You hain't heerd the news? Goodness gracious! I'm so glad. Come along, squire. I'm so glad."

He did look glad—even thankful. We went together to our tree.

"And you hain't heerd it? Goodness gracious! I thought it would a been all over Georgy before this. Let's set down here. Philip Pearch, I think I told you that Jonis Lively war a book. I won't be certing; but I think I did."

He certainly did.

"Is it all over?" I asked.

Mr. Bill smiled at the very idea that I should have expected to get it out of him in that style.

"Don't you forgit what I told you, Philip. Philiminirippip Pearch, let every part have a far chance to be interestin' accordin' to hits circumsances and hits various pro-prowosoes."

He *fixed* himself as comfortably as possible among the roots of the old tree, and thus began:

"Well, you know, squire, I told you that I seed that Cousin Malviny war lookin' up mightly to-wards the old man; which I sposen I oughtn't to say the old man now; but let that go. I seed that she war lookin' up to him, and I knowed that she war thinkin' about of changin' of her conditions. I knowed that she had change 'em twice already befo'; and wimming, when they git in sich a habit, you needn't try to alter 'em. When Cousin Malviny have made up her mind, she take right arfter Mr. Lively with a sharp stick, as it were, as the sayin' is with us town people. Mr. Lively, it seem, war at first surprise, and he rather hold back. It appear like he war hard to understand Cousin Malviny. But the more he hold back, the more Cousin Malviny keep movin' up. Hit were jes' like one feller with two kings, in draffs, a-follerin' of another feller with one king, and him a-retreatin' to a double cornder. He see Cousin Malviny keep sprusen up; but he think he know sich things is common with widders, and he have no sich idee that she war sprusenin' up so for him. But byn-bye he begin to sprusen up hisself, and to get new clothes; and he war monstous free and friendly like with Cousin Malviny, and begin to talk about what ought to be done about fixin' up the house and things in ginilly; and it seem like he and Cousin Malviny war movin' up toler'ble close: and I hain't seed Cousin Malviny so spry and active sence she war a widder befo', and that war when I warn't nothin' but a leetle bit of a boy.

"Well, things kept a-goin' on, and everybody see that they war obleeged to come to a head, and that soon, becase people knowed they was both old enough to know thar own mind; and both of 'em a-livin' in the same place, everything was so convenant like. Mr. Lively begin to spend his money free. He have bought new clothes for hisself, and he have bought a fine silk dress for Cousin Malviny, and he even went so far as to give a right nice muslin and a caliker to Susan. Stick a pin right thar, Pelomenenon, my friend. Oh, he's a book! The very day you all went away, a man come thar from Augusty and fotch a bran new gig, and two fine bedstids, and a bureau and cheers. And he never say a word to Cousin Malviny till they got thar, and he have all the furnitoor put in the office; and Cousin Malviny war delighted, and didn't ast him anything about it, becase she know he war a man of mighty few words, and didn't do things like t'other people nohow, and didn't keer about people astin him too many questions—which I could a told her the same. When all this got thar, people know what was a-comin'; leastways they think they do. As for me, I war lookin' out every day for a invite.

"And now, lo and behold! The next mornin' I war woke up by daylight by wheels a-rattlin'; and our nigger boy, who war makin' me and Mr. Jones's fire, he went to the door, and he come back and he say that it war Mr. Lively in a new gig, and he have a female in thar along with him, and which she have on a white dress and a veil, but which he know it war Cousin Malviny Hodge, and they went a-scootin' on. Thinks I to myself, and I says to Mr. Jones, what's the reason they can't git married at home like t'other people? And Mr. Jones he say that considerin' they war both toler'ble old people, they was in a monstous hurry from the way the wheels was a-rattlin'; and which they 'minded him of what old Mr. Wiggins said in his sarmints about rushin' along Gallio-like, a-keerin' for none o' these things. Shore enough, they goes on to Squire Whaley's at Beaver Dam, and thar they git married.

"I have just git up from breakfast at Spouter's, when, lo and behold! here come that gig a-drivin' up nigh and in and about as fast as it come by the sto'. I know that they was in for a frolic that day, and was bent on havin' of it, and I laughed when I see 'em a-comin'. When they got to the tavern-door, Mr. Lively he hilt up his horse, and it war nice to see how spry the old man hop outen the gig and hand out his wife. And she, why she farly bounce out, and bounce up and down two or three times arfter she lit! I says to myself, Cousin Malviny she think now she about sixteen year old. She have on her white veil till yit, and clean till she got in the house.

"'How do you do, Mr. Williams?' says he to me when I follered in; 'a very fine morning,' says Mr. Lively. Says I, 'How do you do, Mr. Lively; or mout I now say Cousin Jonis? A fine mornin' indeed, I sposen, to you, sir, and 'specially for sich pleasant bizness. I wishes you much joy, Mr. Lively, and also Cousin Malviny. But,' says I, 'I did spect a invite, and I wants to know what made you two run away in that kind o' style; for I calls it nothin' but runnin' away, and I can but ast myself who is they runnin' away from, and who can be runnin' after 'em? Why didn't you have the frolic at home, Cousin Malviny?' says I. And then she ansered me. I tell you, Philinipinimon, she ansered me!"

Mr. Bill paused, and seemed waiting for me to question him further. "Why didn't they marry at home, then?" I inquired.

"Ah, yes; well mout you ast that question, my friend of the sunny hour. When you ast that question you talkin' sense. Well, I'll tell you. One reason why they didn't was becase they couldn't."

"They couldn't?"

"Couldn't. Onpossible. Jest as onpossible as if it had been a bresh-heap and it afire."

"But why not?"

"Becase Cousin Malviny wouldn't a been willin'." This was answered almost in a whisper.

66

"Well, that *is* funny."

"Fun to some people and death to the t'others."

"Why, I should think she would rather marry at home."

"*She*, I think you said, Philip?"

"Yes. *She*."

"Well, Philmon Pearch, will you jes' be kind and condescendin' enough to tell me who it is you're speakin' about at the present?"

"Why, Mrs. Hodge, of course!"

"Oh!" exclaimed Mr. Bill in apparently great surprise. "Oh yes; Cousin Malviny. Yes. Well, I sposen Cousin Malviny, reasonable speakin', she mout ruther git married at home, providin' in cose that people has got homes to git married at. I should ruther suppose that Cousin Malviny mout some ruther git married at home."

"Well, why didn't she do it then?"

"Do what?" Mr. Bill seemed to be growing very much abstracted.

"Get married," said I, quite distinctly.

"Git married! Ah yes. Git married. To who, Philip?"

"To Mr. Lively. What's the matter with you, Mr. Bill?"

Mr. Bill slowly elevated his eyes until they looked into the zenith, and then he lowered them again.

"Oh! Mr. Lively! Well, when Mr. Lively, *he* got married—you see, Philip, when Mr. Lively *he* got married, Cousin Malviny, *she warn't thar*."

I could have put both my fists into Mr. Bill's mouth, and there still would have been room.

"What!" I exclaimed. "Didn't Mr. Lively marry Mrs. Hodge?"

Mr. Bill rose upon his feet, bent his head and knees forward, and roared:

"Na-ee-ii-o-oh-woh!"

"What! Then they didn't get married after all?"

"Yes, they did."

"Why, what do you mean, Mr. Bill? Did Mr. Lively get married?"

"Certing he did. Ef any man ever got married, Mr. Jonis Lively got married that same mornin'."

"Who did he marry, then?"

"Se-oo-woo-woosen!"

"Who?"

"See-oo-woo-woosen, Tem-em-pem-pemple. Susan! Temple!"

"Susan Temple!"

"Yes, *sir*, it war Susan Temple; and I didn't have not the slightest consate of sich a thing tell she lift up her veil and I see her with my own blessed eyes spread out in all her mornin' glories, so to speak. Didn't I tell you, Philerimon Pearch, that that blessed an' ontimely old feller war a book? I'm not so very certing, but I ruther *think* I did."

"But what about Mrs. Hodge?"

67

"Ah now," said Mr. Bill sadly, "now, Philip, you'r astin' sensible questions, but monstous long ones. You must let me git over that first awful and ontimely skene befo' I can anser sich long questions as them about poor Cousin Malviny. Them questions is civil questions, I know, and I shall anser 'em; but they're mighty long questions, Philip, and a body got to have time. Ain't he a book? Come now, Philippippimon, my honest friend, you astes me questions; and far play, I astes you one. Ain't he a book?"

I could but admit that, if ever man was, it was Mr. Lively.

Chapter IX

I had to let Mr. Bill expatiate at length upon his surprise and that of the public at this unexpected match before I could bring him to the finale. Mr. Bill admitted that he was at first not only embarrassed, but speechless. He never had expected to live to see the day when he should be in that condition before Susan Temple. But such it was. We never know what is before us. The longer a man lives to see anything, the more he finds that it is a solemn fact that he can't tell what he may live to see. He had never been so minded of that as at the present; "leastways" on that blessed and "ontimely" morning.

"When I got so I could open my mouth," said Mr. Bill, "in cose I feel like I ought to say somethin', even ef it war but a few lines, and—ah—some perliminary remarks—so to speak. So I goes up to Mr. Lively, I does, and I says to him: 'Mr. Lively,' says I, 'you has took us all by surprise. And you more so, Susan,' says I; 'which I sposen I ought to say Miss Lively, but which it *is* so onexpected that I begs you'll excuse me.' And then I ast 'em, I does, ef Cousin Malviny know of all sich carrin's on. Susan she looked skeerd. And I tell you, Philippimon, that gurl look right scrimptious with them fine things on and them shoes. But Mr. Lively war cool as a kercomber, or, what I mout ruther say, a summer evenin' like, and he said that he sposen not. Then he say that he had stop to git his breakfast, him and Susan, and that arfter breakfast they was goin' out thar; but also that he war first goin' to git Mr. Spouter to send Cousin Malviny word what had become of 'em, and that they was all safe, for he said he was afeerd his Aunt Malviny might be oneasy about 'em. And then I tells Mr. Lively that ef it suited him I would go myself. I tell you, Philip, I wanted to car' that news out thar. Mr. Lively he sorter smile, and say he would be much obleege ef I would. I hurries on to the sto', tells Mr. Jones what's up, and gits leave to go to Cousin Malviny; and I mighty nigh run all the way out thar.

"Cousin Malviny war standin' at the gate. When I git about twenty yards from her I stop to catch a little breath. Cousin Malviny holler out to me, 'Has you seen 'em, Cousin William?' I tried to be calm and cool, and I astes Cousin Malviny to be calm and cool. And I says, 'What's the matter, Cousin Malviny? Ar anything wrong out here? Seed who?' 'Susan,' says Cousin Malviny, 'and Mr. Lively, and Uncle Moses.' 'Uncle Moses!' says I; 'have Uncle Moses gone too?' 'Yes,' says Cousin Malviny; 'I sent Moses on John mule to look for 'em when I heerd they was gone.' At the very minnit here come old Uncle Moses a-trottin' on up on John mule; and I don't know which war the tiredest and solemest, John or Uncle Moses. Cousin Malviny astes Uncle Moses what news. 'Bad, missis,' said Uncle Moses, 'bad nuff. You see, missis, when you tole me git on top o' John an' take arter 'em, I thought fust they was gwine todes Augusty, but, missis, time I got to the creek and t'other side whar the roads forks, I gets off, I does, offen John, and looks close to the ground to find track of 'em an' which road they tuck Day, hit jes' begin to crack a leetle bit; and bless your soul, missis, they hadn't been thar. I rode on back tell I got to our cowpen right yonder; and shore nuff they has been done got down, let down the draw-bars, gone round the cowpen, let down the fence up yonder ontoo the road again, back up yonder, and gone on todes Dukesborough. I tracks 'em in that field thar same as Towser and Loud arter a possum.'

"Cousin Malviny tell Uncle Moses to let possums alone and go on. 'Yes, missis. I war jest tellin' how dee let down our draw-bars an' went through behind the cowpen yonder, an' got ontoo the road agin an whipt on to town.' But, Philip, I couldn't stop for Uncle Moses to tell his tale; it war always astonishin' to me how long it do take a nigger to tell anything. So I tells Uncle Moses to go 'long and put up his mule, and feed him to boot, and hisself too, as I seed they was both of 'em hongry and tired, and that I knowed all about it and would tell Cousin Malviny myself. And so I did tell her the upshot of the whole business. And oh, my honest friend, ef you ever see a person rip an' rar, it war Cousin Malviny; she came nigh an' in an' about as nigh cussin' as she well could, not to say the very words. But which you know she ar a woming, and kin to me—leastways we claims kin; and you mustn't say anything about it. When I told her they was comin' back arfter a little, she declared on her soul that they shouldn't nary one of 'em put their foot into her house ef she could keep 'em from it; and it look like, she said, she ought to be mistiss of her own house. Well, I war natchelly sorry for Cousin Malviny, an' I astes her ef Mr. Lively have promise to marry her. Cousin Malviny say that no, he didn't in ezactly them words; but he have bought furnitoor, an' talk in sich a way about the place an' everything on it as ef he spected to own it hisself; and she war spectin' him to cote her, and then she war goin' to think about it when he did ast: not that she keerd anything about him no way; and now sense he had done gone and made a fool o' hisself, and took up with that poor, good-for-nothin' Susan Temple, he mout go; and as for comin' into her house, she would set Towser and Loud arfter him first. Now I know that war all foolishness; and specially about them dogs, which I knowed they was bitin' dogs, and which I wouldn't a gone out o' that house that night I stayed thar ef I hadn't knew that Uncle Moses have went possum-huntin'; but which I told Cousin Malviny that them dogs warn't goin' to pester Mr. Lively nor Susan, becase they knowed 'em both as well as they knowed her. We was inside the gate, and we was jest a-startin' to go to the house when here drive up Mr. Lively and Susan. 'Here, Towser! here, Loud!' hollers out Cousin Malviny, 'here, here!' Says I to Cousin Malviny, 'Cousin Malviny, ef them dogs bites anybody here to-day, it's a goin' to be me; and I hopes you will stop callin' of 'em.' But bless your soul, my friend Philipiminon, them dogs was round by the kitchen, and they heerd Cousin Malviny and they come a-tarin' and a-yellin'. As soon as they turned the corner o' the house, I seed they thought I was the person they was to git arfter. I jumps back, I does, and runs through the gate and shets it. 'Sick 'em, Towser! Sick 'em, my boys,' says Cousin Malviny—the foolishest that I think I ever see any sensible person ever do sense I war born; but Cousin Malviny, all the eyes she had war upon Mr. Lively, and he war a-gittin' out of the gig cool, and calm, and he give Susan the reins to hold. 'Sick 'em, my boys!' kept hollerin' Cousin Malviny, outen all reason. Well, sir, lo and behold! while old Towser war at the gate a-rippin' and a-roarin' to git out, Loud he run down about thirty steps whar thar war a rail off the yard fence, and he lit over and he come a-chargin'. I says to myself, ef here ain't a responchibility nobody ever had one, and the only way I has to git outen it is to clime that gate-post. So I hops up, one foot on a rail of the fence, hands on the gate-post, and t'other foot on one of the palin's o' the gate. I war climbin' with all that bein' in a hurry that you mout sposen a man in my present sitooation would know he have no time to lose. I has done got one foot on top o' the fence, and war about to jerk the t'other from between the gate palin's, when old Towser he grab my shoe by the toe, inside the yard, and the next minute Loud he have me by my coat-tails outside.

"At this very minute Mr. Lively have farly got down from the gig; and when he seed Loud have me by my last coat-tail (for he have done tore off t'other), he rush up, gin him a lick with his hickory-stick, and speak to Towser, and they let me go. Bless your soul, Philip! I war too mad to see all what follered. Both o' my coat-tails was tore pretty well off; and hadn't been for my shoes bein' so thick, an' tacks in 'em to boot, I should a lost one of my toes, and maybe two. When I got sorter cool I see Mr. Lively tryin' to show Cousin Malviny a paper, and call her *aunty*. When she hear Mr. Lively call her aunty, Cousin Malviny, who have been a-ravin' all this time, she say that war too much; and then she go in the house, and sink in a chair and call for her smellin' phial, and tell 'em to put her anywhar they wants to, ef it even war her grave. She give up farly and squarly.

"Come to find out, Mr. Lively, while I war gittin' back my temper and bein' sorter cool—for I tell you, boy, I war never madder in my life—Mr. Lively have been a-tellin' Cousin Malviny what I'm now a-tellin' of you, that that place and everything on it belong to him now as the husband o' Susan; and which they have jes' t'other day found Hodge's will, which he have hid away in that desk; and which Hodge he give everything thar to Susan and Cousin Malviny jintly, ontell Cousin Malviny's death, and arfterward the whole to Susan; and which he have pinted Mr. Lively his Ezecketer; that is a law word, Philipip—a-meanin' that somebody arfter a man dies have got to tend to the business in ginerly.

"And now, Philip, I tell you that Mr. Lively is a right clever old man arfter all. He is from old North Calliner, shore nuff; and away long time ago he have a plantation thar, and once goin' to marry a gurl over thar, long time ago, but she took sick and died. And then once he got low-sperited like, and sold out and move to Augusty and buy prop'ty, and make more money and buy more prop'ty, tell he got to be worth twenty thousand dollars at least calc'lation. Did you ever see sich a man?

"Well, he got tired livin' in sich a big place, and he want to git back in the country. But somehow he don't feel like goin' back to old North Calliner; and then he git acquainted with Hodge, and he heern about Dukesborough, and so he come here. Well, arfter Hodge he died, Cousin Malviny, you see, she think about changin' her conditions again, and they ain't no doubt but she take arfter Mr. Lively. She deny it now; but wimming can't fool me. Well, Mr. Lively he git somehow to like the place and don't want to go away from it; but he see somethin's obleeged to be done; and he have always like Susan becase he see Cousin Malviny sorter put on her so much. Hodge war sorry for Susan too, and he use to talk to Mr. Lively about her; and he tell Mr. Lively that ef he died he war goin' to 'member her in his will. But shore nuff they couldn't find no will, and Mr. Lively he sposen that Hodge done forgot Susan; and so he make up his mind to cote her, and ef she'd have him he mean to buy out the prop'ty even if he have to pay too much for it. So he go to cotin' Susan the first chance he git; and Susan, not spectin' she war ever goin' to be coted by anybody, think she better say *yes*, and she say yes. It war a quick cotin' and a quick anser. But lo and behold! Susan found in the sto' one day a paper, and she give it to Mr. Lively; and Mr. Lively see it war Hodge's will, as I tell you. But this didn't alter Susan; for when the old man told her about it, and say he'd let her off ef she wanted to, Susan say she don't want to be let off; and you now behold the conshequenches.

"And now, Philip, what make I tell you he's a right clever old feller

71

is this: when Cousin Malviny have sorter come too, and understan' herself and the sitooation she war in, Mr. Lively call Susan in; for I tell you that gurl war not for gittin' out o' that gig till matters got cooler. And then Mr. Lively tell Cousin Malviny that she mout stay right whar she war, and that he war goin' to fix up her house, and she mout keep her same room, only it should have new furnitoor, and he would fix another room for him and Susan; and he war goin' to find everything hisself, and she shouldn't be at no expense; and ef she got married he would give her more'n the will give her in money, and she mout will away her intrust into the bargain and he would pay it in money; only Mr. Lively say that sto' must be broke up, and he will pay her down in cash twice what the stock war worth. Arfter all this, Cousin Malviny gin up for good, and call for Susan. Susan went to her, and they hugged; and Cousin Malviny she laughed, and Susan she cried. I could but notice them two wimming. Hit was the first time them two wimming ever hugged, and I couldn't but notice the difference. One of 'em was a-laughin' and one was a-crying; and which I couldn't see the use nor the sense of nary one. But wimming's wimming, and you can't alter 'em.

"But it war time I war leavin' and goin' back to my business. Thar business war not mine. I bids them wimming good-bye; and I astes Mr. Lively, ef it war not too much trouble, to see me throo the gate and safe from them dogs; becase I told Mr. Lively I didn't want to hurt them dogs, but I wanted 'em not be pesterin' o' me no more. Mr. Lively he go with me about a hundred yards; and as I war about to tell him good-bye, I says to Mr. Lively, says I, 'Mr. Lively, it 'pear like you has plenty o' money; and I don't sposen that you think people ought to lose anything by 'tending to *your* business, when it's none o' theirn. Well, Mr. Lively, it seems like somebody by good rights, reasonable speakin', somebody ought to pay for my coat-tails; for you can see for yourself, that ef this coat is to be of any more use to me it's got to be as a round jacket; and all this business whar it got tore—and I come monstous nigh gittin' dog-bit—war none o' mine, but t'other people's; and it seem like I ought to git paid by somebody.' Mr. Lively smile and say 'of cose,' and asts me about what I sposen them coat-tails was worth; and I tells him I don't think two dollars and a half was high. And then, Philip, ef he didn't pull out a five-dollar bill and give me, I wish I may be dinged!

"And then, what do you sposen that blessed and ontimely old man said to me? Says he, 'Mr. Williams, you did lose your coat-tails, and come very nigh being badly dog-bit while looking on at business which, as you say, was not yours. You've got paid for it. When you were out here before, Mr. Williams, you took occasion to look at some other business—oh, Mr. Williams, I saw your tracks, and you told on yourself next morning at breakfast. Towser and Loud were then gone with

Uncle Moses possum-hunting. Sup-pose they had been at home, and had caught you in the dark at my window. Don't say anything, Mr. Williams, but let this be a lesson to you, my young friend. There's more ways than one of paying for things. I advise you not to talk about what you saw that night to any more people than you can help. I am not anxious to fool people, and haven't done it; but I would ruther people wouldn't *dog* me about. You see how unpleasant it is to be *dogged*, and what Loud got for meddling with your coat-tails. But *he* didn't know any better. *You* do, or ought to. Let Loud's be a example to you, Mr. Williams. Good-day, Mr. Williams.' And he left me befo' I could say a single word.

"Now, Philip, I war never so much nonplushed in all my born days; and which when he talk about how Loud mout be an ezample, I knowed what he mean, becase which I don't have to be knock downstairs befo' I can take a hint. But you see, under all the circumsances, I think it's maybe best not to say anything about the old man's har. Not as I keer for his old hickory-stick, becase thar's plenty o' hickories in the woods; but, it mout git *you* into difficulties; and ef it was to do that, I should jest feel like I ought to take the responchibility, and I should do it. So le's keep still. I hain't told nobody but you and Mr. Jones; and he's a man of mighty few words anyhow, and he ain't goin' to talk. So le's let the old man go, and not interrupt him, and wish him much joy of his young wife. Poor Cousin Malviny! But she look peert as ever. I see her yistiday, and she look peert as old Molly's colt. But wimming's wimming, Philip, and you can't alter 'em."

Richard Malcolm Johnston (1822–1898)

Johnston was born in Powelton, Georgia. Together with the various editions of Dukesborough Tales (1871, 1874, 1883, 1892), Johnston published several other collections of stories, including Mr. Absalom Billingslea and Other Georgia Folk (1888), The Primes and Their Neighbors (1891), Mr. Fortner's Marital Claims and Other Stories (1892), and Old Times in Middle Georgia (1897). "Investigations Concerning Mr. Jonas Lively" is taken from Dukesborough Tales.

Uncle Tom Barker

Charles Henry Smith

UNCLE TOM BARKER was much of a man. He had been wild and reckless, and feared not God nor regarded man, but one day at a campmeeting, while Bishop Gaston was shaking up the sinners and scorching them over the infernal pit, Tom got alarmed, and before the meeting was over he professed religion and became a zealous, outspoken convert, and declared his intention of going forth into the world and preaching the gospel. He was terribly in earnest, for he said he had lost a power of time and must make it up. Tom was a rough talker, but he was a good one, and knew right smart of "scripture," and a good many of the old-fashioned hymns by heart. The conference thought he was a pretty good fellow to send out into the border country among the settlers, and so Tom straddled his old flea-bitten gray, and in due time was circuit riding in North Mississippi.

In course of time Tom acquired notoriety, and from his strong language and stronger gestures, and his muscular eloquence, they called him old "Sledge Hammer," and after awhile, "Old Sledge," for short. Away down in one corner of his territory there was a blacksmith shop and a wagon shop and a whisky shop and a post-office at Bill Jones's cross-roads; and Bill kept all of them, and was known far and wide as "Devil Bill Jones," so as to distinguish him from 'Squire Bill the magistrate. Devil Bill had sworn that no preacher should ever toot a horn or sing a hymn in the settlement, and if one of the cussed hypocrites ever dared to stop at the cross-roads, he'd make him dance a hornpipe and sing a hymn, and whip him besides. And Bill Jones meant just what he said, for he had a mortal hate for the men of God. It was reasonably supposed that Bill could and would do what he said, for his trade at the anvil had made him strong, and everybody knew that he had as much brute courage as was necessary. And so Uncle Tom was advised to take roundance and never tackle the cross-roads.

He accepted this for a time, and left the people to the bad influence of Devil Bill; but it seemed to him he was not doing the Lord's will, and whenever he thought of the women and children living in darkness and growing up in infidelity, he would groan.

One night he prayed over it with great earnestness, and vowed to do the Lord's will if the Lord would give him light, and it seemed to him as he rose from his knees that there was no longer any doubt—he must go. Uncle Tom never dallied about anything when his mind was made up. He went right at it like killing snakes; and so next morning as a "nabor" passed on his way to Bill's shop, Uncle Tom said:

"My friend, will you please carry a message to Bill Jones for me? Do you tell him that if the Lord is willin', I will be at the cross-roads to preach next Saturday at eleven o'clock, and I am shore the Lord is willin'. Tell him to please 'norate' it in the settlement about, and ax the women and children to come. Tell Bill Jones I will stay at his house, God willin', and I'm shore he's willin', and I'll preach Sunday, too, if things git along harmonious."

When Bill Jones got the message he was amazed, astounded, and his indignation knew no bounds. He raved and cursed at the "onsult," as he called it—the "onsulting message of 'Old Sledge'"—and he swore that he would hunt him up, and whip him, for he knowed that he wouldn't dare to come to the cross-roads.

But the "nabors" whispered it around that "Old Sledge" would come, for he was never known to make an appointment and break it; and there was an old horse thief who used to run with Murrel's gang, who said he used to know Tom Barker when he was a sinner and had seen him fight, and he was much of a man.

So it spread like wild-fire that "Old Sledge" was coming, and Devil Bill was "gwine" to whip him and make him dance and sing a "hime," and treat to a gallon of peach and brandy besides.

Devil Bill had his enemies, of course, for he was a hard man, and one way or another had gobbled up all the surplus of the "naborhood," and had given nothing in exchange but whiskey, and these enemies had long hoped for somebody to come and turn him down. They, too, circulated the astounding news, and, without committing themselves to either party, said that h—ll would break loose on Saturday at the cross-roads, and that "Old Sledge" or the devil would have to go under.

On Friday the settlers began to drop into the cross-roads under pretense of business, but really to get the bottom facts of the rumors that were afloat.

Devil Bill knew full well what they came for, and he talked and cursed more furiously than usual, and swore that anybody who would come expecting to see "Old Sledge" tomorrow was an infernal fool, for he wasn't a-coming. He laid bare his strong arms and shook his long hair and said he wished the lying, deceiving hypocrite would come, for it had been nigh onto fourteen years since he had made a preacher dance.

Saturday morning by nine o'clock the settlers began to gather. They came on foot, and on horse-back, and in carts—men, women and children, and before eleven o'clock there were more people at the crossroads than had ever been there before. Bill Jones was mad at their credulity, but he had an eye to business and kept behind his counter and sold more whiskey in an hour than he had sold in a month. As the appointed hour drew near the settlers began to look down the long, straight road that "Old Sledge" would come, if he came at all, and every man whose head came in sight just over the rise of the distant hill was closely scrutinized.

More than once they said, "Yonder he comes—that's him, shore." But no, it wasn't him.

Some half a dozen had old bull's-eye silver watches, and they compared time, and just at 10:55 o'clock the old horse thief exclaimed:

"I see Tom Barker a risin' of the hill. I hain't seed him for eleven years, but, gintlemen, that ar's him, or I'm a liar."

And it was him.

As he got nearer and nearer, a voice seemed to be coming with him, and some said, "He's talkin' to himself," another said, "He's talkin' to God Almighty," and another said, "I'll be durned if he ain't a praying;" but very soon it was decided that he was "singin' of a hime."

Bill Jones was advised of all this, and coming up the front, said: "Darned if he ain't singing before I axed him, but I'll make him sing another tune until he is tired. I'll pay him for his onsulting message. I'm not a-gwine to kill him, boys. I'll leave life in his rotton old carcass, but that's all. If any of you'ens want to hear 'Old Sledge' preach, you'll have to go ten miles from the road to do it."

Slowly and solemnly the preacher came. As he drew near he narrowed down his tune and looked kindly upon the crowd. He was a massive man in frame, and had a heavy suit of dark brown hair, but his face was clean shaved, and showed a nose and lips and chin of great firmness and great determination.

"Look at him, boys, mind your eye," said the horse thief.

"Where will I find my friend, Bill Jones?" inquired "Old Sledge."

All round they pointed him to the man.

Riding up close, he said: "My friend and brother, the good Lord has sent me to you, and I ask your hospitality for myself and beast," and he slowly dismounted and faced his foe as though expecting a kind reply.

The crisis had come, and Bill Jones met it.

"You infernal old hypocrite; you cussed old shaved-faced scoundrel; didn't you know that I had swored an oath that I would make you sing and dance, and whip you besides if you ever dared to pizen these cross-roads with your shoe-tracks?" Now, sing, d—n you, sing and dance as you sing," and he emphasized his command with a ringing slap with his open hand upon the parson's face.

"Old Sledge" recoiled with pain and surprise.

Recovering in a moment, he said:

"Well, Brother Jones, I did not expect so warm a welcome, but if this be your crossroads manners, I suppose I must sing;" and as Devil Bill gave him another slap on his other jaw, he began with:

"My soul, be on thy guard."

And with his long arm he suddenly and swiftly gave Devil Bill an open hander that nearly knocked him off his feet, while the parson continued to sing in a splendid tenor voice:

"Ten thousand foes arise."

Never was a lion more aroused to frenzy than was Bill Jones. With his powerful arm he made at "Old Sledge" as if to annihilate him with one blow, and many horrid oaths, but the parson fended off the stroke as easily as a practised boxer, and with his left hand dealt Bill a settler on his peepers, as he continued to sing:

"Oh, watch, and fight, and pray,
The battle ne'er give o'er."

But Jones was plucky to desperation, and the settlers were watching with bated breath. The crisis was at hand, and he squared himself and his clenched fists flew thick and fast upon the parson's frame, and for awhile disturbed his equilibrium and his song. But he rallied quickly and began the defensive, as he sang:

"Ne'er think the victory won,
Nor lay thine armor down—"

He backed his adversary squarely to the wall of his shop, and seized him by the throat, and mauled him as he sang:

"Fight on, my soul, till death—"

Well, the long and short of it was, that "Old Sledge" whipped him and humbled him to the ground, and then lifted him up and helped to restore him, and begged a thousand pardons.

When Devil Bill had retired to his house and was being cared for by his wife, "Old Sledge" mounted a box in front of the grocery and preached righteousness and temperance, and judgment to come, to that people.

He closed his solemn discourse with a brief history of his own sinful life before his conversion and his humble work for the Lord ever since, and he besought his hearers to stop and think—"Stop, poor sinner, stop and think," he cried in alarming tones.

There were a few men and many women in that crowd whose eyes, long unused to the melting mood, dropped tears of repentance at the preacher's kind and tender exhortation. Bill Jones's wife, poor woman, had crept humbly into the outskirts of the crowd, for she had long treasured the memories of her childhood, when she, too, had gone with her good mother to hear preaching. In secret she had pined and lamented her husband's hatred for religion and preachers. After she had washed the blood from his swollen face and dressed his wounds she asked him if she might go down and hear the preacher. For a minute he was silent and seemed to be dumb with amazement. He had never been whipped before and had suddenly lost confidence in himself and his infidelity.

"Go, 'long, Sally," he answered, "if he can talk like he can fight and sing, maybe the Lord did send him. It's all mighty strange to me," and he groaned in anguish. His animosity seemed to have changed into an anxious, wondering curiosity, and after Sally had gone, he left his bed and drew near to the window where he could hear.

"Old Sledge" made an earnest, soul-reaching prayer, and his pleading with the Lord for Bill Jones's salvation and that of his wife and children reached the window where Bill was sitting, and he heard it. His wife returned in tears and took a seat beside him, and sobbed out her heart's distress, but said nothing. Bill bore it for awhile in thoughtful silence, and then putting his bruised hand in hers, said: "Sally, if the Lord sent 'Old Sledge' here, and maybe he did, I reckon you had better look after his horse." And sure enough "Old Sledge" stayed there that night and held family prayer, and the next day he preached from the piazza to a great multitude, and sang his favorite hymn:

"Am I a soldier of the Cross?"

And when he got to the third verse his untutored but musical voice seemed to be lifted a little higher as he sang:

"Sure I must fight if I would reign,
Increase my courage, Lord."

Devil Bill was converted and became a changed man. He joined the church, and closed his grocery and helped to build a meeting house, and it was always said and believed that "Old Sledge" mauled the grace into his unbelieving soul, and it never would have got in any other way.

Charles Henry Smith ("Bill Arp") (1826-1903)

Smith was born in Lawrenceville, Georgia. Most of his stories and "Bill Arp" letters were published in the following five collections: BILL ARP, SO CALLED (1866), BILL ARP'S PEACE PAPERS (1873), BILL ARP'S SCRAP BOOK: Humor and Philosophy (1884), THE FARM AND THE FIRESIDE: Sketches of Domestic Life in War and Peace (1891), and BILL ARP: From the UnCivil War to Date (1893). "Uncle Tom Barker" is taken from BILL ARP: From the UnCivil War to Date.

Free Joe and the Rest of the World

Joel Chandler Harris

THE NAME OF FREE JOE strikes humorously upon the ear of memory. It is impossible to say why, for he was the humblest, the simplest, and the most serious of all God's living creatures, sadly lacking in all those elements that suggest the humorous. It is certain, moreover, that in 1850 the sober-minded citizens of the little Georgian village of Hillsborough were not inclined to take a humorous view of Free Joe, and neither his name nor his presence provoked a smile. He was a black atom, drifting hither and thither without an owner, blown about by all the winds of circumstance, and given over to shiftlessness.

The problems of one generation are the paradoxes of a succeeding one, particularly if war, or some such incident, intervenes to clarify the atmosphere and strengthen the understanding. Thus, in 1850, Free Joe represented not only a problem of large concern, but, in the watchful eyes of Hillsborough, he was the embodiment of that vague and mysterious danger that seemed to be forever lurking on the outskirts of slavery, ready to sound a shrill and ghostly signal in the impenetrable swamps, and steal forth under the midnight stars to murder, rapine, and pillage,—a danger always threatening, and yet never assuming shape; intangible, and yet real; impossible, and yet not improbable. Across the serene and smiling front of safety, the pale outlines of the awful shadow of insurrection sometimes fell. With this invisible panorama as a background, it was natural that the figure of Free Joe, simple and humble as it was, should assume undue proportions. Go where he would, do what he might, he could not escape the finger of observation and the kindling eye of suspicion. His lightest words were noted, his slightest actions marked.

Under all the circumstances it was natural that his peculiar condition should reflect itself in his habits and manners. The slaves laughed loudly day by day, but Free Joe rarely laughed. The slaves sang at their work and danced at their frolics, but no one ever heard Free Joe sing or saw him dance. There was something painfully plaintive and appealing in his attitude, something touching in his anxiety to please. He was of the friendliest nature, and seemed to be delighted when he could amuse the little children who had made a playground of the public square. At times he would please them by making his little dog Dan perform all sorts of curious tricks, or he would tell them quaint stories of the beasts of the field and birds of the air; and frequently he was coaxed into relating the story of his own freedom. That story was brief, but tragical.

In the year of our Lord 1840, when a negro-speculator of a sportive turn of mind reached the little village of Hillsborough on his way to the Mississippi region, with a caravan of likely negroes of both sexes, he found much to interest him. In that day and at that time there were a number of young men in the village who had not bound themselves over to repentance for the various misdeeds of the flesh. To these young men the negro-speculator (Major Frampton was his name) proceeded to address himself. He was a Virginian, he declared; and, to prove the statement, he referred all the festively inclined young men of Hillsborough to a barrel of peach-brandy in one of his covered wagons. In the minds of these young men there was less doubt in regard to the age and quality of the brandy than there was in regard to the negro-trader's birthplace. Major Frampton might or might not have been born in the Old Dominion,—that was a matter for consideration and inquiry,—but there could be no question as to the mellow pungency of the peach-brandy.

In his own estimation, Major Frampton was one of the most accomplished of men. He had summered at the Virginia Springs; he had been to Philadelphia, to Washington, to Richmond, to Lynchburg, and to Charleston, and had accumulated a great deal of experience which he found useful. Hillsborough was hid in the woods of Middle Georgia, and its general aspect of innocence impressed him. He looked on the young men who had shown their readiness to test his peach-brandy, as overgrown country boys who needed to be introduced to some of the arts and sciences he had at his command. Thereupon the major pitched his tents, figuratively speaking, and became, for the time being, a part and parcel of the innocence that characterized Hillsborough. A wiser man would doubtless have made the same mistake.

The little village possessed advantages that seemed to be providentially arranged to fit the various enterprises that Major Frampton had in view. There was the auction-block in front of the stuccoed court-house, if he desired to dispose of a few of his negroes; there was a quarter-track, laid out to his hand and in excellent order, if he chose to enjoy the pleasures of horse-racing; there were secluded pine thickets within easy reach, if he desired to indulge in the exciting pastime of cock-fighting; and various lonely and unoccupied rooms in the second story of the tavern, if he cared to challenge the chances of dice or cards.

Major Frampton tried them all with varying luck, until he began his famous game of poker with Judge Alfred Wellington, a stately gentleman with a flowing white beard and mild blue eyes that gave him the appearance of a benevolent patriarch. The history of the game in which Major Frampton and Judge Alfred Wellington took part is something more than a tradition in Hillsborough, for there are still living three or four men who sat around the table and watched its progress. It is said that at various stages of the game Major Frampton would destroy the cards with which they were playing, and send for a new pack, but the result was always the same. The mild blue eyes of Judge Wellington, with few exceptions, continued to overlook "hands" that were invincible—a habit they had acquired during a long and arduous course of training from Saratoga to New Orleans. Major Frampton lost his money, his horses, his wagons, and all his negroes but one, his body-servant. When his misfortune had reached this limit, the major adjourned the game. The sun was shining brightly, and all nature was cheerful. It is said that the major also seemed to be cheerful. However this may be, he visited the court-house, and executed the papers that gave his body-servant his freedom. This being done, Major Frampton sauntered into a convenient pine thicket, and blew out his brains.

The negro thus freed came to be known as Free Joe. Compelled, under law, to choose a guardian, he chose Judge Wellington, chiefly because his wife Lucinda was among the negroes won from Major Frampton. For several years Free Joe had what may be called a jovial time. His wife Lucinda was well provided for, and he found it a comparatively easy matter to provide for himself; so that, taking all the circumstances into consideration, it is not matter for astonishment that he became somewhat shiftless.

When Judge Wellington died, Free Joe's troubles began. The judge's negroes, including Lucinda, went to his half-brother, a man named Calderwood, who was a hard master and a rough customer generally,—a man of many eccentricities of mind and character. His neighbors had a habit of alluding to him as "Old Spite"; and the name seemed to fit him so completely, that he was known far and near as "Spite" Calderwood. He probably enjoyed the distinction the name gave him, at any rate, he never resented it, and it was not often that he missed an opportunity to show that he deserved it. Calderwood's place was two or three miles from the village of Hillsborough, and Free Joe visited his wife twice a week, Wednesday and Saturday nights.

One Sunday he was sitting in front of Lucinda's cabin, when Calderwood happened to pass that way.

"Howdy, marster?" said Free Joe, taking off his hat. "Who are you?" exclaimed Calderwood abruptly, halting and staring at the negro.

"I'm name' Joe, marster. I'm Lucindy's ole man."

"Who do you belong to?"

"Marse John Evans is my gyardeen, marster."

"Big name—gyardeen. Show your pass."

Free Joe produced that document, and Calderwood read it aloud slowly, as if he found it difficult to get at the meaning:—

"To whom it may concern: This is to certify that the boy Joe Frampton has my permission to visit his wife Lucinda."

This was dated at Hillsborough, and signed *"John W. Evans."*

Calderwood read it twice, and then looked at Free Joe, elevating his eyebrows, and showing his discolored teeth.

"Some mighty big words in that there. Evans owns this place, I reckon. When's he comin' down to take hold?"

Free Joe fumbled with his hat. He was badly frightened.

"Lucindy say she speck you wouldn't min' my comin', long ez I behave, marster."

Calderwood tore the pass in pieces and flung it away.

"Don't want no free niggers 'round here," he exclaimed.

"There's the big road. It'll carry you to town. Don't let me catch you here no more. Now, mind what I tell you."

Free Joe presented a shabby spectacle as he moved off with his little dog Dan slinking at his heels. It should be said in behalf of Dan, however, that his bristles were up, and that he looked back and growled. It may be that the dog had the advantage of insignificance, but it is difficult to conceive how a dog bold enough to raise his bristles under Calderwood's very eyes could be as insignificant as Free Joe. But both the negro and his little dog seemed to give a new and more dismal aspect to forlornness as they turned into the road and went toward Hillsborough.

After this incident Free Joe appeared to have clearer ideas concerning his peculiar condition. He realized the fact that though he was free he was more helpless than any slave. Having no owner, every man was his master. He knew that he was the object of suspicion, and therefore all his slender resources (ah! how pitifully slender they were!) were devoted to winning, not kindness and appreciation, but toleration; all his efforts were in the direction of mitigating the circumstances that tended to make his condition so much worse than that of the negroes around him,—negroes who had friends because they had masters.

So far as his own race was concerned, Free Joe was an exile. If the slaves secretly envied him his freedom (which is to be doubted, considering his miserable condition), they openly despised him, and lost no opportunity to treat him with contumely. Perhaps this was in some measure the result of the attitude which Free Joe chose to maintain toward them. No doubt his instinct taught him that to hold himself aloof from the slaves would be to invite from the whites the toleration which he coveted, and without which even his miserable condition would be rendered more miserable still.

His greatest trouble was the fact that he was not allowed to visit his wife; but he soon found a way out of this difficulty. After he had been ordered away from the Calderwood place, he was in the habit of wandering as far in that direction as prudence would permit. Near the Calderwood place, but not on Calderwood's land, lived an old man named Micajah Staley and his sister Becky Staley. These people were old and very poor. Old Micajah had a palsied arm and hand; but, in spite of this, he managed to earn a precarious living with his turning-lathe.

When he was a slave Free Joe would have scorned these representatives of a class known as poor white trash, but now he found them sympathetic and helpful in various ways. From the back door of their cabin he could hear the Calderwood negroes singing at night, and he sometimes fancied he could distinguish Lucinda's shrill treble rising above the other voices. A large poplar grew in the woods some distance from the Staley cabin, and at the foot of this tree Free Joe would sit for hours with his face turned toward Calderwood's. His little dog Dan would curl up in the leaves near by, and the two seemed to be as comfortable as possible.

One Saturday afternoon Free Joe, sitting at the foot of this friendly poplar, fell asleep. How long he slept, he could not tell; but when he awoke little Dan was licking his face, the moon was shining brightly, and Lucinda his wife stood before him laughing. The dog, seeing that Free Joe was asleep, had grown somewhat impatient, and he concluded to make an excursion to the Calderwood place on his own account. Lucinda was inclined to give the incident a twist in the direction of superstition.

"I 'uz settin' down front er de fireplace," she said, "cookin' me some meat, w'en all of a sudden I year sumpin at de do'—scratch, scratch. I tuck'n tu'n de meat over, en make out I aint year it. Bimeby it come dar 'gin—scratch, scratch. I up en open de do', I did, en, bless de Lord! dar wuz little Dan, en it look like ter me dat his ribs done grow tergeer. I gin 'im some bread, en den, w'en he start out, I tuck'n foller 'im, kaze, I say ter myse'f, maybe my nigger man mought be some'rs 'roun'. Dat ar little dog got sense, mon."

Free Joe laughed and dropped his hand lightly on Dan's head. For a long time after that he had no difficulty in seeing his wife. He had only to sit by the poplar-tree until little Dan could run and fetch her. But after a while the other negroes discovered that Lucinda was meeting Free Joe in the woods, and information of the fact soon reached Calderwood's ears. Calderwood was what is called a man of action. He said nothing; but one day he put Lucinda in his buggy, and carried her to Macon, sixty miles away. He carried her to Macon, and came back without her; and nobody in or around Hillsborough, or in that section, ever saw her again.

For many a night after that Free Joe sat in the woods and waited. Little Dan would run merrily off and be gone a long time, but he always came back without Lucinda. This happened over and over again. The "willis-whistlers" would call and call, like phantom huntsmen wandering on a far-off shore; the screech-owl would shake and shiver in the depths of the woods; the night-hawks, sweeping by on noiseless wings, would snap their beaks as though they enjoyed the huge joke of which Free Joe and little Dan were the victims; and the whip-poor-wills would cry to each other through the gloom. Each night seemed to be lonelier than the preceding, but Free Joe's patience was proof against loneliness. There came a time, however, when little Dan refused to go after Lucinda. When Free Joe motioned him in the direction of the Calderwood place, he would simply move about uneasily and whine; then he would curl up in the leaves and make himself comfortable.

One night, instead of going to the poplar-tree to wait for Lucinda, Free Joe went to the Staley cabin, and, in order to make his welcome good, as he expressed it, he carried with him an armful of fat-pine splinters. Miss Becky Staley had a great reputation in those parts as a fortune-teller, and the schoolgirls, as well as older people, often tested her powers in this direction, some in jest and some in earnest. Free Joe placed his humble offering of light-wood in the chimney-corner, and then seated himself on the steps, dropping his hat on the ground outside.

"Miss Becky," he said presently, "whar in de name er gracious you reckon Lucindy is?"

"Well, the Lord he'p the nigger!" exclaimed Miss Becky, in a tone that seemed to reproduce, by some curious agreement of sight with sound, her general aspect of peakedness. "Well, the Lord he'p the nigger! haint you been a-seein' her all this blessed time? She's over at old Spite Calderwood's, if she's anywheres, I reckon."

"No'm, dat I aint, Miss Becky. I aint seen Lucindy in now gwine on mighty nigh a mont'."

"Well, it haint a-gwine to hurt you," said Miss Becky, somewhat sharply. "In my day an' time it wuz allers took to be a bad sign when niggers got to honeyin' 'roun' an' gwine on."

"Yessum," said Free Joe, cheerfully assenting to the proposition—"yessum, dat's so, but me an' my ole 'oman, we 'us raise tergeer, en dey aint bin many days w'en we 'uz 'way fum one 'n'er like we is now."

"Maybe she's up an' took up wi' some un else," said Micajah Staley from the corner. "You know what the sayin' is, 'New Master, new nigger.'"

"Dat's so, dat's de sayin', but tain't wid my ole 'oman like 'tis wid yuther niggers. Me en her wuz des natally raise up tergeer. Dey's lots likelier niggers dan w'at I is," said Free Joe, viewing his shabbiness with a critical eye, "but I knows Lucindy mos' good ez I does little Dan dar— dat I does."

There was no reply to this, and Free Joe continued,—

"Miss Becky, I wish you please, ma'am, take en run yo' kyards en see sump'n n'er 'bout Lucindy; kaze ef she sick, I'm gwine dar. Dey ken take en take me up en gimme a stroppin', but I'm gwine dar."

Miss Becky got her cards, but first she picked up a cup, in the bottom of which were some coffee-grounds. These she whirled slowly round and round, ending finally by turning the cup upside down on the hearth and allowing it to remain in that position.

"I'll turn the cup first," said Miss Becky, "and then I'll run the cards and see what they say."

As she shuffled the cards the fire on the hearth burned low, and in its fitful light the gray-haired, thin-featured woman seemed to deserve the weird reputation which rumor and gossip had given her. She shuffled the cards for some moments, gazing intently in the dying fire; then, throwing a piece of pine on the coals, she made three divisions of the pack, disposing them about in her lap. Then she took the first pile, ran the cards slowly through her fingers—and studied them carefully. To the first she added the second pile. The study of these was evidently not satisfactory. She said nothing, but frowned heavily; and the frown deepened as she added the rest of the cards until the entire fifty-two had passed in review before her. Though she frowned, she seemed to be deeply interested. Without changing the relative position of the cards, she ran them all over again. Then she threw a larger piece of pine on the fire, shuffled the cards afresh, divided them into three piles, and subjected them to the same careful and critical examination.

"I can't tell the day when I've seed the cards run this a-way," she said after a while. "What is an' what aint, I'll never tell you; but I know what the cards sez."

"W'at does dey say, Miss Becky?" the negro inquired, in a tone the solemnity of which was heightened by its eagerness.

"They er runnin' quare. These here that I'm a-lookin' at," said Miss Becky, "they stan' for the past. Them there, they er the present; and the t'others, they er the future. Here's a bundle,"— tapping the ace of clubs with her thumb,—"an' here's a journey as plain as the nose on a man's face. Here's Lucinda—"

"Whar she, Miss Becky?"

"Here she is—the queen of spades."

Free Joe grinned. The idea seemed to please him immensely.

"Well, well, well!" he exclaimed. "Ef dat don't beat my time! De queen er spades! W'en Lucindy year dat hit'll tickle 'er, sho'!"

Miss Becky continued to run the cards back and forth through her fingers.

"Here's a bundle an' a journey, and here's Lucinda. An' here's ole Spite Calderwood."

She held the cards toward the negro and touched the king of clubs.

"De Lord he'p my soul!" exclaimed Free Joe with a chuckle.

"De faver's dar. Yesser, dat's him! W'at de matter 'long wid all un um, Miss Becky?"

The old woman added the second pile of cards to the first, and then the third, still running them through her fingers slowly and critically. By this time the piece of pine in the fireplace had wrapped itself in a mantle of flame, illuminating the cabin and throwing into strange relief the figure of Miss Becky as she sat studying the cards. She frowned ominously at the cards and mumbled a few words to herself. Then she dropped her hands in her lap and gazed once more into the fire. Her shadow danced and capered on the wall and floor behind her, as if, looking over her shoulder into the future, it could behold a rare spectacle. After a while she picked up the cup that had been turned on the hearth. The coffee-grounds, shaken around, presented what seemed a most intricate map.

"Here's the journey," said Miss Becky, presently; "here's the big road, here's rivers to cross, here's the bundle to tote." She paused and sighed. "They haint no names writ here, an' what it all means I'll never tell you. Cajy, I wish you'd be so good as to han' me my pipe."

"I haint no hand wi' the kyards," said Cajy, as he handed the pipe, "but I reckon I can patch out your misinformation, Becky, bekaze the other day, whiles I was a-finishin' up Mizzers Perdue's rollin'-pin, I hearn a rattlin' in the road. I looked out, an' Spite Calderwood was a-drivin' by in his buggy, an' thar sot Lucinda by him. It'd in-about drapt out er my min'."

Free Joe sat on the door-sill and fumbled at his hat, flinging it from one hand to the other.

"You aint see um gwine back, is you, Mars Cajy?" he asked after a while.

"Ef they went back by this road," said Mr. Staley, with the air of one who is accustomed to weigh well his words, "it must 'a' bin endurin' of the time whiles I was asleep, bekaze I haint bin no furder from my shop than to yon bed."

"Well, sir!" exclaimed Free Joe in an awed tone, which Mr. Staley seemed to regard as a tribute to his extraordinary powers of statement.

"Ef it's my beliefs you want," continued the old man, "I'll pitch 'em at you fair and free. My beliefs is that Spite Calderwood is gone an' took Lucindy outen the county. Bless your heart and soul! when Spite Calderwood meets the Old Boy in the road they'll be a turrible scuffle. You mark what I tell you."

Free Joe, still fumbling with his hat, rose and leaned against the door-facing. He seemed to be embarrassed. Presently he said,—

"I speck I better be gittin' 'long. Nex' time I see Lucindy, I'm gwine tell 'er w'at Miss Becky say 'bout de queen er spades—dat I is. Ef dat don't tickle 'er, dey ain't no nigger 'oman never bin tickle'."

He paused a moment, as though waiting for some remark or comment, some confirmation of misfortune, or, at the very least, some indorsement of his suggestion that Lucinda would be greatly pleased to know that she had figured as the queen of spades; but neither Miss Becky nor her brother said any thing.

"One minnit ridin' in de buggy 'longside er Mars Spite, en de nex' highfalutin' 'roun' playin' de queen er spades. Mon, deze yer nigger gals gittin' up in de pictur's; dey sholy is."

With a brief "Good-night, Miss Becky, Mars Cajy," Free Joe went out into the darkness, followed by little Dan. He made his way to the poplar, where Lucinda had been in the habit of meeting him, and sat down. He sat there a long time; he sat there until little Dan, growing restless, trotted off in the direction of the Calderwood place. Dozing against the poplar, in the gray dawn of the morning, Free Joe heard Spite Calderwood's fox-hounds in full cry a mile away.

"Shoo!" he exclaimed, scratching his head, and laughing to himself, "dem ar dogs is des a-warmin' dat old fox up."

But it was Dan the hounds were after, and the little dog came back no more. Free Joe waited and waited, until he grew tired of waiting. He went back the next night and waited, and for many nights thereafter. His waiting was in vain, and yet he never regarded it as in vain. Careless and shabby as he was, Free Joe was thoughtful enough to have his theory. He was convinced that little Dan had found Lucinda, and that some night when the moon was shining brightly through the trees, the dog would rouse him from his dreams as he sat sleeping at the foot of the poplar-tree, and he would open his eyes and behold Lucinda standing over him, laughing merrily as of old; and then he thought what fun they would have about the queen of spades.

How many long nights Free Joe waited at the foot of the poplar-tree for Lucinda and little Dan, no one can ever know. He kept no account of them, and they were not recorded by Micajah Staley nor by Miss Becky. The season ran into summer and then into fall. One night he went to the Staley cabin, cut the two old people an armful of wood, and seated himself on the door-steps, where he rested. He was always thankful—and proud, as it seemed—when Miss Becky gave him a cup of coffee, which she was sometimes thoughtful enough to do. He was especially thankful on this particular night.

"You er still layin' off for to strike up wi' Lucindy out thar in the woods, I reckon," said Micajah Staley, smiling grimly. The situation was not without its humorous aspects.

"Oh, dey er comin', Mars Cajy, dey er comin', sho," Free Joe replied. "I boun' you dey'll come; en w'en dey does come, I'll des take en fetch um yer, whar you kin see um wid you own eyes, you en Miss Becky."

"No," said Mr. Staley, with a quick and emphatic gesture of disapproval. "Don't! don't fetch 'em anywheres. Stay right wi' 'em as long as may be."

Free Joe chuckled, and slipped away into the night, while the two old people sat gazing in the fire. Finally Micajah spoke.

"Look at that nigger; look at 'im. He's pine-blank as happy now as a killdee by a mill-race. You can't 'faze 'em. I'd in-about give up my other hand ef I could stan' flat-footed, an' grin at trouble like that there nigger."

"Niggers is niggers," said Miss Becky, smiling grimly, "an' you can't rub it out; yit I lay I've seed a heap of white people lots meaner'n Free Joe. He grins,—an' that's nigger,—but I've ketched his under jaw a-trimblin' when Lucindy's name uz brung up. An' I tell you," she went on, bridling up a little, and speaking with almost fierce emphasis, "the Old Boy's done sharpened his claws for Spite Calderwood. You'll see it."

"Me, Rebecca?" said Mr. Staley, hugging his palsied arm; "Me? I hope not."

"Well, you'll know it then," said Miss Becky, laughing heartily at her brother's look of alarm.

The next morning Micajah Staley had occasion to go into the woods after a piece of timber. He saw Free Joe sitting at the foot of the poplar, and the sight vexed him somewhat.

"Git up from there," he cried, "an' go an' arn your livin'. A mighty purty pass it's come to, when great big buck niggers can lie a-snorin' in the woods all day, when t'other folks is got to be up an' a-gwine. Git up from there!"

Receiving no response, Mr. Staley went to Free Joe, and shook him by the shoulder; but the negro made no response. He was dead. His hat was off, his head was bent, and a smile was on his face. It was as if he had bowed and smiled when death stood before him, humble to the last. His clothes were ragged; his hands were rough and callous; his shoes were literally tied together with strings; he was shabby in the extreme. A passer-by, glancing at him, could have no idea that such a humble creature had been summoned as a witness before the Lord God of Hosts.

The Wonderful Tar-Baby Story

Joel Chandler Harris

"DIDN'T THE FOX *never* catch the rabbit, Uncle Remus?" asked the little boy the next evening.

"He come mighty nigh it, honey, sho's you bawn—Brer Fox did. One day atter Brer Rabbit fool 'im wid dat calamus root, Brer Fox went ter wuk en got 'im some tar, en mix it wid some turkentime, en fix up a contrapshun wat he call a Tar-Baby, en he tuck dish yer Tar-Baby en he sot 'er in de big road, en den he lay off in de bushes fer ter see wat de news wuz gwineter be. En he didn't hatter wait long, nudder, kaze bimeby here come Brer Rabbit pacin' down de road—lippity-clippity, clippity-lippity—dez ez sassy ez a jay-bird. Brer Fox, he lay low. Brer Rabbit come prancin' 'long twel he spy de Tar-Baby, en den he fotch up on his behime legs like he wuz 'stonished. De Tar-Baby, she sot dar, she did, en Brer Fox, he lay low.

"'Mawnin'!' sez Brer Rabbit, sezee—'nice wedder dis mawnin',' sezee.

"Tar-Baby ain't sayin' nuthin', en Brer Fox, he lay low.

"'How duz yo' smy'tums seem ter segashuate?' sez Brer Rabbit, sezee.

"Brer Fox, he wink his eye slow, en lay low, en de Tar-Baby, she ain't sayin' nuthin'.

"'How you come on, den? Is you deaf?' sez Brer Rabbit, sezee. 'Kaze if you is, I kin holler louder,' sezee.

"Tar-Baby stay still, en Brer Fox, he lay low.

"'Youer stuck up, dat's w'at you is,' sez Brer Rabbit, sezee, 'en I'm gwineter kyore you, dat's w'at I'm a gwineter do,' sezee.

"Brer Fox, he sorter chuckle in his stummuck, he did, but Tar-Baby ain't sayin' nuthin'.

"'I'm gwineter larn you howter talk ter 'specttubble fokes ef hit's de las' ack,' sez Brer Rabbit, sezee. 'Ef you don't take off dat hat en tell me howdy, I'm gwineter bus' you wide open,' sezee.

"Tar-Baby stay still, en Brer Fox, he lay low.

"Brer Rabbit keep on axin' 'im, en de Tar-Baby, she keep on sayin' nuthin', twel present'y Brer Rabbit draw back wid his fis', he did, en blip he tuck 'er side er de head.

Right dar's whar he broke his merlasses jug. His fis' stuck, en he can't pull loose. De tar hilt 'im. But Tar-Baby, she stay still, en Brer Fox, he lay low.

"'Ef you don't lemme loose, I'll knock you agin,' sez Brer Rabbit, sezee, en wid dat he fotch 'er a wipe wid de udder han', en dat stuck. Tar-Baby, she ain't sayin' nuthin', en Brer Fox he lay low.

"'Tu'n me loose, fo' I kick de natal stuffin' outen you,' sez Brer Rabbit, sezee, but de Tar-Baby, she ain't sayin' nuthin'. She des hilt on, en den Brer Rabbit lose de use er his feet in de same way. Brer Fox, he lay low. Den Brer Rabbit squall out dat ef de Tar-Baby don't tu'n 'im loose he butt 'er cranksided. En den he butted, en his head got stuck. Den Brer Fox, he sa'ntered fort', lookin' des ez innercent ez wunner yo' mammy's mockin' birds.

"'Howdy, Brer Rabbit,' sez Brer Fox, sezee. 'You look sorter stuck up dis mawnin',' sezee, en den he rolled on de groun', en laft en laft twel he couldn't laff no mo'. 'I speck you'll take dinner wid me dis time, Brer Rabbit. I done laid in some calamus root, en I ain't gwineter take no skuse,' sez Brer Fox, sezee."

Here Uncle Remus paused, and drew a two-pound yam out of the ashes.

"Did the fox eat the rabbit?" asked the little boy to whom the story had been told.

"Dat's all de fur de tale goes," replied the old man. "He mout, en den again he moutent. Some say Jedge B'ar come 'long en loosed 'im—some say he didn't. I hear Miss Sally callin'. You better run 'long."

How Mr. Rabbit Was Too Sharp for Mr. Fox

"Uncle Remus," said the little boy one evening, when he had found the old man with little or nothing to do, "did the fox kill and eat the rabbit when he caught him with the Tar-Baby?"

"Law, honey, ain't I tell you 'bout dat?" replied the old darkey, chuckling slyly. "I 'clar ter grashus I ought er tole you dat, but ole man Nod wuz ridin' on my eyeleds 'twel a leetle mo'n I'd a dis'member'd my own name, en den on to dat here come yo' mammy a hollerin' atter you.

"W'at I tell you w'en I fus' begin? I tole you Brer Rabbit wuz a monstus soon creetur; leas'ways dat's w'at I laid out fer ter tell you. Well, den, honey, don't you go en make no udder calkalashuns, kaze in dem days Brer Rabbit en his family wuz at de head er de gang w'en enny racket wuz on han', en dar dey stayed. 'Fo' you begins fer ter wipe yo' eyes 'bout Brer Rabbit, you wait en see whar'bouts Brer Rabbit gwineter fetch up at. But dat's needer yer ner dar.

"W'en Brer Fox fine Brer Rabbit mixt up wid de Tar-Baby, he feel mighty good, en he roll on de groun' en laff. Bimeby he up'n say, sezee:

"'Well, I speck I got you dis time, Brer Rabbit,' sezee; 'maybe I ain't, but I speck I is. You been runnin' roun' here sassin' after me a mighty long time, but I speck you done come ter de een' er de row. You bin cuttin' up yo' capers en bouncin' 'roun' in dis neighborhood ontwel you come ter b'leeve you'sef de boss er de whole gang. En den youer allers som'ers whar you got no bizness,' sez Brer Fox, sezee. 'Who ax you fer ter come en strike up a 'quaintance wid dish yer Tar-Baby? En who stuck you up dar whar you iz? Nobody in di roun' worril. You des tuck en jam yo'se'f on dat Tar-Baby widout waitin' fer enny invite,' sez Brer Fox, sezee, 'en dar you is, en dar you'll stay twel I fixes up a bresh-pile and fires her up, kaze I'm gwineter bobbycue you dis day, sho,' sez Brer Fox, sezee.

"Den Brer Rabbit talk mighty 'umble.

"'I don't keer w'at you do wid me, Brer Fox,' sezee, 'so you don't fling me in dat brier-patch. Roas' me, Brer Fox,' sezee, 'but don't fling me in dat brier-patch,' sezee.

"'Hit's so much trouble fer ter kindle a fier,' sez Brer Fox, sezee, 'dat I speck I'll hatter hang you,' sezee.

"'Hang me des ez high as you please, Brer Fox,' sez Brer Rabbit, sezee, 'but do fer de Lord's sake don't fling me in dat brier-patch,' sezee.

"'I ain't got no string,' sez Brer Fox, sezee, 'en now I speck I'll hatter drown you,' sezee.

"'Drown me des ez deep ez you please, Brer Fox,' sez Brer Rabbit, sezee, 'but do don't fling me in dat brier-patch,' sezee.

"'Dey ain't no water nigh,' sez Brer Fox, sezee, 'en now I speck I'll hatter skin you,' sezee.

"'Skin me, Brer Fox,' sez Brer Rabbit, sezee, 'snatch out my eyeballs, t'ar out my years by de roots, en cut off my legs,' sezee, 'but do please, Brer Fox, don't fling me in dat brier-patch,' sezee.

"Co'se Brer Fox wanter hurt Brer Rabbit bad ez he kin, so he cotch 'im by de behime legs en slung 'im right in de middle er de brier-patch. Dar wuz a considerbul flutter whar Brer Rabbit struck de bushes, en Brer Fox sorter hang 'roun' fer ter see w'at wuz gwineter happen. Bimeby he hear somebody call 'im, en way up de hill he see Brer Rabbit settin' cross-legged on a chinkapin log koamin' de pitch outen his har wid a chip. Den Brer Fox know dat he bin swop off mighty bad. Brer Rabbit wuz bleedzed fer ter fling back some er his sass, en he holler out:

"'Bred en bawn in a brier-patch, Brer Fox—bred en bawn in a brier-patch!' en wid dat he skip out des ez lively ez a cricket in de embers."

Joel Chandler Harris (1848-1908)

Harris was born in Eatonton, Georgia. Best known as the author of the Uncle Remus stories, Harris wrote many books, including UNCLE REMUS: His Songs and His Sayings (1880), NIGHTS WITH UNCLE REMUS: Myths and Legends of the Old Plantation (1883), MINGO AND OTHER SKETCHES IN BLACK AND WHITE (1884), FREE JOE AND OTHER GEORGIAN SKETCHES (1887), BALAAM AND HIS MASTER AND OTHER SKETCHES AND STORIES (1891), and GABRIEL TOLLIVER: A Story of Reconstruction (1902). "Free Joe and the Rest of the World" is taken from FREE JOE AND OTHER GEORGIAN SKETCHES. "The Wonderful Tar-Baby Story," combining the two linked chapters "The Wonderful Tar-Baby Story" and "How Mr. Rabbit was Too Sharp for Mr. Fox," is taken from UNCLE REMUS: His Songs and His Sayings.

The Heresy of Abner Calihan

Will N. Harben

NEIL FILMORE'S STORE was at the crossing of the Big Cabin and Rock Valley roads. Before the advent of Sherman into the South it had been a grist-mill, to which the hardy mountaineers had regularly brought their grain to be ground, in wagons, on horseback, or on their shoulders, according to their conditions. But the Northern soldiers had appropriated the miller's little stock of toll, had torn down the long wooden sluice which had conveyed the water from the race to the mill, had burnt the great wheel and crude wooden machinery, and rolled the massive grinding-stones into the deepest part of the creek.

After the war nobody saw any need for a mill at that point, and Neil Filmore had bought the property from its impoverished owner and turned the building into a store. It proved to be a fair location, for there was considerable travel along the two main roads, and as Filmore was postmaster his store became the general meeting-point for everybody living within ten miles of the spot. He kept for sale, as he expressed it, "a little of everything, from shoe-eyes to a sack of guano." Indeed, a sight of his rough shelves and unplaned counters, filled with cakes of tallow, beeswax and butter, bolts of calico, sheeting and ginghams, and the floor and porch heaped with piles of skins, cases of eggs, coops of chickens, and cans of lard, was enough to make an orderly housewife shudder with horror.

But Mrs. Filmore had grown accustomed to this state of affairs in the front part of the house, for she confined her domestic business, and whatever neatness and order were possible, to the room in the rear, where, as she often phrased it, she did the "eatin' an' cookin', an' never interfeer with pap's part except to lend 'im my cheers when thar is more'n common waitin' fer the mail-carrier."

And her chairs were often in demand, for Filmore was a deacon in Big Cabin Church, which stood at the foot of the green-clad mountain a mile down the road, and it was at the store that his brother deacons frequently met to transact church business.

One summer afternoon they held an important meeting. Abner Calihan, a member of the church and a good, industrious citizen, was to be tried for heresy.

"It has worried me more'n anything that has happened sence them two Dutchmen over at Cove Spring swapped wives an' couldn't be convinced of the'r error," said long, lean Bill Odell, after he had come in and borrowed a candle-box to feed his mule in, and had given the animal eight ears of corn from the pockets of his long-tailed coat, and left the mule haltered at a hitching-post in front of the store.

"Ur sence the widder Dill swore she was gwine to sue Hank Dobb's wife fer witchcraft," replied Filmore, in a hospitable tone. "Take a cheer; it must be as hot as a bake-oven out thar in the sun."

Bill Odell took off his coat and folded it carefully and laid it across the beam of the scales, and unbuttoned his vest and sat down, and proceeded to mop his perspiring face with a red bandanna. Toot Bailey came in next, a quiet little man of about fifty, with a dark face, straggling gray hair, and small, penetrating eyes. His blue jean trousers were carelessly stuck into the tops of his clay-stained boots, and he wore a sack-coat, a "hickory" shirt, and a leather belt. Mrs. Filmore put her red head and broad, freckled face out of the door of her apartment to see who had arrived, and the next moment came out dusting a "split-bottomed" chair with her apron.

"How are ye, Toot?" was her greeting as she placed the chair for him between a jar of fresh honey and a barrel of sorghum molasses. "How is the sore eyes over yore way?"

"Toler'ble," he answered, as he leaned back against the counter and fanned himself with his slouch hat. "Mine is about through it, but the Tye childern is a sight. Pizen-oak hain't a circumstance."

"What did ye use?"

"Copperas an' sweet milk. It is the best thing I've struck. I don't want any o' that peppery eye-wash 'bout my place. It'd take the hide off'n a mule's hind leg."

"Now yore a-talkin'," and Bill Odell went to the water-bucket on the end of the counter. He threw his tobacco-quid away, noisily washed out his mouth, and took a long drink from the gourd dipper. Then Bart Callaway and Amos Sanders, who had arrived half an hour before and had walked down to take a look at Filmore's fish-pond, came in together. Both were whittling sticks and looking cool and comfortable.

"We are all heer," said Odell, and he added his hat to his coat and the pile of weights on the scale-beam, and put his right foot on the rung of his chair. "I reckon we mought as well proceed." At these words

96

the men who had arrived last carefully stowed their hats away under their chairs and leaned forward expectantly. Mrs. Filmore glided noiselessly to a corner behind the counter, and with folded arms stood ready to hear all that was to be said.

"Did anybody inform Ab of the object of this meeting?" asked Odell.

They all looked at Filmore, and he transferred their glances to his wife. She flushed under their scrutiny and awkwardly twisted her fat arms together.

"Sister Calihan wuz in here this mornin'," she deposed in an uneven tone. "I 'lowed somebody amongst 'em ort to know what you-uns wuz up to, so I up an' told 'er."

"What did she have to say?" asked Odell, bending over the scales to spit at a crack in the floor, but not removing his eyes from the witness.

"Law, I hardly know what she didn't say! I never seed a woman take on so. Ef the last bit o' kin she had on earth wuz suddenly wiped from the face o' creation, she couldn't 'a' tuk it more to heart. Sally wuz with 'er, an' went on wuss 'an her mammy."

"What ailed Sally?"

Mrs. Filmore smiled irrepressibly. "I reckon you ort to know, Brother Odell," she said, under the hand she had raised to hide her smile. "Do you reckon she hain't heerd o' yore declaration that Eph cayn't marry in no heretic family while yo're above ground? It wuz goin' the round at singin'-school two weeks ago, and thar hain't been a thing talked sence."

"I hain't got a ioty to retract," replied Odell, looking down into the upturned faces for approval. "I'd as soon see a son o' mine in his box. Misfortune an' plague is boun' to foller them that winks at infidelity in any disguise ur gyarb."

"Oh, shucks! don't fetch the young folks into it, Brother Odell," gently protested Bart Callaway. "Them two has been a-settin' up to each other ever sence they wuz knee-high to a duck. They hain't responsible fer the doin's o' the old folks."

"I hain't got nothin' to take back, an' Eph knows it," thundered the tall deacon, and his face flushed angrily. "Ef the membership sees fit to excommunicate Ab Calihan, none o' his stock'll ever come into my family. But this is dilly-dallyin' over nothin'. You fellers 'll set thar cocked up, an' chaw an' spit, an' look knowin', an' let the day pass 'thout doin' a single thing. Ab Calihan is either fitten or unfitten, one ur t'other. Brother Filmore, you've seed 'im the most, now what's he let fall that's undoctrinal?"

Filmore got up and laid his clay pipe on the counter and kicked back his chair with his foot.

"The fust indications I noticed," he began, in a raised voice, as if he were speaking to some one outside, "wuz the day Liz Wambush died. Bud Thorn come in while I wuz weighing up a side o' bacon fur Ab, an' 'lowed that Liz couldn't live through the night. I axed 'im ef she had made her peace, and he 'lowed she had, entirely, that she wuz jest a-lyin' thar shoutin' Glory ever' breath she drawed, an' that they all wuz glad to see her reconciled, fer you know she wuz a hard case speritually. Well, it wuz right back thar at the fireplace while Ab wuz warmin' hisse'f to start home that he 'lowed that he hadn't a word to say agin Liz's marvelous faith, nur her sudden speritual spurt, but that in his opinion the doctrine o' salvation through faith without actual deeds of the flesh to give it backbone wuz all shucks, an' a dangerous doctrine to teach to a risin' gineration. Them wuz his words as well as I can remember, an' he cited a good many cases to demonstrate that the members o' Big Cabin wuzn't any more ready to help a needy neighbor than a equal number outside the church. He wuz mad kase last summer when his wheat wuz spilin' everybody that come to he'p wuz uv some other denomination, an' the whole lot o' Big Cabin folks made some excuse ur other. He 'lowed that you—"

Filmore hesitated, and the tall man opposite him changed countenance.

"Neil, hain't you got a bit o' sense?" put in Mrs. Filmore, sharply.

"What did he say ag'in' me—the scamp?" asked Odell, firing up.

Filmore turned his back to his scowling wife, and took an egg from a basket on the counter and looked at it closely, as he rolled it over and over in his fingers.

"Lots that he ortn't to, I reckon," he said, evasively.

"Well, what wuz *some* of it? I hain't a-keerin' what he says about me."

"He 'lowed, fer one thing, that yore strict adheerance to doctrine had hardened you some, wharas religious conviction, ef thar wuz any divine intention in it, ort, in reason, to have a contrary effect. He 'lowed you wuz money-lovin' and' uncharitable an' unfergivin' an', a heap o' times, un-Christian in yore persecution o' the weak an' helpless— them that has no food an' raiment—when yore crib an' smokehouse is always full. Ab is a powerful talker, an'—"

"It's the devil in 'im a-talkin'," interrupted Odell, angrily, "an' it's plain enough that he ort to be churched. Brother Sanders, you intimated that you'd have a word to say; let us have it."

Sanders, a heavy-set man, bald-headed and red-bearded, rose. He took a prodigious quid of tobacco from his mouth and dropped it on the floor at the side of his chair. His remarks were crisp and to the point.

"My opinion is that Ab Calihan hain't a bit more right in our church than Bob Inglesel. He's got plumb crooked."

"What have you heerd 'im say? That's what we want to git at," said

Odell, his leathery face brightening.

"More'n I keered to listen at. He has been readin' stuff he ortn't to. He give up takin' the *Advocate*, an' wouldn't go in Mary Bank's club when they've been takin' it in his family fer the last five year, an' has been subscribin' fer the *True Light* sence Christmas. The last time I met 'im at Big Cabin, I think it wuz the second Sunday, he couldn't talk o' nothin' else but what this great man an' t'other had writ somewhar up in Yankeedom, an' that ef we all keep along in our little rut we'll soon be the laughin'-stock of all the rest of the enlightened world. Ab is a slippery sort of a feller, an' it's mighty hard to ketch 'im, but I nailed 'im on one vital p'int."

Sanders paused for a moment, stroked his beard, and then continued: "He got excited sorter, an' 'lowed that he had come to the conclusion that hell warn't no literal, burnin' one nohow, that he had too high a regyard fer the Almighty to believe that He would amuse Hisse'f roastin' an' feedin' melted lead to His creatures jest to see 'em squirm."

"He disputes the Bible, then," said Odell, conclusively, looking first into one face and then another. "He sets his puny self up ag'in' the Almighty. The Book that has softened the pillers o' thousands; the Word that has been the consolation o' millions an' quintillions o' mortals of sense an' judgment in all ages an' countries is a pack o' lies from kiver to kiver. I don't see a bit o' use goin' furder with this investigation."

Just then Mrs. Filmore stepped out from her corner.

"I hain't been axed to put in," she said, warmly; "but ef I wuz you-uns I'd go slow with Abner Calihan. He's nobody's fool. He's too good a citizen to be hauled an' drug about like a dog with a rope round his neck. He fit on the right side in the war, an' to my certain knowledge has done more to'ds keepin' peace an' harmony in this community than any other three men in it. He has set up with the sick an' toted medicine to 'em, an' fed the pore an' housed the homeless. Here only last week he got hisse'f stung all over the face an' neck helpin' that lazy Joe Sebastian hive his bees, an' Joe an' his triflin' gang didn't git a scratch. You may see the day you'll regret it ef you run dry shod over that man."

"We simply intend to do our duty, Sister Filmore," said Odell, slightly taken aback; "but you kin see that church rules must be obeyed. I move we go up thar in a body an' lay the case squar before 'im. Ef he is willin' to take back his wild assertions an' go 'long quietly without tryin' to play smash with the religious order of the whole community, he may stay in on probation. What do you-uns say?"

"It's all we kin do now," said Sanders; and they all rose and reached for their hats.

"You'd better stay an' look atter the store," Filmore called back to his wife from the outside; "somebody mought happen along." With a reluctant nod of her head she acquiesced, and came out on the little porch and looked after them as they trudged along the hot road toward Abner Calihan's farm. When they were out of sight she turned back into the store. "Well," she muttered, "Abner Calihan *may* put up with that triflin' layout a-interfeerin' with 'im when he is busy a-savin' his hay, but ef he don't set his dogs on 'em he is a better Christian 'an I think he is' an' he's a good un. They are a purty-lookin' set to be a-dictatin' to a man like him."

A little wagon-way, which was not used enough to kill the stubbly grass that grew on it, ran from the main road out to Calihan's house. The woods through which the little road had been cut were so thick and the foliage so dense that the overlapping branches often hid the sky.

Calihan's house was a four-roomed log building which had been weather-boarded on the outside with upright unpainted planks. On the right side of the house was an orchard, and beneath some apple-trees near the door stood an old-fashioned cider-press, a pile of acid-stained rocks which had been used as weights in the press, and numerous tubs, barrels, jugs, and jars, and piles of sour-smelling refuse, over which buzzed a dense swarm of honey-bees, wasps, and yellow-jackets. On the other side of the house, in a chip-strewn yard, stood cords upon cords of wood, and several piles of rich pine-knots and charred pine-logs, which the industrious farmer had on rainy days hauled down from the mountains for kindling-wood. Behind the house was a great log barn and a stable-yard, and beyond them lay the cornfields and the lush green meadow, where a sinuous line of willows and slender cane-brakes marked the course of a little creek.

The approach of the five visitors was announced to Mrs. Calihan and her daughter by a yelping rush toward the gate of half a dozen dogs which had been napping and snapping at flies on the porch. Mrs. Calihan ran out into the yard and vociferously called the dogs off, and with awed hospitality invited the men into the little sitting-room.

Those of them who cared to inspect their surroundings saw a rag carpet, walls of bare, hewn logs, the cracks of which had been filled with yellow mud, a little table in the center of the room, and a cottage organ against the wall near the small window. On the mantel stood a new clock and a glass lamp, the globe of which held a piece of red flannel and some oil. The flannel was to give the lamp color. Indeed, lamps with flannel in them were very much in vogue in that part of the country.

"Me an' Sally wuz sorter expectin' ye," said Mrs. Calihan, as she gave them seats and went around and took their hats from their knees and laid them on a bed in the next room. "I don't know what to make of Mr. Calihan," she continued, plaintively. "He never wuz this away before. When we wuz married he could offer up the best prayer of any young man in the settlement. The Mount Zion meetin'-house couldn't hold protracted meetin' without 'im. He fed more preachers an' the'r hosses than anybody else, an' some 'lowed that he wuz jest too natcherly good to pass away like common folks, an' that when his time come he'd jest disappear body an' all." She was now wiping her eyes on her apron, and her voice had the suggestion of withheld emotions. "I never calculated on him bringin' such disgrace as this on his family."

"Whar is he now?" asked Odell, preliminarily.

"Down thar stackin' hay. Sally begun on 'im ag'in at dinner about yore orders to Eph, an' he went away 'thout finishin' his dinner. She's been a-cryin' an' a-poutin' an' takin' on fer a week, an' won't tech a bite to eat. I never seed a gal so bound up in anybody as she is in Eph. It has mighty nigh driv her pa distracted, kase he likes Eph, an' Sally's his pet." Mrs. Calihan turned her head toward the adjoining room: "Sally, oh, Sally! are ye listenin'? Come heer a minute!"

There was silence for a moment, then a sound of heavy shoes on the floor of the next room, and a tall rather good-looking girl entered. Her eyes and cheeks were red, and she hung her head awkwardly, and did not look at any one but her mother.

"Did you call me, ma?"

"Yes, honey; run an' tell yore pa they are all heer,—the last one of 'em an' fer him to hurry right on to the house an' not keep 'em a-waitin'."

"Yes-sum!" And without any covering for her head the visitors saw her dart across the back yard toward the meadow.

With his pitchfork on his shoulder, a few minutes later Abner Calihan came up to the back door of his house. He wore no coat, and but one frayed suspender supported his patched and baggy trousers. His broad, hairy breast showed through the opening in his shirt. His tanned cheeks and neck were corrugated, his hair and beard long and reddish brown. His brow was high and broad, and a pair of blue eyes shone serenely beneath his shaggy brows.

"Good evenin'," he said, leaning his pitchfork against the door-jamb outside and entering. Without removing his hat he went around and gave a damp hand to each visitor. "It is hard work savin' hay sech weather as this."

No one replied to this remark, though they all nodded and looked as if they wanted to give utterance to something struggling within them. Calihan swung a chair over near the door, and sat down and leaned back against the wall, and looked out at the chickens in the yard and the gorgeous peacock strutting about in the sun. No one seemed quite ready to speak, so, to cover his embarrassment, he looked farther over in the yard to his potato-bank and pig-pens, and then up into the clear sky for indications of rain.

"I reckon you know our business, Brother Calihan," began Odell, in a voice that broke the silence harshly.

"I reckon I could make a purty good guess," and Calihan spit over his left shoulder into the yard. "I hain't heerd nothin' else fer a week. From all the talk, a body'd 'low I'd stole somebody's hawgs."

"We jest *had* to take action," affirmed the self-constituted speaker for the others. "The opinions you have expressed," and Odell at once began to warm up to his task," are so undoctrinal an' so p'int blank ag'in' the articles of faith that, believin' as you seem to believe, you are plumb out o' j'int with Big Cabin Church, an' a resky man in any God-feerin' community. God Almighty"—and those who saw Odell's twitching upper lip and indignantly flashing eye knew that the noted "exhorter" was about to become mercilessly personal and vindictive—"God Almighty is the present ruler of the universe, but sence you have set up to run ag'in' Him it looks like you'd need a wider scope of territory to transact business in than jest heer in this settlement."

The blood had left Calihan's face. His eyes swept from one stern, unrelenting countenance to another till they rested on his wife and daughter, who sat side by side, their faces in their aprons, their shoulders quivering with soundless sobs. They had forsaken him. He was an alien in his own house, a criminal convicted beneath his own roof. His rugged breast rose and fell tumultuously as he strove to command his voice.

"I hain't meant no harm—not a speck," he faltered, as he wiped the perspiration from his quivering chin. "I hain't no hand to stir up strife in a community. I've tried to be law-abidin' an' honest, but it don't seem like a man kin he'p thinkin'. He—"

"But he kin keep his thinkin' to hisse'f," interrupted Odell, sharply; and a pause came after his words.

In a jerky fashion Calihan spit over his shoulder again. He looked at his wife and daughter for an instant, and nodded several times as if acknowledging the force of Odell's words. Bart Callaway took out his tobacco-quid and nervously shuffled it about in his palm as if he had half made up his mind that Odell ought not to do all the talking, but he remained mute, for Mrs. Calihan had suddenly looked up.

"That's what I told him," she whimpered, bestowing a tearful glance on her husband. "He mought 'a' kep' his idees to hisse'f ef he had to have 'em, and not 'a' fetched calumny an' disgrace down on me an' Sally. When he used to set thar atter supper an' pore over the *True Light* when ever'body else wuz in bed, I knowed it'd bring trouble, kase some o' the doctrine wuz scand'lous. The next thing I knowed he had lost intrust in prayer-meetin', an' 'lowed that Brother Washburn's sermons wuz the same thing over an' over, an' that they mighty nigh put him to sleep. An' then he give up axin' the blessin' at the table— somethin' that has been done in my fam'ly as fur back as the oldest one kin remember. An' he talked his views, too, fer it got out, an' me nur Sally narry one never cheeped it, fer we wuz ashamed. An' then ever' respectable woman in Big Cabin meetin'-house begun to sluff away from us as ef they wuz afeerd o' takin' some dreadful disease. It wuz hard enough on Sally at the start, but when Eph up an' tol' her that you had give him a good tongue-lashin', an' had refused to deed him the land you promised him ef he went any further with her, it mighty nigh prostrated her. She hain't done one thing lately but look out at the road an' pine an' worry. The blame is all on her father. My folks has all been good church members as fur back as kin be traced, an' narry one wuz ever turned out."

Mrs. Calihan broke down and wept. Calihan was deeply touched; he could not bear to see a woman cry. He cleared his throat and tried to look unconcerned.

"What step do you-uns feel called on to take next to—to what you are a-doin' of now?" he stammered.

"We 'lowed," replied Odell, "ef we couldn't come to some sort o' understandin' with you now, we'd fetch up the case before preachin' to-morrow an' let the membership vote on it. The verdict would go ag'in' you, Ab, fer thar hain't a soul in sympathy with you."

The sobbing of the two women broke out in renewed volume at the mention of this dreadful ultimatum, which, despite their familiarity with the rigor of Big Cabin Church discipline, they had up to this moment regarded as a vague contingent rather than a tangible certainty.

Calihan's face grew paler. Whatever struggle might have been going on in his mind was over. He was conquered.

"I am ag'in' bringin' reproach on my wife an' child," he conceded, a lump in his throat and a tear in his eye. "You all know best. I reckon I have been too forward an' too eager to heer myself talk." He got up and looked out toward the towering cliffy mountains and into the blue indefiniteness above them, and without looking at the others he finished awkwardly: "Ef it's jest the same to you-uns you may let the charge drap, an'—an' in future I'll give no cause fer complaint."

"That's the talk" said Odell, warmly, and he got up and gave his hand to Calihan. The others followed his example.

"I'll make a little speech before preachin' in the mornin'," confided Odell to Calihan after congratulations were over. "You needn't be thar unless you want to. I'll fix you up all right."

Calihan smiled faintly and looked shame-facedly toward the meadow, and reached outside and took hold of the handle of his pitch-fork.

"I want to try to git through that haystack 'fore dark," he said, awkwardly. "Ef you-uns will be so kind as to excuse me now I'll run down and finish up. I'd sorter set myself a task to do, an' I don't like to fall short o' my mark."

Down in the meadow Calihan worked like a tireless machine, not pausing for a moment to rest his tense muscles. He was trying to make up for the time he had lost with his guests. Higher and smaller grew the great haystack as it slowly tapered toward its apex. The red sun sank behind the mountain and began to draw in its long streamers of light. The gray of dusk, as if fleeing from its darker self, the monster night, crept up from the east, and with a thousand arms extended moved on after the receding light.

Calihan worked on till the crickets began to shrill and the frogs in the marshes to croak, and the hay beneath his feet felt damp with dew. The stack was finished. He leaned on his fork and inspected his work mechanically. It was a perfect cone. Every outside straw and blade of grass lay smoothly downward, like the hair on a well-groomed horse. Then with his fork on his shoulder he trudged slowly up the narrow field-road toward the house. He was vaguely grateful for the darkness; a strange, new, childish embarrassment was on him. For the first time in life he was averse to meeting his wife and child.

"I've been spanked an' told to behave ur it 'ud go wuss with me," he muttered. "I never wuz talked to that away before by nobody, but I jest had to take it. Sally an' her mother never would 'a heerd the last of it ef I had let out jest once. No man, I reckon, has a moral right to act so as to make his family miserable. I crawfished, I know, an' on short notice; but law me! I wouldn't have Bill Odell's heart in me fer ever' acre o' bottom-lan' in this valley. I wouldn't 'a talked to a houn' dog as he did to me right before Sally an' her mother." He was very weary when he leaned his fork against the house and turned to wash his face and hands in the tin basin on the bench at the side of the steps. Mrs. Calihan came to the door, her face beaming.

"I wuz afeerd you never would come," she said, in a sweet, winning tone. "I got yore beans warmed over an' some o' yore brag yam taters cooked. Come on in 'fore the coffee an' biscuits git cold."

"I'll be thar in a minute," he said; and he rolled up his sleeves and plunged his hot hands and face into the cold spring water.

"Here's a clean towel, pa; somebody has broke the roller." It was Sally. She had put on her best white muslin gown and braided her rich, heavy hair into two long plaits which hung down her back. There was no trace of the former redness about her eyes, and her face was bright and full of happiness. He wiped his hands and face on the towel she held, and took a piece of comb from his vest pocket and hurriedly raked his coarse hair backward. He looked at her tenderly and smiled in an abashed sort of way.

"Anybody comin' to-night?"

"Yes, sir."

"Eph Odell, I'll bet my hat!"

The girl nodded, and blushed and hung her head.

"How do you know?"

"Mr. Odell 'lowed I mought look fer him."

Abner Calihan laughed slowly and put his arm around his daughter, and together they went toward the steps of the kitchen door.

"You seed yore old daddy whipped clean out to-day," he said, tentatively. "I reckon yo're ashamed to see him sech a coward an' have him sneak away like a dog with his tail tucked 'tween his legs. Bill Odell is a power in this community."

She laughed with him, but she did not understand his banter, and preceded him into the kitchen. It was lighted by a large tallow-dip in the center of the table. There was much on the white cloth to tempt a hungry laborer's appetite—a great dish of greasy string-beans, with pieces of bacon, a plate of smoking biscuits, and a platter of fried ham in brown gravy. But he was not hungry. Slowly and clumsily he drew up his chair and sat down opposite his wife and daughter. He slid a quivering thumb under the edge of his inverted plate and turned it half over, but noticing that they had their hands in their laps and had reverently bowed their heads, he cautiously replaced it. In a flash he comprehended what was expected of him. The color surged into his homely face. He played with his knife for a moment, and then stared at them stubbornly, almost defiantly. They did not look up, but remained motionless and patiently expectant. The dread of the protracted silence, for which he was becoming more and more responsible, conquered him. He lowered his head and spoke in a low, halting tone:

"Good Lord, Father of us all, have mercy on our sins, and make us thankful fer these, Thy many blessings. Amen."

Will N. Harben (1858–1912)

Harben was born in Dalton, Georgia. He wrote more than twenty novels, including ABNER DANIEL (1902), ANN BOYD (1906), MAM' LINDA (1907), and THE TRIUMPH (1917). His most important book, however, remains NORTHERN GEORGIA SKETCHES, the collection of short stories he published in 1900. "The Heresy of Abner Calihan" is taken from NORTHERN GEORGIA SKETCHES.

Rachel and Her Children

Frances Newman

EVERYONE AGREED that a perfect stranger could not have seen Mrs. Foster's funeral without realizing that Mrs. Foster had lived a well-rounded life. There was her husband in the front pew, vainly struggling to conceal his grief so that he could console Mrs. Foster's mother, old Mrs. Overton. There were her two sons, vainly struggling to conceal their grief so that they could console Mrs. Foster's daughters-in-law, their wives. There were her four little grandchildren, as downcast as any one could ask. There were her six faithful servants, as heartbroken as her daughters-in-law. The society of Colonial Dames was there, in a body, and the Daughters of the Confederacy were there in a body. The Woman's Club was there, in a body, and even the Chamber of Commerce was there, in a body. There was all of the Social Register which did not happen to be on its yachts, or in sanatoria, or abroad. And there were the wreaths, and the harps, and the crescents, and the sheaves of all those bodies and of all those personages.

The hearts of the community went out to every member of Mrs. Foster's stricken family, so the rector told his audience and his God. But in particular it went out to Mrs. Foster's mother, for not a month before she had stood by her only son's open grave, and now she was about to stand beside her only daughter's open grave. She sat among them in the church—as the rector said, like Rachel weeping for her children. But she was veiled in English crêpe of excellent quality and so the most acute eyes of the community could not count the number of her tears. It was fortunate, indeed, that Mr. Foster could afford that excellent quality of crêpe, for old Mrs. Overton was not actually weeping like Rachel—in fact, she was not weeping at all.

Old Mrs. Overton had dreamed indirectly of Mrs. Foster's funeral on at least a hundred different nights. Thus she had now no difficulty in realizing that her brilliant daughter's mortal remains were reposing in that gray coffin which was so magnificently concealed by its blanket of lilies and pink roses. Old Mrs. Overton was seventy-four years old; she belonged to a generation which believed that dreaming of a funeral was a sign of a wedding, and that dreaming of a wedding was a sign of a funeral. She had never read the works of Dr. Siegmund Freud—she had, in fact, never heard of Dr. Freud—and so she had no idea what Dr. Freud's disciples would have entered on the card describing her case. Old Mrs. Overton sat comfortably in the best corner of the cushioned pew and, in the pleasant shelter of her well-draped veil, thought about things.

She thought of the time when she was sixteen, back in 1864. She thought of Captain Ashby, with his black plume and his black horse. They had stood in the box garden, and she had fairly ached with adoration of his six feet, his black hair, his black eyes, of the wound in some vaguely invisible spot that no Southern lady could even think about, of his gallant war record, not yet embalmed in the Confederate Museum. She was familiar with the works of Mr. Dickens and Mr. Thackeray and Sir Walter Scott, but she had never been allowed to read the story of Jane Eyre and Mr. Rochester. She flutteringly expected...she flutteringly hoped...that one night soon, perhaps that very night, Captain Ashby would drop on his gray-trousered knees, and implore her to do him the great honour of becoming his wife. She would accept the great honour, she would beg him not to kneel before one so unworthy, and Captain Ashby would rise. He would timidly bend down and kiss her respectfully on the forehead. And then Captain Ashby and his betrothed would walk in to his betrothed's father, and Captain Ashby would ask her hand in marriage. That was what Mr. Dickens and Mr. Thackeray led one to expect, and that was what her mother, who had been twice married and therefore twice engaged, led her to expect.

But that was not what happened. Captain Ashby stopped talking. Even eager questions about his recent heroic deeds were barely answered. The moment might be approaching. Sally had no desire to postpone it, and so she stopped asking the eager questions. Captain Ashby seized her in a passionate embrace, he covered her face with passionate kisses, he kissed her under her soft chin, and just below the brown curls on her neck. It was instantly obvious to Sally that Captain Ashby did not love her. Ivanhoe would never have kissed the fair Rowena like that; David Copperfield would never have kissed the angelic Agnes like that, or even Dora who could not keep her accounts straight. Sally's heart was broken. She tore herself from the embrace of this man who had proved that he did not love her by kissing her, she rushed into her father's house, and up the stairs to her own four-poster. She wept there until her mother came to find her, and to hear the tragic tale. And her mother, though she had been twice married and twice engaged, confirmed Sally's belief that she had been insulted. And Captain Ashby rode away on his black horse.

Mrs. Overton sighed a little under the crêpe veil. She had waited six months for the black horse to gallop back up the avenue between the magnolias, but it had been years before she discovered that a kiss before proposal did not necessarily insult a great love. Meanwhile, her mother had decided to marry her to a certain Colonel Overton, and had had no great difficulty in overcoming Colonel Overton's intention of being legally faithful to the memory of his Julia. Sally's heart, of course, was broken, but that was no reason for being a forlorn old maid, and she thought it would be rather pleasant to decide for herself what frock she would wear, and whether she would go to the Springs in the summer, and how she would do her hair. Elderly husbands were said to be tractable, and Sally had been very tired of talking only when Mama didn't want to talk, or only to people Mama didn't want to talk to, and of always sitting with her back to the horses like an inconsequential Prince Consort. She had been convinced that the dignity of marriage would offset its disadvantages, and, besides, she had no very clear idea of marriage except that it meant a change of name and of residence, and sitting at the head of one's own table, behind one's own silver tea service. People hardly talked then of the boredom of sitting at the other end of the table from the wrong man every morning; certainly they never talked of the occasions when there wasn't a table between one and the wrong man.

The choir was singing "Lead, Kindly Light," which had been Mrs. Foster's favourite hymn, and which, she always mentioned, was written by the late Cardinal Newman before he became a Catholic, much less a Cardinal. Old Mrs. Overton shivered a little under her veil when they came to

And with the morn those angel faces smile
That I have loved long since and lost awhile.

Mrs. Overton had no doubt that Mama, tulle cap, black bombazine, and all, and Colonel Overton, beard, temper, and all, would be smiling among those angels, and the idea was not cheering. She had been an old man's darling, but she had also been an old man's slave, a carefully treasured harem of one. Colonel Overton had been fond of saying, of declaiming, that he did not believe in the honour of any man, or the virtue of any woman. Sally had never thought of deceiving him even about the price of a new gown, but even if she had been the most abandoned creature she would have been saved in spite of herself. When she went to a dentist, Colonel Overton was beside her. When she bought a new hat, Colonel Overton was there to protect her from the shop's manager and also from an unbecoming bonnet. Sally had never danced even the Virginia Reel or the Lancers after the morning when Colonel Overton had confirmed her idea of respectful proposals by asking the honour of her hand in marriage and then kissing her chastely on the brow.

Now she looked at the lilies and pink roses that concealed Mrs. Foster's coffin under their expensive fragrance. She was thinking of the day Mrs. Foster was born—something less than a year after the respectful proposal. It was not a coincidence that the baby, now a corpse, had been christened Cornelia for the maternal grandmother whose capacity for being obeyed she had inherited. Mrs. Overton's mother had not waited to receive a namesake with that pleased surprise which ordinarily greets namesakes and proposals and legacies. She had taken the name for granted, quite audibly, on the day when a granddaughter's probable advent was announced to her. The younger Cornelia had justified her grandmother. She allowed her mother to sit in her own carriage facing her own horses, and she allowed her to continue filling her own cups with tea and coffee from her own silver urn. That was the correct thing, and Cornelia always did the correct thing, in all matters from sleeves and shoes to husbands and religions. But after Cornelia was four years old, her mother was never allowed to talk to the people she wanted to talk to about the things she wanted to talk about—not even when her husband permitted her the luxury of an unchaperoned feminine visit. And when Colonel Overton very unwillingly died, Cornelia had seen that her mother was faithful to his memory.

Cornelia was nineteen when that event took place, and just in the process of marrying herself to a rising young lawyer named Henry Foster. The marriage took place shortly afterward, with a simple elegance which the newspaper notices attributed to the recent bereavement in the bride's family. But the simplicity of the elegance at Cornelia's marriage was really due to the disappearance of the late colonel's prosperity rather than to the disappearance of the late colonel himself. His wife and his daughter and his son knew that their acquaintances attributed part of this disappearance to the colonel's extraordinary gratitude to a prepossessing coloured—just barely coloured—nurse, who had been the comfort of his declining years. But Mrs. Overton had never been so indiscreet as to mention this theory to her daughter, even on the most tempting occasions.

Mrs. Overton had been as faithful to her husband as her sex required in the days when a good woman had no history except that recorded in the parish register. Her husband, she supposed, had been no more faithful to her than his sex will continue to require until nature changes her ways. But her daughter was inexpressibly shocked when she began to show signs of considering a second alliance.

Mrs. Overton, at that time, was still sufficiently under forty not to have begun comparing the corners of her eyes and the line under her chin with those of her contemporaries. The aspiring Mr. Robinson was not an Overton, but the war had been over long enough for prosperous Robinsons and impoverished Overtons to marry each other without scandal. Mrs. Overton would have liked to sit behind her own silver tea service again, and in her own drawing room, and Mr. Robinson would have been so honoured by the gift of her hand in marriage that she would at last have been able to talk to the people she wanted to talk to about the things she wanted to talk about. But Cornelia disapproved of second marriages so positively that people who did not know her might well have thought she was sorry that she had been born. Cornelia was then expecting the birth of that son who was now trying to conceal his own grief so that he could console her first daughter-in-law. And Cornelia had been thrown into such a state by her mother's announcement that Mrs. Overton had felt obliged to give up the idea.

So she had continued to sit on the side of her daughter's table for nine months of every year, and on the side of her son William's table for three months of every year. Even when tea services on breakfast tables went out, and round tables came in, tables continued to have a head and a side, and Mrs. Overton had continued to grieve for her own tea service and her own table. She had never ceased to long for a house where a ringing telephone would mean that someone in the world wanted to talk with her badly enough to go through the trouble of getting a telephone number; where a ringing door bell would mean that someone wanted to see her, if it were only a book agent, or the laundry man.

For thirty-four years Mrs. Overton had spoken to Daughters of the American Revolution and Daughters of the Confederacy and newspaper reporters and officers of those clubs which seem to exist chiefly to elect officers. But she had spoken only to tell them that Mrs. Foster was lunching or dining or presiding at some house or some club where she either could or could not be called to the telephone. She had talked to a great many callers, but she had talked to callers of no consequence, while Mrs. Foster talked to callers of great consequence—local, if not international. And then Mrs. Foster had fallen ill. And William Overton had fallen ill. And old Mrs. Overton began to be Rachel weeping for her children.

Mrs. Foster was ill, desperately ill, for six months. For their convenience, if not for hers, the doctors decreed that Mrs. Foster must be in a hospital, and that she must receive no visitors. Old Mrs.

Overton suffered with her daughter, but she revived the pleasant old custom of pouring the breakfast coffee from her own silver urn, and Mr. Foster was delighted. She carried the pantry keys, and the silver-closet keys, and the linen-room keys; she went to market alone; she went shopping alone. All the ladies of high position, and all the officers of all Mrs. Foster's clubs came to call on Mrs. Overton—to ask about Mrs. Foster, of course, but even on such occasions other subjects are discussed, and Mrs. Overton must be cheered and strengthened for the ordeal she was undergoing. Then William Overton was mercifully released from his sufferings. And then Mrs. Foster was mercifully released from her longer sufferings.

Old Mrs. Overton had received hundred of notes. She had scores of callers, and she had felt herself able to receive them all—decorously, in her own bedroom, one or two at a time. Her fortitude was considered remarkable. She had ordered delicate lunches for the faithful friends who were downstairs receiving the wreaths and the sheaves of Mrs. Overton's other friends and of all her societies. And she had ordered her own veil of the best English crêpe.

The choir was singing "Asleep in Jesus," and Mrs. Foster's funeral was nearly over. Mrs. Overton began to look about a little, under the shadow of her veil. She was thinking of all the visitors she would have the next day and the next week; of the days the granddaughters-in-law and the great-grandchildren would spend with her, of the birthday party she would give for little Cornelia in the spring—Mrs. Foster would want her namesake to have the party she had promised her. She was thinking of all the people who would beg her and Mr. Foster to come and have dinner with them, very quietly—since they, too, had loved Mrs. Foster.

And then Mrs. Overton happened to look across the aisle at Mrs. Turner, and Mrs. Turner was looking beyond her at Mr. Foster. Mrs. Turner's look was only a decorous look of heartfelt sympathy, but Mrs. Overton suddenly felt cold and forlorn. She remembered how attentive Mrs. Turner had been to her and to Mr. Foster. And she remembered that Mrs. Turner had lost Mr. Turner three years before. And she remembered how many of the kind women who had come to cheer her for her great ordeal, who had received the flowers that were banked about the chancel, had lost their husbands three or four or five years before. She remembered the statistics of the number of widows in the state that she had read for one of Mrs. Foster's erudite club papers. The whole church, the whole world, seemed to be filled with widows—widows whose daughters would not discourage their mothers from taking names different from their own.

Mrs. Overton had no doubt that in a year she would go back to the side of another Mrs. Foster's table, that she would receive telephone messages for another Mrs. Foster—and that this Mrs. Foster would not even be her daughter.

That last prayer was over. The eight eminent pallbearers were gathering. Mr. Foster rose and offered his arm to his mother-in-law. Mrs. Overton stood up, shaking with bitter sobs, and took the offered arm. She walked up the aisle behind the blanket of lilies and pink roses that covered Mrs. Foster's coffin. All the hearts of the community went out to old Mrs. Overton, weeping like Rachel for her children.

Frances Newman (1883-1928)

Newman was born in Atlanta. Author of two novels, THE HARD-BOILED VIRGIN (1926) and DEAD LOVERS ARE FAITHFUL LOVERS (1928), and editor of an anthology of short stories, THE SHORT STORY'S MUTATIONS (1924), her own stories have never been collected in a single volume. "Rachel and Her Children" was first published in the magazine AMERICAN MERCURY in 1924.

The Life and Death of Cousin Lucius

John Donald Wade

HE REMEMBERED ALL HIS LIFE the feel of the hot sand on his young feet on that midsummer day. He was very young then, but he knew that he was very tired of riding primly beside his mother in the carriage. So his father let him walk for a little, holding him by his small hand. On went the carriage, on went the wagons behind the carriage, with the slaves, loud with greetings for young master. In the back of the last wagon his father set him down till he could himself find a seat there. Then his father, still holding his hand, lowered him to the road, and let him run along as best he could, right where the mules had gone. The slaves shouted in their pride of him, and in their glee, and the sport was unquestionably fine, but the sand was hot, too hot, and he was happy to go back to his prim station next the person who ruled the world.

That was all he remembered of that journey. He did not remember the look of the soil, black at times with deep shade, nor the far-reaching cotton-fields running down to the wagon ruts in tangles of blackberry bushes and morning-glories. He knew, later, that they had forded streams on that journey, that they had set out with a purpose, from a place—as travelers must—and that they had at last arrived. But all that came to him later. In his memory there was chiefly the hot sand.

What he learned later was this—that in 1850 his father had left his home in lower South Carolina and followed an uncle of his—Uncle Daniel—to a new home in Georgia. His father was then only twenty or so, and when he inherited some land and slaves he decided to go on to Georgia, where land, said Uncle Daniel, was cheap and fresh, and where with thrift one might reasonably hope to set up for oneself almost a little nation of one's own.

The next thing actually in his memory was also about slaves. In South Carolina, Aunt Amanda, an aunt of his mother's, had lately died. What that might mean was a mystery, but one clear result of the transaction was that Aunt Amanda had no further use for her slaves, and, in accordance with her will, they had been sent to him in Georgia. Their arrival his memory seized upon for keeps. They were being rationed—so much meal, so much meat, so much syrup, so much rice. But not enough rice. "Li'l' master," said one of his new chattels to him, "you min' askin' master to let us swap back all our meal for mo' rice?" He remembered that he thought it would be delightful to make that request, and he remembered that it was granted.

Next he remembered seeing the railway train. There it came with all its smoke, roaring, with its bell ringing and its shrill whistle. It was stopping on Uncle Daniel's place to get wood, the same wood that all that morning he had watched the slaves stacking into neat piles. It seemed to him indeed fine to have an uncle good enough to look after the hungry train's wants. That train could pull nearly anything, and it took cotton bales away so easily to the city that people did not have to use their mules any longer, at all, for such long hauls.

But in some things the railroad did not seem so useful. For when it nosed farther south into the state, after resting its southern terminus for a year or two at a town some miles beyond Uncle Daniel's, the town went down almost overnight, almost as suddenly as a blown bladder goes down, pricked.

Then a war came, and near Uncle Daniel's, where the road crossed the railroad and there were some little shops, some men walked up and down and called themselves drilling. That seemed a rare game to him, and he never forgot what a good joke it seemed to them, and to him, for them to mutter over and over as they set down their feet, corn-foot, shuck-foot, corn-foot, shuck-foot—on and on. At last the men went away from the crossroads, and Cousin James and Cousin Edwin went with them—Uncle Daniel's son and his daughter's son. His own father did not go and Lucius was very glad, but very sorry too, in a way. He did not go, he said, because he could hardly leave Lucius's mother and the baby girls—for somehow two baby girls had come, from somewhere. Lucius thought his father very considerate, but he wondered whether the girls were, after all, of a degree of wit that would make them miss their father very much.—But before he had done wondering, off his father went also.

That war was a queer thing. It was away, somewhere, farther than he had come from when he came first to Georgia. He heard no end of talk about it, but most of that talk confused itself later in his mind with his mature knowledge. He clearly remembered that there were such people as refugees, women and children mostly, who had come that far south because their own land was overrun by hundreds and hundreds of men, like Cousin James and Cousin Edwin, who were up there fighting hundreds and hundreds of other men, called Yankees.

They were really fighting, not playing merely. They were shooting at one another, with guns, just as people shot a beef down when time came. But after they shot a man they did not put him to any use at all.

One day he went with Uncle Daniel to see a lot of soldiers who were going by, on their way north to help whip the Yankees. Uncle Daniel said that the soldiers were the noblest people in the world, and Lucius understood why it was that he took his gold-headed cane and wore his plush hat, as if he were going to church, when he went to say his good wishes to such noble people. As the train stopped and as he and Uncle Daniel stood there cheering, one of the soldiers called out to Uncle Daniel, boisterously: "Hey," he said, "what did you make your wife mad about this morning?"—"I was not aware, sir," said Uncle Daniel, "that I had angered her."—"Well," the soldier said, and he pointed at the plush hat, "I see she crowned you with the churn." Lucius wished very much that Uncle Daniel would say something sharp back to him, but he did not. He simply stood there looking a little red, saying, "Ah, sir, ah, sir," in the tone of voice used in asking questions but never coming out with any question whatever.

Once Lucius was with his mother in the garden. She was directing a number of negro women who were gathering huge basketfuls of vegetables. The vegetables, his mother told him, were being sent to Andersonville, where a lot of Yankees the soldiers had caught were being kept in prison. He asked his mother why they had not shot the Yankees, but she told him that it would have been very un-Christian to shoot them, because these particular Yankees had surrendered, and it was one's duty to be kind to them.

Years later he searched his mind for further memories of the war, but little else remained. Except, of course, about Cousin Edwin. He was at Cousin Edwin's mother's, Cousin Elvira's. It was a spring morning and everything was fresh with new flowers, and there were more birds flying in more trees, chirping, than a boy could possibly count. And at the front gate two men stopped with a small wagon.

He called to Cousin Elvira and she came from the house, down to the gate with him to see what was wanted. She was combing her hair; it was hanging down her back and the comb was in her hand so that he had to go round and take the other hand. What those men had in that wagon was Cousin Edwin's dead body. Cousin Elvira had not known that he was dead. Only that morning she had had a letter from him. He had been killed. How Cousin Elvira wept! He, too, wept bitterly, and the wagon men wept also. But Cousin Edwin was none the better off for all their tears. Nor was Cousin Elvira, for her part, much better off, either. She lived forty years after that day, and she told him often how on spring mornings all her life long she went about, or seemed to go about, numb through all her body and holding in her right hand a rigid comb that would not be cast away.

He was a big boy when the war ended, nearly fifteen, and the passing of days and weeks seemed increasingly more rapid. As he looked back and thought of the recurrent seasons falling upon the world it seemed to him that they had come to the count, over and over, of Hard Times, Hard Times, Hard Times, more monotonous, more unending, than the count of the soldiers, muttering as they marched, years before, in the town which had before been called only the crossroads.

He went to school to Mr. and Mrs. Pixley, who taught in town, some three miles from his father's plantation. Both of them, he learned, were Yankees, but it seemed, somehow, that they were good Yankees. And he took with him to Mr. Pixley's his two sisters. There was a brother, too, and there was a sister younger still, but they were not yet old enough to leave home.

One day his mother was violently ill. He heard her cry aloud in her agony—as he had before heard her cry, he remembered, two or three distinct times. She was near dying, he judged, for very pain—but they had told him not to come where she was and he waited, himself in anguish for her wretchedness. That day as she bore another child into the world, that lady quit the world once and for all. He thought that he would burst with rage and sorrow. Wherever he turned, she seemed to speak to him, and he cursed himself for his neglect of her. Surrounded by a nation of her husband's kin, she had not always escaped their blame. She had known that times were hard, well, well; but she had insisted that some things she must have while her children were still young. She had saved her round dollars and sent them to Philadelphia to be moulded into spoons; she had somehow managed to find some books, and and piano she *would* have. Well, she was dead now, and it seemed to Lucius that the world would be always dark to him, and that things more rigid, more ponderous, more relentlessly adhesive than combs are, would drag his hands downward to earth all his life.

It would not do, then, he decided, to take anybody quite for granted. Already he had learned, as a corollary of the war, that *things* are not dependable; even institutions almost universally the base of people's lives could not, from the fact that they were existent in 1860, be counted upon to be existent also in 1865. He knew now that people also are like wind that blows, and then, inexplicably, is still.

He examined his father, coldly, impersonally, for the first time— not as a fixed body like the earth itself. His father had obviously many elements of grandeur. He was honest and kind and capable. He was introspective, but not sure always to arrive by his self-analysis at judgments that Lucius believed valid. By the Methodist church, which he loved, he was stimulated wisely in his virtues and led to battle against a certain native irascibleness. But in that church such a vast emphasis is set on preaching, that the church is likely to be thought of as little more than a house big enough for the preacher's audience. Lucius learned before long that many of the preachers he was expected to emulate might with more justice be set to emulate him, let alone his father. But his father could not be brought to such a viewpoint, and indeed, if Lucius had dared to suggest his conclusions very pointedly, it might have proved the worse for him.

Soon Lucius was sent to a college maintained by Georgia Methodists, and he stayed till he was graduated. The college was in a tiny town remote from the railroad, and it was such a place that if the generation of Methodists who had set it there some forty years earlier had looked down upon it from Elysium, they would have been happy. Whatever virtues Methodism attained in the South were as manifest there as they were anywhere, and whatever defects it had were less vocal. The countless great oaks on the campus, lightened by countless white columns, typified, appropriately, in his mind the strength and the disciplined joyousness that life might come to. His teachers were usually themselves Methodist ministers, like those who had come periodically to his father's church at home, but the burden of their talk was different. The books they were constantly reading and the white columns among the oaks and the tangible memories thereabout of one or two who had really touched greatness, had somehow affected all who walked in that paradise.

In his studies the chief characters he met were Vergil and Horace and other Romans, who seemed in that atmosphere, as he understood them, truly native. More recent than they were Cervantes and Shakespeare, and the English Lord Byron, the discrepancies of whose life one could overlook in view of his inspiring words about liberty. Hardly dignified enough, because of their modernity, to be incorporated into the curriculum of his college, these writers were none the less current in the college community.

Lucius knew many other boys like himself. In his fraternity, dedicated to God and ladies, he talked much about their high patron and their patronesses, and in his debating society he joined in many windy dissertations on most subjects known to man. In spite of all the implication about him regarding the transiency of earth, in spite of the despair evident in some quarters regarding the possible future of the South, Lucius and his fellows and even his teachers speculated frequently and long on mundane matters. They were large-hearted men, in way of being philosophic, and they felt a pity for their own people, in their poverty and in their political banishment from a land that they had governed—no one in his senses would say meanly—through Jefferson and Calhoun and Lee.

Once he went as a delegate from his fraternity to a meeting held at the state university, where an interest in this world as apart from heaven was somewhat more openly sanctioned than at his own college. The chief sight he saw there was Alexander Stephens, crippled and emaciated and shockingly treble. As he spoke, a young negro fanned him steadily and gave him from time to time a resuscitating toddy. That man's eyes burned with a kind of fire that Lucius knew was fed by a passionate integrity and a passionate love for all mankind. He was obviously the center of a legend, the type to which would gravitate men's memories of other heroes who had been in their way great, but never so great as he was.

Many young men whom Lucius met at the state university acknowledged the complexities of that legend when they attempted to follow it; when they rose to speak—as people were so frequently doing in those days at such conventions—they behaved themselves with a grandiloquence and declaimed with a gilded ardor that matched the legend of Stephens better than it matched the iron actuality. But Lucius did not know that. He admired the fervid imitations. He regretted that he could never send a majestic flight of eagles soaring across a peroration without having dart though his mind a flight of creatures as large as they, but of less dignified suggestion. He was sure that he could never speak anything in final earnestness without tending to stutter a little. His virtues were of the sort that can be recognized at their entire value only after one has endured the trampling of years which reduce a man to a patriarch.

When Lucius finally had A.B. appended to his name with all the authority of his college, he went home again. Hard Times met him at the train. For indeed the stress of life was great upon his father. Cotton was selling low and the birth rate had been high. Sister Cordelia was already at a Methodist college for girls, and Sister Mary would be going soon. And behind Mary was Brother Andrew. Lucius's father had married again, his first cousin, the widowed Cousin Elvira. And in the house was Cousin Elvira's ward, her sister's daughter, Lucius's third cousin. Her name was Caroline, and she was nineteen, and she had recently, like Lucius, returned home from college.

It was time for Lucius to go to work, and there was not much work one could do. The cities had begun to grow much more rapidly than in times past, and some of his classmates at college had gone to the cities for jobs. The fathers of some of them were in a position to help their sons with money till they could get on their feet, but Lucius felt that it would be unjust, in his case, to his younger brothers and sisters for him to expect anything further from his father. About the only thing left was to help his father on the farm, but his father was in the best of health, and as vigorous and capable an executive as ever. He really did not need a lieutenant, and the thought of becoming a private soldier of the farm no more entered Lucius's mind than the thought of becoming executioner to the Tsar. While he was still undecided where to turn, he heard one day of the death of Mr. Pixley. Temporarily, then, at least, he could be Mr. Pixley's successor.

So with his father's help he took over Mr. Pixley's academy, naming it neither for its late owner nor, as his father wished, for Bishop Asbury. Instead he named it for the frail man with the burning eyes whom he had seen at the state university, Stephens.

All that fall and winter and into the next spring he managed his academy—one woman assistant and some eighty youngsters ranging from seven to twenty-one. And just as summer came round the year following he married Cousin Caroline.

So life went with him, year in, year out. Children came to him and Cousin Caroline in God's plenty, and children, less intimately connected with him, flocked to the academy. He was determined to make all these youngsters come to something. After all, his lines were cast as a teacher. At least he could make a livelihood at that work, and very likely, there, as well as in another place, he could urge himself and the world about him into the strength and the disciplined joyousness which he had come to prize and which he believed would surely bring with them a fair material prosperity. If the children were amenable, he was pleased; if they were dull, he was resolute, unwilling to condemn them as worse than lazy. When night came he was tired—like a man who has spent the day ploughing; but perhaps, he thought, in a little while the situation would become easier.

After the war, nearly all the owners of plantations moved into town, and land that had formerly made cotton for Uncle Daniel gradually turned into streets and building lots. Lucius felt that the thing he had learned at college, and had caught, somehow, from the burning eyes of Mr. Stephens, involved him in a responsibility to that town that could not be satisfied by his giving its youth a quality of instruction that he, if not they, recognized as better than its money's worth. He organized among the citizens a debating society such as he had seen away at school, and he operated in connection with it a lending library. Shakespeare and Cervantes and the English Lord Byron were at the beck of his fellow townsmen—and Addison and Swift and Sterne and Sir Walter Scott, and even Dickens and Thackeray and George Eliot. Lucius managed to make people think (the men as well as the women—he stood out for that) that without the testimony and the comment of such spirits on this life they would all find this life less invigorating.

He found abettors in this work—his father and Uncle Daniel and others of the same mind—but he was its captain. His school, then, affected not merely those who were of an age appropriate for his academy, and it was not long before he was known almost universally in his village as "Cap"—for Captain.

His father turned over about two hundred and fifty acres to him as a sort of indefinite loan, and he became in a fashion a farmer as well as a teacher. That possibly was an error, for when word of his pedagogic ability and energy spread far, and he was offered an important teaching position in a neighboring city, he decided not to accept it because of his farm. But possibly all that was not an error. An instinct for the mastery of land was in his blood, and he knew few pleasures keener than that of roaming over his place, in the afternoons, when school was out, exulting in the brave world and shouting to the dogs that followed him.

There is no doubt that Lucius was gusty. He shouted not only to his dogs, but to himself, occasionally, when he had been reading alone for a long time, during vacations, on his shaded veranda. And he shouted, too, when the beauty of the red sinking sun over low hills, or of clean dogwood blossoms in a dense brake, seemed to him too magnificent not to be magnificently saluted.

Hard Times shadowed him night and day, thwarting in his own life more generous impulses than he could number. Hard Times also, singly or perhaps in collusion with other forces, thwarted in the lives of his neighbors activities that he felt strenuously should be stimulated. What did people mean, in a land where all delectable fruits would grow for the mere planting, by planting never a fruit tree? His father had fruit trees, Uncle Daniel had, all of the older men, in fact, commanded for their private use, not for commercial purposes, orchards of pears and peaches, and vineyards, and many a row of figs and pomegranates. But only he of all the younger men would trouble to plant them.

Lucius pondered that matter. Of course there was the small initial expense of the planting, but it was very small or he himself could not have mustered it. Of course there was the despair, the lassitude of enduring poverty. He would shake his head violently when talking about this with his father—like a man coming from beneath water—but for all that gesture could find no clear vision.

It seemed to him, as he considered the world he was a part of, that common sense was among the rarest of qualities—that when it should assert itself most vigorously, it was most likely to lie sleeping. The prevalent economic order was tight and apparently tightening, yet the more need people had to provide themselves with simple assuagements—like pomegranates, for example—the more they seemed paralyzed and inactive. The bewildering necessity of actual money drove everyone in the farm community to concern himself exclusively with the only crop productive of actual money. The more cotton a man grew, the cheaper it went, and the more it became necessary to sustain one's livestock and oneself with dearly purchased grain and meat that had been produced elsewhere. Sometimes when Lucius considered these complexities, and ran over in his mind the actual want of money of his friends, and the cruel deprivation that many of them subjected themselves to in order to send their children away to colleges which were themselves weak with penury—at such times he was almost beside himself with a sort of blind anger.

It was lucky that his anger saved him from despair. He was not built for despair, from the beginning, and he was, after all, the husband of Cousin Caroline, and between her and despair there was no shadow of affinity. In every regard he could think of except money, Cousin Caroline had brought him as his wife everything that he, or any man, might ask for.

She knew how to summon a group of people from the town and countryside, and how, on nothing, apparently, to provide them with enough food and enough merriment to bring back to all of them the tradition of generous living that seemed native to them. He often thought that she, who was at best but a frail creature, was the strongest hope he knew for the perpetuation of that bright tradition against the ceaseless, clamorous, insensate piracies of Hard Times. He was sure that the sum total of her character presented aspects of serenity and splendor that demanded, more appropriately than it did anything else, a sort of worship.

Cousin Caroline had religion. She was made for religion from the beginning, and she was, after all, the wife of Cousin Lucius, and in every regard she could think of except money, Cousin Lucius, had brought her as her husband, everything that she, or any woman, might ask for. To many beside those two it seemed that Cousin Lucius, because he never quite accepted the Methodist Church, had no religion whatever, that, having only charity and integrity for his currency, he would fare badly at last with St. Peter as concerned tolls. But Cousin Caroline thought better of St. Peter's fundamental discernment than to believe he would quibble about the admission of one who was so plainly one of God's warriors.

Among the best things Cousin Caroline did for him was to bring him to a fuller appreciation of his father. Always fond of him, always loyal to him, Cousin Lucius had never quite understood his apparent satisfaction with the offerings of Methodism. He was affected inescapably when the Methodists presented his father, on his completing twenty-five years as superintendent of their Sunday school, with a large silver pitcher. Most of the people who had helped purchase it were harried by need, and their contributions were all the fruit of sacrifice.

But it was Cousin Caroline's satisfaction, as well as his father's, with the offerings of Methodism that did most to quiet his misgivings in that quarter. Anything that two lofty souls—or indeed one lofty soul, he conceded—can be fain of, must itself be somehow worthy. And if it is worthy, an adherence to it on the part of one person should never stand as a barrier between that disciple and an honest soul who is unable to achieve that particular discipleship. As cousin Lucius grew older, then, his love and admiration of his father, while no greater perhaps than they had been formerly, were certainly more active, less hampered by reservations. His father, he knew, had doted on him in a fashion so prideful that it had seemed a little ridiculous, but that surely could be no barrier between them, and the two men loved each other very tenderly.

Occasionally on trips to this or that city, he encountered friends whom he had known at college. Most of them were prosperous, and some of them were so rich and eminent that news of them seeped down constantly to the stagnant community that was his demesne. He was conscious, as he talked with some of them, of a sort of condescension for him as one who had not justified the promise of his youth. Friendly, aware soon that the old raciness and the old scope of his mind were still operative, one and another of them suggested his coming, still, to live in a city, where he might wrestle with the large affairs that somebody *must* wrestle with, and that he seemed so peculiarly fitted to control.

He learned pointedly through these people what was stirring in the great world. All of them recognized that the condition of Georgia, and of all the South, was indeed perilous, for acquaintance with Hard Times had taught them that Hard Times is a cruel master, who will brutalize, in time, even the stoutest-hearted victim. Somehow the tyrant must be cast down.

In the meantime Cousin Lucius saw the Literary and Debating Society, with its library, gradually go to pieces. It had lasted twenty years. People could not afford the bare expenses of its operation. He saw men resort to subterfuges and to imitations for so long that they at last believed in them; and he, for one, while opposed to anything that was not true, was too sorry for them not to be in part glad that they could persevere in their hallucination. He saw the negroes, inescapably dependent on the whites, sag so far downward, as the whites above them sagged, that final gravity, he feared, would seize the whole swinging structure of society and drag it fatally to earth. He saw the best of people, identified with as good a tradition as English civilization had afforded, moving he feared unswervably, toward a despair from which they never might be lifted.

A small daughter of his, one day, chattering to him, said a thing that made him cold with anger. She used the word "city" as an adjective, and as an adjective so inclusively commendatory that he knew she implied that whatever was the opposite of "city" was inclusively culpable. He knew that she reflected a judgment that was becoming dangerously general, and he wondered how long he himself could evade it. For days after that he went about fortifying himself by his knowledge of history and of ancient fable, telling himself that man had immemorially drawn his best strength from the earth that mothered him, that the farmer, indeed until quite recently, in the South, had been the acknowledged lord; the city man most often a tradesman. "But what have history and ancient fable," the fiend whispered, "to do with the present?" Cousin Lucius admitted that they apparently had little to do with it, but he believed they *must* have something to do with it if it were not to go amuck past all remedy.

Some of Cousin Lucius's friends thought that the solution of their troubles was to adopt frankly the Northern way of life; and others thought that the solution was to band themselves with discontented farmer sections elsewhere in the country, and so by fierce force to wrest the national organization to a pattern that would favor farmers for a while at the expense of industrialists. On the whole, philosophically, he hoped that farming would continue paramount in his Georgia. He knew little of the philosophy of industrialism, but he knew some people who had grown up to assume that it was the normal order of the world, and he knew that those people left him without comfort. Yet he doubted the wisdom of fierce force, anywhere, and he disliked the renunciation of individualism necessary to attain fierce force. And he observed that in the camp of his contemporaries who relied on that expedient there were many who favored socialistic measures he could not condone, and more whose ignorance and selfishness he could not stomach. The only camp left for him, in his political thinking, was the totally unorganized—and perhaps unorganizable—camp of those who could not bring themselves to assert the South either by means of abandoning much that was peculiarly Southern or by means of affiliating themselves with many who had neither dignity nor wisdom nor honesty.

Cousin Lucius was nearly fifty by now, but he had not yet reconciled himself to the rarity with which power and virtue go hand in hand, leading men with them to an Ultimate who embodies all that our poor notions of virtue and power dimly indicate to us. When he was at college, among the great oaks and the columns, it had seemed to him that those two arbiters were inseparable, as he observed them along the shaded walks. And he had taught school too long—Euclid and Plato were more real to him than Ulysses Grant and William McKinley.

About 1890 one of Cousin Lucius's friends sent some peaches to New York in refrigerated boxes. They sold well. And slowly, cautiously,

Cousin Lucius and all the people in his community began putting more and more of their land into orchards. It took a long time for them to adopt the idea that peaches were a better hope for them than cotton. Old heads wagged sagely about the frequent winters that were too cold for the tender buds, young heads told of the insect scourges likely to infest any large scale production; and every sad prophecy came true. In spite of all, the industry proceeded. Farm after farm that had been sowed to crops afresh each year since being cleared of the forests was set now in interminable rows of peach trees. In spring, when the earth was green with a low cover-crop and each whitewashed stalk of tree projected upward to the loveliest pink cloud of blossom, Lucius was like a boy again for sheer delight. And in summer, when the furious activity of marketing the fruit spurred many of the slow-going Georgians to the point of pettishness, his own vast energy became, it seemed, utterly tireless. What he saw made him believe that the master compromise had been achieved, that an agricultural community could fare well in a dance where the fiddles were all buzz-saws and the horns all steam-whistles.

An instinct, perhaps, made all of Cousin Lucius's children less confident of that compromise than he was. Without exception they revered him; and persuaded, all of them, of his conviction that the test of a society is the kind of men it produces, they could not think poorly of the system that had him as a part of it. But they could not gain their own consent also to live in that system. And one by one they went away to cities, and they all prospered.

An instinct, too, perhaps, made the people of his community restive under the demands he made of school children. He had yielded to the community judgment to the extent of turning his academy into a public school, but he could not believe that the transformation was more than nominal. That is where circumstance tricked him. The people had lost faith in the classics as a means to better living, or had come to think of *better living* in a restricted, tangible sense that Cousin Lucius would not contemplate. And to teach anything less than the classics seemed to him to involve a doubt as to the value of teaching anything. He wondered why people did not send their children to "business colleges" and be done with it. So he was repudiated as a teacher, after thirty faithful years. The times, he thought, and not any individuals he knew, were responsible and he was in no way embittered. It was, of course, a consideration that he would no longer draw his hundred dollars a month, but the farm was more remunerative than it had been since the Civil War. And before long the village bank was reorganized and he was made its president.

Money was really coming into the community, and it was sweet not to be stifled always with a sense of poverty. But sometimes he felt that money was like a narcotic that, once tasted, drives men to make any sacrifice in order to taste more of it. All around him, for instance, many gentlemen whom he had long recognized as persons of dignity were behaving themselves with a distressing lack of dignity. On the advice of New York commission merchants they were attaching to each of their peach-crates a gaudy label, boasting that peaches of that particular brand were better than peaches of any other brand. There were gentlemen who were actually shipping the same sort of peaches, from the same orchard, under two distinct brands. Cousin Lucius was sure that such conduct was not native with them, and he was at a loss to know what they meant. What if the commission merchants had said that such practice was "good business"? Who were the commission merchants, anyway?

Another by-and-by had come round and Hard Times was no longer knocking at the door. Cousin Lucius saw men and women, whose heads had been held up by a feat of will only, holding their heads high, at last, naturally. He thought they should hold them higher still. By the Eternal, these people were as good as any people anywhere, and it had not been right, he believed, nor in accord with the intent of God, for them to be always supplicants.

It made him glad to see the girls of various families with horses and phaetons of their own. When a group of citizens promoted a swimming club, he exulted with the happiness of one who loved swimming for itself and who loved it in this special case as a symbol of liberation. The water that he cavorted in on the summer afternoons, while he whooped from time to time to the ecstatic shrieks of a hundred children, plopped no more deliciously upon his body than upon his spirit. For forty years he and his kind had wandered through a dense wilderness, with little external guidance either of cloud or fire. He told himself that by the light of their own minds they had wandered indeed bravely, but he was unashamedly glad that help had come, and that other men and cities were at last visible.

His father lived on, hale at ninety. He had become in the eyes of everybody who knew him a benign and indomitable saint. Shortly before his death he was in extreme pain and feebleness, and Cousin Lucius, for one, while he was saddened, could not be wholly sad to have the old man go on to whatever might await him. As he ran over in his mind the events of the long life just ended, one thing he had not before thought of stuck in his memory. His father had continued superintendent of the Methodist Sunday School until his death, and yet when he had rounded out his fifty years, though his flock was less hard pressed by far than it had been twenty-five years earlier, there was no silver pitcher offered in recognition of that cycle of effort. He believed that his father, too, had let the anniversary go unnoticed.

Yet Cousin Lucius felt that the omission meant something, most likely something that people were not conscious of. To all appearances the Methodists were never so active. Like the Baptists—and as incompletely as he indorsed the Methodists, it truly grieved him for them to execute their reforms Baptistward—they had replaced their rather graceful wooden church with a contorted creation, Gothic molded, in red brick. Most of their less material defects remained constant. But the church's neglect of his father's fifty years of service made him know that in spite of its bustling works, it was bored upon from within by something that looked to him curiously like mortality. And the most alarming part of the situation was that the church could not be persuaded of its malady. People simply did not look to it any longer as to the center of all their real hopes. He felt that for the great run of men the church is an indispensable symbol of the basic craving of humanity for an integrity which it must aspire to, if it can never quite exemplify.

He dimly felt that in its zeal to maintain itself as that symbol it had adopted so many of the methods of the men about it, that men had concluded it too much like themselves to be specially needful. It had become simply the most available agent for their philanthropies. For its continued services on that score they paid it the tribute of executing its ceremonies, but they believed, in their hearts, if they were not aware that they did, that all those ceremonies were quite barren. Cousin Lucius, too, had felt that they were barren, but rather because they understated the degree of his humility than because they overstated it. It seemed to him that most of his contemporaries, who were in fact, by now, almost all his juniors, felt that those ceremonies needlessly belittled creatures who were in fact not necessarily little at all.

He did not solve those questions, but he held them in his mind, to couple them, if occasion came, with facts that he might run upon that seemed related.

So the new day was not altogether cloudless. Cousin Lucius felt that people were going too fast, that, villagers, they were trying to keep the pace of people they considered, but whom he could not consider, the best people in the great cities. He believed that the people who had represented in an urban civilization in 1850 what his family had represented at that time in a rural civilization were most likely as little disposed as he was to endorse the new god, who was so mobile that he had lost all his stability.

Tom and Dick and the butcher and the baker and others were all shooting fiercely about in automobiles, and Europe was trying to destroy itself in a great war—and then America was driven into the war, too. As a banker, he urged Tom and Dick to buy government bonds to sustain the war, but most of them were more concerned to buy something else. Perhaps the older families in the cities were protesting as he protested—and to as little purpose. And people would not read any more. Well-to-do again, they would not listen to his efforts to reorganize the old Library. They would swim with him, they would set up a golf club, but they would not read Cervantes because they were too busy going to the movies.

That war in Europe, with the clamorous agencies that swung to its caissons, woman's suffrage and "socialism" and prohibition, was a puzzle to him. His knowledge of history taught him that most of the avowed objects of any war prove inevitably, in the event, not to have been the real objects. As for woman's suffrage, despite his fervor for justice, he was sure that the practice of a perfectly sound "right" often involves the practicer, and with him others, in woes incomparably more galling than the renunciation of that right.

Socialism meant to him at bottom the desire of the laboring classes for a more equable share of the world's goods, and the laboring classes that he knew were negro farm hands. It seemed to him that in all conscience they shared quite as fully as justice might demand in the scant dole of the world's goods handed down to their white overlords.

For many years Georgia had had prohibition, and he had voted for it long before it was established. He believed that it was mainly an expedient for furthering good relations between the whites and negroes. It was not practical for a rural community to command adequate police protection, and he was willing to sacrifice his right to resort to liquor openly, in order to make it less available to persons who were likely to use it to the point of madness.

But national prohibition, involving the effort to force upon urban communities, and upon rural communities with a homogeneous population, a system designed peculiarly for the rural South, seemed to him as foolhardy and as vicious as the efforts of alien New England to control the ballot-box in the South. The law was passed in spite of him, and for a while—stickler as he was for law—he grudgingly abided by it. But he soon learned that he was alone, with scarcely anybody except women for company, and that made him restless. He remembered his initial objection to the program, and reminded himself of the statute books cluttered with a thousand laws inoperative because people did not believe in them, and at last, so far as he was concerned, repealed the national prohibition law altogether and abided by the prohibition law of Georgia, only, as he had before abided by it, with wisdom and temperance.

One day he was sitting in his brother's store, and he heard some men—they had all been students of his—talking lustily among themselves out on the sidewalk. "What this town needs," said one of them, "is looser credit. Look at every town up and down the road—booming! Look at us—going fast to nothing. What we need is a factory, with a big payroll every Saturday. Naturally we haven't got the capital to float the thing from the start, but, good Lord! how would anything ever start if people waited till they had cash enough to meet every possible expense? In this man's world you've got to take chances. The root of our trouble"—and here Cousin Lucius listened earnestly. He was president of the bank, and though he had not thought the town was disintegrating, he recognized that comparatively it was at a standstill—"the root of our trouble," continued his economist, "is old-man Lucius. Fine old fellow and all that kind of thing, but, my God! what an old fogy! I'll tell you, it's like the fellow said, what this town needs most is one or two first-class funerals!"

Cousin Lucius was pretty well dazed. He did not know whether to go out and defend himself, or to hold his peace, and later, when appropriate, to clarify his position as best he could for a race that had become so marvelously aggressive. He was afraid that if he went he would not be able to talk calmly. He had fairly mastered his trait of stuttering, but he felt sure that before any speech he might make just then he would do well to fill his mouth with pebbles and to plant himself by the roaring surf.

He knew well what that bounding youngster had in mind. He wanted, without effort, things that have immemorially come as the result of effort only. His idea of happiness was to go faster and faster on less and less, and Cousin Lucius was bound to admit that that idea was prevalent nearly everywhere. He did not know, for sure, where it had come from, but it was plainly subjugating Georgia, and if reports were faithful, it was lord everywhere in America. He did not care, he told himself, if it was lord everywhere in the hypothecated universe, it should win no submission from him. The true gods might be long in reasserting themselves, but life is long enough to wait. For that which by reason of strength may run to fourscore years, by reason of other forces may run farther. He would not concede that we are no better than flaring rockets, and he would never get it into his old-fashioned head that anything less than a complete integrity will serve as a right basis for anything that is intended to mount high and to keep high.

He would not say all that now. He believed that the peach business would be constantly remunerative, but he remembered that it had been in existence less than twenty-five years, and he knew that many things of longer lease than that, on men's minds, had suddenly crashed into nothingness. For that reason he was glad that his community had undertaken the commercial production of asparagus and pecans as well as peaches and the older dependence, cotton. He did not anticipate the collapse of all those industries. All that he insisted on was that the expansion of his community be an ordered response to actual demands—not a response so violently stimulated to meet artificial demands that it created new demands faster than it could satisfy the old ones.

The peach crop in 1919 was a complete failure—for reasons not yet determined. The fruit was inferior; the costs of production and transportation, high; the market, lax. And in turn other crops were almost worthless. Next year, everybody said, things would be better. And pretty soon it was plain to Cousin Lucius that his faith in the compromise between farming and industrialism had in its foundations mighty little of reality.

He was himself cautious and thrifty and he had not spent by any means all that the fat years just past had brought to him. He had saved money—and bought more land. He blamed, in a fashion, the people who had lived on all they had made, but against his will he had to admit to himself that he did not blame them very much. Gravely impoverished for years, holding in their land a capital investment that in theory, only, amounted to anything, they had toiled to feed and clothe a boisterous nation which had become rankly rich and which had reserved for itself two privileges: to drive such iron bargains with the Southern farmer that he could scarcely creep, and to denounce him from time to time for his oppression of the negro. Seeing all that, Cousin Lucius could hardly blame the grasshoppers for flitting during the short and, after all, only half-hearted summer of the peach industry. But he considered that he was weak not to blame them more, and he was torn to know whether he should promise the people a better day, which he could not descry, or berate them about the duties of thrift.

The towns in the peach area which had committed themselves to the looser credits he had heard advocated were in worse condition now, by far, than his own town. The same people who had called Cousin Lucius an old fogy began now to say that he was a wise old bird. And he accepted their verdict to this extent—he was wise in seeing the folly that a farm community surely enacts in attempting to live as if it were an industrial community. While he conceded that no community could in his day be any longer purely agrarian, he felt—when he heard people urging a universal acceptance of the industrial program—that that program was not suitable even for an industrial community if it was made up of human beings as he knew them. He recognized that his wisdom was only negative, that there were basic phases of the question that lay too deep for his perceiving.

The farmer, it seemed to him, was in the hard position of having to win the suffrage of a world that had got into the industrialists' motor-car and gone riding. He could run alongside the car, or hang on behind the car, or sit beside the road and let the car go on whither it would—with destination unannounced and, one might suspect, un-considered.

The case was illustrated by some towns he knew. One of them had continued to grow cotton exclusively—and the world had forgotten it. Many of them had run as hard as ever they could to keep up with the world, and they had fallen exhausted. His own town had hung on as best it could, and though the industrialists might grumble, it managed not to be dislodged. That was a half victory indeed.

He thought as a matter of justice to the farmer and as a matter of well-being for the world, that that motor-car should be controlled not always by the industrialists but sometimes by an agency that would be less swift, more ruminative. A truly wise bird would bring *that* about, and Cousin Lucius knew that that lay clean beyond him.

One might speculate on these things interminably, but what Cousin Lucius actually saw was that the economic structure of his community was falling down, like London Bridge, or like the little town which, as a child, he had seen burst, bladder like, when the railroad pushed on beyond it. He heard doctrinaire persons, sent down by the government, explain that the trouble lay wholly in the commitment of the people to one crop only. That infuriated him. His community was not committed to a one-crop system; it had four crops. But he found the doctrinaire persons hopelessly obtuse.

Four crops! They had five crops, worse luck, for the countryside everywhere was being stripped of its very forests, so that the people in the cities might have more lumber. That was a chance of getting some money, and one could not let it pass. Woods he had roamed, calculat-ing—as he had learned to do at college—their cubic content in timber per acre, were to his dismay being operated upon in actuality, as he had often fondly, with no thought of sacrilege, operated on them in fancy. It seemed that people could not be happy unless they were felling trees.

One day the young school superintendent began chopping some oaks on the school grounds, for the high purpose of making an out-of-door basketball court. Cousin Lucius had not a shred of authority to stop the young man, but when he found that the persons who did have authority would not interfere, he interfered himself. At first Cousin Lucius reasoned with him calmly, but the superintendent would not be convinced. There was much talk.

"I have the authority of the Board of Education," said the super-intendent, concluding the matter. But Cousin Lucius was determined that that should not conclude the matter. "Authority or no authority," said he, flustered, stuttering a little, "you will take them down, sir, at your peril." Then he walked away.

The superintendent knew that Cousin Lucius had no mandate of

132

popular sentiment behind him, but knew also *one* person who did not mean to risk that old man's displeasure. The trees were spared.

The sacrifice of the forests was a symbol to Cousin Lucius, and a sad one. He knew by it how grave, once more, was the extremity of his friends—how fully it meant the arrival once more of Hard Times as their master. Even now they retained a plenty of most things they actually needed, but lacked the means of acquiring anything in addition. Of course they had wanted too much, and had curbed their desires in general less successfully than he had done, and they were consequently harder pressed. But they were a people not bred to peasant viewpoints. Traditionally they were property owners. They worked faithfully, they maintained holdings upon the value of which was predicated the entire economic structure of the nation. Society would not in either decency or sense deny that value, and it never did. What it did—by some process Cousin Lucius could not encompass— was to make the revenues from that value quite valueless—or at least quite valueless as compared with the revenues from equal amounts of capital invested elsewhere.

Once again he saw inaugurated the old process, checked for a while, of people leaving their farms and putting out for the cities. And he observed that those who went prospered, while those who stayed languished. Formerly, the more or less gradual development of the cities made them incapable of offering work to all who came, and many of his younger neighbors kept to their farms through necessity. Now the cities were growing like mad—precisely, he thought, like mad— and most of the old families he knew were moving off, losing their connection with their old home. Some survived their difficulties, but many, after lapsing deeper and deeper into debt, finally turned over their holdings to one or another mortgage firm, and went away. And the mortgage firms turned over the land to aliens, people from here and yon- der, whose grandfathers never owned a slave nor planted a pomegranate.

Even the negroes, conscious at last of the insatiate capacity of the new cities, were moving away. The Southern cities had absorbed as many negroes as they could use, but the Northern cities had much work of the sort they felt negroes were suited for. It saddened Cousin Lucius to see them go. Men and women whose parents had come with his parents from Carolina, and who lived in the same houses all their lives, were going away—to Detroit, to Akron, to Pittsburgh. Well, God help them.

The prospect was not cheerful, but Cousin Lucius thought that as a human being he was superior to any prospect whatever. When he preached that doctrine to some of his friends they taunted him with the idea that his particular bravery was sustained by certain government bonds he had, and it was true that he had the bonds. He and

Cousin Caroline had not stinted themselves during the fat years all for nothing, and he had kept out a small share of his savings to go into Liberty Bonds. But he told those who mourned, and he told himself, that even if he had not saved the bonds, he would still have asserted his humanity over the shackling activities of mere circumstance.

It was a fine sight to see him early on a summer morning walking the mile-long street between his home and the bank. On one side there were great oaks bordering his path, and the other side was a row of houses. In front of nearly every house a woman was stirring among her flowers, and Cousin Lucius had some words for nearly all of them. "Nice morning, ma'am," he would say. "I hope you all are well this morning." And then he would pass on, and often he would sniff the cool air greedily into his nostrils. "My, my," he would say, "sweet! How sweet the air is this morning!" And when a breeze blew, he would stretch out his arms directly into it—for of all the good things to have up one's sleeve he considered a summer breeze among the usefulest.

The time came round when he and Cousin Caroline had been married fifty years. And they gave a great party, and all their children came home, and people from all that section came to say good wishes to them. Cousin Caroline sat most of the evening, lovely in her black dress and with her flowers, and Cousin Lucius—sure that Cousin Caroline would pay for the two of them whatever was owing to propriety—sat nowhere, nor was indeed still for a moment anywhere. He looked very elegant, as young, almost, as his youngest son, and he was as vigorous, apparently, as anybody in all that company. Cousin Lucius had never lost a moment in his whole life from having drunk too much liquor, but he had always kept some liquor on hand, and he felt that that night surely justified his touching it a little more freely than was his custom. So he summoned by groups all the gentlemen present into his own backroom, and had a toast with them. Now the room was small and there were many groups and that involved Cousin Lucius's having many toasts, but he used his head and came through the operation with the dignity that was a part of him.

Not everybody was satisfied with his conduct. Some of the ladies especially who had men-folk less well balanced than they might have been, thought the situation scandalous. They had been indoctrinated fully with the dogma which says that life must be made safe for everybody at the cost, if necessary, of shutting the entire world into a back yard with high palings, and they believed that somebody prone to sottishness might be wrecked by Cousin Lucius's example. They did not realize the complexities of life which baffle those who have eyes to see, and make them despair at times of saving even the just and wise—much less the weak and foolish.

Those ladies were not shadowed—nor glorified—by a sense of

tragic vision, and they were not capable—not indeed aware—of philosophic honesty, but they were good and angry with Cousin Lucius and they went to Cousin Caroline and told her that she should curb him. That lady was not dismayed. The thought of being angry with Cousin Lucius did not once occur to her, but for the briefest moment she realized that she was having to check herself not to be outraged against the little ladies who had constituted themselves his guardians. "Oh," she said, "you know Lucius! What can I do with Lucius? My dear, where *did* you find that lovely dress. You always show such exquisite taste. I am so happy to have you here. No friends, you know, like old ones. I am *so* happy."

The next winter Cousin Lucius and Cousin Caroline both had influenza, and Cousin Lucius's sister, who came to look after them, had it too. They all recovered, but Cousin Lucius *would* violate directions and go back to work at the bank before he was supposed to go. And as spring came on it was evident that something ailed him, very gravely. It was his heart, but he refused to recognize the debility that was patent to everybody else, and went on.

And when summer came, and the jaded people began again to market the peaches they felt sure—and rightly—would be profitless, he, with the rest, set his operations in motion. One of his sons, Edward, was at home on a visit, and early one morning the father and son went out to the farm, with the intention of coming back home for breakfast. Only the negro foreman, Anthony, was at the packing-house, where they stopped, and Edward strolled down into the orchard, leaving Cousin Lucius to talk over the day's plans with Anthony. A little way down one of the rows between the peach trees, Edward almost stumbled upon some quail. And the quail fluttered up and flew straight toward the packing-house.

He heard his father shout at them as they went by, the fine lusty shout that he remembered as designed especially for sunsets and clean dogwood blossoms. And then there was perfect silence. And then he heard the frantic voice of Anthony: "Oh, Mas' Edward! Help, help, Mas' Edward! Mas' Lucius! O Lord! help, Mas' Edward!" Stark fright slugged him. He was sick and he could scarcely walk, but he ran, and after unmeasured time, it seemed to him, he rounded the corner of the packing-house and saw Anthony, a sort of maniac between grief and terror, half weeping, half shouting, stooping, holding in his arms Cousin Lucius's limp body. "Oh, Mas' Edward! Mas' Edward! Fo' God, I believe Mas' Lucius done dead!"

He *was* dead. And all who wish to think that he lived insignificantly and that the sum of what he was is negligible are welcome to think so. And may God have mercy on their souls.

John Donald Wade (1892-1963)

Wade was born in Marshallville, Georgia. Among his works are two biographies, JOHN WESLEY (1930) and AUGUSTUS BALDWIN LONGSTREET: A Study of the Development of Culture in the South (1924), and many essays. "The Life and Death of Cousin Lucius" was his contribution to the Southern Agrarian manifesto I'LL TAKE MY STAND: The South and the Agrarian Tradition (1930).

"The Life and Death of Cousin Lucius" by John Donald Wade. Reprinted by permission of Anne Wade Rittenberry.

Blood-Burning Moon

Jean Toomer

1

Up from the skeleton stone walls, up from the rotting floor boards and the solid hand-hewn beams of oak of the pre-war cotton factory, dusk came. Up from the dusk the full moon came. Glowing like a fired pine-knot, it illumined the great door and soft showered the Negro shanties aligned along the single street of factory town. The full moon in the great door was an omen. Negro women improvised songs against its spell.

Louisa sang as she came over the crest of the hill from the white folks' kitchen. Her skin was the color of oak leaves on young trees in fall. Her breasts, firm and up-pointed like ripe acorns. And her singing had the low murmur of winds in fig trees. Bob Stone, younger son of the people she worked for, loved her. By the way the world reckons things, he had won her. By measure of that warm glow which came into her mind at thought of him, he had won her. Tom Burwell, whom the whole town called Big Boy, also loved her. But working in the fields all day, and far away from her, gave him no chance to show it. Though often enough of evenings he had tried to. Somehow, he never got along. Strong as he was with hands upon the ax or plow, he found it difficult to hold her. Or so he thought. But the fact was the he held her to factory town more firmly than he thought for. His black balanced, and pulled against, the white of Stone, when she thought of them. And her mind was vaguely upon them as she came over the crest of the hill, coming from the white folks' kitchen. As she sang softly at the evil face of the full moon.

A strange stir was in her. Indolently, she tried to fix upon Bob or Tom as the cause of it. To meet Bob in the canebrake, as she was going to do an hour or so later, was nothing new. And Tom's proposal which she felt on its way to her could be indefinitely put off. Separately, there was no unusual significance to either one. But for some reason, they jumbled when her eyes gazed vacantly at the rising moon. And from the jumble came the stir that was strangely within her. Her lips trembled. The slow rhythm of her song grew agitant and restless. Rusty black and tan spotted hounds, lying in the dark corners of porches or prowling around back yards, put their noses in the air and caught its tremor. They began plaintively to yelp and howl. Chickens woke up and cackled. Intermittently, all over the countryside dogs barked and roosters crowed as if heralding a weird dawn or some ungodly awakening. The women sang lustily. Their songs were cotton-wads to stop their ears. Louisa came down into factory town and sank wearily upon the step before her home. The moon was rising towards a thick cloudbank which soon would hide it.

> Red nigger moon. Sinner!
> Blood-burning moon. Sinner!
> Come out that fact'ry door.

2

Up from the deep dusk of a cleared spot on the edge of the forest a mellow glow arose and spread fan-wise into the low-hanging heavens. And all around the air was heavy with the scent of boiling cane. A large pile of cane-stalks lay like ribboned shadows upon the ground. A mule, harnessed to a pole, trudged lazily round and round the pivot of the grinder. Beneath a swaying oil lamp, a Negro alternately whipped out at the mule, and fed cane-stalks to the grinder. A fat boy waddled pails of fresh ground juice between the grinder and the boiling stove. Steam came from the copper boiling pan. The scent of cane came from the copper pan and drenched the forest and the hill that sloped to factory town, beneath its fragrance. It drenched the men in circle seated around the stove. Some of them chewed at the white pulp of stalks, but there was no need for them to, if all they wanted was to taste the cane. One tasted it in factory town. And from factory town one could see the soft haze thrown by the glowing stove upon the low-hanging heavens.

Old David Georgia stirred the thickening syrup with a long ladle, and ever so often drew it off. Old David Georgia tended his stove and told tales about the white folks, about moonshining and cotton picking, and about sweet nigger gals, to the men who sat there about his stove to listen to him. Tom Burwell chewed cane-stalk and laughed with the others till some one mentioned Louisa. Till some one said something about Louisa and Bob Stone, about the silk stockings she must have gotten from him. Blood ran up Tom's neck hotter than the glow that flooded from the stove. He sprang up. Glared at the men and said, "She's my gal." Will Manning laughed. Tom strode over to him. Yanked him up and knocked him to the ground. Several of Manning's friends got up to fight for him. Tom whipped out a long knife and would have cut them to shreds if they hadnt ducked into the woods. Tom had had enough. He nodded to Old David Georgia and swung down the path to factory town. Just then, the dogs started barking and the roosters began to crow. Tom felt funny. Away from the fight, away from the stove, chill got to him. He shivered. He shuddered when he saw the full moon rising towards the cloud-bank. He who didnt give a godam for the fears of old women. He forced his mind to fasten on Louisa. Bob Stone. Better not be. He turned into the street and saw Louisa sitting before her home. He went towards her, ambling, touched the brim of a marvelously shaped, spotted, felt hat, said he wanted to say something to her, and then found that he didnt know what he had to say, or if he did, that he couldnt say it. He shoved his big fists in his overalls, grinned, and started to move off.

"Youall want me, Tom?"

"Thats what us wants, sho, Louisa."

"Well, here I am—"

"An here I is, but that aint ahelpin none, all th same."

"You wanted to say something? . ."

"I did that, sho. But words is like th spots on dice: no matter how y fumbles em, there's times when they jes wont come. I dunno why. Seems like th love I feels fo yo done stole m tongue. I got it now. Whee! Louisa, honey, I oughtnt tell y, I feel I oughtnt cause yo is young an goes t church an I has had other gals, but Louisa I sho do love y. Lil gal, Ise watched y from them first days when youall sat right here befo yo door befo th well an sang sometimes in a way that like t broke m heart. Ise carried y with me into th fields, day after day, an after that, an I sho can plow when yo is there, an I can pick cotton. Yassur! Come near beatin Barlo yesterday. I sho did. Yassur! An next year if ole Stone'll trust me, I'll have a farm. My own. My bales will buy yo what y gets from white folks now. Silk stockings an purple dresses—course I dont believe what some folks been whisperin as t how y gets them things now. White folks always did do for niggers what they likes. An they jes cant help alikin yo, Louisa. Bob Stone likes y. Course he does. But not th way folks is awhisperin. Does he, hon?"

"I dont know what you mean, Tom."

"Course y dont. Ise already cut two niggers. Had t hon, t tell em so. Niggers always tryin t make somethin out a nothin. An then besides, white folks aint up t them tricks so much nowadays. Godam better not be. Leastawise not with yo. Cause I wouldnt stand f it. Nassur."

"What would you do, Tom?"

"Cut him jes like I cut a nigger."

"No, Tom—"

"I said I would an there aint no mo to it. But that aint th talk f now. Sing, honey Louisa, an while I'm listenin t y I'll be makin love."

Tom took her hand in his. Against the tough thickness of his own, hers felt soft and small. His huge body slipped down to the step beside her. The full moon sank upward into the deep purple of the cloud-bank. An old woman brought a lighted lamp and hung it on the common well whose bulky shadow squatted in the middle of the road, opposite Tom and Louisa. The old woman lifted the well-lid, took hold the chain, and began drawing up the heavy bucket. As she did so, she sang. Figures shifted, restlesslike, between lamp and window in the front rooms of the shanties. Shadows of the figures fought each other on the gray dust of the road. Figures raised the windows and joined the old woman in song. Louisa and Tom, the whole street, singing:

> Red nigger moon. Sinner!
> Blood-burning moon. Sinner!
> Come out that fact'ry door.

3

Bob Stone sauntered from his veranda out into the gloom of fir trees and magnolias. The clear white of his skin paled, and the flush of his cheeks turned purple. As if to balance this outer change, his mind became consciously a white man's. He passed the house with its huge open hearth which, in the days of slavery, was the plantation cookery. He saw Louisa bent over that hearth. He went in as a master should and took her. Direct, honest, bold. None of this sneaking that he had to go through now. The contrast was repulsive to him. His family had lost ground. Hell no, his family still owned the niggers, practically. Damned if they did, or he wouldnt have to duck around so. What would they think if they knew? His mother? His sister? He shouldnt mention them, shouldnt think of them in this connection. There in the dusk he blushed at doing so. Fellows about town were all right, but how about his friends up North? He could see them incredible, repulsed. They didnt know. The thought first made him laugh. Then, with their eyes still upon him, he began to feel embarrassed. He felt the need of explaining things to them. Explain hell. They wouldnt understand, and moreover, who ever heard of a Southerner getting on his knees to any Yankee, or anyone. No sir. He was going to see Louisa to-night, and love her. She was lovely—in her way. Nigger way. What way was that? Damned if he knew. Must know. He'd known her long enough to know. Was there something about niggers that you couldnt know? Listening to them at church didnt tell you anything. Looking at them didnt tell you anything. Talking to them didnt tell you anything—unless it was gossip, unless they wanted to talk. Of course, about farming, and licker, and craps—but those werent nigger. Nigger was something more. How much more? Something to be afraid of, more? Hell no. Who ever heard of being afraid of a nigger? Tom Burwell. Cartwell had told him that Tom went with Louisa after she reached home. No sir. No nigger had ever been with his girl. He'd like to see one try. Some position for him to be in. Him, Bob Stone, of the the old Stone family, in a scrap with a nigger over a nigger girl. In the good old days . . . Ha! Those were the days. His family had lost ground. Not so much, though. Enough for him to have to cut through old Lemon's canefield by way of the woods, that he might meet her. She was worth it. Beautiful nigger gal. Why nigger? Why not, just gal? No, it was because she was nigger that he went to her. Sweet . . . The scent of boiling cane came to him. Then he saw the rich glow of the stove. He heard the voices of the men circled around it. He was about to skirt the clearing when he heard his own name mentioned. He stopped. Quivering. Leaning against a tree, he listened.

"Bad nigger. Yassur, he sho is one bad nigger when he gets started."

"Tom Burwell's been on th gang three times fo cuttin men."

"What y think he's agwine t do t Bob Stone?"

"Dunno yet. He aint found out. When he does—Baby!"

"Aint no tellin."

"Young Stone aint no quitter an I ken tell y that. Blood of th old uns in his veins."

"Thats right. He'll scrap, sho."

"Be gettin too hot f niggers round this away."

"Shut up, nigger. Y dont know what y talkin bout."

Bob Stone's ears burned as though he had been holding them over the stove. Sizzling heat welled up within him. His feet felt as if they rested on red-hot coals. They stung him to quick movement. He circled the fringe of the glowing. Not a twig cracked beneath his feet. He reached the path that led to factory town. Plunged furiously down it. Halfway along, a blindness within him veered him aside. He crashed into the bordering canebrake. Cane leaves cut his face and lips. He tasted blood. He threw himself down and dug his fingers in the ground. The earth was cool. Cane-roots took the fever from his hands. After a long while, or so it seemed to him, the thought came to him that it must be time to see Louisa. He got to his feet and walked calmly to their meeting place. No Louisa. Tom Burwell had her. Veins in his forehead bulged and distended. Saliva moistened the dried blood on his lips. He bit down on his lips. He tasted blood. Not his own blood; Tom Burwell's blood. Bob drove through the cane and out again upon the road. A hound swung down the path before him towards factory town. Bob couldnt see it. The dog loped aside to let him pass. Bob's blind rushing made him stumble over it. He fell with a thud that dazed him. The hound yelped. Answering yelps came from all over the countryside. Chickens cackled. Roosters crowed, heralding the blood-shot eyes of southern awakening. Singers in the town were silenced. They shut their windows down. Palpitant between the rooster crows, a chill hush settled upon the huddled forms of Tom and Louisa. A figure rushed from the shadow and stood before them. Tom popped to his feet,

"Whats y want?"

"I'm Bob Stone."

"Yassur—an I'm Tom Burwell. Whats y want?"

Bob lunged at him. Tom side-stepped, caught him by the shoulder, and flung him to the ground. Straddled him.

"Let me up."

"Yassur—but watch yo doins, Bob Stone."

A few dark figures, drawn by the sound of scuffle, stood about them. Bob sprang to his feet.

"Fight like a man, Tom Burwell, an I'll lick y."

Again he lunged. Tom side-stepped and flung him to the ground. Straddled him.

"Get off me, you godam nigger you."

"Yo sho has started somethin now. Get up."

Tom yanked him up and began hammering at him. Each blow sounded as if it smashed into a precious, irreplaceable soft something. Beneath them, Bob staggered back. He reached in his pocket and whipped out a knife.

"Thats my game, sho."

Blue flash, a steel blade slashed across Bob Stone's throat. He had a sweetish sick feeling. Blood began to flow. Then he felt a sharp twitch of pain. He let his knife drop. He slapped one hand against his neck. He pressed the other on top of his head as if to hold it down. He groaned. He turned, and staggered towards the crest of the hill in the direction of white town. Negroes who had seen the fight slunk into their homes and blew the lamps out. Louisa, dazed, hysterical, refused to go indoors. She slipped, crumbled, her body loosely propped against the woodwork of the well. Tom Burwell leaned against it. He seemed rooted there.

Bob reached Broad Street. White men rushed up to him. He collapsed in their arms.

"Tom Burwell . . . ."

White men like ants upon a forage rushed about. Except for the taut hum of their moving, all was silent. Shotguns, revolvers, rope, kerosene, torches. Two high-powered cars with glaring searchlights. They came together. The taut hum rose to a low roar. Then nothing could be heard but the flop of their feet in the thick dust of the road. The moving body of their silence preceded them over the crest of the hill into factory town. It flattened the Negroes beneath it. It rolled to the wall of the factory, where it stopped. Tom knew that they were coming. He couldnt move. And then he saw the search-lights of the two cars glaring down on him. A quick shock went through him. He stiffened. He started to run. A yell went up from the mob. Tom wheeled about and faced them. They poured down on him. They swarmed. A large man with dead-white face and flabby cheeks came to him and almost jabbed a gun-barrel through his guts.

"Hands behind y, nigger."

Tom's wrists were bound. The big man shoved him to the well. Burn him over it, and when the woodwork caved in, his body would drop to the bottom. Two deaths for a godam nigger. Louisa was driven back. The mob pushed in. Its pressure, its momentum was too great. Drag him to the factory. Wood and stakes already there. Tom moved in the direction indicated. But they had to drag him. They reached the great door. Too many to get in there. The mob divided and flowed around the walls to either side. The big man shoved him through the door. The mob pressed in from the sides. Taut humming. No words. A stake was sunk into the ground. Rotting floor boards piled around it. Kerosene poured on the rotting floor boards. Tom bound to the stake. His breast was bare. Nails' scratches let little lines of blood trickle down and mat into the hair. His face, his eyes were set and stony. Except for irregular breathing, one would have thought him already dead. Torches were flung onto the pile. A great flare muffled in black smoke shot upward. The mob yelled. The mob was silent. Now Tom could be seen within the flames. Only his head, erect, lean, like a blackened stone. Stench of burning flesh soaked the air. Tom's eyes popped. His head settled downward. The mob yelled. Its yell echoed against the skeleton stone walls and sounded like a hundred yells. Like a hundred mobs yelling. Its yell thudded against the thick front wall and fell back. Ghost of a yell slipped through the flames and out the great door of the factory. It fluttered like a dying thing down the single street of factory town. Louisa, upon the step before her home, did not hear it, but her eyes opened slowly. They saw the full moon glowing in the great door. The full moon, an evil thing, an omen, soft showering the homes of folks she knew. Where were they, these

people? She'd sing, and perhaps they'd come out and join her.
Perhaps Tom Burwell would come. At any rate, the full moon in the
great door was an omen which she must sing to:

> Red nigger moon. Sinner!
> Blood-burning moon. Sinner!
> Come out that fact'ry door.

Jean Toomer (1894–1967)

Toomer was born in Washington, D.C. Drawn to his father's home state of Georgia,
Toomer taught school for several months in Sparta, Georgia, an experience that led
to his writing of CANE (1923), a unified collection of stories, poems, and a play. Much
of his work was left unpublished at his death. "Blood-Burning Moon" is taken from
CANE.

Diah on Lost Island

Cecile Matschat

STILLNESS HUNG over the little clearing by the side of the lagoon. The only visible motion was silent—a buzzard soaring above the island. Diah shivered as the winged shadow swept across the water. "Hit be the quiet," he decided, tilting back his head to watch the bird's flight. The late afternoon light shone clearly on the vulture's naked, crimson head and spreading wings of dusky black.

The pond, not more than fifty feet across and about two hundred yards long, was merely an extension of the run, hardly wider than his boat, which Diah had followed from the marsh. Large pines, their branches fringed with blackish green needles, and a few gum and water oaks grew down to its banks. No lily pads floated on the dark water, and no reeds grew along the shore. Not a fish splashed, not a frog croaked. "Water must be plenty deep," Diah reflected as he filled his coffeepot. "Whole place hain't natural. Hain't no flowers, hain't no birds, hain't no snakeses, nuther." He climbed up the muddy bank and peered around uneasily. The silver moss grew longer and thicker here, he noted, than anywhere he had seen it except in the depths of cypress bays. The air seemed heavy, stagnant.

Although sundown was two hours away, he set about his preparations for the night. "Bein' so warm like, won't need a big fire," he thought, striking a light under some dry pine knobs to cook his bear steaks and coffee. He skewered long strips of the red flesh on a gum sapling and stuck the butt of the sapling in the ground at an angle, so that the meat would broil evenly from all sides. He had eaten nothing since morning, and was ravenously hungry.

Blockie pressed close against his legs and whined uneasily. He gave the puppy a reassuring pat, and then ordered him to lie down by his dignified father, Scavenger, the best bearhound in the country. "Guard, boy," he told the big dog. Scavenger obediently crouched close to the carcass of the bear, which was piled at the foot of a water oak. Diah glanced at the low-growing branches; it would be easy to hoist the meat up to them later, out of the way of preying animals. "Scavenger acts queer," he thought, for he noticed that the dog held his head up steadily, sniffing at the air and staring into the depth of the forest. He picked up his gun and broke it open, to make certain that it was loaded.

This island was strange to him, and as yet he had seen no familiar animal signs. It appeared barren of life, but he knew that the jungle was always deceptive, its dense bush and hanging moss affording shelter for many creatures whose presence no eye could detect. The thought came to him that this might even be the famous Lost Island, said to have been a Seminole hideaway in the wars and, afterwards, a sanctuary for moonshiners and criminals. Long ago, a Scotch trapper had discovered the old Indian trail to the island; but he was too canny to lead others to his new fur grounds. No one had ever been able to find the hidden run again. Diah was excited by the idea. He had followed a bear wallow from early morning until midafternoon; then he came up with the animal, a two-year-old male, in a brier thicket and shot it. But he had strayed far on the long chase and was in an unknown part of the swamp. So he poled out of the marsh and glided down the first open run he came to, a long slender thread of current between massed green walls, which had brought him into this deep, narrow lagoon. Tomorrow he would explore the island thoroughly.

During supper he could hear the dogs moving restlessly behind him, but they were too well trained to leave their posts without permission. After eating, he cut chunks of underdone meat for Scavenger and smaller pieces for Blockie, but neither dog ate, although, like himself, they had been long without food. The puppy crouched close beside his master, whimpering in fear, but Scavenger stood stiffly upright, a growl rumbling deep in his throat. "Likely they smells a live b'ar too, some'eres nigh," Diah thought, and tried to quiet them.

The light dimmed gradually as the sun sank toward the west. A queer green mist seeped through the clearing. Selecting a comfortable spot beneath the oak, he placed his gun close at hand and sat down to rest. There would be at least another hour of daylight, and plenty of time to hang up the meat. Suddenly Blockie threw back his head and howled, a long-drawn-out cry of distress. Diah spoke to him sharply; but as he turned he caught a glimpse of a gray body, which faded like a wraith into the smoky background of drooping moss. Scavenger had seen it, too; the thick fur stood up in a line along his back, and he snarled defiance.

And then, before Diah could raise his gun, they were all around him. In his terror, it seemed as though the place swarmed with the ferocious piney woods rooters. Their small cloven hoofs pattered on the dead leaves of the oaks as they came nearer—and, slowly, nearer—held in check by the sight of the savage hound. Instinctively, Diah muttered, "Down, boy," and Blockie crouched motionless behind a protruding root of the tree, frozen with fear.

For a few seconds Diah was unable to realize that death stared at him from dozens of small, wicked eyes. "Hit's the b'ar meat," he thought mechanically, as the leader of the pack, an old gray boar, moved a pace or two toward him. The beast lowered its massive head so that, even in the dimmer light beneath the trees, he could see plainly the long, raised bristles that covered its powerful high shoulders and sloping, narrow hams. Scavenger quivered in every limb, and a rasping snarl poured steadily from his throat. The boar answered now with hoarse grunts. Its tusks, four keen-edged sickles of gleaming ivory, clicked in challenge until bloody foam dripped from its jaws.

The whole herd pattered closer now, spreading in a wide half circle. Diah felt a dank moisture break out all over him: he was trapped. At his first move the leader of the pack would charge. Its curving tusks would rip open his body as easily as they slit the belly of a deer. The boar took the few mincing steps forward, which always precede the charge. With a wild yell Diah jumped to his feet, just as the vicious beast launched at him. Swift as the boar was, Scavenger was swifter. He flung himself between his master and the rooter, his teeth reaching for the throat-hold which would give him the advantage.

While Scavenger wrestled with the boar, rolling over and over on the ground in a death grapple, Diah swung himself quickly into the low branches of the oak. His breath came in gasps and the gun, which he raised to his shoulder, wavered in his hands. Under his bough a dozen big sows rushed together. Gaunt with hunger, they tore savagely at the bear meat, paying no attention to the fight between the hound and their leader. They were not yet aware of Blockie. The puppy was hidden from their sight by the big root; and they did not scent him because their sense of smell, which is never so keen as that of deer or most other wild animals, was glutted with bear's blood. But the yearling shotes squealed and pranced about the fighters, waiting their chance to be in at the kill.

Diah lowered his gun in despair. He knew he could do no good by shooting. Besides, he had only two extra shells in his pocket; the others were in the boat. There were fully two dozen rooters in the pack, and a shot would only draw their attention to him. Perhaps if he kept very quiet they would forget about him, finish their meal, and go away. He knew hunters who had been treed by rooters for hours. They had been rescued eventually, but no one would come to help him, for no one knew where he was.

All this flashed through his mind in an instant. Scavenger was weakening, his struggles growing less and less. Diah saw a young shote tear one of the hound's long ears from its head. With a hoarse, guttural howl of pain the dog wrenched himself loose from his tormentors and stood, swaying on his feet, his eyes blinded by blood. His neck and shoulders were slashed and bleeding, his remaining ear was cut to ribbons, and blood and froth dripped from his mouth. In the second before they could launch themselves upon him again, he raised his head and looked straight toward the master he could no longer see. Diah's breath tore through him with something like a sob. He threw the gun to his shoulder, sighted, and pulled the trigger. Scavenger dropped, twitched, and was still. The boars sprang upon him, squealing, and the hound disappeared from sight beneath the stamping pack. Diah knew that the rooters would look around soon for more meat to devour. They would find Blockie, unless he took the desperate chance that might save him.

He wedged his gun among the branches, moved cautiously, without shaking the boughs, to a low limb directly above the terrified dog, and dropped noiselessly to the ground behind the tree. Then he caught the puppy up in his hands and threw him, with all his strength, into a wide crotch high above his head. And Blockie, who could always git a idee, clawed frantically for a foothold, and clung trembling to his perch. But, in putting forth all his effort to hoist Blockie to safety, Diah's foot slipped on some rotted leaves and he went down on one knee. The old boar saw him and charged.

Diah flung himself to one side and the boar rushed past. It turned quickly and darted back, its slavering mouth emitting high-pitched squeals of rage; but the instant's delay had given the boy time to pull himself up to the lowest limb. He was safe for a little while; he lay there panting, feeling sick and weak. Blockie whined in the crotch above him. Diah climbed carefully and settled himself against the trunk with the quivering dog draped across his knees. The old boar lunged about in rage at the foot of the tree, but Diah resisted the temptation to use one of the two remaining shells on him.

The clouds above the lagoon had turned to violet; he watched while they faded to mauve, then gray, and darkness began to shut down on the lonely island. The old boars' grunts and squeals must carry a long way, he thought. The females fed more quietly, with less fighting among themselves. He leaned back wearily against the trunk and closed his eyes. "Starved," he muttered; "that be why no varmints." The marsh near by was filled with gator holes. The rooters must have been penned on the island so long that they had killed or driven off all the small game; even the young pines had been eaten clean away. He knew that piney woods rooters would not willingly cross water so infested with alligators, whose favorite food is pig meat.

Sometime later he opened his eyes; the dark had lightened, and a full moon looked down from the top of a longleaf pine. Diah saw now that a large black log lay near the edge of the water on the opposite bank. The trained swamper thought it was strange—and keerless—that he should not have noticed it before, when he made camp in the last afternoon light. Blockie stiffened suddenly and growled, and Diah forgot the log as he pulled the dog closer, quieted him, and searched the dark with sharp eyes. Before him the forest loomed pitch black. Suddenly, at the edge of the clearing, two reddish lights, spaced far apart, gleamed for an instant, and disappeared. Then two more, of a greenish tint, shone in the shadows, and others came and went, seemingly rising and falling in the dark, until the clearing was ringed with a circle of twin lights—two, four, six, seven pairs, he counted—with the odd red ones spaced farther apart than the others. He heard no sound, although his ears were keen. The short hairs on the back of his neck stood up in fear. "Be hants," he whispered.

The old gray boar had pulled part of the bear's carcass close to the edge of the clearing and was crunching and gnawing at the bones, too busy to notice that the largest of the paired lights had stopped close behind him. Watching, in chill awe of the supernatural visitation, Diah presently discerned the outline of a large black shape with ridged back and long, tapering, plated tail moving into the moonlight. "A gator!" he breathed in excitement and relief, "they hain't hants! They be gators! Lotsa gators! 'Spect they be crossin' the island from hole to hole in the marsh, an' heerd the squealin'." He climbed higher in the tree, with Blockie clutched firmly beneath one arm, the better to watch the battle he knew was to come. "Hope they kill all ye-uns," he ground out vindictively to the rooters. Were the alligators bringing salvation to him and Blockie? Or only another death? He would know soon. He knew already that he would not be treed by the famished swine for days, until he dropped from weakness! At least, he could see a very slim chance for his life now. The moonlight was as bright as day.

Diah was familiar with the methods of alligators hunting on land, but he had never witnessed a hunt like this—with himself, also, as quarry. However awkward their gait, they can travel quickly, he knew. "Een winter couldn't freeze me no colder," he muttered, and gripped the bough tighter. His teeth chattered and he clenched his jaws as the stalk in the moonlight began and the malevolent reddish eyes came nearer, then a little nearer, to the unsuspecting boar. Stealthily, and it seemed to him without making a sound in the grass, the bull gator moved forward on its four bowed legs. Once or twice, during that inexorable advance, the boar raised his head—perhaps the noise of the amphibian's breathing had reached him during the grunting orgy about him—and the gator sank instantly to the floor of the clearing, and the long black body became one with the shadows. The starved boar fed once more, and the gator crept on. The distance lessened rapidly between them. It seemed incredible how swiftly the alligator moved on those stunted legs: twenty feet, eighteen, fourteen, ten, eight. Its head swung up, its mouth opening; the moonlight glinted on a livid throat and on yellow snaglike teeth for a second before they boomed shut upon the old boar. With a squeal of pain and terror the boar flung his two hundred pounds to one side, but the resistless jaws ground together, shearing him apart like paper.

The rooters heard their leader's death cry and scattered, racing for the shelter of the woods; but the gators hemmed them in. "Sartin hit's a battle sich-like no man has seed afore," Diah whispered. The squeals of the rooters mingled with the arrogant booming bellow of the bull gator. The female saurians stalked and fought silently, except for the sound of their breathing—like brief gusts of wind, low keyed. One young boar, caught by a hind foot, twisted beneath his captor and drove his sharp tusks through her throat in a ripping thrust, then swung around and gashed her side with his tusks, only to be knocked across the clearing by a smashing blow from her tail. Again and again the bull gator bellowed his hoarse challenge.

Blockie was frantic with terror. Diah held him tight in his arms, feeling his heart pounding so that it shook the small body. He took off his coat and wrapped the puppy in it; after a while the warmth and his soothing mutter had their effect, only an occasional long shudder showing the fear Blockie still felt.

From his high perch Diah watched the few pigs that could still move make off into the forest. That danger, at least, was past. He leaned over and looked down upon the alligators beneath him. The wounded female was dragging herself weakly toward the water; the blood that dripped from her throat left a dark trail behind her. She breathed laboriously as she struggled on. Diah had decided that she would reach the comparative safety of the lagoon, after all, when he noticed that two females and the bull had left their meal and were stalking her in their typical stiff-legged manner. She lashed at them with her tail and tried to threaten them with her jaws, but they gripped her and tore her apart.

Diah heard a loud, long-drawn hiss. He knew that it did not come from the alligators, now feeding on the dismembered female. He lifted his head and looked carefully about him. The moonlight shown full upon the lagoon, which was still and placid. But on the farther bank a long, low shadow stirred. The big log was moving, blending so perfectly with the dark shore that it seemed as though a part of the ground itself had risen on stout, bowed legs and was sliding silently into the silver water, with scarcely a ripple. Only an inky patch was visible on the pool.

It floated slowly toward the island. Three knobs showed above the surface, and then, as it came closer, Diah could see the whole of a big ungainly head. The two knobs at the back of the head were eyes, he knew, and the third was the rounded snout; but aside from knowing that the alligator must be very old and massive, because of the wide space between the eyes, he was unable to guess its length. The flat tail moved smoothly through the water, without ripples. Then the monster heaved itself ponderously upon the bank; water dripped from its gleaming armored back and formed little pools around it.

Diah's eyes bulged in amazement and he clung desperately to the limb. "Must be nigh sixteen foot!" he chattered. Its enormous mouth, pink-lined and filled with yellow snags, yawned wide and emitted a roar that seemed to make the whole island tremble. At the sound the smaller bull whirled, his ridged back arched like a bow. With a snap he shut his mouth to a crooked slit and hurled himself straight toward the invader.

The two heavy bodies struck the ground with smashing force. Diah, clinging to his refuge, felt the stem shake and saw the moon-silvered tips of the forest wave like feathers. A moment afterwards a blow sent the smaller gator crashing against his oak shelter. Insane with rage, the reptile struck blow after blow against the trunk, making the oak quiver and sway, while Diah clutched desperately at the limb and the little dog. If the great saurian joined the other in his attack on the tree, the trunk must surely crack, he thought. Directly below him he could see the savage eyes of the younger bull, gleaming with rage. The fiery red, he knew, was always the color of the bulls' eyes in the mating season, when their temper is more ferocious than at any other time.

Then the giant gator used his plated tail like a scythe. The young bull, unable to stand the force of the cutting strokes, tried to back away, but his enemy waddled forward on bowed legs and grabbed him by one foot. Superior weight told, and slowly the bull dragged his twelve-foot rival to the water's edge, his red eyes gleaming malevolently. The smaller reptile dug into the mud of the bank and bellowed, but still the slow, relentless dragging continued, until with a thunderous splash, which drove the spray high into the air, they fell together into the lagoon.

The female gators had drawn back under the oak, and were calmly finishing their meal, indifferent to the fate of their former lord. In his excitement, Diah forgot his fear, and leaned as far from the tree as he could to see the finish of the battle. He yelled and howled in glee as first one ridged body, then another, broke the surface of the water. "Big ole un's nigh about fifty years," he thought, recalling what the natural-ist to whom he had acted as guide had told him. Fifty-six years was the longest time an alligator had been known to live in captivity, he remembered; but the man had said that they might easily live twice as long in a state of nature—nobody really knew. Diah understood, from his own observations, why the big gator had dragged the other to the pool. It was because his cave was beneath the water, and here he would take his prey to soften until he chose to eat it.

Suddenly, out of the churning, spraying water, the smaller head appeared and came up over the rim of the island. The young gator had managed to break away and reach the shore, being quicker in turning than his foe. He was already partly out of the pool, when the other seized him by a foot, tearing the leg nearly from its socket with the fury of his rush.

The old gator pulled the younger bull back under the water and the battle began again. The monster's long tail appeared high above the surface in an arch, rose higher and higher, then sank, and the enormous, yawning jaws appeared and flashed downward again, a second later, with a hollow booming clang as they closed on the other's throat. Diah could see the large piece of whitish, scaly flesh that was ripped from the smaller bull, and the blood pouring from his throat into the swirl of water. The air was heavy with the scent of musk as the torn scent glands gushed out jets of vapor; the smell made Diah feel sick and faint. Once, twice, again the big gator rolled the dying bull over. The victim's flailing tail smote the water in wild, aimless blows; its head rolled back and forth in agony, while from its open jaws came a long, moaning hiss. The huge alligator triumphed and pulled the smaller bull down beneath the surface.

Diah watched the lagoon closely, to see if the fighters would reappear; but the ripples widened and lapped the shore with a gentle sound. It seemed to him that only a few minutes passed before the moon gleamed on still water, and there was silence.

The female gators had remained beneath the oak, eating steadily during the battle. Now they lay at ease in the moonlight near the edge of the pool. Bones and chunks of flesh littered the clearing, but they had had their fill. Presently two black knobs showed above the surface at the far side of the lagoon, and a coughing, snoring bellow of command came to their ears. They rose and slid, almost without a ripple, into the water to join their new master.

Black clouds floated up and hid the moon from view. Diah could hear wind across the marsh beyond the island, like surf beating on the ocean shore, or the roll of a primitive water drum; but here in the pines the air was still. His father had told him that the reverberating boom of the wind through the grass was due to the fact that only a thin layer of quaking earth overlay the water beneath. He had listened to it often, as now, from among still branches. But tonight the sound in the grasses, which stretched from the base of the silent woods, seemed unnatural and fearsome, as if an army of hants were drumming underground.

Soon it was dark. The exaltation he had felt in watching the battle faded, and terror came back upon him. The thick enveloping blackness seemed to be hiding something from him, and he could have screamed aloud in fright.

Then from below he heard the soft pad, pad of heavy feet. Around and around they went, until he felt the blood pound in his ears in rhythm with their march. Pad, pad, and then a soft, coughing snuffle, and he knew that a painter was feeding on the gators' leavings. Pad, pad—and the crunch of breaking bones. If he could only see! But in the pitch darkness, he might waste both his shells. It still seemed to him that his one chance of ever reaching his boat again was to keep still. Then the sound ceased; but there came another, which chilled his hair roots—the scratch of claws against the bark of the tree. If he made a move for his gun now the creature would be on him with one bound. He pressed his hand over the muzzle of the little dog snuggled beneath his coat, to prevent its whining. "Lord, could I pray!" Diah thought, but to his fear-stricken mind came only a prayer he had learned years ago from his grandmother. He had remembered it because it was a rhyme:

Now I lay me down to sleep,
I pray the Lord my soul to keep.

The scratching sound was louder. Was the panther climbing, or only stretching itself?

If I should die afore I wake,
I pray the Lord my soul to take.

Over and over he said the little verse. The scratching ceased. Once he heard the big cat yawn loudly, and a grating, fuzzy sound as its rough tongue licked the coarse hairs of its paws clean. And then it scratched on the bark again. But the animal was not choosing his oak for a lookout tonight. The padding of feet on the leaves presently told him that the painter was going off into the forest. He waited perhaps an hour before he moved from his cramped position.

The island and the lagoon were black, and there was no sound. He slid stiffly from the tree, put the dog down, and pulled on his coat. The air was fetid, sickening! His feet slid on bloody muck and crushed bones.

"In, boy!" Blockie jumped into the boat and Diah followed him. He took up the pole with stiff, awkward fingers and pushed out onto the pond.

He did not know where he was, and he could see nothing; the nearest thing to light in the scene was the polished black surface of the water. But it was the law of the swamp that its waters moved. The boat would drift into the run he had come in by, or another; and with daylight he could find his bearings.

"Iffen yon be Lost Island, Blockie," he said to the dog, which was nosing his arm and whimpering softly with relief, "'t is a fitten name for hit. We-uns don' hanker to see hit agin. Nuvver!"

Cecile Hulse Matschat (1895-1976)

Matschat was born in New York. She was a botanist and author who wrote several novels and documentary studies, including HIGHWAY TO HEAVEN (1942), LAND OF THE BIG SWAMP (1954), and TAVERN IN THE TOWN (1942). She lived for several months in the Okefenokee Swamp, where the first half of her finest book, SUWANNEE RIVER: *Strange Green Land*, is set. SUWANNEE RIVER was first published in 1938 in the Rivers of America series. "Diah on Lost Island" is taken from SUWANNEE RIVER.

Candy-Man Beechum

Erskine Caldwell

IT WAS TEN MILES out of the Ogeechee swamps, from the sawmill to the top of the ridge, but it was just one big step to Candy-Man. The way he stepped over those Middle Georgia gullies was a sight to see.

"Where you goin', Candy-Man?"

"Make way for these flapping feet, boy, because I'm going for to see my gal. She's standing on the tips of her toes waiting for me now."

The rabbits lit out for the hollow logs where those stomping big feet couldn't get nowhere near them.

"Don't tread on no white-folks' toes, Candy-Man," Little Bo said, "Because the white-folks is first-come."

Candy-Man Beechum flung a leg over the rail fence just as if it had been a hoe handle to straddle. He stood for a minute astride the fence, looking at the black boy. It was dark in the swamps, and he had ten miles to go.

"Me and white-folks don't mix," Candy-Man told him, "just as long as they leave me be. I skin their mules for them, and I snake their cypress logs, but when the day is done, I'm long gone where the white-folks ain't are."

Owls in the trees began to take on life. Those whooing birds were glad to see that setting sun.

The black boy in the mule yard scratched his head and watched the sun go down. If he didn't have all those mules to feed, and if he had had a two-bit piece in his pocket, he'd have liked to tag along with Candy-Man. It was Saturday night, and there'd be a barrelful of catfish frying in town that evening. He wished he had some of that good-smelling cat.

"Before the time ain't long," Little Bo said, "I'm going to get me myself a gal."

"Just be sure she ain't Candy-Man's, boy, and I'll give you a helping hand."

He flung the other leg over the split-rail fence and struck out for the high land. Ten miles from the swamps to the top of the ridge, and his trip would be done. The bushes whipped around his legs, where his legs had been. He couldn't be waiting for the back-strike of no swamp-country bushes. Up the log road, and across the bottom land, taking three corn rows at a stride, Candy-Man Beechum was on his way.

There were some colored boys taking their time in the big road. He was up on them before they had time to turn their heads around.

"Make way for these flapping feet, boys," he shouted. "Here I come!"

"Where you going, Candy-Man?"

They had to do a lot of running to keep up with him. They had to hustle to match those legs four feet long. He made their breath come short.

"Somebody asked me where I'm going," Candy-Man said. "I got me a yellow gal, and I'm on my way to pay her some attention."

"You'd better toot your horn, Candy-Man, before you open her door. Yellow gals don't like to be taken by surprise."

"Boy, you're tooting the truth, except that you don't know the whyfor of what you're saying. Candy-Man's gal always waits for him right at the door."

"Saturday-night bucks sure have to hustle along. They have to strike pay before the Monday-morning whistle starts whipping their ears."

The boys fell behind, stopping to blow and wheeze. There was no keeping up, on a Saturday night, with the seven-foot mule skinner on his way.

The big road was too crooked and curvy for Candy-Man. He struck out across the fields, headed like a plumb line for a dishful of frying catfish. The lights of the town came up to meet him in the face like a swarm of lightning bugs. Eight miles to town, and two more to go, and he'd be rapping on that yellow gal's door.

Back in the big road, when the big road straightened out, Candy-Man swung into town. The old folks riding, and the young ones walking, they all made way for those flapping feet. The mules to the buggies and the sports in the middle of the road all got aside to let him through.

"What's you big hurry, Candy-Man?"

"Take care my dust don't choke you blind, niggers. I'm on my way."

"Where to, Candy-Man?"

"I got a gal what's waiting right at her door. She don't like for to be kept waiting."

"Better slow down and cool those heels, Candy-Man, because you're coming to the white-folks' town. They don't like niggers stepping on their toes."

"When the sun goes down, I'm on my own. I can't be stopping to see what color people be."

The old folks clucked, and the mules began to trot. They didn't like the way that big coon talked.

"How about taking me along, Candy-Man?" the young bucks begged. "I'd like to grab me a chicken off a hen-house roost."

"Where I'm going I'm the cock of the walk. I gouge my spurs in all strange feathers. Stay away, black boy, stay away."

Down the street he went, sticking to the middle of the road. The sidewalks couldn't hold him when he was in a hurry like that. A plateful of frying catfish, and he would be on his way. That yellow gal was waiting, and there was no time to lose. Eight miles covered, and two short ones to go. That sawmill fireman would have to pull on that Monday-morning whistle like it was the rope to the promised land.

The smell of the fish took him straight to the fish-house door. Maybe they were mullets, but they smelled just as good. There wasn't enough time to order up a special dish of fins.

He had his hand on the restaurant door. When he had his supper, he would be on his way. He could see that yellow gal waiting for him only a couple of miles away.

All those boys were sitting at their meal. The room was full of hungry people just like him. The stove was full of frying fish, and the barrel was only halfway used. There was enough good eating for a hundred hungry men.

He still had his hand on the fish-house door, and his nose was soaking it in. If he could have his way about it, some of these days he was going to buy himself a whole big barrel of catfish and eat them every one.

"What's your hurry, Candy-Man?"

"No time to waste, white-boss. Just let me be."

The night policeman snapped open the handcuffs, and reached for his arms. Candy-Man stepped away.

"I reckon I'd better lock you up. It'll save a lot of trouble. I'm getting good and tired of chasing fighting niggers all over town every Saturday night."

"I never hurt a body in all my life, white-boss. And I sure don't pick fights. You must have the wrong nigger, white-boss. You sure has got me wrong. I'm just passing through for to see my gal."

"I reckon I'll play safe and lock you up till Monday morning just the same. Reach out your hands for these cuffs, nigger."

Candy-Man stepped away. His yellow gal was on his mind. He didn't feel like passing her up for no iron-bar jail. He stepped away.

"I'll shoot you down, nigger. One more step, and I'll blast away."

"White-boss, please just let me be. I won't even stop to get my supper, and I'll shake my legs right out of town. Because I just got to see my gal before the Monday-morning sun comes up."

Candy-Man stepped away. The night policeman threw down the handcuffs and jerked out his gun. He pulled the trigger at Candy-Man, and Candy-Man fell down.

"There wasn't no cause for that, white-boss. I'm just a big black nigger with itching feet. I'd a heap rather be traveling than standing still."

The people came running, but some of them turned around and went the other way. Some stood and looked at Candy-Man while he felt his legs to see if they could hold him up. He still had two miles to go before he could reach the top of the ridge.

The people crowded around, and the night policeman put away his gun. Candy-Man tried to get up so he could be getting on down the road. That yellow gal of his was waiting for him at her door, straining on the tips of her toes.

"White-boss, I sure am sorry you had to go and shoot me down. I never bothered white-folks, and they sure oughtn't bother me. But there ain't much use in living if that's the way it's going to be. I reckon I'll just have to blow out the light and fade away. Just reach me a blanket so I can cover my skin and bones."

"Shut up, nigger," the white-boss said. "If you keep on talking with that big mouth of yours, I'll just have to pull out my gun again and hurry you on."

The people drew back to where they wouldn't be standing too close. The night policeman put his hand on the butt of his gun, where it would be handy, in case.

"If that's the way it's to be, then make way for Candy-Man Beechum, because here I come."

Erskine Caldwell (1903-1987)

Caldwell was born in Coweta County, Georgia. Among his many novels and collections of short stories, the following stand out: AMERICAN EARTH (1931), TOBACCO ROAD (1932), WE ARE THE LIVING (1933), GOD'S LITTLE ACRE (1933), KNEEL TO THE RISING SUN (1935), JOURNEYMAN (1935), SOUTHWAYS (1938), TROUBLE IN JULY (1940), GEORGIA BOY (1944), and TRAGIC GROUND (1944). "Candy-Man Beechum" was first published in ESQUIRE in 1935.

The Ballad of the Sad Café

Carson McCullers

THE TOWN ITSELF is dreary; not much is there except the cotton mill, the two-room houses where the workers live, a few peach trees, a church with two colored windows, and a miserable main street only a hundred yards long. On Saturdays the tenants from the near-by farms come in for a day of talk and trade. Otherwise the town is lonesome, sad, and like a place that is far off and estranged from all other places in the world. The nearest train stop is Society City, and the Greyhound and White Bus Lines use the Forks Fall Road which is three miles away. The winters here are short and raw, the summer white with glare and fiery hot.

If you walk along the main street on an August afternoon there is nothing whatsoever to do. The largest building, in the very center of the town, is boarded up completely and leans so far to the right that it seems bound to collapse at any minute. The house is very old. There is about it a curious, cracked look that is very puzzling until you suddenly realize that at one time, and long ago, the right side of the front porch had been painted, and part of the wall—but the painting was left unfinished and one portion of the house is darker and dingier than the other. The building looks completely deserted. Nevertheless, on the second floor there is one window which is not boarded; sometimes in the late afternoon when the heat is at its worst a hand will slowly open the shutter and a face will look down on the town. It is a face like the terrible dim faces known in dreams—sexless and white, with two gray crossed eyes which are turned inward so sharply that they seem to be exchanging with each other one long and secret gaze of grief. The shutters are closed once more, and as likely as not there will not be another soul to be seen along the main street. These August afternoons—when your shift is finished there is absolutely nothing to do; you might as well walk down to the Forks Falls Road and listen to the chain gang.

However, here in this very town there was once a café. And this old boarded-up house was unlike any other place for many miles around. There were tables with cloths and paper napkins, colored streamers from the electric fans, great gatherings on Saturday nights. The owner of the place was Miss Amelia Evans. But the person most responsible for the success and gaiety of the place was a hunchback called Cousin Lymon. One other person had a part in the story of this café—he was the former husband of Miss Amelia, a terrible character who returned to the town after a long term in the penitentiary, caused ruin, and then went on his way again. The café has long since been closed, but it is still remembered.

The place was not always a café. Miss Amelia inherited the building from her father, and it was a store that carried mostly feed, guano, and staples such as meal and snuff. Miss Amelia was rich. In addition to the store she operated a still three miles back in the swamp, and ran out the best liquor in the county. She was a dark, tall woman with bones and muscles like a man. Her hair was cut short and brushed back from the forehead, and there was about her sunburned face a tense, haggard quality. She might have been a handsome woman if, even then, she was not slightly cross-eyed. There were those who would have courted her, but Miss Amelia cared nothing for the love of men and was a solitary person. Her marriage had been unlike any other marriage ever contracted in this county—it was a strange and dangerous marriage, lasting only for ten days, that left the whole town wondering and shocked. Except for this queer marriage, Miss Amelia had lived her life alone. Often she spent whole nights back in her shed in the swamp, dressed in overalls and gum boots, silently guarding the low fire of the still.

With all things which could be made by the hands Miss Amelia prospered. She sold chitterlins and sausage in the town near-by. On fine autumn days, she ground sorghum, and the syrup from her vats was dark golden and delicately flavored. She built the brick privy behind her store in only two weeks and was skilled in carpentering. It was only with people that Miss Amelia was not at ease. People, unless they are nilly-willy or very sick, cannot be taken into the hands and changed overnight to something more worthwhile and profitable. So that the only use that Miss Amelia had for other people was to make money out of them. And in this she succeeded. Mortgages on crops and property, a sawmill, money in the bank—she was the richest woman for miles around. She would have been rich as a congressman if it were not for her one great failing, and that was her passion for lawsuits and the courts. She would involve herself in long and bitter litigation over just a trifle. It was said that if Miss Amelia so much as stumbled over a rock in the road she would glance around instinctively as though looking for something to sue about it. Aside from these lawsuits she lived a steady life and every day was very much like the day that had gone before. With the exception of her ten-day marriage, nothing happened to change this until the spring of the year that Miss Amelia was thirty years old.

It was toward midnight on a soft quiet evening in April. The sky was the color of a blue swamp iris, the moon clear and bright. The crops that spring promised well and in the past weeks the mill had run a night shift. Down by the creek the square brick factory was yellow with light, and there was the faint, steady hum of the looms. It was such a night when it is good to hear from faraway, across the dark fields, the slow song of a Negro on his way to make love. Or when it is pleasant to sit quietly and pick a guitar; or simply to rest alone and think of nothing at all. The street that evening was deserted, but Miss Amelia's store was lighted and on the porch outside there were five people. One of these was Stumpy MacPhail, a foreman with a red face and dainty, purplish hands. On the top step were two boys in overalls, the Rainey twins—both of them lanky and slow, with white hair and sleepy green eyes. The other man was Henry Macy, a shy and timid person with gentle manners and nervous ways, who sat on the edge of the bottom step. Miss Amelia herself stood leaning against the side of the open door, her feet crossed in their big swamp boots, patiently untying knots in a rope she had come across. They had not talked for a long time.

One of the twins, who had been looking down the empty road, was the first to speak. "I see something coming," he said.

"A calf got loose," said his brother.

The approaching figure was still too distant to be clearly seen. The moon made dim, twisted shadows of the blossoming peach trees along the side of the road. In the air the odor of blossoms and sweet spring grass mingled with the warm, sour smell of the near-by lagoon.

"No. It's somebody's youngun," said Stumpy MacPhail.

Miss Amelia watched the road in silence. She had put down her rope and was fingering the straps of her overalls with her brown bony hand. She scowled, and a dark lock of hair fell down on her forehead. While they were waiting there, a dog from one of the houses down the road began a wild, hoarse howl that continued until a voice called out and hushed him. It was not until the figure was quite close, within the range of the yellow light from the porch, that they saw clearly what had come.

The man was a stranger, and it is rare that a stranger enters the town on foot at that hour. Besides, the man was a hunchback. He was scarcely more than four feet tall and he wore a ragged, dusty coat that reached only to his knees. His crooked little legs seemed too thin to carry the weight of his great warped chest and the hump that sat on his shoulders. He had a very large head, with deep-set blue eyes and a sharp little mouth. His face was both soft and sassy—at the moment his pale skin was yellowed by dust and there were lavender shadows beneath his eyes. He carried a lopsided old suitcase which was tied with a rope.

"Evening," said the hunchback, and he was out of breath.

Miss Amelia and the men on the porch neither answered his greeting nor spoke. They only looked at him.

"I am hunting for Miss Amelia Evans."

Miss Amelia pushed back her hair from her forehead and raised her chin. "How come?"

"Because I am kin to her," the hunchback said.

The twins and Stumpy MacPhail looked up at Miss Amelia.

"That's me," she said. "How do you mean 'kin'?"

"Because—" the hunchback began. He looked uneasy, almost as though he was about to cry. He rested the suitcase on the bottom step, but did not take his hand from the handle. "My mother was Fanny Jesup and she come from Cheehaw. She left Cheehaw some thirty years ago when she married her first husband. I remember hearing her tell how she had a half-sister named Martha. And back in Cheehaw today they tell me that was your mother."

Miss Amelia listened with her head turned slightly aside. She ate her Sunday dinners by herself; her place was never crowded with a flock of relatives, and she claimed kin with no one. She had had a great-aunt who owned the livery stable in Cheehaw, but that aunt was now dead. Aside from her there was only one double first cousin who lived in a town twenty miles away, but this cousin and Miss Amelia did not get on so well, and when they chanced to pass each other they spat on the side of the road. Other people had tried very hard, from time to time, to work out some kind of far-fetched connection with Miss Amelia, but with absolutely no success.

The hunchback went into a long rigmarole, mentioning names and places that were unknown to the listeners on the porch and seemed to have nothing to do with the subject. "So Fanny and Martha Jesup were half-sisters. And I am the son of Fanny's third husband. So that would make you and I—" He bent down and began to unfasten his suitcase. His hands were like dirty sparrow claws and they were trembling. The bag was full of all manner of junk—ragged clothes and odd rubbish that looked like parts out of a sewing machine, or something just as worthless. The hunchback scrambled among these belongings and brought out an old photograph. "This is a picture of my mother and her half-sister."

Miss Amelia did not speak. She was moving her jaw slowly from side to side, and you could tell from her face what she was thinking about. Stumpy MacPhail took the photograph and held it out toward the light. It was a picture of two pale, withered-up little children of about two and three years of age. The faces were tiny white blurs, and it might have been an old picture in anyone's album.

Stumpy MacPhail handed it back with no comment. "Where you come from?" he asked.

The hunchback's voice was uncertain. "I was traveling."

Still Miss Amelia did not speak. She just stood leaning against the side of the door, and looked down at the hunchback. Henry Macy winked nervously and rubbed his hands together. Then quietly he left the bottom step and disappeared. He is a good soul, and the hunchback's situation had touched his heart. Therefore he did not want to wait and watch Miss Amelia chase this newcomer off her property and run him out of town. The hunchback stood with his bag open on the bottom step; he sniffled his nose, and his mouth quivered. Perhaps he began to feel his dismal predicament. Maybe he realized what a miserable thing it was to be a stranger in the town with a suitcase full of junk, and claiming kin with Miss Amelia. At any rate he sat down on the steps and suddenly began to cry.

It was not a common thing to have an unknown hunchback walk to the store at midnight and then sit down and cry. Miss Amelia rubbed back her hair from her forehead and the men looked at each other uncomfortably. All around the town was very quiet.

At last one of the twins said: "I'll be damned if he ain't a regular Morris Finestein."

Everyone nodded and agreed, for that is an expression having a certain special meaning. But the hunchback cried louder because he could not know what they were talking about. Morris Finestein was a person who had lived in the town years before. He was only a quick, skipping little Jew who cried if you called him Christ-killer, and ate light bread and canned salmon every day. A calamity had come over him and he had moved away to Society City. But since then if a man were prissy in any way, or if a man ever wept, he was known as a Morris Finestein.

"Well, he is afflicted," said Stumpy MacPhail. "There is some cause."

Miss Amelia crossed the porch with two slow, gangling strides. She went down the steps and stood looking thoughtfully at the stranger. Gingerly, with one long brown forefinger, she touched the hump on his back. The hunchback still wept, but he was quieter now. The night was silent and the moon still shone with a soft, clear light— it was getting colder. Then Miss Amelia did a rare thing; she pulled out

163

a bottle from her hip pocket and after polishing off the top with the palm of her hand she handed it to the hunchback to drink. Miss Amelia could seldom be persuaded to sell her liquor on credit, and for her to give so much as a drop away free was almost unknown.

"Drink," she said. "It will liven your gizzard."

The hunchback stopped crying, neatly licked the tears from around his mouth, and did as he was told. When he was finished, Miss Amelia took a slow swallow, warmed and washed her mouth with it, and spat. Then she also drank. The twins and the foreman had their own bottle they had paid for.

"It is smooth liquor," Stumpy MacPhail said. "Miss Amelia, I have never known you to fail."

The whisky they drank that evening (two big bottles of it) is important. Otherwise, it would be hard to account for what followed. Perhaps without it there would never have been a café. For the liquor of Miss Amelia has a special quality of its own. It is clean and sharp on the tongue, but once down a man it glows inside him for a long time afterward. And that is not all. It is known that if a message is written with lemon juice on a clean sheet of paper there will be no sign of it. But if the paper is held for a moment to the fire then the letters turn brown and the meaning becomes clear. Imagine that the whisky is the fire and that the message is that which is known only in the soul of a man—then the worth of Miss Amelia's liquor can be understood. Things that have gone unnoticed, thoughts that have been harbored far back in the dark mind, are suddenly recognized and comprehended. A spinner who has thought only of the loom, the dinner pail, the bed, and then the loom again—this spinner might drink some on a Sunday and come across a marsh lily. And in his palm he might hold this flower, examining the golden dainty cup, and in him suddenly might come a sweetness keen as pain. A weaver might look up suddenly and see for the first time the cold, weird radiance of midnight January sky, and a deep fright at his own smallness stop his heart. Such things as these, then, happen when a man has drunk Miss Amelia's liquor. He may suffer, or he may be spent with joy—but the experience has shown the truth; he has warmed his soul and seen the message hidden there.

They drank until it was past midnight, and the moon was clouded over so that the night was cold and dark. The hunchback still sat on the bottom steps, bent over miserably with his forehead resting on his knee. Miss Amelia stood with her hands in her pockets, one foot resting on the second step of the stairs. She had been silent for a long time. Her face had the expression often seen in slightly cross-eyed persons who are thinking deeply, a look that appears to be both very wise and very crazy. At last she said: "I don't know your name."

"I'm Lymon Willis," said the hunchback.

"Well, come on in," she said. "Some supper was left in the stove and you can eat."

Only a few times in her life had Miss Amelia invited anyone to eat with her, unless she were planning to trick them in some way, or make money out of them. So the men on the porch felt there was something wrong. Later, they said among themselves that she must have been drinking back in the swamp the better part of the afternoon. At any rate she left the porch, and Stumpy MacPhail and the twins went on off home. She bolted the front door and looked all around to see that her goods were in order. Then she went to the kitchen, which was at the back of the store. The hunchback followed her, dragging his suitcase, sniffing and wiping his nose on the sleeve of his dirty coat.

"Sit down," said Miss Amelia. "I'll just warm up what's here."

It was a good meal they had together on that night. Miss Amelia was rich and she did not grudge herself food. There was fried chicken (the breast of which the hunchback took on his own plate), mashed rootabeggars, collard greens, and hot, pale golden, sweet potatoes. Miss Amelia ate slowly and with the relish of a farm hand. She sat with both elbows on the table, bent over the plate, her knees spread wide apart and her feet braced on the rungs of the chair. As for the hunchback, he gulped down his supper as though he had not smelled food in months. During the meal one tear crept down his dingy cheek—but it was just a little leftover tear and meant nothing at all. The lamp on the table was well-trimmed, burning blue at the edges of the wick, and casting a cheerful light in the kitchen. When Miss Amelia had eaten her supper she wiped her plate carefully with a slice of light bread, and then poured her own clear, sweet syrup over the bread. The hunchback did likewise—except that he was more finicky and asked for a new plate. Having finished, Miss Amelia tilted back her chair, tightened her fist, and felt the hard, supple muscles of her right arm beneath the clean, blue cloth of her shirtsleeves—an unconscious habit with her, at the close of a meal. Then she took the lamp from the table and jerked her head toward the staircase as an invitation for the hunchback to follow after her.

Above the store there were the three rooms where Miss Amelia had lived during all her life—two bedrooms with a large parlor in between. Few people had even seen these rooms, but it was generally known that they were well-furnished and extremely clean. And now Miss Amelia was taking up with her a dirty little hunchbacked stranger, come from God knows where. Miss Amelia walked slowly, two steps at a time, holding the lamp high. The hunchback hovered so close behind her that the swinging light made on the staircase wall one great, twisted shadow of the two of them. Soon the premises above the store were dark as the rest of the town.

The next morning was serene, with a sunrise of warm purple mixed with rose. In the fields around the town the furrows were newly plowed, and very early the tenants were at work setting out the young, deep green tobacco plants. The wild crows flew down close to the fields, making swift blue shadows on the earth. In town the people set out early with their dinner pails, and the windows of the mill were blinding gold in the sun. The air was fresh and the peach trees light as March clouds with their blossoms.

Miss Amelia came down at about dawn, as usual. She washed her head at the pump and very shortly set about her business. Later in the morning she saddled her mule and went to see about her property, planted with cotton, up near the Forks Falls Road. By noon, of course, everybody had heard about the hunchback who had come to the store in the middle of the night. But no one as yet had seen him. The day soon grew hot and the sky was a rich, midday blue. Still no one had laid an eye on this strange guest. A few people remembered that Miss Amelia's mother had had a half-sister—but there was some difference of opinion as to whether she had died or had run off with a tobacco stringer. As for the hunchback's claim, everyone thought it was a trumped-up business. And the town, knowing Miss Amelia, decided that surely she had put him out of the house after feeding him. But toward evening, when the sky had whitened, and the shift was done, a woman claimed to have seen a crooked face at the window of one of the rooms up over the store. Miss Amelia herself said nothing. She clerked in the store for a while, argued for an hour with a farmer over a plow shaft, mended some chicken wire, locked up near sundown, and went to her rooms. The town was left puzzled and talkative.

The next day Miss Amelia did not open the store, but stayed locked up inside her premises and saw no one. Now this was the day that the rumor started—the rumor so terrible that the town and all the country about were stunned by it. The rumor was started by a weaver called Merlie Ryan. He is a man of not much account—sallow, shambling, and with no teeth in his head. He has the three-day malaria, which means that every third day the fever comes on him. So on two days he is dull and cross, but on the third day he livens up and sometimes has an idea or two, most of which are foolish. It was while Merlie Ryan was in his fever that he turned suddenly and said:

"I know what Miss Amelia done. She murdered that man for something in that suitcase."

He said this in a calm voice, as a statement of fact. And within an hour the news had swept through the town. It was a fierce and sickly tale the town built up that day. In it were all the things which cause the heart to shiver—a hunchback, a midnight burial in the swamp, the dragging of Miss Amelia through the streets of the town on the way to prison, the squabbles over what would happen to her property—all told in hushed voices and repeated with some fresh and weird detail. It rained and women forgot to bring in the washing from the lines. One or two mortals, who were in debt to Miss Amelia, even put on Sunday clothes as though it were a holiday. People clustered together on the main street, talking and watching the store.

It would be untrue to say that all the town took part in the evil festival. There were a few sensible men who reasoned that Miss Amelia, being rich, would not go out of her way to murder a vagabond for a few trifles of junk. In the town there were even three good people, and they did not want this crime, not even for the sake of the interest and the great commotion it would entail; it gave them no pleasure to think of Miss Amelia holding to the bars of the penitentiary and being electrocuted in Atlanta. These good people judged Miss Amelia in a different way from what the others judged her. When a person is as contrary in every single respect as she was and when the sins of a person have amounted to such a point that they can hardly be remembered all at once—then this person plainly requires a special judgment. They remembered that Miss Amelia had been born dark and somewhat queer of face, raised motherless by her father who was a solitary man, that early in youth she had grown to be six feet two inches tall which in itself is not natural for a woman, and that her ways and habits of life were too peculiar ever to reason about. Above all, they remembered her puzzling marriage, which was the most unreasonable scandal ever to happen in this town.

So these good people felt toward her something near to pity. And when she was out on her wild business, such as rushing in a house to drag forth a sewing machine in payment for a debt, or getting herself worked up over some matter concerning the law—they had toward her a feeling which was a mixture of exasperation, a ridiculous little inside tickle, and a deep, unnamable sadness. But enough of the good people, for there were only three of them; the rest of the town was making a holiday of this fancied crime the whole of the afternoon.

Miss Amelia herself, for some strange reason, seemed unaware of all this. She spent most of her day upstairs. When down in the store, she prowled around peacefully, her hands deep in the pockets of her overalls and head bent so low that her chin was tucked inside the collar of her shirt. There was no bloodstain on her anywhere. Often she stopped and just stood somberly looking down at the cracks on the floor, twisting a lock of her short-cropped hair, and whispering something to herself. But most of the day was spent upstairs.

167

Dark came on. The rain that afternoon had chilled the air, so that the evening was bleak and gloomy as in wintertime. There were no stars in the sky, and a light, icy drizzle had set in. The lamps in the houses made mournful, wavering flickers when watched from the street. A wind had come up, not from the swamp side of the town but from the cold black pinewoods to the north.

The clocks in the town struck eight. Still nothing had happened. The bleak night, after the gruesome talk of the day, put a fear in some people, and they stayed home close to the fire. Others were gathered in groups together. Some eight or ten men had convened on the porch of Miss Amelia's store. They were silent and were indeed just waiting about. They themselves did not know what they were waiting for, but it was this: in times of tension, when some great action is impending, men gather and wait in this way. And after a time there will come a moment when all together they will act in unison, not from thought or from the will of any one man, but as though their instincts had merged together so that the decision belongs to no single one of them, but to the group as a whole. At such a time, no individual hesitates. And whether the matter will be settled peaceably, or whether the joint action will result in ransacking, violence, and crime, depends on destiny. So the men waited soberly on the porch of Miss Amelia's store, not one of them realizing what they would do, but knowing inwardly that they must wait, and that the time had almost come.

Now the door to the store was open. Inside it was bright and natural-looking. To the left was the counter where slabs of white meat, rock candy, and tobacco were kept. Behind this were shelves of salted white meat and meal. The right side of the store was mostly filled with farm implements and such. At the back of the store, to the left, was the door leading up the stairs, and it was open. And at the far right of the store there was another door which led to a little room that Miss Amelia called her office. This door was also open. And at eight o'clock that evening Miss Amelia could be seen there sitting before her rolltop desk, figuring with a fountain pen and some pieces of paper.

The office was cheerfully lighted, and Miss Amelia did not seem to notice the delegation on the porch. Everything around her was in great order, as usual. This office was a room well-known, in a dreadful way, throughout the country. It was there Miss Amelia transacted all business. On the desk was a carefully covered typewriter which she knew how to run, but used only for the most important documents. In the drawers were literally thousands of papers, all filed according to the alphabet. This office was also the place where Miss Amelia received sick people, for she enjoyed doctoring and did a great deal of it. Two whole shelves were crowded with bottles and various paraphernalia. Against the wall was a bench where the patients sat.

She could sew up a wound with a burnt needle so that it would not turn green. For burns she had a cool, sweet syrup. For unlocated sickness there were any number of different medicines which she had brewed herself from unknown recipes. They wrenched loose the bowels very well, but they could not be given to small children, as they caused bad convulsions; for them she had an entirely separate draught, gentler and sweet-flavored. Yes, all in all, she was considered a good doctor. Her hands, though very large and bony, had a light touch about them. She possessed great imagination and used hundreds of different cures. In the face of the most dangerous and extraordinary treatment she did not hesitate, and no disease was so terrible but what she would undertake to cure it. In this there was one exception. If a patient came with a female complaint she could do nothing. Indeed at the mere mention of the words her face would slowly darken with shame, and she would stand there craning her neck against the collar of her shirt, or rubbing her swamp boots together, for all the world like a great, shamed, dumb-tongued child. But in other matters people trusted her. She charged no fees whatsoever and always had a raft of patients.

On this evening, Miss Amelia wrote with her fountain pen a good deal. But even so she could not be forever unaware of the group waiting out there on the dark porch, and watching her. From time to time she looked up and regarded them steadily. But she did not holler out to them to demand why they were loafing around her property like a sorry bunch of gabbies. Her face was proud and stern, as it always was when she sat at the desk of her office. After a time their peering in like that seemed to annoy her. She wiped her cheek with a red handkerchief, got up, and closed the office door.

Now to the group on the porch this gesture acted as a signal. The time had come. They had stood for a long while with the night raw and gloomy in the street behind them. They had waited long and just at that moment the instinct to act came on them. All at once, as though moved by one will, they walked into the store. At that moment the eight men looked very much alike—all wearing blue overalls, most of them with whitish hair, all pale of face, and all with a set, dreaming look in the eye. What they would have done next no one knows. But at that instant there was a noise at the head of the staircase. The men looked up and then stood dumb with shock. It was the hunchback, whom they had already murdered in their minds. Also, the creature was not at all as had been pictured to them—not a pitiful and dirty little chatterer, alone and beggared in this world. Indeed, he was like nothing any man among them had ever beheld until that time. The room was still as death.

The hunchback came down slowly with the proudness of one who owns every plank of the floor beneath his feet. In the past days he had greatly changed. For one thing he was clean beyond words. He still wore his little coat, but it was brushed off and neatly mended. Beneath this was a fresh red and black checkered shirt belonging to Miss Amelia. He did not wear trousers such as ordinary men are meant to wear, but a pair of tight-fitting little knee-length breeches. On his skinny legs he wore black stockings, and his shoes were of a special kind, being queerly shaped, laced up over the ankles, and newly cleaned and polished with wax. Around his neck, so that his large, pale ears were almost completely covered, he wore a shawl of lime-green wool, the fringes of which almost touched the floor.

The hunchback walked down the store with his stiff little strut and then stood in the center of the group that had come inside. They cleared a space about him and stood looking with hands loose at their sides and eyes wide open. The hunchback himself got his bearings in an odd manner. He regarded each person steadily at his own eye-level, which was about belt line for an ordinary man. Then with shrewd deliberation he examined each man's lower regions—from the waist to the sole of the shoe. When he had satisfied himself he closed his eyes for a moment and shook his head, as though in his opinion what he had seen did not amount to much. Then with assurance, only to confirm himself, he tilted back his head and took in the halo of faces around him with one long, circling stare. There was a half-filled sack of guano on the left side of the store, and when he had found his bearings in this way, the hunchback sat down upon it. Cozily settled, with his little legs crossed, he took from his coat pocket a certain object.

Now it took some moments for the men in the store to regain their ease. Merlie Ryan, he of the three-day fever who had started the rumor that day, was the first to speak. He looked at the object which the hunchback was fondling, and said in a hushed voice:

"What is it you have there?"

Each man knew well what it was the hunchback was handling. For it was the snuffbox which had belonged to Miss Amelia's father. The snuffbox was of blue enamel with a dainty embellishment of wrought gold on the lid. The group knew it well and marveled. They glanced warily at the closed office door, and heard the low sound of Miss Amelia whistling to herself.

"Yes, what is it, Peanut?"

The hunchback looked up quickly and sharpened his mouth to speak. "Why, this is a lay-low to catch meddlers."

The hunchback reached in the box with his scrambly little fingers and ate something, but he offered no one around him a taste. It was not even proper snuff which he was taking, but a mixture of sugar and cocoa. This he took, though, as snuff, pocketing a little wad of it beneath his lower lip and licking down neatly into this with a flick of his tongue which made a frequent grimace come over his face.

"The very teeth in my head have always tasted sour to me," he said in explanation. "That is the reason why I take this kind of sweet snuff."

The group still clustered around, feeling somewhat gawky and bewildered. This sensation never quite wore off, but it was soon tempered by another feeling—an air of intimacy in the room and a vague festivity. Now the names of the men of the group there on that evening were as follows: Hasty Malone, Robert Calvert Hale, Merlie Ryan, Reverend T. M. Willin, Rosser Cline, Rip Wellborn, Henry Ford Crimp, and Horace Wells. Except for Reverend Willin, they are all alike in many ways as has been said—all having taken pleasure from something or other, all having wept and suffered in some way, most of them tractable unless exasperated. Each of them worked in the mill, and lived with others in a two- or three-room house for which the rent was ten dollars or twelve dollars a month. All had been paid that afternoon, for it was Saturday. So, for the present, think of them as a whole.

The hunchback, however, was already sorting them out in his mind. Once comfortably settled he began to chat with everyone, asking questions such as if a man was married, how old he was, how much his wages came to in an average week, et cetera—picking his way along to inquiries which were downright intimate. Soon the group was joined by others in the town, Henry Macy, idlers who had sensed something extraordinary, women come to fetch their men who lingered on, and even one loose, towhead child who tiptoed into the store, stole a box of animal crackers, and made off very quietly. So the premises of Miss Amelia were soon crowded, and she herself had not yet opened her office door.

There is a type of person who has a quality about him that sets him apart from other and more ordinary human beings. Such a person has an instinct which is usually found only in small children, an instinct to establish immediate and vital contact between himself and all things in the world. Certainly the hunchback was of this type. He had only been in the store half an hour before an immediate contact had been established between him and each other individual. It was as though he had lived in the town for years, was a well-known character, and had been sitting and talking there on that guano sack for countless evenings. This, together with the fact that it was Saturday night, could account for the air of freedom and illicit gladness in the store. There was a tension, also, partly because of the oddity of the situation and because Miss Amelia was still closed off in her office and had not yet made her appearance.

She came out that evening at ten o'clock. And those who were expecting some drama at her entrance were disappointed. She opened the door and walked in with her slow, gangling swagger. There was a streak of ink on one side of her nose, and she had knotted the red handkerchief about her neck. She seemed to notice nothing unusual. Her gray, crossed eyes glanced over to the place where the hunchback was sitting, and for a moment lingered there. The rest of the crowd in her store she regarded with only a peaceable surprise.

"Does anyone want waiting on?" she asked quietly.

There were a number of customers, because it was Saturday night, and they all wanted liquor. Now Miss Amelia had dug up an aged barrel only three days past and had siphoned it into bottles back by the still. This night she took the money from the customers and counted it beneath the bright light. Such was the ordinary procedure. But after this what happened was not ordinary. Always before, it was necessary to go around to the dark back yard, and there she would hand out your bottle through the kitchen door. There was no feeling of joy in the transaction. After getting his liquor the customer walked off into the night. Or, if his wife would not have it in the home, he was allowed to come back around to the front porch of the store and guzzle there or in the street. Now, both the porch and the street before it were the property of Miss Amelia, and no mistake about it—but she did not regard them as her premises; the premises began at the front door and took in the entire inside of the building. There she had never allowed liquor to be opened or drunk by anyone but herself. Now for the first time she broke this rule. She went to the kitchen, with the hunchback close at her heels, and she brought back the bottles into the warm, bright store. More than that she furnished some glasses and opened two boxes of crackers so that they were there hospitably in a platter on the counter and anyone who wished could take one free.

She spoke to no one but the hunchback, and she only asked him in a somewhat harsh and husky voice: "Cousin Lymon, will you have yours straight, or warmed in a pan with water on the stove?"

"If you please, Amelia," the hunchback said. (And since what time had anyone presumed to address Miss Amelia by her bare name, without a title of respect?—Certainly not her bridegroom and her husband of ten days. In fact not since the death of her father, who for some reason had always called her Little, had anyone dared to address her in such a familiar way.) "If you please, I'll have it warmed."

Now, this was the beginning of the café. It was as simple as that. Recall that the night was gloomy as in wintertime, and to have sat around the property outside would have made a sorry celebration. But inside there was the company and a genial warmth. Someone had rattled up the stove in the rear, and those who bought bottles shared their liquor with friends. Several women were there and they had twists of licorice, a Nehi, or even a swallow of the whisky. The hunchback was still a novelty and his presence amused everyone. The bench in the office was brought in, together with several extra chairs. Other people leaned against the counter or made themselves comfortable on barrels and sacks. Nor did the opening of liquor on the premises cause any rambunctiousness, indecent giggles, or misbehavior whatsoever. On the contrary the company was polite even to the point of a certain timidness. For people in this town were then unused to gathering together for the sake of pleasure. They met to work in the mill. Or on Sunday there would be an all-day camp meeting—and though that is a pleasure, the intention of the whole affair is to sharpen your view of Hell and put into you a keen fear of the Lord Almighty. But the spirit of a café is altogether different. Even the richest, greediest old rascal will behave himself, insulting no one in a proper café. And poor people look about them gratefully and pinch up the salt in a dainty and modest manner. For the atmosphere of a proper café implies these qualities: fellowship, the satisfactions of the belly, and a certain gaiety and grace of behavior. This had never been told to the gathering in Miss Amelia's store that night. But they knew it of themselves, although never, of course, until that time had there been a café in the town.

Now, the cause of all this, Miss Amelia, stood most of the evening in the doorway leading to the kitchen. Outwardly she did not seem changed at all. But there were many who noticed her face. She watched all that went on, but most of the time her eyes were fastened lonesomely on the hunchback. He strutted about the store, eating from his snuffbox, and being at once sour and agreeable. Where Miss Amelia stood, the light from the chinks of the stove cast a glow, so that her brown, long face was somewhat brightened. She seemed to be looking inward. There was in her expression pain, perplexity, and uncertain joy. Her lips were not so firmly set as usual, and she swallowed often. Her skin had paled and her large empty hands were sweating. Her look that night, then, was the lonesome look of the lover.

This opening of the café came to an end at midnight. Everyone said good-bye to everyone else in a friendly fashion. Miss Amelia shut the front door of her premises, but forgot to bolt it. Soon everything— the main street with its three stores, the mill, the houses—all the town, in fact—was dark and silent. And so ended three days and nights in which had come an arrival of a stranger, an unholy holiday, and the start of the café.

Now time must pass. For the next four years are much alike. There are great changes, but these changes are brought about bit by bit, in simple steps which in themselves do not appear to be important. The hunchback continued to live with Miss Amelia. The café expanded in a gradual way. Miss Amelia began to sell her liquor by the drink, and some tables were brought into the store. There were customers every evening, and on Saturday a great crowd. Miss Amelia began to serve fried catfish suppers at fifteen cents a plate. The hunchback cajoled her into buying a fine mechanical piano. Within two years the place was a store no longer, but had been converted into a proper café, open every evening from six until twelve o'clock.

Each night the hunchback came down the stairs with the air of one who has a grand opinion of himself. He always smelled slightly of turnip greens, as Miss Amelia rubbed him night and morning with pot liquor to give him strength. She spoiled him to a point beyond reason, but nothing seemed to strengthen him; food only made his hump and his head grow larger while the rest of him remained weakly and deformed. Miss Amelia was the same in appearance. During the week she still wore swamp boots and overalls, but on Sunday she put on a dark red dress that hung on her in a most peculiar fashion. Her manners, however, and her way of life were greatly changed. She still loved a fierce lawsuit, but she was not so quick to cheat her fellow man and to exact cruel payments. Because the hunchback was so extremely sociable, she even went about a little—to revivals, to funerals, and so forth. Her doctoring was as successful as ever, her liquor even finer than before, if that were possible. The café itself proved profitable and was the only place of pleasure for many miles around.

So for the moment regard these years from random and disjointed views. See the hunchback marching in Miss Amelia's footsteps when on a red winter morning they set out for the pinewoods to hunt. See them working on her properties—with Cousin Lymon standing by and doing absolutely nothing, but quick to point out any laziness among the hands. On autumn afternoons they sat on the back steps chopping sugar cane. The glaring summer days they spent back in the swamp where the water cypress is a deep black green, where beneath the tangled swamp trees there is a drowsy gloom. When the path leads through a bog or a stretch of blackened water see Miss Amelia bend down to let Cousin Lymon scramble on her back—and see her wading forward with the hunchback settled on her shoulders, clinging to her ears or to her broad forehead. Occasionally Miss Amelia cranked up the Ford which she had bought and treated Cousin Lymon to a picture-show in Cheehaw, or to some distant fair or cockfight; the hunchback took a passionate delight in spectacles. Of course, they were in their café every morning, they would often sit for hours together by the fireplace in the parlor upstairs. For the hunchback was sickly at night and dreaded to lie looking into the dark. He had a deep fear of death.

And Miss Amelia would not leave him by himself to suffer with this fright. It may even be reasoned that the growth of the café came about mainly on this account; it was a thing that brought him company and pleasure and that helped him through the night. So compose from such flashes an image of these years as a whole. And for a moment let it rest.

Now some explanation is due for all this behavior. The time has come to speak about love. For Miss Amelia loved Cousin Lymon. So much was clear to everyone. They lived in the same house together and were never seen apart. Therefore, according to Mrs. MacPhail, a warty-nosed old busybody who is continually moving her sticks of furniture from one part of the front room to another; according to her and to certain others, these two were living in sin. If they were related, they were only a cross between first and second cousins, and even that could in no way be proved. Now, of course, Miss Amelia was a powerful blunderbuss of a person, more than six feet tall—and Cousin Lymon a weakly little hunchback reaching only to her waist. But so much the better for Mrs. Stumpy MacPhail and her cronies, for they and their kind glory in conjunctions which are ill-matched and pitiful. So let them be. The good people thought that if those two had found some satisfaction of the flesh between themselves, then it was a matter concerning them and God alone. All sensible people agreed in their opinion about this conjecture—and their answer was a plain, flat no. What sort of thing, then, was this love?

First of all, love is a joint experience between two persons—but the fact that it is a joint experience does not mean that it is a similar experience to the two people involved. There are the lover and the beloved, but these two come from different countries. Often the beloved is only a stimulus for all the stored-up love which has lain quiet within the lover for a long time hitherto. And somehow every lover knows this. He feels in his soul that his love is a solitary thing. He comes to know a new, strange loneliness and it is this knowledge which makes him suffer. So there is only one thing for the lover to do. He must house his love within himself as best he can; he must create for himself a whole new inward world—a world intense and strange, complete in himself. Let it be added here that this lover about whom we speak need not necessarily be a young man saving for a wedding ring—this lover can be man, woman, child, or indeed any human creature on this earth.

Now, the beloved can also be of any description. The most outlandish people can be the stimulus for love. A man may be a doddering great-grandfather and still love only a strange girl he saw in the streets of Cheehaw one afternoon two decades past. The preacher may love a fallen woman. The beloved may be treacherous, greasy-headed, and given to evil habits. Yes, and the lover may see this as clearly as anyone else—but that does not affect the evolution of his love one whit. A most mediocre person can be the object of a love which is wild, extravagant, and beautiful as the poison lilies of the swamp. A good man may be the stimulus for a love both violent and debased, or a jabbering madman may bring about in the soul of someone a tender and simple idyll. Therefore, the value and quality of any love is determined solely by the lover himself.

It is for this reason that most of us would rather love than be loved. Almost everyone wants to be the lover. And the curt truth is that, in a deep secret way, the state of being beloved is intolerable to many. The beloved fears and hates the lover, and with the best of reasons. For the lover is forever trying to strip bare his beloved. The lover craves any possible relation with the beloved, even if this experience can cause him only pain.

It has been mentioned before that Miss Amelia was once married. And this curious episode might as well be accounted for at this point. Remember that it all happened long ago, and that it was Miss Amelia's only personal contact, before the hunchback came to her, with this phenomenon—love.

The town then was the same as it is now, except there were two stores instead of three and the peach trees along the street were more crooked and smaller than they are now. Miss Amelia was nineteen years old at the time, and her father had been dead for many months. There was in the town at the time a loom-fixer named Marvin Macy. He was the brother of Henry Macy, although to know them you would never guess that those two could be kin. For Marvin Macy was the handsomest man in this region—being six feet one inch tall, hard-muscled, and with slow gray eyes and curly hair. He was well off, made good wages, and had a gold watch which opened in the back to a picture of a waterfall. From the outward and worldly point of view Marvin Macy was a fortunate fellow; he needed to bow and scrape to no one and always got just what he wanted. But from a more serious and thoughtful viewpoint Marvin Macy was not a person to be envied, for he was an evil character. His reputation was as bad, if not worse, than that of any young man in the county. For years, when he was a boy, he had carried about with him the dried and salted ear of a man he had killed in a razor fight. He had chopped off the tails of squirrels in the pinewoods just to please his fancy, and in his left hip pocket he carried forbidden marijuana weed to tempt those who were discouraged and drawn toward death. Yet in spite of his well-known reputation he was the beloved of many females in this region—and there were at the time several young girls who were clean-haired and soft-eyed, with tender sweet little buttocks and charming ways. These gentle young girls he degraded and shamed. Then finally, at the age of twenty-two, this Marvin Macy chose Miss Amelia. That solitary gangling, queer-eyed girl was the one he longed for. Nor did he want her because of her money, but solely out of love.

And love changed Marvin Macy. Before the time when he loved Miss Amelia it could be questioned if such a person had within him a heart and soul. Yet there is some explanation for the ugliness of his character, for Marvin Macy had had a hard beginning in this world. He was one of seven unwanted children whose parents could hardly be called parents at all; these parents were wild younguns who liked to fish and roam around the swamp. Their own children, and there was a new one almost every year, were only a nuisance to them. At night when they came home from the mill they would look at the children as though they did not know wherever they had come from. If the children cried they were beaten, and the first thing they learned in this world was to seek the darkest corner of the room and try to hide themselves as best they could. They were as thin as little whitehaired ghosts, and they did not speak, not even to each other. Finally, they were abandoned by their parents altogether and left to the mercies of the town. It was a hard winter, with the mill closed down almost three months, and much misery everywhere. But this is not a town to let white orphans perish in the road before your eyes. So here is what came about: the eldest child, who was eight years old, walked into Cheehaw and disappeared—perhaps he took a freight train somewhere and went out into the world, nobody knows. Three other children were boarded out amongst the town, being sent around from one kitchen to another, and as they were delicate they died before Easter time. The last two children were Marvin Macy and Henry Macy, and they were taken into a home. There was a good woman in the town named Mrs. Mary Hale, and she took Marvin Macy and Henry Macy and loved them as her own. They were raised in her household and treated well.

But the hearts of small children are delicate organs. A cruel beginning in this world can twist them into curious shapes. The heart of a hurt child can shrink so that forever afterward it is hard and pitted as the seed of a peach. Or again, the heart of such a child may fester and swell until it is a misery to carry within the body, easily chafed and hurt by the most ordinary things. This last is what happened to Henry Macy, who is so opposite to his brother, is the kindest and gentlest man in town. He lends his wages to those who are unfortunate, and in the old days he used to care for the children whose parents were at the café on Saturday night. But he is a shy man, and he has the look of one who has a swollen heart and suffers. Marvin Macy, however, grew to be bold and fearless and cruel. His heart turned tough as the horns of Satan, and until the time when he loved Miss Amelia he brought to his brother and the good woman who raised him nothing but shame and trouble.

But love reversed the character of Marvin Macy. For two years he loved Miss Amelia, but he did not declare himself. He would stand near the door of her premises, his cap in his hand, his eyes meek and longing and misty gray. He reformed himself completely. He was good to his brother and foster mother, and he saved his wages and learned thrift. Moreover, he reached out toward God. No longer did he lie around on the floor of the front porch all day Sunday, singing and playing his guitar; he attended church services and was present at all religious meetings. He learned good manners; he trained himself to rise and give his chair to a lady, and he quit swearing and fighting and using holy names in vain. So for two years he passed through this transformation and improved his character in every way. Then at the end of the two years he went one evening to Miss Amelia, carrying a bunch of swamp flowers, a sack of chitterlins, and a silver ring—that night Marvin Macy declared himself.

And Miss Amelia married him. Later everyone wondered why. Some said it was because she wanted to get herself some wedding presents. Others believed it came about through the nagging of Miss Amelia's great-aunt in Cheehaw, who was a terrible old woman. Anyway, she strode with great steps down the aisle of the church wearing her dead mother's bridal gown, which was of yellow satin and at least twelve inches too short for her. It was a winter afternoon and the clear sun shown through the ruby windows of the church and put a curious glow on the pair before the altar. As the marriage lines were read Miss Amelia kept making an odd gesture—she would rub the palm of her right hand down the side of her satin wedding gown. She was reaching for the pocket of her overalls, and being unable to find it her face became impatient, bored, and exasperated. At last when the lines were spoken and the marriage prayer was done Miss Amelia hurried out of the church, not taking the arm of her husband, but walking at least two paces ahead of him.

The church is no distance from the store so the bride and groom walked home. It is said that on the way Miss Amelia began to talk about some deal she had worked up with a farmer over a load of kindling wood. In fact, she treated her groom in exactly the same manner she would have used with some customer who had come into the store to buy a pint from her. But so far all had gone decently enough; the town was gratified, as people had seen what this love had done to Marvin Macy and hoped that it might also reform his bride. At least, they counted on the marriage to tone down Miss Amelia's temper, to put a bit of bride-fat on her, and to change her at last into a calculable woman.

They were wrong. The young boys who watched through the window on that night said that this is what actually happened: The bride and groom ate a grand supper prepared by Jeff, the old Negro who cooked for Miss Amelia. The bride took second servings of everything, but the groom picked with his food. Then the bride went about her ordinary business—reading the newspaper, finishing an inventory of the stock in the store, and so forth. The groom hung about in the doorway with a loose, foolish, blissful face and was not noticed. At eleven o'clock the bride took a lamp and went upstairs. The groom followed close behind her. So far all had gone decently enough, but what followed after was unholy.

Within half an hour Miss Amelia had stomped down the stairs in breeches and a khaki jacket. Her face had darkened so that it looked quite black. She slammed the kitchen door and gave it an ugly kick. Then she controlled herself. She poked up the fire, sat down, and put her feet up on the kitchen stove. She read the Farmer's Almanac, drank coffee, and had a smoke with her father's pipe. Her face was hard, stern, and had now whitened to its natural color. Sometimes she paused to jot down some information from the Almanac on a piece of paper. Toward dawn she went into her office and uncovered her typewriter, which she had recently bought and was only just learning how to run. That was the way in which she spent the whole of her wedding night. At daylight she went out to her yard as though nothing whatsoever had occurred and did some carpentering on a rabbit hutch which she had begun the week before and intended to sell somewhere.

A groom is in a sorry fix when he is unable to bring his well-beloved bride to bed with him, and the whole town knows it. Marvin Macy came down that day still in his wedding finery, and with a sick face. God knows how he had spent the night. He moped about the yard, watching Miss Amelia, but keeping some distance away from her. Then toward noon an idea came to him and he went off in the direction of Society City. He returned with presents—an opal ring, a pink enamel doreen of the sort which was then in fashion, a silver bracelet with two hearts on it, and a box of candy which had cost two dollars and a half. Miss Amelia looked over these fine gifts and opened the box of candy, for she was hungry. The rest of the presents she judged shrewdly for a moment to sum up their value—then she put them in the counter out for sale. The night was spent in much the same manner as the preceding one—except that Miss Amelia brought her feather mattress to make a pallet by the kitchen stove, and she slept fairly well.

Things went on like this for three days. Miss Amelia went about her business as usual, and took great interest in some rumor that a bridge was to be built some ten miles down the road. Marvin Macy still followed her about around the premises, and it was plain from his face how he suffered. Then on the fourth day he did an extremely simple-minded thing: he went to Cheehaw and came back with a lawyer. Then in Miss Amelia's office he signed over to her the whole of his worldly goods, which was ten acres of timberland which he had bought with the money he had saved. She studied the paper sternly to make sure there was no possibility of a trick and filed it soberly in the drawer of her desk. That afternoon Marvin Macy took a quart bottle of whisky and went with it alone out in the swamp while the sun was still shining. Toward evening he came in drunk, went up to Miss Amelia with wet wide eyes, and put his hand on her shoulder. He was trying to tell her something, but before he could open his mouth she had swung once with her fist and hit his face so hard that he was thrown back against the wall and one of his front teeth was broken.

The rest of this affair can only be mentioned in bare outline. After this first blow Miss Amelia hit him whenever he came within arm's reach of her, and whenever he was drunk. At last she turned him off the premises altogether, and he was forced to suffer publicly. During the day he hung around just outside the boundary line of Miss Amelia's property and sometimes with a drawn crazy look he would fetch his rifle and sit there cleaning it, peering at Miss Amelia steadily. If she was afraid she did not show it, but her face was sterner than ever, and often she spat on the ground. His last foolish effort was to climb in the window of her store one night and to sit there in the dark, for no purpose whatsoever, until she came down the stairs next morning. For this Miss Amelia set off immediately to the courthouse in Cheehaw with some notion that she could get him locked in the penitentiary for trespassing. Marvin Macy left the town that day, and no one saw him go, or knew just where he went. On leaving he put a long curious letter, partly written in pencil and partly with ink, beneath Miss Amelia's door. It was a wild love letter—but in it were also included threats, and he swore that in his life he would get even with her. His marriage had lasted for ten days. And the town felt the special satisfaction that people feel when someone has been thoroughly done in by some scandalous and terrible means.

Miss Amelia was left with everything that Marvin Macy had ever owned—his timberwood, his gilt watch, every one of his possessions. But she seemed to attach little value to them and that spring she cut up his Klansman's robe to cover her tobacco plants. So all that he had ever done was to make her richer and to bring her love. But, strange to say, she never spoke of him but with a terrible and spiteful bitterness. She never once referred to him by name but always mentioned him scornfully as "that loom-fixer I was married to."

And later, when horrifying rumors concerning Marvin Macy reached the town, Miss Amelia was very pleased. For the true character of Marvin Macy finally revealed itself, once he had freed himself of his love. He became a criminal whose picture and whose name were in all the papers in the state. He robbed three filling stations and held up the A & P store of Society City with a sawed-off gun. He was suspected of the murder of Slit-Eye Sam who was a noted highjacker. All these crimes were connected with the name of Marvin Macy, so that his evil became famous through many counties. Then finally the law captured him, drunk, on the floor of a tourist cabin, his guitar by his side, and fifty-seven dollars in his right shoe. He was tried, sentenced, and sent off to the penitentiary near Atlanta. Miss Amelia was deeply gratified.

Well, all this happened a long time ago, and it is the story of Miss Amelia's marriage. The town laughed a long time over this grotesque affair. But though the outward facts of this love are indeed sad and ridiculous, it must be remembered that the real story was that which took place in the soul of the lover himself. So who but God can be the final judge of this or any other love? On the very first night of the café there were several who suddenly thought of this broken bridegroom, locked in the gloomy penitentiary, many miles away. And in the years that followed, Marvin Macy was not altogether forgotten in the town. His name was never mentioned in the presence of Miss Amelia or the hunchback. But the memory of his passion and his crimes, and the thought of him trapped in his cell in the penitentiary, was like a troubling undertone beneath the happy love of Miss Amelia and the gaiety of the café. So do not forget this Marvin Macy, as he is to act a terrible part in the story which is yet to come.

During the four years in which the store became a café the rooms upstairs were not changed. This part of the premises remained exactly as it had been all of Miss Amelia's life, as it was in the time of her father, and most likely his father before him. The three rooms, it is already known, were immaculately clean. The smallest object had its exact place, and everything was wiped and dusted by Jeff, the servant of Miss Amelia, each morning. The front room belonged to Cousin Lymon— it was the room where Marvin Macy had stayed during the few nights he was allowed on the premises, and before that it was the bedroom of Miss Amelia's father. The room was furnished with a large chifforobe, a bureau covered with a stiff white linen cloth crocheted at the edges, and a marble-topped table. The bed was immense, an old fourposter made of carved, dark rosewood. On it were two feather mattresses, bolsters, and a number of handmade comforts. The bed was so high that beneath it were two wooden steps—no occupant had ever used these steps before, but Cousin Lymon drew them out each night and walked up in state. Beside the steps, but pushed modestly out of view, there was a china chamber-pot painted with pink roses. No rug covered the dark, polished floor and the curtains were of some white stuff, also crocheted at the edges.

On the other side of the parlor was Miss Amelia's bedroom, and it was smaller and very simple. The bed was narrow and made of pine. There was a bureau for her breeches, shirts, and Sunday dress, and she had hammered two nails in the closet wall on which to hang her swamp boots. There were no curtains, rugs, or ornaments of any kind.

The large middle room, the parlor, was elaborate. The rosewood sofa, upholstered in threadbare green silk, was before the fireplace. Marble-topped tables, two Singer sewing machines, a big vase of pampas grass—everything was rich and grand. The most important piece of furniture in the parlor was a big, glass-doored cabinet in which was kept a number of treasures and curios. Miss Amelia had added two objects to this collection—one was a large acorn from a water oak, the other a little velvet box holding two small, grayish stones. Sometimes when she had nothing much to do, Miss Amelia would take out this velvet box and stand by the window with the stones in the palm of her hand, looking down at them with a mixture of fascination, dubious respect, and fear. They were the kidney stones of Miss Amelia herself, and had been taken from her by the doctor in Cheehaw some years ago. It had been a terrible experience, from the first minute to the last, and all she had got out of it were those two little stones; she was bound to set great store by them, or else admit to a mighty sorry bargain. So she kept them and in the second year of Cousin Lymon's stay with her she had them set as ornaments in a watch chain which she gave to him. The other object she had added to the collection, the large acorn, was precious to her—but when she looked at it her face was always saddened and perplexed.

"Amelia, what does it signify?" Cousin Lymon asked her.

"Why, it's just an acorn," she answered. "Just an acorn I picked up on the afternoon Big Papa died."

"How do you mean?" Cousin Lymon insisted.

"I mean it's just an acorn I spied on the ground that day. I picked it up and put it in my pocket. But I don't know why."

"What a peculiar reason to keep it," Cousin Lymon said.

The talks of Miss Amelia and Cousin Lymon in the rooms upstairs, usually in the first few hours of the morning when the hunchback could not sleep, were many. As a rule, Miss Amelia was a silent woman, not letting her tongue run wild on any subject that happened to pop into her head. There were certain topics of conversation, however, in which she took pleasure. All these subjects had one point in common—they were interminable. She liked to contemplate problems which could be worked over for decades and still remain insoluble. Cousin Lymon, on the other hand, enjoyed talking on any subject whatsoever, as he was a great chatterer. Their approach to any conversation was altogether different. Miss Amelia always kept to the broad, rambling generalities of the matter, going on endlessly in a low, thoughtful voice and getting nowhere—while Cousin Lymon would interrupt her suddenly to pick up, magpie fashion, some detail which, even if unimportant, was at least concrete and bearing on some practical facet close at hand. Some of the favorite subjects of Miss Amelia were: the stars, the reason why Negroes are black, the best treatment for cancer, and so forth. Her father was also an interminable subject which was dear to her.

"Why, Law," she would say to Lymon. "Those days I slept. I'd go to bed just as the lamp was turned on and sleep—why, I'd sleep like I was drowned in warm axle grease. Then come daybreak Big Papa would walk in and put his hand down on my shoulder. 'Get stirring, Little,' he would say. Then later he would holler up the stairs from the kitchen when the stove was hot. 'Fried grits,' he would holler. 'White meat and gravy. Ham and eggs.' And I'd run down the stairs and dress by the hot stove while he was out washing at the pump. Then off we'd go to the still or maybe——"

"The grits we had this morning was poor," Cousin Lymon said. "Fried too quick so that the inside never heated."

"And when Big Papa would run off the liquor in those days——" The conversation would go on endlessly, with Miss Amelia's long legs stretched out before the hearth; for winter or summer there was always a fire in the grate, as Lymon was cold-natured. He sat in a low chair across from her, his feet not quite touching the floor and his torso usually well-wrapped in a blanket or the green wool shawl. Miss Amelia never mentioned her father to anyone else except Cousin Lymon.

That was one of the ways in which she showed her love for him. He had her confidence in the most delicate and vital matters. He alone knew where she kept the chart that showed where certain barrels of whisky were buried on a piece of property near by. He alone had access to her bank-book and the key to the cabinet of curios. He took money from the cash register, whole handfuls of it, and appreciated the loud jingle it made inside his pockets. He owned almost everything on the premises, for when he was cross Miss Amelia would prowl about and find him some present—so that now there was hardly anything left close at hand to give him. The only part of her life that she did not want Cousin Lymon to share with her was the memory of her ten-day marriage. Marvin Macy was the one subject that was never, at any time, discussed between the two of them.

So let the slow years pass and come to a Saturday evening six years after the time when Cousin Lymon came first to the town. It was

August and the sky had burned above the town like a sheet of flame all day. Now the green twilight was near and there was a feeling of repose. The street was coated an inch deep with dry golden dust and the little children ran about half-naked, sneezed often, sweated, and were fretful. The mill had closed down at noon. People in the houses along the main street sat resting on their steps and the women had palmetto fans. At Miss Amelia's there was a sign at the front of the premises saying CAFE. The back porch was cool with latticed shadows and there Cousin Lymon sat turning the ice-cream freezer—often he unpacked the salt and ice and removed the dasher to lick a bit and see how the work was coming on. Jeff cooked in the kitchen. Early that morning Miss Amelia had put a notice on the wall of the front porch reading: Chicken Dinner—Twenty Cents Tonite. The café was already open and Miss Amelia had just finished a period of work in her office. All the eight tables were occupied and from the mechanical piano came a jingling tune.

In a corner near the door and sitting at a table with a child, was Henry Macy. He was drinking a glass of liquor, which was unusual for him, as liquor went easily to his head and made him cry or sing. His face was very pale and his left eye worked constantly in a nervous tic, as it was apt to do when he was agitated. He had come into the café sidewise and silent, and when he was greeted he did not speak. The child next to him belonged to Horace Wells, and he had been left at Miss Amelia's that morning to be doctored.

Miss Amelia came out from her office in good spirits. She attended to a few details in the kitchen and entered the café with the pope's nose of a hen between her fingers, as that was her favorite piece. She looked about the room, saw that in general all was well, and went over to the corner table by Henry Macy. She turned the chair around and sat straddling the back, as she only wanted to pass the time of day and was not yet ready for her supper. There was a bottle of Kroup Kure in the hip pocket of her overalls—a medicine made from whisky, rock candy, and a secret ingredient. Miss Amelia uncorked the bottle and put it to the mouth of the child. Then she turned to Henry Macy and, seeing the nervous winking of his left eye, she asked:

"What ails you?"

Henry Macy seemed on the point of saying something difficult, but, after a long look into the eyes of Miss Amelia, he swallowed and did not speak.

So Miss Amelia returned to her patient. Only the child's head showed above the table top. His face was very red, with the eyelids half-closed and the mouth partly open. He had a large, hard, swollen boil on his thigh, and had been brought to Miss Amelia so that it could be opened. But Miss Amelia used a special method with children; she did not like to see them hurt, struggling, and terrified. So she had kept the child around the premises all day, giving him licorice and frequent doses of the Kroup Kure, and toward evening she tied a napkin around his neck and let him eat his fill of the dinner. Now as he sat at the table his head wobbled slowly from side to side and sometimes as he breathed there came from him a little worn-out grunt.

There was a stir in the café and Miss Amelia looked around quickly. Cousin Lymon had come in. The hunchback strutted into the café as he did every night, and when he reached the exact center of the room he stopped short and looked shrewdly around him, summing up the people and making a quick pattern of the emotional material at hand that night. The hunchback was a great mischief-maker. He enjoyed any kind of to-do, and without saying a word he could set the people at each other in a way that was miraculous. It was due to him that the Rainey twins had quarreled over a jacknife two years past, and had not spoken one word to each other since. He was present at the big fight between Rip Wellborn and Robert Calvert Hale, and every other fight for that matter since he had come into the town. He nosed around everywhere, knew the intimate business of everybody, and trespassed every waking hour. Yet, queerly enough, in spite of this it was the hunchback who was most responsible for the great popularity of the café. Things were never so gay as when he was around. When he walked into the room there was always a quick feeling of tension, because with this busybody about there was never any telling what might descend on you, or what might suddenly be brought to happen in the room. People are never so free with themselves and so recklessly glad as when there is some possibility of commotion or calamity ahead. So when the hunchback marched into the café everyone looked around at him and there was a quick outburst of talking and a drawing of corks.

Lymon waved his hand to Stumpy MacPhail who was sitting with Merlie Ryan and Henry Ford Crimp. "I walked to Rotten Lake today to fish," he said. "And on the way I stepped over what appeared at first to be a big fallen tree. But then as I stepped over I felt something stir and I taken this second look and there I was straddling this here alligator long as from the front door to the kitchen and thicker than a hog."

The hunchback chattered on. Everyone looked at him from time to time, and some kept track of his chattering and others did not. There were times when every word he said was nothing but lying and bragging. Nothing he said tonight was true. He had lain in bed with a summer quinsy all day long, and had only got up in the late afternoon in order to turn the ice-cream freezer. Everybody knew this, yet he stood there in the middle of the café and held forth with such lies and boasting that it was enough to shrivel the ears.

Miss Amelia watched him with her hands in her pockets and her head turned to one side. There was a softness about her gray, queer eyes and she was smiling gently to herself. Occasionally she glanced from the hunchback to the other people in the café—and then her look was proud, and there was in it the hint of a threat, as though daring anyone to try to hold him to account for all his foolery. Jeff was bringing in the suppers, already served on the plates, and the new electric fans in the café made a pleasant stir of coolness in the air.

"The little youngun is asleep," said Henry Macy finally.

Miss Amelia looked down at the patient beside her, and composed her face for the matter in hand. The child's chin was resting on the table edge and a trickle of spit or Kroup Kure had bubbled from the corner of his mouth. His eyes were quite closed, and a little family of gnats had clustered peacefully in the corners. Miss Amelia put her hand on his head and shook it roughly, but the patient did not awake. So Miss Amelia lifted the child from the table, being careful not to touch the sore part of his leg, and went into the office. Henry Macy followed after her and they closed the office door.

Cousin Lymon was bored that evening. There was not much going on, and in spite of the heat the customers in the café were good-humored. Henry Ford Crimp and Horace Wells sat at the middle table with their arms around each other, sniggering over some long joke—but when he approached them he could make nothing of it as he had missed the beginning of the story. The moonlight brightened the dusty road, and the dwarfed peach trees were black and motionless: there was no breeze. The drowsy buzz of swamp mosquitoes was like an echo of the silent night. The town seemed dark, except far down the road to the right there was the flicker of a lamp. Somewhere in the darkness a woman sang in a high wild voice and the tune had no start and no finish and was made up of only three notes which went on and on and on. The hunchback stood leaning against the banister of the porch, looking down the empty road as though hoping that someone would come along.

There were footsteps behind him, then a voice: "Cousin Lymon, your dinner is set out upon the table."

"My appetite is poor tonight," said the hunchback, who had been eating sweet snuff all the day. "There is a sourness in my mouth."

"Just a pick," said Miss Amelia. "The breast, the liver, and the heart."

Together they went back into the bright café, and sat down with Henry Macy. Their table was the largest one in the café, and on it there was a bouquet of swamp lilies in a Coca Cola bottle. Miss Amelia had finished with her patient and was satisfied with herself. From behind the closed office door there had come only a few sleepy whimpers, and before the patient could wake up and become terrified it was all over. The child was now slung across the shoulder of his father, sleeping deeply, his little arms dangling loose along his father's back, and his puffed-up face very red—they were leaving the café to go home.

Henry Macy was still silent. He ate carefully, making no noise when he swallowed, and was not a third as greedy as Cousin Lymon who claimed to have no appetite and was now putting down helping after helping of the dinner. Occasionally Henry Macy looked across at Miss Amelia and again held his peace.

It was a typical Saturday night. An old couple who had come in from the country hesitated for a moment at the doorway, holding each other's hand, and finally decided to come inside. They had lived together so long, this old country couple, that they looked as similar as twins. They were brown, shriveled, and like two little walking peanuts. They left early, and by midnight most of the other customers were gone. Rosser Cline and Merlie Ryan still played checkers, and Stumpy MacPhail sat with a liquor bottle on his table (his wife would not allow it in the home) and carried on peaceable conversations with himself. Henry Macy had not yet gone away, and this was unusual, as he almost always went to bed soon after nightfall. Miss Amelia yawned sleepily, but Lymon was restless and she did not suggest that they close up for the night.

Finally, at one o'clock, Henry Macy looked up at the corner of the ceiling and said quietly to Miss Amelia: "I got a letter today."

Miss Amelia was not one to be impressed by this, because all sorts of business letters and catalogues came addressed to her.

"I got a letter from my brother," said Henry Macy.

The hunchback, who had been goose-stepping about the café with his hands clasped behind his head, stopped suddenly. He was quick to sense any change in the atmosphere of a gathering. He glanced at each face in the room and waited.

Miss Amelia scowled and hardened her right fist. "You are welcome to it," she said.

"He is on parole. He is out of the penitentiary."

The face of Miss Amelia was very dark, and she shivered although the night was warm. Stumpy MacPhail and Merlie Ryan pushed aside their checker game. The café was very quiet.

"Who?" asked Cousin Lymon. His large, pale ears seemed to grow on his head and stiffen. "What?"

Miss Amelia slapped her hands palm down on the table. "Because Marvin Macy is a——" But her voice hoarsened and after a few moments she only said: "He belongs to be in that penitentiary the balance of his life."

"What did he do?" asked Cousin Lymon.

There was a long pause, as no one knew exactly how to answer this. "He robbed three filling stations," said Stumpy MacPhail. But his words did not sound complete and there was a feeling of sins left unmentioned.

The hunchback was impatient. He could not bear to be left out of anything, even a great misery. The name Marvin Macy was unknown to him, but it tantalized him as did any mention of subjects which others knew about and of which he was ignorant—such as any reference to the old sawmill that had been torn down before he came, or a chance word about poor Morris Finestein, or the recollection of any event that had occurred before his time. Aside from this inborn curiosity, the hunchback took a great interest in robbers and crimes of all varieties. As he strutted around the table he was muttering the words "released on parole" and "penitentiary" to himself. But although he questioned insistently, he was unable to find anything, as nobody would dare to talk about Marvin Macy before Miss Amelia in the café.

"The letter did not say very much," said Henry Macy. "He did not say where he was going."

"Humph!" said Amelia, and her face was still hardened and very dark. "He will never set his split hoof on my premises."

She pushed back her chair from the table, and made ready to close the café. Thinking about Marvin Macy may have set her to brooding, for she hauled the cash register back to the kitchen and put it in a private place. Henry Macy went off down the dark road. But Henry Ford Crimp and Merlie Ryan lingered for a time on the front porch. Later Merlie Ryan was to make certain claims, to swear that on that night he had a vision of what was to come. But the town paid no attention, for that was just the sort of thing that Merlie Ryan would claim. Miss Amelia and Cousin Lymon talked for a time in the parlor. And when at last the hunchback thought that he could sleep she arranged the mosquito netting over his bed and waited until he had finished with his prayers. Then she put on her long nightgown, smoked two pipes, and only after a long time went to sleep.

That autumn was a happy time. The crops around the countryside were good, and over at the Forks Falls market the price of tobacco held firm that year. After the long hot summer the first cool days had a clean bright sweetness. Goldenrod grew along the dusty roads, and the sugar cane was ripe and purple. The bus came each day from Cheehaw to carry off a few of the younger children to the consolidated school to get an education. Boys hunted foxes in the pinewoods, winter quilts were aired out on the wash lines, and sweet potatoes bedded in the ground with straw against the colder months to come. In the evening, delicate shreds of smoke rose from the chimneys, and the moon was round and orange in the autumn sky. There is no stillness like the quiet of the first cold nights in the fall. Sometimes, late in the night when there was no wind, there could be heard in the town the thin wild whistle of the train that goes through Society City on its way far off to the North.

For Miss Amelia Evans this was a time of great activity. She was at work from dawn until sundown. She made a new and bigger condenser for her still, and in one week ran off enough liquor to souse the whole county. Her old mule was dizzy from grinding so much sorghum, and she scalded her Mason jars and put away pear preserves. She was looking forward greatly to the first frost, because she had traded for three tremendous hogs, and intended to make much barbecue, chitterlins, and sausage.

During these weeks there was a quality about Miss Amelia that many people noticed. She laughed often, with a deep ringing laugh, and her whistling had a sassy, tuneful trickery. She was forever trying out her strength, lifting up heavy objects, or poking her tough biceps with her finger. One day she sat down to her typewriter and wrote a story—a story in which there were foreigners, trap doors, and millions of dollars. Cousin Lymon was with her always, traipsing along behind her coat-tails, and when she watched him her face had a bright, soft look, and when she spoke his name there lingered in her voice the undertone of love.

The first cold spell came at last. When Miss Amelia awoke one morning there were frost flowers on the windowpanes, and rime had silvered the patches of grass in the yard. Miss Amelia built a roaring fire in the kitchen stove, then went out of doors to judge the day. The air was cold and sharp, the sky pale green and cloudless. Very shortly people began to come in from the country to find out what Miss Amelia thought of the weather; she decided to kill the biggest hog, and word got round the countryside. The hog was slaughtered and a low oak fire started in the barbecue pit. There was the warm smell of pig blood and smoke in the back yard, the stamp of footsteps, the ring of voices in the winter air. Miss Amelia walked around giving orders and soon most of the work was done.

She had some particular business to do in Cheehaw that day, so after making sure that all was going well, she cranked up her car and got ready to leave. She asked Cousin Lymon to come with her, in fact, she asked him seven times, but he was loath to leave the commotion and wanted to remain. This seemed to trouble Miss Amelia, as she always liked to have him near to her, and was prone to be terribly homesick when she had to go any distance away. But after asking him seven times, she did not urge him any further. Before leaving she found a stick and drew a heavy line all around the barbecue pit, about two feet back from the edge, and told him not to trespass beyond that boundary. She left after dinner and intended to be back before dark.

Now, it is not so rare to have a truck or an automobile pass along the road and through the town on the way from Cheehaw to somewhere else. Every year the tax collector comes to argue with rich people such as Miss Amelia. And if somebody in the town, such as Merlie Ryan, takes a notion that he can connive to get a car on credit, or to pay down three dollars and have a fine electric icebox such as they advertise in the store windows of Cheehaw, then a city man will come out asking meddlesome questions, finding out all his troubles, and ruining his chances of buying anything on the installment plan. Sometimes, especially since they are working on the Forks Falls highway, the cars hauling the chain gang come through the town. And frequently people in automobiles get lost and stop to inquire how they can find the right road again. So, late that afternoon it was nothing unusual to have a truck pass the mill and stop in the middle of the road near the café of Miss Amelia. A man jumped down from the back of the truck, and the truck went on its way.

The man stood in the middle of the road and looked about him. He was a tall man, with brown curly hair, and slow-moving, deep-blue eyes. His lips were red and he smiled the lazy, half-mouthed smile of the braggart. The man wore a red shirt, and a wide belt of tooled leather; he carried a tin suitcase and a guitar. The first person in the town to see this newcomer was Cousin Lymon, who had heard the shifting gears and come around to investigate. The hunchback stuck his head around the corner of the porch, but did not step out altogether into full view. He and the man stared at each other, and it was not the look of two strangers meeting for the first time and swiftly summing up each other. It was a peculiar stare they exchanged between them, like the look of two criminals who recognize each other. Then the man in the red shirt shrugged his left shoulder and turned away. The face of the hunchback was very pale as he watched the man go down the road, and after a few moments he began to follow along carefully, keeping many paces away.

It was immediately known throughout the town that Marvin Macy had come back again. First, he went to the mill, propped his elbows lazily on a window sill and looked inside. He liked to watch others hard at work, as do all born loafers. The mill was thrown into a sort of numb confusion. The dyers left the hot vats, the spinners and weavers forgot about their machines, and even Stumpy MacPhail, who was foreman, did not know exactly what to do. Marvin Macy still smiled his wet half-mouthed smiles, and when he saw his brother, his bragging expression did not change. After looking over the mill Marvin Macy went down the road to the house where he had been raised, and left his suitcase and guitar on the front porch. Then he walked around the millpond, looked over the church, the three stores, and the rest of the town. The hunchback trudged along quietly at some distance behind him, his hands in his pockets, and his little face still very pale.

It had grown late. The red winter sun was setting, and to the west the sky was deep gold and crimson. Ragged chimney swifts flew to their nests; lamps were lighted. Now and then there was the smell of smoke, and the warm rich odor of the barbecue slowly cooking in the pit behind the café. After making the rounds of the town Marvin Macy stopped before Miss Amelia's premises and read the sign above the porch. Then, not hesitating to trespass, he walked through the side yard. The mill whistle blew a thin, lonesome blast, and the day's shift was done. Soon there were others in Miss Amelia's back yard beside Marvin Macy—Henry Ford Crimp, Merlie Ryan, Stumpy MacPhail, and any number of children and people who stood around the edges of the property and looked on. Very little was said. Marvin Macy stood by himself on one side of the pit, and the rest of the people clustered together on the other side. Cousin Lymon stood somewhat apart from everyone, and he did not take his eyes from the face of Marvin Macy.

"Did you have a good time in the penitentiary?" asked Merlie Ryan, with a silly giggle.

Marvin Macy did not answer. He took from his hip pocket a large knife, opened it slowly, and honed the blade on the seat of his pants. Merlie Ryan grew suddenly very quiet and went to stand directly behind the broad back of Stumpy MacPhail.

Miss Amelia did not come home until almost dark. They heard the rattle of her automobile while she was still a long distance away, then the slam of the door and a bumping noise as though she were hauling something up the front steps of her premises. The sun had already set, and in the air there was the blue smoky glow of early winter evenings. Miss Amelia came down the back steps slowly, and the group in her yard waited very quietly. Few people in this world could stand up to Miss Amelia, and against Marvin Macy she had this special and bitter hate. Everyone waited to see her burst into a terrible holler, snatch up some dangerous object, and chase him altogether out of town. At first she did not see Marvin Macy, and her face had the relieved and dreamy expression that was natural to her when she reached home after having gone some distance away.

Miss Amelia must have seen Marvin Macy and Cousin Lymon at the same instant. She looked from one to the other, but it was not the wastrel from the penitentiary on whom she finally fixed her gaze of sick amazement. She, and everyone else, was looking at Cousin Lymon, and he was a sight to see.

The hunchback stood at the end of the pit, his pale face lighted by the soft glow from the smoldering oak fire. Cousin Lymon had a very peculiar accomplishment, which he used whenever he wished to ingratiate himself with someone. He would stand very still, and with just a little concentration, he could wiggle his large pale ears with marvelous quickness and ease. This trick he always used when he wanted to get something special out of Miss Amelia, and to her it was irresistible. Now as he stood there the hunchback's ears were wiggling furiously on his head, but it was not Miss Amelia at whom he was looking this time. The hunchback was smiling at Marvin Macy with an entreaty that was near to desperation. At first Marvin Macy paid no attention to him, and when he did finally glance at the hunchback it was without any appreciation whatsoever.

"What ails this Brokeback?" he asked with a rough jerk of his thumb.

No one answered. And Cousin Lymon, seeing that his accomplishment was getting him nowhere, added new efforts of persuasion. He fluttered his eyelids, so that they were like pale, trapped moths in his sockets. He scraped his feet around on the ground, waved his hands about, and finally began doing a little trotlike dance. In the last gloomy light of the winter afternoon he resembled the child of a swamphaunt.

Marvin Macy, alone of all the people in the yard, was unimpressed.

"Is the runt throwing a fit?" he asked, and when no one answered he stepped forward and gave Cousin Lymon a cuff on the side of the head. The hunchback staggered, then fell back on the ground. He sat where he had fallen, still looking up at Marvin Macy, and with great effort his ears managed one last forlorn little flap.

Now everyone turned to Miss Amelia to see what she would do. In all these years no one had so much as touched a hair of Cousin Lymon's head, although many had had the itch to do so. If anyone even spoke crossly to the hunchback, Miss Amelia would cut off this rash mortal's credit and find ways of making things go hard for him a long time afterward. So now if Miss Amelia had split open Marvin Macy's head with the ax on the back porch no one would have been surprised. But she did nothing of the kind.

There were times when Miss Amelia seemed to go into a sort of trance. And the cause of these trances was usually known and understood. For Miss Amelia was a fine doctor, and did not grind up swamp roots and other untried ingredients and give them to the first patient who came along; whenever she invented a new medicine she always tried it out first on herself. She would swallow an enormous dose and spend the following day walking thoughtfully back and forth from the café to the brick privy. Often, when there was a sudden keen gripe, she would stand quite still, her queer eyes staring down at the ground and her fists clenched; she was trying to decide which organ was being worked upon, and what misery the new medicine might be most likely to cure. And now as she watched the hunchback and Marvin Macy, her face wore this same expression, tense with reckoning some inward pain, although she had taken no new medicine that day.

"That will learn you, Brokeback," said Marvin Macy.

Henry Macy pushed back his limp whitish hair from his forehead and coughed nervously. Stumpy MacPhail and Merlie Ryan shuffled their feet, and the children and black people on the outskirts of the property made not a sound. Marvin Macy folded the knife he had been honing, and after looking about him fearlessly he swaggered out of the yard. The embers in the pit were turning to grey feather ashes and it was now quite dark.

That was the way Marvin Macy came back from the penitentiary. Not a living soul in all the town was glad to see him. Even Mrs. Mary Hale, who was a good woman and had raised him with love and care— at the first sight of him even this old foster mother dropped the skillet she was holding and burst into tears. But nothing could faze that Marvin Macy. He sat on the back steps of the Hale house, lazily picking his guitar, and when the supper was ready, he pushed the children of the household out of the way and served himself a big meal, although there had been barely enough hoecakes and white meat to go round. After eating he settled himself in the best and warmest sleeping place in the front room and was untroubled by dreams.

Miss Amelia did not open the café that night. She locked the doors and all the windows very carefully, nothing was seen of her and Cousin Lymon, and a lamp burned in her room all the night long.

Marvin Macy brought with him bad fortune, right from the first, as could be expected. The next day the weather turned suddenly, and it became hot. Even in the early morning there was a sticky sultriness in the atmosphere, the wind carried the rotten smell of the swamp, and delicate shrill mosquitoes webbed the green millpond. It was unseasonable, worse than August, and much damage was done. For nearly everyone in the county who owned a hog had copied Miss Amelia and slaughtered the day before. And what sausage could keep in such weather as this? After a few days there was everywhere the smell of slowly spoiling meat, and an atmosphere of dreary waste. Worse yet, a family reunion near the Forks Falls highway ate pork roast and died, every one of them. It was plain that their hog had been infected—and who could tell whether the rest of the meat was safe or not? People were torn between the longing for the good taste of pork, and the fear of death. It was a time of waste and confusion.

The cause of all this, Marvin Macy, had no shame in him. He was seen everywhere. During work hours he loafed about the mill, looking in at the windows, and on Sundays he dressed in his red shirt and paraded up and down the road with his guitar. He was still handsome—with his brown hair, his red lips, and his broad strong shoulders; but the evil in him was now too famous for his good looks to get him anywhere. And this evil was not measured only by the actual sins he had committed. True, he had robbed those filling stations. And before that he had ruined the tenderest girls in the county, and laughed about it. Any number of wicked things could be listed against him, but quite apart from these crimes there was about him a secret meanness that clung to him almost like a smell. Another thing—he never sweated, not even in August, and that surely is a sign worth pondering over.

Now it seemed to the town that he was more dangerous than he had ever been before, as in the penitentiary in Atlanta he must have learned the method of laying charms. Otherwise how could his effect on Cousin Lymon be explained? For since first setting eyes on Marvin Macy the hunchback was possessed by an unnatural spirit. Every minute he wanted to be following along behind this jailbird, and he was full of silly schemes to attract attention to himself. Still Marvin Macy either treated him hatefully or failed to notice him at all. Sometimes the hunchback would give up, perch himself on the banister of the front porch much as a sick bird huddles on a telephone wire, and grieve publicly.

"But why?" Miss Amelia would ask, staring at him with her crossed, gray eyes, and her fists closed tight.

"Oh, Marvin Macy," groaned the hunchback, and the sound of the name was enough to upset the rhythm of his sobs so that he hiccuped. "He has been to Atlanta."

Miss Amelia would shake her head and her face was dark and hardened. To begin with she had no patience with any traveling; those who had made the trip to Atlanta or traveled fifty miles from home to see the ocean—those restless people she despised. "Going to Atlanta does no credit to him."

"He has been to the penitentiary," said the hunchback, miserable with longing.

How are you going to argue against such envies as these? In her perplexity Miss Amelia did not herself sound any too sure of what she was saying. "Been to the penitentiary, Cousin Lymon? Why, a trip like that is no travel to brag about."

During these weeks Miss Amelia was closely watched by everyone. She went about absent-mindedly, her face remote as though she had lapsed into one of her gripe trances. For some reason, after the day of Marvin Macy's arrival, she put aside her overalls and wore always the red dress she had before this time reserved for Sundays, funerals, and sessions of the court. Then as the weeks passed she began to take some steps to clear up the situation. But her efforts were hard to understand. If it hurt her to see Cousin Lymon follow Marvin Macy about the town, why did she not make the issues clear once and for all, and tell the hunchback that if he had dealings with Marvin Macy she would turn him off the premises? That would have been simple, and Cousin Lymon would have had to submit to her, or else face the sorry business of finding himself loose in the world. But Miss Amelia seemed to have lost her will; for the first time in her life she hesitated as to just what course to pursue. And, like most people in such a position of uncertainty, she did the worst thing possible—she began following several courses at once, all of them contrary to each other.

The café was opened every night as usual, and, strangely enough, when Marvin Macy came swaggering through the door, with the hunchback at his heels, she did not turn him out. She even gave him free drinks and smiled at him in a wild, crooked way. At the same time she set a terrible trap for him out in the swamp that surely would have killed him if he had got caught. She let Cousin Lymon invite him to Sunday dinner, and then tried to trip him up as he went down the steps. She began a great campaign of pleasure for Cousin Lymon—making exhausting trips to various spectacles being held in distant places, driving the automobile thirty miles to a Chautauqua, taking him to Forks Falls to watch a parade. All in all it was a distracting time for Miss Amelia. In the opinion of most people she was well on her way in the climb up fools' hill, and everyone waited to see how it would all turn out.

The weather turned cold again, the winter was upon the town, and night came before the last shift in the mill was done. Children kept on all their garments when they slept, and women raised the backs of their skirts to toast themselves dreamily at the fire. After it rained, the mud in the road made hard frozen ruts, there were faint flickers of lamplight from the windows of the houses, the peach trees were scrawny and bare. In the dark, silent nights of winter-time the café was the warm center point of the town, the lights shining so brightly that they could be seen a quarter of a mile away. The great iron stove at the back of the room roared, crackled, and turned red. Miss Amelia had made red curtains for the windows, and from a salesman who passed through the town she bought a great bunch of paper roses that looked very real.

But it was not only the warmth, the decorations, and the brightness, that made the café what it was. There is a deeper reason why the café was so precious to this town. And this deeper reason has to do with a certain pride that had not hitherto been known in these parts.

To understand this new pride the cheapness of human life must be kept in mind. There were always plenty of people clustered around a mill—but it was seldom that every family had enough meal, garments, and fat back to go the rounds. Life could become one long dim scramble just to get the things needed to keep alive. And the confusing point is this: All useful things have a price, and are bought only with money, as that is the way the world is run. You know without having to reason about it the price of a bale of cotton, or a quart of molasses. But no value has been put on human life; it is given to us free and taken without being paid for. What is it worth? If you look around, at times the value may seem to be little or nothing at all. Often after you have sweated and tried and things are not better for you, there comes a feeling deep down in the soul that you are not worth much.

But the new pride that the café brought to this town had an effect on almost everyone, even the children. For in order to come to the café you did not have to buy the dinner, or a portion of the liquor. There were cold bottled drinks for a nickel. And if you could not even afford that, Miss Amelia had a drink called Cherry Juice which sold for a penny a glass, and was pink-colored and very sweet. Almost everyone, with the exception of Reverend T. M. Willin, came to the café at least once during the week. Children love to sleep in houses other than their own, and to eat at a neighbor's table; on such occasions they behave themselves decently and are proud. The people in the town were likewise proud when sitting at the tables in the café. They washed before coming to Miss Amelia's, and scraped their feet very politely on the threshold as they entered the café. There, for a few hours at least, the deep bitter knowing that you are not worth much in this world could be laid low.

The café was a special benefit to bachelors, unfortunate people, and consumptives. And here it may be mentioned that there was some reason to suspect that Cousin Lymon was consumptive. The brightness of his gray eyes, his insistence, his talkativeness, and his cough—these were all signs. Besides, there is generally supposed to be some connection between a hunched spine and consumption. But whenever this subject had been mentioned to Miss Amelia she had become furious; she denied these symptoms with bitter vehemence, but on the sly she treated Cousin Lymon with hot chest platters, Kroup Kure, and such. Now this winter the hunchback's cough was worse, and sometimes even on cold days he would break out in a heavy sweat. But this did not prevent him from following along after Marvin Macy.

Early every morning he left the premises and went to the back door of Mrs. Hale's house, and waited and waited—as Marvin Macy was a lazy sleeper. He would stand there and call out softly. His voice was just like the voices of children who squat patiently over those tiny little holes in the ground where doodlebugs are thought to live, poking the hole with a broom straw, and calling plaintively: "Doodlebug, Doodlebug—fly away home. Mrs. Doodlebug, Mrs. Doodlebug. Come out, come out. Your house is on fire and all your children are burning up." In just such a voice—at once sad, luring, and resigned—would the hunchback call Marvin Macy's name each morning. Then when Marvin Macy came out for the day, he would trail him about the town, and sometimes they would be gone for hours together out in the swamp.

And Miss Amelia continued to do the worst thing possible: that is, to try to follow several courses at once. When Cousin Lymon left the house she did not call him back, but only stood in the middle of the road and watched lonesomely until he was out of sight. Nearly every day Marvin Macy turned up with Cousin Lymon at dinnertime, and ate at her table. Miss Amelia opened the pear preserves, and the table was well-set with ham or chicken, great bowls of hominy grits, and winter peas. It is true that on one occasion Miss Amelia tried to poison Marvin Macy—but there was a mistake, the plates were confused, and it was she herself who got the poisoned dish. This she quickly realized by the slight bitterness of the food, and that day she ate no dinner. She sat tilted back in her chair, feeling her muscle, and looking at Marvin Macy.

Every night Marvin Macy came to the café and settled himself at the best and largest table, the one in the center of the room. Cousin Lymon brought him liquor, for which he did not pay a cent. Marvin Macy brushed the hunchback aside as if he were a swamp mosquito, and not only did he show no gratitude for these favors, but if the hunchback got in his way he would cuff him with the back of his hand, or say: "Out of my way, Brokeback—I'll snatch you bald-headed." When this happened Miss Amelia would come out from behind her counter and approach Marvin Macy very slowly, her fists clenched, her peculiar red dress hanging awkwardly around her bony knees. Marvin Macy would also clench his fists and they would walk slowly and meaningfully around each other. But, although everyone watched breathlessly, nothing ever came of it. The time for the fight was not yet ready.

There is one particular reason why this winter is remembered and still talked about. A great thing happened. People woke up on the second of January and found the whole world about them altogether changed. Little ignorant children looked out of the windows, and they were so puzzled that they began to cry. Old people harked back and could remember nothing in these parts to equal the phenomenon. For in the night it had snowed. In the dark hours after midnight the dim flakes started falling softly on the town. By dawn the ground was covered, and the strange snow banked the ruby windows of the church, and whitened the roofs of the houses. The snow gave the town a drawn, bleak look. The two-room houses near the mill were dirty, crooked, and seemed about to collapse, and somehow everything was dark and shrunken. But the snow itself—there was a beauty about it few people around here had ever known before. The snow was not white, as Northerners had pictured it to be; in the snow there were soft colors of blue and silver; the sky was a gentle shining gray. And the dreamy quietness of falling snow—when had the town been so silent?

People reacted to the snowfall in various ways. Miss Amelia, on looking out of her window, thoughtfully wiggled the toes of her bare foot, gathered close to her neck the collar of her nightgown. She stood there for some time, then commenced to draw the shutters and lock every window on the premises. She closed the place completely, lighted the lamps, and sat solemnly over her bowl of grits. The reason for this was not that Miss Amelia feared the snowfall. It was simply that she was unable to form an immediate opinion of this new event, and unless she knew exactly and definitely what she thought of the matter (which was nearly always the case) she preferred to ignore it. Snow had never fallen in this county in her lifetime, and she had never thought about it one way or the other. But if she admitted this snowfall she would have to come to some decision, and in those days there was enough distraction in her life as it was already. So she poked about the gloomy, lamp-lighted house and pretended that nothing had happened. Cousin Lymon, on the contrary, chased around in the wildest excitement, and when Miss Amelia turned her back to dish him some breakfast he slipped out of the door.

Marvin Macy laid claim to the snowfall. He said that he knew snow, had seen it in Atlanta, and from the way he walked about the town that day it was as though he owned every flake. He sneered at the little children who crept timidly out of the houses and scooped up handfuls of snow to taste. Reverend Willin hurried down the road with a furious face, as he was thinking deeply and trying to weave the snow into his Sunday sermon. Most people were humble and glad about this marvel; they spoke in hushed voices and said "thank you" and "please" more than was necessary. A few weak characters, of course, were demoralized and got drunk—but they were not numerous. To everyone this was an occasion and many counted their money and planned to go to the café that night.

Cousin Lymon followed Marvin Macy about all day, seconding his claim to the snow. He marveled that snow did not fall as does rain, and stared up at the dreamy, gently falling flakes until he stumbled from dizziness. And the pride he took on himself, basking in the glory of Marvin Macy—it was such that many people could not resist calling out to him: "'Oho,' said the fly on the chariot wheel. 'What a dust we do raise.'"

Miss Amelia did not intend to serve dinner. But when, at six o'clock, there was the sound of footsteps on the porch she opened the front door cautiously. It was Henry Ford Crimp, and though there was no food, she let him sit at a table and served him a drink. Others came. The evening was blue, bitter, and though the snow fell no longer there was a wind from the pine trees that swept up delicate flurries from the ground. Cousin Lymon did not come until after dark, with him Marvin Macy, and he carried his tin suitcase and his guitar.

"So you mean to travel?" said Miss Amelia quickly.

Marvin Macy warmed himself at the stove. Then he settled down at his table and carefully sharpened a little stick. He picked his teeth, frequently taking the stick out of his mouth to look at the end and wipe it on the sleeve of his coat. He did not bother to answer.

The hunchback looked at Miss Amelia, who was behind the counter. His face was not in the least beseeching; he seemed quite sure of himself. He folded his hands behind his back and perked up his ears confidently. His clothes were soggy wet. "Marvin Macy is going to visit a spell with us," he said.

Miss Amelia made no protest. She only came out from behind the counter and hovered over the stove, as though the news had made her suddenly cold. She did not warm her backside modestly, lifting her skirt only an inch or so, as do most women when in public. There was not a grain of modesty about Miss Amelia, and she frequently seemed to forget altogether that there were men in the room. Now as she stood warming herself, her red dress was pulled up quite high in the back so that a piece of her strong, hairy thigh could be seen by anyone who cared to look at it. Her head was turned to one side, and she had begun talking with herself, nodding and wrinkling her forehead, and there was the tone of accusation and reproach in her voice although the words were not plain. Meanwhile, the hunchback and Marvin Macy had gone upstairs—up to the parlor with the pampas grass and the two sewing machines, to the private rooms where Miss Amelia had lived the whole of her life. Down in the café you could hear them bumping around, unpacking Marvin Macy, and getting him settled.

That is the way Marvin Macy crowded into Miss Amelia's home. At first Cousin Lymon, who had given Marvin Macy his own room, slept on the sofa in the parlor. But the snowfall had a bad effect on him; he caught a cold that turned into a winter quinsy, so Miss Amelia gave up her bed to him. The sofa in the parlor was much too short for her, her feet lapped over the edges, and often she rolled off onto the floor. Perhaps it was this lack of sleep that clouded her wits; everything she tried to do against Marvin Macy rebounded on herself. She got caught in her own tricks, and found herself in many pitiful positions. But still she did not put Marvin Macy off the premises, as she was afraid that she would be left alone. Once you have lived with another, it is a great torture to have to live alone. The silence of a firelit room when suddenly the clock stops ticking, the nervous shadows in an empty house—it is better to take in your mortal enemy than face the terror of living alone.

The snow did not last. The sun came out and within two days the town was just as it had always been before. Miss Amelia did not open her house until every flake had melted. Then she had a big house cleaning and aired everything out in the sun. But before that, the very first thing she did on going out again into her yard, was to tie a rope to the largest branch of the chinaberry tree. At the end of the rope she tied a crocus sack tightly stuffed with sand. This was the punching bag she made for herself and from that day on she would box with it out in her yard every morning. Already she was a fine fighter—a little heavy on her feet, but knowing all manner of mean holds and squeezes to make up for this.

Miss Amelia, as has been mentioned, measured six feet two inches in height. Marvin Macy was one inch shorter. In weight they were about even—both of them weighing close to a hundred and sixty pounds. Marvin Macy had the advantage in slyness of movement, and in toughness of chest. In fact from the outward point of view the odds were altogether in his favor. Yet almost everybody in the town was betting on Miss Amelia; scarcely a person would put up money on Marvin Macy. The town remembered the great fight between Miss Amelia and a Fork Falls lawyer who had tried to cheat her. He had been a huge strapping fellow, but he was left three-quarters dead when she had finished with him. And it was not only her talent as a boxer that had impressed everyone—she could demoralize her enemy by making terrifying faces and fierce noises, so that even the spectators were sometimes cowed. She was brave, she practiced faithfully with her punching bag, and in this case she was clearly in the right. So people had confidence in her, and they waited. Of course there was no set date for this fight. There were just the signs that were too plain to be overlooked.

During these times the hunchback strutted around with a pleased little pinched-up face. In many delicate and clever ways he stirred up trouble between them. He was constantly plucking at Marvin Macy's trouser leg to draw attention to himself. Sometimes he followed in Miss Amelia's footsteps—but these days it was only in order to imitate her awkward long-legged walk; he crossed his eyes and aped her gestures in a way that made her appear to be a freak. There was something so terrible about this that even the silliest customers of the café, such as Merlie Ryan, did not laugh. Only Marvin Macy drew up the left corner of his mouth and chuckled. Miss Amelia, when this happened, would be divided between two emotions. She would look at the hunchback with a lost, dismal reproach—then turn toward Marvin Macy with her teeth clamped.

"Bust a gut!" she would say bitterly.

And Marvin Macy, most likely, would pick up the guitar from the floor beside his chair. His voice was wet and slimy, as he always had too much spit in his mouth. And the tunes he sang glided slowly from his throat like eels. His strong fingers picked the strings with dainty skill, and everything he sang both lured and exasperated. This was usually more than Miss Amelia could stand.

"Bust a gut!" she would repeat, in a shout.

But always Marvin Macy had the answer ready for her. He would cover the strings to silence the quivering leftover tones, and reply with slow, sure insolence.

"Everything you holler at me bounces back on yourself. Yah! Yah!"

Miss Amelia would have to stand there helpless, as no one has ever invented a way out of this trap. She could not shout out abuse that would bounce back on herself. He had the best of her, there was nothing she could do.

So things went on like this. What happened between the three of them during the nights in the rooms upstairs nobody knows. But the café became more and more crowded every night. A new table had to be brought in. Even the Hermit, the crazy man named Rainer Smith, who took to the swamps years ago, heard something of the situation and came one night to look in at the window and brood over the gathering in the bright café. And the climax each evening was the time when Miss Amelia and Marvin Macy doubled their fists, squared up and glared at each other. Usually this did not happen after any especial argument, but it seemed to come about mysteriously, by means of some instinct on the part of both of them. At these times the café would become so quiet that you could hear the bouquet of paper roses rustling in the draft. And each night they held this fighting stance a little longer than the night before.

The fight took place on Ground Hog Day, which is the second of February. The weather was favorable, being neither rainy nor sunny, and with a neutral temperature. There were several signs that this was the appointed day, and by ten o'clock the news spread all over the county. Early in the morning Miss Amelia went out and cut down her punching bag. Marvin Macy sat on the back step with a tin can of hog fat between his knees and carefully greased his arms and his legs. A hawk with a bloody breast flew over the town and circled twice around the property of Miss Amelia. The tables in the café were moved out to the back porch, so that the whole big room was cleared for the fight. There was every sign. Both Miss Amelia and Marvin Macy ate four helpings of half-raw roast for dinner, and then lay down in the afternoon to store up strength. Marvin Macy rested in the big room upstairs, while Miss Amelia stretched herself out on the bench in her office. It was plain from her white stiff face what a torment it was for her to be lying still and doing nothing, but she lay there quiet as a corpse with her eyes closed and her hands crossed on her chest.

Cousin Lymon had a restless day, and his little face was drawn and tightened with excitement. He put himself up a lunch, and set out to find the ground hog—within an hour he returned, the lunch eaten, and said that the ground hog had seen his shadow and there was to be bad weather ahead. Then, as Miss Amelia and Marvin Macy were both resting to gather strength, and he was left to himself, it occurred to him that he might as well paint the front porch. The house had not been painted for years—in fact, God knows if it had ever been painted at all. Cousin Lymon scrambled around, and soon he had painted half the floor of the porch a gay bright green. It was a loblolly job, and he smeared himself all over. Typically enough he did not even finish the floor, but changed over to the walls, painting as high as he could reach and then standing on a crate to get up a foot higher. When the paint ran out, the right side of the floor was bright green and there was a jagged portion of wall that had been painted. Cousin Lymon left it at that.

There was something childish about his satisfaction with his painting. And in this respect a curious fact should be mentioned. No one in the town, not even Miss Amelia, had any idea how old the hunchback was. Some maintained that when he came to town he was about twelve years old, still a child—others were certain that he was well past forty. His eyes were blue and steady as a child's but there were lavender crêpy shadows beneath these blue eyes that hinted of age. It was impossible to guess his age by his hunched queer body. And even his teeth gave no clue—they were all still in his head (two were broken from cracking a pecan), but he had stained them with so much sweet snuff that it was impossible to decide whether they were old teeth or young teeth. When questioned directly about his age the hunchback professed to know absolutely nothing—he had no idea how long he had been on the earth, whether for ten years or a hundred! So his age remained a puzzle.

Cousin Lymon finished his painting at five-thirty o'clock in the afternoon. The day had turned colder and there was a wet taste in the air. The wind came up from the pinewoods, rattling windows, blowing an old newspaper down the road until at last it caught upon a thorn tree. People began to come in from the country; packed automobiles that bristled with the poked-out heads of children, wagons drawn by old mules who seemed to smile in a weary, sour way and plodded along with their tired eyes half-closed. Three young boys came from Society City. All three of them wore yellow rayon shirts and caps put on backward—they were as much alike as triplets, and could always be seen at cock fights and camp meetings. At six o'clock the mill whistle sounded the end of the day's shift and the crowd was complete. Naturally, among the newcomers there were some riffraff, unknown characters, and so forth—but even so the gathering was quiet. A hush was on the town and the faces of people were strange in the fading light. Darkness hovered softly; for a moment the sky was a pale clear yellow against which the gables of the church stood out in dark and bare outlines, then the sky died slowly and the darkness gathered into night.

Seven is a popular number, and especially it was a favorite with Miss Amelia. Seven swallows of water for hiccups, seven runs around the millpond for cricks in the neck, seven doses of Amelia Miracle Mover as a worm cure—her treatment nearly always hinged on this number. It is a number of mingled possibilities, and all who love mystery and charms set store by it. So the fight was to take place at seven o'clock. This was known to everyone, not by announcement or words, but understood in the unquestioning way that rain is understood, or an evil odor from the swamp. So before seven o'clock everyone gathered gravely around the property of Miss Amelia. The cleverest got into the café itself and stood lining the walls of the room. Others crowded onto the front porch, or took a stand in the yard.

Miss Amelia and Marvin Macy had not yet shown themselves. Miss Amelia, after resting all afternoon on the office bench, had gone upstairs. On the other hand Cousin Lymon was at your elbow every minute, threading his way through the crowd, snapping his fingers nervously, and batting his eyes. At one minute to seven o'clock he squirmed his way into the café and climbed up on the counter. All was very quiet.

It must have been arranged in some manner beforehand. For just at the stroke of seven Miss Amelia showed herself at the head of the stairs. At the same instant Marvin Macy appeared in front of the café and the crowd made way for him silently. They walked toward each other with no haste, their fists already gripped, and their eyes like the eyes of dreamers. Miss Amelia had changed her red dress for her old overalls, and they were rolled up to the knees. She was barefooted and she had an iron strengthband around her right wrist. Marvin Macy had also rolled his trouser legs—he was naked to the waist and heavily greased; he wore the heavy shoes that had been issued him when he left the penitentiary. Stump MacPhail stepped forward from the crowd and slapped their hip pockets with the palm of his right hand to make sure there would be no sudden knives. Then they were alone in the cleared center of the bright café.

There was no signal, but they both struck out simultaneously. Both blows landed on the chin, so that the heads of Miss Amelia and Marvin Macy bobbed back and they were left a little groggy. For a few seconds after the first blows they merely shuffled their feet around on the bare floor, experimenting with various positions, and making mock fists. Then, like wildcats, they were suddenly on each other. There was the sound of knocks, panting, and thumpings on the floor. They were so fast that it was hard to take in what was going on—but once Miss Amelia was hurled backward so that she staggered and almost fell, and another time Marvin Macy caught a knock on the shoulder that spun him around like a top. So the fight went on in this wild violent way with no sign of weakening on either side.

During a struggle like this, when the enemies are as quick and strong as these two, it is worth-while to turn from the confusion of the fight itself and observe the spectators. The people had flattened back as close as possible against the walls. Stumpy MacPhail was in a corner, crouched over and with his fists tight in sympathy, making strange noises. Poor Merlie Ryan had his mouth so wide open that a fly buzzed into it, and was swallowed before Merlie realized what had happened. And Cousin Lymon—he was worth watching. The hunchback still stood on the counter, so that he was raised up above everyone else in the café. He had his hands on his hips, his big head thrust forward, and his little legs bent so that the knees jutted outward. The excitement had made him break out in a rash, and his pale mouth shivered.

Perhaps it was half an hour before the course of the fight shifted. Hundreds of blows had been exchanged, and there was still a deadlock. Then suddenly Marvin Macy managed to catch hold of Miss Amelia's left arm and pinion it behind her back. She struggled and got a grasp around his waist; the real fight was now begun. Wrestling is the natural way of fighting in this county—as boxing is too quick and requires much thinking and concentration. And now that Miss Amelia and Marvin were locked in a hold together the crowd came out of its daze and pressed in closer. For a while the fighters grappled muscle to muscle, their hipbones braced against each other. Backward and forward, from side to side, they swayed in this way. Marvin Macy still had not sweated, but Miss Amelia's overalls were drenched and so much sweat had trickled down her legs that she left wet footprints on the floor. Now the test had come, and in these moments of terrible effort, it was Miss Amelia who was the stronger. Marvin Macy was greased and slippery, tricky to grasp, but she was stronger. Gradually she bent him over backward, and inch by inch she forced him to the floor. It was a terrible thing to watch and their deep hoarse breaths were the only sound in the café. At last she had him down, and straddled; her strong big hands were on his throat.

But at that instant, just as the fight was won, a cry sounded in the café that caused a shrill bright shiver to run down the spine. And what took place has been a mystery ever since. The whole town was there to testify what happened, but there were those who doubted their own eyesight. For the counter on which Cousin Lymon stood was at least twelve feet from the fighters in the center of the café. Yet at the instant Miss Amelia grasped the throat of Marvin Macy the hunchback sprang forward and sailed through the air as though he had grown hawk wings. He landed on the broad strong back of Miss Amelia and clutched at her neck with his clawed little fingers.

The rest is confusion. Miss Amelia was beaten before the crowd could come to their senses. Because of the hunchback the fight was won by Marvin Macy, and at the end Miss Amelia lay sprawled on the floor, her arms flung outward and motionless. Marvin Macy stood over her, his face somewhat popeyed, but smiling his old half-mouthed smile. And the hunchback, he had suddenly disappeared. Perhaps he was frightened about what he had done, or maybe he was so delighted that he wanted to glory with himself alone—at any rate he slipped out of the café and crawled under the back steps. Someone poured water on Miss Amelia, and after a time she got up slowly and dragged herself into her office. Through the open door the crowd could see her sitting at her desk, her head in the crook of her arm, and she was sobbing with the last of her grating, winded breath. Once she gathered her right fist together and knocked it three times on the top of her office desk, then her hand opened feebly and lay palm upward and still. Stumpy MacPhail stepped forward and closed the door.

The crowd was quiet, and one by one the people left the café. Mules were waked up and untied, automobiles cranked, and the three boys from Society City roamed off down the road on foot. This was not a fight to hash over and talk about afterward; people went home and pulled the covers up over their heads. The town was dark, except for the premises of Miss Amelia, but every room was lighted there the whole night long.

Marvin Macy and the hunchback must have left the town an hour or so before daylight. And before they went away this is what they did:

They unlocked the private cabinet of curios and took everything in it.

They broke the mechanical piano.

They carved terrible words on the café tables.

They found the watch that opened in the back to show a picture of a waterfall and took that also.

They poured a gallon of sorghum syrup all over the kitchen floor and smashed the jars of preserves.

They went out in the swamp and completely wrecked the still, ruining the big new condenser and the cooler, and setting fire to the shack itself.

They fixed a dish of Miss Amelia's favorite food, grits with sausage, seasoned it with enough poison to kill off the county, and placed this dish temptingly on the café counter.

They did everything ruinous they could think of without actually breaking into the office where Miss Amelia stayed the night. Then they went off together, the two of them.

That was how Miss Amelia was left alone in the town. The people would have helped her if they had known how, as people in this town will as often as not be kindly if they have a chance. Several housewives nosed around with brooms and offered to clear up the wreck. But Miss Amelia only looked at them with lost crossed eyes and shook her head. Stumpy MacPhail came in on the third day to buy a plug of Queenie tobacco, and Miss Amelia said the price was one dollar. Everything in the café had suddenly risen in price to be worth one dollar. And what sort of a café is that? Also, she changed very queerly as a doctor. In all the years before she had been much more popular than the Cheehaw doctor. She had never monkeyed with a patient's soul, taking away from him such real necessities as liquor, tobacco, and so forth. Once in a great while she might carefully warn a patient never to eat fried watermelon or some such dish it had never occurred to a person to want in the first place. Now all this wise doctoring was over. She told one-half of her patients that they were going to die outright, and to the remaining half she recommended cures so far-fetched and agonizing that no one in his right mind would consider them for a moment.

Miss Amelia let her hair grow ragged, and it was turning gray. Her face lengthened, and the great muscles of her body shrank until she was thin as old maids are thin when they go crazy. And those gray eyes—slowly day by day they were more crossed, and it was as though they sought each other out to exchange a little glance of grief and lonely recognition. She was not pleasant to listen to; her tongue had sharpened terribly.

When anyone mentioned the hunchback she would say only this: "Ho! if I could lay hand to him I would rip out his gizzard and throw it to the cat!" But it was not so much the words that were terrible, but the voice in which they were said. Her voice had lost its old vigor; there was none of the ring of vengeance it used to have when she would mention "that loom-fixer I was married to," or some other enemy. Her voice was broken, soft, and sad as the wheezy whine of the church pump-organ.

For three years she sat out on the front steps every night, alone and silent, looking down the road and waiting. But the hunchback never returned. There were rumors that Marvin Macy used him to climb into windows to steal, and other rumors that Marvin Macy had sold him into a side show. But both these reports were traced back to Merlie Ryan. Nothing true was ever heard of him. It was in the fourth year that Miss Amelia hired a Cheehaw carpenter and had him board up the premises, and there in those closed rooms she has remained ever since.

Yes, the town is dreary. On August afternoons the road is empty, white with dust, and the sky above is bright as glass. Nothing moves—there are no children's voices, only the hum of the mill. The peach trees seem to grow more crooked every summer, and the leaves are dull gray and of a sickly delicacy. The house of Miss Amelia leans so much to the right that it is now only a question of time when it will collapse completely, and people are careful not to walk around the yard. There is no good liquor to be bought in the town; the nearest still is eight miles away, and the liquor is such that those who drink it grow warts on their livers the size of goobers, and dream themselves into a dangerous inward world. There is absolutely nothing to do in the town. Walk around the millpond, stand kicking at a rotten stump, figure out what you can do with the old wagon wheel by the side of the road near the church. The soul rots with boredom. You might as well go down to the Forks Falls highway and listen to the chain gang.

The Twelve Mortal Men

The Forks Falls highway is three miles from the town, and it is here the chain gang has been working. The road is of macadam, and the county decided to patch up the rough places and widen it at a certain dangerous place. The gang is made up of twelve men, all wearing black and white striped prison suits, and chained at the ankles. There is a guard, with a gun, his eyes drawn to red slits by the glare. The gang works all the day long, arriving huddled in the prison cart soon after daybreak, and being driven off again in the gray August twilight. All day there is the sound of the picks striking into the clay earth, hard sunlight, the smell of sweat. And every day there is music. One dark voice will start a phrase, half-sung, and like a question. And after a moment another voice will join in, soon the whole gang will be singing. The voices are dark in the golden glare, the music intricately blended, both somber and joyful. The music will swell until at last it seems that the sound does not come from the twelve men on the gang, but from the earth itself, or the wide sky. It is music that causes the heart to broaden and the listener to grow cold with ecstasy and fright. Then slowly the music will sink down until at last there remains one lonely voice, then a great hoarse breath, the sun, the sound of the picks in the silence.

And what kind of gang is this that can make such music? Just twelve mortal men, seven of them black and five of them white boys from this county. Just twelve mortal men who are together.

Carson McCullers (1917-1967)

McCullers was born in Columbus, Georgia. Her novels include THE HEART IS A LONELY HUNTER (1940), REFLECTIONS IN A GOLDEN EYE (1941), THE MEMBER OF THE WEDDING (1946), and A CLOCK WITHOUT HANDS (1961). Her major short stories are collected in THE BALLAD OF THE SAD CAFÉ (1951). "The Ballad of the Sad Café" is taken from this latter volume.

Revelation

Flannery O'Connor

THE DOCTOR'S WAITING ROOM, which was very small, was almost full when the Turpins entered and Mrs. Turpin, who was very large, made it look even smaller by her presence. She stood looming at the head of the magazine table set in the center of it, a living demonstration that the room was inadequate and ridiculous. Her little bright black eyes took in all the patients as she sized up the seating situation. There was one vacant chair and a place on the sofa occupied by a blond child in a dirty blue romper who should have been told to move over and make room for the lady. He was five or six, but Mrs. Turpin saw at once that no one was going to tell him to move over. He was slumped down in the seat, his arms idle at his sides and his eyes idle in his head; his nose ran unchecked.

Mrs. Turpin put a firm hand on Claud's shoulder and said in a voice that included anyone who wanted to listen, "Claud, you sit in that chair there," and gave him a push down into the vacant one. Claud was florid and bald and sturdy, somewhat shorter than Mrs. Turpin, but he sat down as if he were accustomed to doing what she told him to.

Mrs. Turpin remained standing. The only man in the room besides Claud was a lean stringy old fellow with a rusty hand spread out on each knee, whose eyes were closed as if he were asleep or dead or pretending to be so as not to get up and offer her his seat. Her gaze settled agreeably on a well-dressed gray-haired lady whose eyes met hers and whose expression said: if that child belonged to me, he would have some manners and move over—there's plenty of room there for you and him too.

Claud looked up with a sigh and made as if to rise.

"Sit down," Mrs. Turpin said. "You know you're not supposed to stand on that leg. He has an ulcer on his leg," she explained.

Claud lifted his foot onto the magazine table and rolled his trouser leg up to reveal a purple swelling on a plump marble-white calf.

"My!" the pleasant lady said. "How did you do that?"

"A cow kicked him," Mrs. Turpin said.

"Goodness!" said the lady.

Claud rolled his trouser leg down.

"Maybe the little boy would move over," the lady suggested, but the child did not stir.

"Somebody will be leaving in a minute," Mrs. Turpin said. She could not understand why a doctor—with as much money as they made charging five dollars a day to just stick their head in the hospital door and look at you—couldn't afford a decent-sized waiting room. This one was hardly bigger than a garage. The table was cluttered with limp-looking magazines and at one end of it there was a big green glass ash tray full of cigarette butts and cotton wads with little blood spots on them. If she had had anything to do with the running of the place, that would have been emptied every so often. There were no chairs against the wall at the head of the room. It had a rectangular-shaped panel in it that permitted a view of the office where the nurse came and went and the secretary listened to the radio. A plastic fern in a gold pot sat in the opening and trailed its fronds down almost to the floor. The radio was softly playing gospel music.

Just then the inner door opened and a nurse with the highest stack of yellow hair Mrs. Turpin had ever seen put her face in the crack and called for the next patient. The woman sitting beside Claud grasped the two arms of her chair and hoisted herself up; she pulled her dress free from her legs and lumbered through the door where the nurse had disappeared.

Mrs. Turpin eased into the vacant chair, which held her tight as a corset. "I wish I could reduce," she said, and rolled her eyes and gave a comic sigh.

"Oh, *you* aren't fat," the stylish lady said.

"Ooooo I am too," Mrs. Turpin said. "Claud he eats all he wants to and never weighs over one hundred and seventy-five pounds, but me I just look at something good to eat and I gain some weight," and her stomach and shoulders shook with laughter. "You can eat all you want to, can't you, Claud?" she asked, turning to him.

Claud only grinned.

"Well, as long as you have such a good disposition," the stylish lady said, "I don't think it makes a bit of difference what size you are. You just can't beat a good disposition."

Next to her was a fat girl of eighteen or nineteen, scowling into a thick blue book which Mrs. Turpin saw was entitled *Human Development*. The girl raised her head and directed her scowl at Mrs. Turpin as if she did not like her looks. She appeared annoyed that anyone should speak while she tried to read. The poor girl's face was blue with acne and Mrs. Turpin thought how pitiful it was to have a face like that at that age. She gave the girl a friendly smile but the girl only scowled the harder. Mrs. Turpin herself was fat but she had always had good skin, and, though she was forty-seven years old, there was not a wrinkle in her face except around her eyes from laughing too much.

Next to the ugly girl was the child, still in exactly the same position, and next to him was a thin leathery old woman in a cotton print dress. She and Claud had three sacks of chicken feed in their pump house that was in the same print. She had seen from the first that the child belonged with the old woman. She could tell by the way they sat—kind of vacant and white-trashy, as if they would sit there until Doomsday if nobody called and told them to get up. And at right angles but next to the well-dressed pleasant lady was a lank-faced woman who was certainly the child's mother. She had on a yellow sweat shirt and wine-colored slacks, both gritty-looking, and the rims of her lips were stained with snuff. Her dirty yellow hair was tied behind with a little piece of red paper ribbon. Worse than niggers any day, Mrs. Turpin thought.

The gospel hymn playing was, "When I looked up and He looked down," and Mrs. Turpin, who knew it, supplied the last line mentally, "And wona these days I know I'll we-eara crown."

Without appearing to, Mrs. Turpin always noticed people's feet. The well-dressed lady had on red and gray suede shoes to match her dress. Mrs. Turpin had on her good black patent leather pumps. The ugly girl had on Girl Scout shoes and heavy socks. The old woman had on tennis shoes and the white-trashy mother had on what appeared to be bedroom slippers, black straw with gold braid threaded through them—exactly what you would have expected her to have on.

Sometimes at night when she couldn't go to sleep, Mrs. Turpin would occupy herself with the question of who she would have chosen to be if she couldn't have been herself. If Jesus had said to her before he made her, "There's only two places available for you. You can either be a nigger or white-trash," what would she have said? "Please, Jesus, please," she would have said, "just let me wait until there's another place available," and he would have said, "No, you have to go right now and I have only those two places so make up your mind." She would have wiggled and squirmed and begged and pleaded but it would have been no use and finally she would have said, "All right, make me a nigger then—but that don't mean a trashy one." And he would have made her a neat clean respectable Negro woman, herself but black.

Next to the child's mother was a red-headed youngish woman, reading one of the magazines and working a piece of chewing gum, hell for leather, as Claud would say. Mrs. Turpin could not see the woman's feet. She was not white-trash, just common. Sometimes Mrs. Turpin occupied herself at night naming the classes of people. On the bottom of the heap were most colored people, not the kind she would have been if she had been one, but most of them; then next to them—not above, just away from—were the white-trash; then above them were the home-owners, and above them the home-and-land owners, to which she and Claud belonged. Above she and Claud were people with a lot of money and much bigger houses and much more land. But here the complexity of it would begin to bear in on her, for some of the people with a lot of money were common and ought to be below she and Claud and some of the people who had good blood had lost their money and had to rent and then there were colored people who owned their homes and land as well. There was a colored dentist in town who had two red Lincolns and a swimming pool and a farm with registered white-face cattle on it. Usually by the time she had fallen asleep all the classes of people were moiling and roiling around in her head, and she would dream they were all crammed in together in a box car, being ridden off to be put in a gas oven.

"That's a beautiful clock," she said and nodded to her right. It was a big wall clock, the face encased in a brass sunburst.

"Yes, it's very pretty," the stylish lady said agreeably. "And right on the dot too," she added, glancing at her watch.

The ugly girl beside her cast an eye upward at the clock, smirked, then looked directly at Mrs. Turpin and smirked again. Then she returned her eyes to her book. She was obviously the lady's daughter because, although they didn't look anything alike as to disposition, they both had the same shape of face and the same blue eyes. On the lady they sparkled pleasantly but in the girl's seared face they appeared alternately to smolder and to blaze.

What if Jesus had said, "All right, you can be white-trash or a nigger or ugly"!

Mrs. Turpin felt an awful pity for the girl, though she thought it was one thing to be ugly and another to act ugly.

The woman with the snuff-stained lips turned around in her chair and looked up at the clock. Then she turned back and appeared to look a little to the side of Mrs. Turpin. There was a cast in one of her eyes. "You want to know wher you can get you one of themther clocks?" she asked in a loud voice.

"No, I already have a nice clock," Mrs. Turpin said. Once somebody like her got a leg in the conversation, she would be all over it.

"You can get you one with green stamps," the woman said. "That's most likely wher he got hisn. Save you up enough, you can get you most anythang. I got me some joo'ry."

Ought to have got you a wash rag and some soap, Mrs. Turpin thought.

212

"I get contour sheets with mine," the pleasant lady said.

The daughter slammed her book shut. She looked straight in front of her, directly through Mrs. Turpin and on through the yellow curtain and the plate glass window which made the wall behind her. The girl's eyes seemed lit all of a sudden with a peculiar light, an unnatural light like night road signs give. Mrs. Turpin turned her head to see if there was anything going on outside that she should see, but she could not see anything. Figures passing cast only a pale shadow through the curtain. There was no reason the girl should single her out for her ugly looks.

"Miss Finley," the nurse said, cracking the door. The gum-chewing woman got up and passed in front of her and Claud and went into the office. She had on red high-heeled shoes.

Directly across the table, the ugly girl's eyes were fixed on Mrs. Turpin as if she had some very special reason for disliking her.

"This is wonderful weather, isn't it?" the girl's mother said.

"It's good weather for cotton if you can get the niggers to pick it," Mrs. Turpin said, "but niggers don't want to pick cotton any more. You can't get the white folks to pick it and now you can't get the niggers—because they got to be right up there with the white folks."

"They gonna *try* anyways," the white-trash woman said, leaning forward.

"Do you have one of the cotton-picking machines?" the pleasant lady asked.

"No," Mrs. Turpin said, "they leave half the cotton in the field. We don't have much cotton anyway. If you want to make it farming now, you have to have a little of everything. We got a couple of acres of cotton and a few hogs and chickens and just enough white-face that Claud can look after them himself."

"One thang I don't want," the white-trash woman said, wiping her mouth with the back of her hand. "Hogs. Nasty stinking things, a-gruntin and a-rootin all over the place."

Mrs. Turpin gave her the merest edge of her attention. "Our hogs are not dirty and they don't stink," she said. "They're cleaner than some children I've seen. Their feet never touch the ground. We have a pig-parlor—that's where you raise them on concrete," she explained to the pleasant lady, "and Claud scoots them down with the hose every afternoon and washes off the floor." Cleaner by far than that child right there, she thought. Poor nasty little thing. He had not moved except to put the thumb of his dirty hand into his mouth.

The woman turned her face away from Mrs. Turpin. "I know I wouldn't scoot down no hog with no hose," she said to the wall.

You wouldn't have no hog to scoot down, Mrs. Turpin said to herself.

"A-gruntin and a-rootin and a-groanin," the woman muttered.

"We got a little of everything," Mrs. Turpin said to the pleasant lady. "It's no use in having more than you can handle yourself with help like it is. We found enough niggers to pick our cotton this year but Claud he has to go after them and take them home again in the evening. They can't walk that half a mile. No they can't. I tell you," she said and laughed merrily, "I sure am tired of buttering up niggers, but you got to love em if you want em to work for you. When they come in the morning, I run out and I say, 'Hi yawl this morning?' and when Claud drives them off to the field I just wave to beat the band and they just wave back." And she waved her hand rapidly to illustrate.

"Like you read out of the same book," the lady said, showing she understood perfectly.

"Child, yes," Mrs. Turpin said. "And when they come in from the field, I run out with a bucket of icewater. That's the way it's going to be from now on," she said. "You may as well face it."

"One thang I know," the white-trash woman said. "Two thangs I ain't going to do: love no niggers or scoot down no hog with no hose." And she let out a bark of contempt.

The look that Mrs. Turpin and the pleasant lady exchanged indicated they both understood that you had to *have* certain things before you could *know* certain things. But every time Mrs. Turpin exchanged a look with the lady, she was aware that the ugly girl's peculiar eyes were still on her, and she had trouble bringing her attention back to the conversation.

"When you got something," she said, "you got to look after it." And when you ain't got a thing but breath and britches, she added to herself, you can afford to come to town every morning and just sit on the Court House coping and spit.

A grotesque revolving shadow passed across the curtain behind her and was thrown palely on the opposite wall. Then a bicycle clattered down against the outside of the building. The door opened and a colored boy glided in with a tray from the drugstore. It had two large red and white paper cups on it with tops on them. He was a tall, very black boy in discolored white pants and a green nylon shirt. He was chewing gum slowly, as if to music. He set the tray down in the office opening next to the fern and stuck his head through to look for the secretary. She was not in there. He rested his arms on the ledge and waited, his narrow bottom stuck out, swaying to the left and right. He raised a hand over his head and scratched the base of his skull.

"You see that button there, boy?" Mrs. Turpin said. "You can punch that and she'll come. She's probably in the back somewhere."

"Is thas right?" the boy said agreeably, as if he had never seen the button before. He leaned to the right and put his finger on it. "She sometime out," he said and twisted around to face his audience, his elbows behind him on the counter. The nurse appeared and he twisted back again. She handed him a dollar and he rooted in his pocket and made the change and counted it out to her. She gave him fifteen cents for a tip and he went out with the empty tray. The heavy door swung to slowly and closed at length with the sound of suction. For a moment no one spoke.

"They ought to send all them niggers back to Africa," the white-trash woman said. "That's wher they come from in the first place."

"Oh, I couldn't do without my good colored friends," the pleasant lady said.

"There's a heap of things worse than a nigger," Mrs. Turpin agreed. "It's all kinds of them just like it's all kinds of us."

"Yes, and it takes all kinds to make the world go round," the lady said in her musical voice.

As she said it, the raw-complexioned girl snapped her teeth together. Her lower lip turned downwards and inside out, revealing the pale pink inside her mouth. After a second it rolled back up. It was the ugliest face Mrs. Turpin had ever seen anyone make and for a moment she was certain that the girl had made it at her. She was looking at her as if she had known and disliked her all her life—all of Mrs. Turpin's life, it seemed too, not just all the girl's life. Why, girl, I don't even know you, Mrs. Turpin said silently.

She forced her attention back to the discussion. "It wouldn't be practical to send them back to Africa," she said. "They wouldn't want to go. They got it too good here."

"Wouldn't be what they wanted—if I had anythang to do with it," the woman said.

"It wouldn't be a way in the world you could get all the niggers back over there," Mrs. Turpin said. "They'd be hiding out and lying down and turning sick on you and wailing and hollering and raring and pitching. It wouldn't be a way in the world to get them over there."

"They got over here," the trashy woman said. "Get back like they got over."

"It wasn't so many of them then," Mrs. Turpin explained.

The woman looked at Mrs. Turpin as if here was an idiot indeed but Mrs. Turpin was not bothered by the look, considering where it came from.

"Nooo," she said, "they're going to stay here where they can go to New York and marry white folks and improve their color. That's what they all want to do, every one of them, improve their color."

"You know what comes of that, don't you?" Claud asked.

"No, Claud, what?" Mrs. Turpin said.

Claud's eyes twinkled. "White-faced niggers," he said with never a smile.

Everybody in the office laughed except the white-trash and the ugly girl. The girl gripped the book in her lap with white fingers. The trashy woman looked around her from face to face as if she thought they were all idiots. The old woman in the feed sack dress continued to gaze expressionless across the floor at the high-top shoes of the man opposite her, the one who had been pretending to be asleep when the Turpins came in. He was laughing heartily, his hands still spread out on his knees. The child had fallen to the side and was lying now almost face down in the old woman's lap.

While they recovered from their laughter, the nasal chorus on the radio kept the room from silence.

> "You go to blank blank
> And I'll go to mine
> But we'll all blank blank
> To-geth-ther,
> And all along the blank
> We'll hep eachother out
> Smile-ling in any kind of
> Weath-ther!"

Mrs. Turpin didn't catch every word but she caught enough to agree with the spirit of the song and it turned her thoughts sober. To help anybody out that needed it was her philosophy of life. She never spared herself when she found somebody in need, whether they were white or black, trash or decent. And of all she had to be thankful for, she was most thankful that this was so. If Jesus had said, "You can be high society and have all the money you want and be thin and svelte-like, but you can't be a good woman with it," she would have had to say, "Well don't make me that then. Make me a good woman and it don't matter what else, how fat or how ugly or how poor!" Her heart rose. He had not made her a nigger or white-trash or ugly! He had made her herself and given her a little of everything. Jesus, thank you! she said. Thank you thank you thank you! Whenever she counted her blessings she felt as buoyant as if she weighed one hundred and twenty-five pounds instead of one hundred and eighty.

"What's wrong with your little boy?" the pleasant lady asked the white-trashy woman.

"He has a ulcer," the woman said proudly. "He ain't give me a minute's peace since he was born. Him and her are just alike," she said, nodding at the old woman, who was running her leathery fingers through the child's pale hair. "Look like I can't get nothing down them two but Co' Cola and candy."

That's all you try to get down em, Mrs. Turpin said to herself. Too lazy to light the fire. There was nothing you could tell her about people like them that she didn't know already. And it was not just that they didn't have anything. Because if you gave them everything, in two weeks it would all be broken or filthy or they would have chopped it up for lightwood. She knew all this from her own experience. Help them you must, but help them you couldn't.

All at once the ugly girl turned her lips inside out again. Her eyes fixed like two drills on Mrs. Turpin. This time there was no mistaking that there was something urgent behind them.

Girl, Mrs. Turpin exclaimed silently, I haven't done a thing to you! The girl might be confusing her with somebody else. There was no need to sit by and let herself be intimidated. "You must be in college," she said boldly, looking directly at the girl. "I see you reading a book there."

The girl continued to stare and pointedly did not answer.

Her mother blushed at this rudeness. "The lady asked you a question, Mary Grace," she said under her breath.

"I have ears," Mary Grace said.

The poor mother blushed again. "Mary Grace goes to Wellesley College," she explained. She twisted one of the buttons on her dress. "In Massachusetts," she added with a grimace. "And in the summer she just keeps right on studying. Just reads all the time, a real book worm. She's done real well at Wellesley; she's taking English and Math and History and Psychology and Social Studies," she rattled on, "and I think it's too much. I think she ought to get out and have fun."

The girl looked as if she would like to hurl them all through the plate glass window.

"Way up north," Mrs. Turpin murmured and thought, well, it hasn't done much for her manners.

"I'd almost rather to have him sick," the white-trash woman said, wrenching the attention back to herself. "He's so mean when he ain't. Look like some children just take natural to meanness. It's some gets bad when they get sick but he was the opposite. Took sick and turned good. He don't give me no trouble now. It's me waitin to see the doctor," she said.

If I was going to send anybody back to Africa, Mrs. Turpin thought, it would be your kind, woman. "Yes, indeed," she said aloud, but looking up at the ceiling, "it's a heap of things worse than a nigger." And dirtier than a hog, she added to herself.

"I think people with bad dispositions are more to be pitied than anyone on earth," the pleasant lady said in a voice that was decidedly thin.

"I thank the Lord he has blessed me with a good one," Mrs. Turpin said. "The day has never dawned that I couldn't find something to laugh at."

"Not since she married me anyways," Claud said with a comical straight face.

Everybody laughed except the girl and the white-trash.

Mrs. Turpin's stomach shook. "He's such a caution," she said, "that I can't help but laugh at him."

The girl made a loud ugly noise through her teeth.

Her mother's mouth grew thin and tight. "I think the worst thing in the world," she said, "is an ungrateful person. To have everything and not appreciate it. I know a girl," she said, "who has parents who would give her anything, a little brother who loves her dearly, who is getting a good education, who wears the best clothes, but who can never say a kind word to anyone, who never smiles, who just criticizes and complains all day long."

"Is she too old to paddle?" Claud asked.

The girl's face was almost purple.

"Yes," the lady said, "I'm afraid there's nothing to do but leave her to her folly. Some day she'll wake up and it'll be too late."

"It never hurt anyone to smile," Mrs. Turpin said. "It just makes you feel better all over."

"Of course," the lady said sadly, "but there are just some people you can't tell anything to. They can't take criticism."

"If it's one thing I am," Mrs. Turpin said with feeling, "it's grateful. When I think who all I could have been besides myself and what all I got, a little of everything, and a good disposition besides, I just feel like shouting, 'Thank you, Jesus, for making everything the way it is!' It could have been different!" For one thing, somebody else could have got Claud. At the thought of this, she was flooded with gratitude and a terrible pang of joy ran through her. "Oh thank you, Jesus, Jesus, thank you!" she cried aloud.

The book struck her directly over her left eye. It struck almost at the same instant that she realized the girl was about to hurl it. Before she could utter a sound, the raw face came crashing across the table toward her, howling. The girl's fingers sank like clamps into the soft flesh of her neck. She heard the mother cry out and Claud shout, "Whoa!" There was an instant when she was certain that she was about to be in an earthquake.

All at once her vision narrowed and she saw everything as if it were happening in a small room far away, or as if she were looking at it through the wrong end of a telescope. Claud's face crumpled and fell out of sight. The nurse ran in, then out, then in again. Then the gangling figure of the doctor rushed out of the inner door. Magazines flew this way and that as the table turned over. The girl fell with a thud and Mrs. Turpin's vision suddenly reversed itself and she saw everything large instead of small. The eyes of the white-trashy woman were staring hugely at the floor. There the girl, held down on one side by the nurse and on the other by her mother, was wrenching and turning in their grasp. The doctor was kneeling astride her, trying to hold her arm down. He managed after a second to sink a long needle into it.

Mrs. Turpin felt entirely hollow except for her heart which swung from side to side as if it were agitated in a great empty drum of flesh.

"Somebody that's not busy call for the ambulance," the doctor said in the off-hand voice young doctors adopt for terrible occasions.

Mrs. Turpin could not have moved a finger. The old man who had been sitting next to her skipped nimbly into the office and made the call, for the secretary still seemed to be gone.

"Claud!" Mrs. Turpin called.

He was not in his chair. She knew she must jump up and find him but she felt like some one trying to catch a train in a dream, when everything moves in slow motion and the faster you try to run the slower you go.

"Here I am," a suffocated voice, very unlike Claud's, said.

He was doubled up in the corner on the floor, pale as paper, holding his leg. She wanted to get up and go to him but she could not move. Instead, her gaze was drawn slowly downward to the churning face on the floor, which she could see over the doctor's shoulder.

The girl's eyes stopped rolling and focused on her. They seemed a much lighter blue than before, as if a door that had been tightly closed behind them was now open to admit light and air.

Mrs. Turpin's head cleared and her power of motion returned. She leaned forward until she was looking directly into the fierce brilliant eyes. There was no doubt in her mind that the girl did know her, knew her in some intense and personal way, beyond time and place and condition. "What you got to say to me?" she asked hoarsely and held her breath, waiting, as for a revelation.

The girl raised her head. Her gaze locked with Mrs. Turpin's. "Go back to hell where you came from, you old wart hog," she whispered. Her voice was low but clear. Her eyes burned for a moment as if she saw with pleasure that her message had struck its target.

Mrs. Turpin sank back in her chair.

After a moment the girl's eyes closed and she turned her head wearily to the side.

The doctor rose and handed the nurse the empty syringe. He leaned over and put both hands for a moment on the mother's shoulders, which were shaking. She was sitting on the floor, her lips pressed together, holding Mary Grace's hand in her lap. The girl's fingers were gripped like a baby's around her thumb. "Go on to the hospital," he said. "I'll call and make the arrangements."

"Now let's see that neck," he said in a jovial voice to Mrs. Turpin.

He began to inspect her neck with his first two fingers. Two little moon-shaped lines like pink fish bones were indented over her windpipe. There was the beginning of an angry red swelling above her eye. His fingers passed over this also.

"Lea' me be," she said thickly and shook him off. "See about Claud. She kicked him."

"I'll see about him in a minute," he said and felt her pulse. He was a thin gray-haired man, given to pleasantries. "Go home and have yourself a vacation the rest of the day," he said and patted her on the shoulder.

Quit your pattin me, Mrs. Turpin growled to herself.

"And put an ice pack over that eye," he said. Then he went and squatted down beside Claud and looked at his leg. After a moment he pulled him up and Claud limped after him into the office.

Until the ambulance came, the only sounds in the room were the tremulous moans of the girl's mother, who continued to sit on the floor. The white-trash woman did not take her eyes off the girl. Mrs. Turpin looked straight ahead at nothing. Presently the ambulance drew up, a long dark shadow, behind the curtain. The attendants came in and set the stretcher down beside the girl and lifted her expertly onto it and carried her out. The nurse helped the mother gather up her things. The shadow of the ambulance moved silently away and the nurse came back in the office.

"That ther girl is going to be a lunatic, ain't she?" the white-trash woman asked the nurse, but the nurse kept on to the back and never answered her.

"Yes, she's going to be a lunatic," the white-trash woman said to the rest of them.

"Po' critter," the old woman murmured. The child's face was still in her lap. His eyes looked idly out over her knees. He had not moved during the disturbance except to draw one leg up under him.

"I thank Gawd," the white-trash woman said fervently, "I ain't a lunatic."

Claud came limping out and the Turpins went home.

As their pick-up truck turned into their own dirt road and made the crest of the hill, Mrs. Turpin gripped the window ledge and looked out suspiciously. The land sloped gracefully down through a field dotted with lavender weeds and at the start of the rise their small yellow frame house, with its little flower beds spread out around it like a fancy apron, sat primly in its accustomed place between two giant hickory trees. She would not have been startled to see a burnt wound between two blackened chimneys.

Neither of them felt like eating so they put on their house clothes and lowered the shade in the bedroom and lay down, Claud with his leg on a pillow and herself with a damp washcloth over her eye. The instant she was flat on her back, the image of a razor-backed hog with warts on its face and horns coming out behind its ears snorted into her head. She moaned, a low quiet moan.

"I am not," she said tearfully, "a wart hog. From hell." But the denial had no force. The girl's eyes and her words, even the tone of her voice, low but clear, directed only to her, brooked no repudiation. She had been singled out for the message, though there was trash in the room to whom it might justly have been applied. The full force of this fact struck her only now. There was a woman there who was neglecting her own child but she had been overlooked. The message had been given to Ruby Turpin, a respectable, hard-working, church-going woman. The tears dried. Her eyes began to burn instead with wrath.

She rose on her elbow and the washcloth fell into her hand. Claud was lying on his back, snoring. She wanted to tell him what the girl had said. At the same time, she did not wish to put the image of herself as a wart hog from hell into his mind.

"Hey, Claud," she muttered and pushed his shoulder.

Claud opened one pale baby blue eye.

She looked into it warily. He did not think about anything. He just went his way.

"Wha, whasit?" he said and closed the eye again.

"Nothing," she said. "Does your leg pain you?"

"Hurts like hell," Claud said.

"It'll quit terreckly," she said and lay back down. In a moment Claud was snoring again. For the rest of the afternoon they lay there. Claud slept. She scowled at the ceiling. Occasionally she raised her fist and made a small stabbing motion over her chest as if she was defending her innocence to invisible guests who were like the comforters of Job, reasonable-seeming but wrong.

About five-thirty Claud stirred. "Got to go after those niggers," he sighed, not moving.

She was looking straight up as if there were unintelligible handwriting on the ceiling. The protuberance over her eye had turned a greenish-blue. "Listen here," she said.

"What?"

"Kiss me."

Claud leaned over and kissed her loudly on the mouth. He pinched her side and their hands interlocked. Her expression of ferocious concentration did not change. Claud got up, groaning and growling, and limped off. She continued to study the ceiling.

She did not get up until she heard the pick-up truck coming back with the Negroes. Then she rose and thrust her feet in her brown oxfords, which she did not bother to lace, and stumped out onto the back porch and got her red plastic bucket. She emptied a tray of ice cubes into it and filled it half full of water and went out into the back yard. Every afternoon after Claud brought the hands in, one of the boys helped him put out hay and the rest waited in the back of the truck until he was ready to take them home. The truck was parked in the shade under one of the hickory trees.

"Hi yawl this evening?" Mrs. Turpin asked grimly, appearing with the bucket and the dipper. There were three women and a boy in the truck.

"Us doin nicely," the oldest woman said. "Hi you doin?" and her gaze stuck immediately on the dark lump on Mrs. Turpin's forehead. "You done fell down, ain't you?" she asked in a solicitous voice. The old woman was dark and almost toothless. She had on an old felt hat of Claud's set back on her head. The other two women were younger and lighter and they both had new bright green sunhats. One of them had hers on her head; the other had taken hers off and the boy was grinning beneath it.

Mrs. Turpin set the bucket down on the floor of the truck. "Yawl hep yourselves," she said. She looked around to make sure Claud had gone. "No, I didn't fall down," she said, folding her arms. "It was something worse than that."

"Ain't nothing bad happen to you!" the old woman said. She said it as if they all knew that Mrs. Turpin was protected in some special way by Divine Providence. "You just had you a little fall."

"We were in town at the doctor's office for where the cow kicked Mr. Turpin," Mrs. Turpin said in a flat tone that indicated they could leave off their foolishness. "And there was this girl there. A big fat girl with her face all broke out. I could look at that girl and tell she was peculiar but I couldn't tell how. And me and her mama was just talking and going along and all of a sudden WHAM! She throws this big book she was reading at me and..."

"Naw!" the old woman cried out.

"And then she jumps over the table and commences to choke me."

"Naw!" they all exclaimed, "naw!"

"Hi come she do that?" the old woman asked. "What ail her?"

Mrs. Turpin only glared in front of her.

"Somethin ail her," the old woman said.

"They carried her off in an ambulance," Mrs. Turpin continued, "but before she went she was rolling on the floor and they were trying to hold her down to give her a shot and she said something to me." She paused. "You know what she said to me?"

"What she say?" they asked.

"She said," Mrs. Turpin began, and stopped, her face very dark and heavy. The sun was getting whiter and whiter, blanching the sky overhead so that the leaves of the hickory tree were black in the face of it. She could not bring forth the words. "Something real ugly," she muttered.

"She sho shouldn't said nothin ugly to you," the old woman said. "You so sweet. You the sweetest lady I know."

"She pretty too," the one with the hat on said.

"And stout," the other one said. "I never knowed no sweeter white lady."

"That's the truth befo' Jesus," the old woman said. "Amen! You des as sweet and pretty as you can be."

Mrs. Turpin knew exactly how much Negro flattery was worth and it added to her rage. "She said," she began again and finished this time with a fierce rush of breath, "that I was an old wart hog from hell."

There was an astounded silence.

"Where she at?" the youngest woman cried in a piercing voice. "Lemme see her. I'll kill her!"

"I'll kill her with you!" the other one cried.

"She b'long in the sylum," the old woman said emphatically. "You the sweetest white lady I know."

"She pretty too," the other two said. "Stout as she can be and sweet. Jesus satisfied with her!"

"Deed he is," the old woman declared.

Idiots! Mrs. Turpin growled to herself. You could never say anything intelligent to a nigger. You could talk at them but not with them. "Yawl ain't drunk your water," she said shortly. "Leave the bucket in the truck when you're finished with it. I got more to do than just stand around and pass the time of day," and she moved off and into the house.

She stood for a moment in the middle of the kitchen. The dark protuberance over her eye looked like a miniature tornado cloud which might any moment sweep across the horizon of her brow. Her lower lip protruded dangerously. She squared her massive shoulders. Then she marched into the front of the house and out the side door and started down the road to the pig parlor. She had the look of a woman going single-handed, weaponless, into battle.

The sun was deep yellow now like a harvest moon and was riding westward very fast over the far tree line as if it meant to reach the hogs before she did. The road was rutted and she kicked several good-sized stones out of her path as she strode along. The pig parlor was on a little knoll at the end of a lane that ran off from the side of the barn. It was a square of concrete as large as a small room, with a board fence about four feet high around it. The concrete floor sloped slightly so that the hog wash could drain off into a trench where it was carried to the field for fertilizer. Claud was standing on the outside, on the edge of the concrete, hanging onto the top board, hosing down the floor inside. The hose was connected to the faucet of a water trough nearby.

Mrs. Turpin climbed up beside him and glowered down at the hogs inside. There were seven long-snouted bristly shoats in it—tan with liver-colored spots—and an old sow a few weeks off from farrowing. She was lying on her side grunting. The shoats were running about shaking themselves like idiot children, their little slit pig eyes searching the floor for anything left. She had read that pigs were the most intelligent animal. She doubted it. They were supposed to be smarter than dogs. There had even been a pig astronaut. He had performed his assignment perfectly but died of a heart attack afterwards because they left him in his electric suit, sitting upright throughout his examination when naturally a hog should be on all fours.

A-gruntin and a-rootin and a-groanin.

"Gimme that hose," she said, yanking it away from Claud. "Go on and carry them niggers home and then get off that leg."

"You look like you might have swallowed a mad dog," Claud observed, but he got down and limped off. He paid no attention to her humors.

Until he was out of earshot, Mrs. Turpin stood on the side of the pen, holding the hose and pointing the stream of water at the hind quarters of any shoat that looked as if it might try to lie down. When he had had time to get over the hill, she turned her head slightly and her wrathful eyes scanned the path. He was nowhere in sight. She turned back again and seemed to gather herself up. Her shoulders rose and she drew in her breath.

"What do you send me a message like that for?" she said in a low fierce voice, barely above a whisper but with the force of a shout in its concentrated fury. "How am I a hog and me both? How am I saved and from hell too?" Her free fist was knotted and with the other she gripped the hose, blindly pointing the stream of water in and out of the eye of the old sow whose outraged squeal she did not hear.

The pig parlor commanded a view of the back pasture where their twenty beef cows were gathered around the hay-bales Claud and the boy had put out. The freshly cut pasture sloped down to the highway. Across it was their cotton field and beyond that a dark green dusty wood which they owned as well. The sun was behind the wood, very red, looking over the paling of trees like a farmer inspecting his own hogs.

"Why me?" she rumbled. "It's no trash around here, black or white, that I haven't given to. And break my back to the bone every day working. And do for the church."

She appeared to be the right size woman to command the arena before her. "How am I a hog?" she demanded. "Exactly how am I like them?" and she jabbed the stream of water at the shoats. "There was plenty of trash there. It didn't have to be me.

"If you like trash better, go get yourself some trash then," she railed. "You could have made me trash. Or a nigger. If trash is what you wanted why didn't you make me trash?" She shook her fist with the hose in it and a watery snake appeared momentarily in the air. "I could quit working and take it easy and be filthy," she growled. "Lounge about the sidewalks all day drinking root beer. Dip snuff and spit in every puddle and have it all over my face. I could be nasty.

"Or you could have made me a nigger. It's too late for me to be a nigger," she said with deep sarcasm, "but I could act like one. Lay down in the middle of the road and stop traffic. Roll on the ground."

In the deepening light everything was taking on a mysterious hue. The pasture was growing a peculiar glassy green and the streak of highway had turned lavender. She braced herself for a final assault and this time her voice rolled out over the pasture. "Go on," she yelled, "call me a hog! Call me a hog again. From hell. Call me a wart hog from hell. Put that bottom rail on top. There'll still be a top and bottom!"

A garbled echo returned to her.

A final surge of fury shook her and she roared, "Who do you think you are?"

The color of everything, field and crimson sky, burned for a moment with a transparent intensity. The question carried over the pasture and across the highway and the cotton field and returned to her clearly like an answer from beyond the wood.

She opened her mouth but no sound came out of it.

A tiny truck, Claud's, appeared on the highway, heading rapidly out of sight. Its gears scraped thinly. It looked like a child's toy. At any moment a bigger truck might smash into it and scatter Claud's and the niggers' brains all over the road.

Mrs. Turpin stood there, her gaze fixed on the highway, all her muscles rigid, until in five or six minutes the truck reappeared, returning. She waited until it had had time to turn into their own road. Then like a monumental statue coming to life, she bent her head slowly and gazed, as if through the very heart of mystery, down into the pig parlor at the hogs. They had settled all in one corner around the old sow who was grunting softly. A red glow suffused them. They appeared to pant with a secret life.

Until the sun slipped finally behind the treeline, Mrs. Turpin remained there with her gaze bent to them as if she were absorbing some abysmal life-giving knowledge. At last she lifted her head. There was only a purple streak in the sky, cutting through a field of crimson and leading, like an extension of the highway, into the descending dusk. She raised her hands from the side of the pen in a gesture hieratic and profound. A visionary light settled in her eyes. She saw the streak as a vast swinging bridge extending upward from the earth through a field of living fire. Upon it a vast horde of souls were rumbling toward heaven. There were whole companies of white-trash, clean for the first time in their lives, and bands of black niggers in white robes, and battalions of freaks and lunatics shouting and clapping and leaping like frogs. And bringing up the end of the procession was a tribe of people whom she recognized at once as those who, like herself and Claud, had always had a little of everything and the God-given wit to use it right. She leaned forward to observe them closer. They were marching behind the others with great dignity, accountable as they had always been for good order and common sense and respectable behavior. They alone were on key. Yet she could see by their shocked and altered faces that even their virtues were being burned away. She lowered her hands and gripped the rail of the hog pen, her eyes small but fixed unblinkingly on what lay ahead. In a moment the vision faded but she remained where she was, immobile.

At length she got down and turned off the faucet and made her slow way on the darkening path to the house. In the woods around her the invisible cricket choruses had struck up, but what she heard were the voices of the souls climbing upward into the starry field and shouting hallelujah.

Flannery O'Connor (1925-1964)

Flannery O'Connor was born in Savannah, Georgia, but lived for most of her life in Milledgeville. She is the author of two novels, WISE BLOOD (1952) and THE VIOLENT BEAR IT AWAY (1960), and three collections of short stories, A GOOD MAN IS HARD TO FIND (1955), EVERYTHING THAT RISES MUST CONVERGE (1965), and COMPLETE STORIES (1971). "Revelation" is taken from EVERYTHING THAT RISES MUST CONVERGE.

A Long Wait

Harry Crews

THE OLD MAN looked out the window at the darkened fields slipping past in the rain and said, "Tonight, you ring the bell before supper. I want to eat with him one more time."

Sarah Nell sat stiff on the seat, both hands holding firmly to the steering wheel, and did not answer. Out of the corner of her eye she could see her father's twisted profile. No matter how hard she concentrated on the road, his face was always there like a piece of gravel under the lid.

The old man turned on the seat toward her, half of his face melting away into shadow.

"You ain't fer it, are you?" he asked.

"You're Pa, so I ain't against it," she said. "It's you that's got to care it around, that's going to bed with it and gittin up with it, so I cain't be against it."

"You always was a sensible girl," he said.

"I just don't know about tollin Gaff in and shutting the door on him like you'd pen a hog. He ain't gone understand that."

"He don't have to understand," said the old man. "I'm the only one who has to understand. I'm sick to death of doctors."

"Don't put it on him," she said. "Dr. Threadly's a good man."

"He's a fool and I'm worse. When it gits that time, you go. That's all there is to it. All there ever was to it." His voice was soft, the words slightly blurred, as though coming from a great distance. "Remember your Ma, an how he wagged his wonderful tongue over her an how we follered her right on down to the grave with him still talking."

Sarah Nell caught at the word "Ma" and held it to her as though it were a talisman. She moved her lips over the sound of it, breathing it into the darkness and sucking it back again until finally the sound and the word became an odor and an image; and the image burned cleanly before her: hot blue eyes, dry and faded with pain, set above high cheek-bones over which the thin flesh stretched like parchment.

"But Ma never rung a bell for Gaff," she said, the words bursting from her lips before she knew she would say them. "Never a bell for Gaff to take me to Big Creek Church."

"That was your Ma, and she had me," he said. "Besides, women can walk up face to face with things that men can only back up to."

"I'll pray," she said softly, almost inaudibly.

"For me?" he asked.

"No," she said. "For Gaff and me."

She turned the car into the lane leading down from the big road, through old, winter-naked pecan trees, past the lot where the hesitant bray of a mule joined the sound of the wind. A great, brindle-colored mastiff waited at the yard fence. He had not barked when they drove up, and sat now with his huge head hanging forward. The old man spoke to him softly as he passed through the gate and the dog raised himself, long and lean, his belly curving sharply upward from his chest. The old man lifted his arm in the direction of the mule barn and the mastiff turned and walked away in the rain.

In the kitchen her father sat silently with his elbows on the faded oilcloth of the table, his chin propped in his hands, while Sarah Nell set out cold meat and bread.

"Is they clabber?" he asked through the web of his fingers.

"Yessir," answered Sarah Nell.

"Set it," he said.

She set the clabber out and put an earthen bowl beside his plate. In the yellow light of the kerosene lamp, the surface of the clabber took on a bluish tinge. He turned his eyes on the bowl and gently his fingers drummed the bandages partially covering his mouth where cancer had broken through in an open sore. Slivers of cheek and segments of gum had been removed leaving the right side of his face concave as though his jawbone had been half split away. As it always did when he was about to eat, his odor grew stronger, the heavy, half-sweet odor of decay that swarmed about him like flies.

"Git that syrup, too," he said, the words far away, muffled by the bandage.

She took the syrup bucket down from the screen-wire safe, pried up the lid with a case knife, and set it beside him. Before she could sit down at her place, he said without looking up from the bucket, "Ring the bell for Gaff."

She stepped out onto the porch, and the night air met her cold and clean. She stood a moment breathing deeply against the scent in her nostrils, but it was no good. On her tongue was the taste of decay and it drew her mouth like alum. The rain had stopped, but a mist still hung in the air as fine as fog. There were no stars now, no moon. The lamp from the kitchen window gave enough light to see the triangular rod of iron hanging from a piece of hay wire at the end of the porch. She struck it three times with an iron cylinder. The sound came back again and again, bouncing out of the black forest of pine that bordered the field at the back of the house.

"I ain't there, I'm here."

Sarah Nell shrank into herself, the breath catching at the base of her throat, her hand still poised to strike. The voice had come out of the darkness at the edge of the porch.

"Gaff?"

"Yeah. I've already come. I was just waiting out there for the bell." The voice was at the steps now; then the sound of his booted feet was on the porch and she saw him, tall, his felt hat pushed back, his brow very smooth and damp.

"How...?" she began.

"Seen the lights of the automobile when it come up," he said.

"He's waiting," she said.

Gaff went into the kitchen ahead of her, stooping slightly in the door, the black hat still on his head.

"That was quick," her father said without looking up from the clabber he had dipped and was now stirring.

"I was out there waiting," said Gaff.

Sarah Nell sat at the table opposite her father. Gaff remained standing just inside the door.

"You had your supper?" asked her father.

Gaff shifted his weight and reached up and pulled his hat farther down on his forehead.

"No sir, I ain't," he said, "But I don't..."

"Git him a plate Sarah Nell."

Gaff was rock-still now, his back pressed into the wall by the door.

"I ain't hongry," he said evenly.

"You said you didn't eat," said her father, still without looking at him. "Set and be welcome."

Sarah Nell set a plate, a bowl, and a spoon at the end of the table, and then the three of them sat very still, their plates empty, while the old man loosened the bandage at the right side of his face so he could eat. Both Gaff and Sarah Nell looked directly at him, at his fingers working slowly and delicately as though unwrapping a fine and treasured secret.

He was the first to eat and the clabber had to be kept in the left side of his mouth because the right cheek had been partially cut away to expose the grinding teeth.

"You want some of this clabber?" asked the old man, gesturing toward the bowl at his elbow.

"No sir, I don't," said Gaff. He had put a biscuit in the middle of his plate and was making an effort to keep his eyes on it, but the naked, working spot in the old man's face was too fascinating, and his eyes would invariably come off his plate and slowly move up the denim work shirt to the dry, seamed neck to the teeth.

"It's mighty good with a little syrup."

"Yessir," Gaff said, his eyes trying to make it back to the biscuit, "But I really ain't too hongry."

"You ain't, huh?"

"No sir, I ain't and if it's the same to you, I'll just step to the door and smoke till you ready to talk."

"No, no," said the old man quickly. "Smoke there if you like. And's for talking, now's as good as any."

Gaff took out a book of cigarette leaves and a can of tobacco.

"Did you start breaking the back field yet?

"Yessir, I did."

"And did you get the cloth on the beds all right?"

"Yessir."

"Any sign of blue mold?"

"No sir."

The old man had cleared his mouth of food and his words were more distinct now.

"Good, good. You're a worker Gaff. Always have been. What you need is a wife."

The cigarette broke in Gaff's fingers, and the tobacco dribbled off onto his lap. He looked at Sarah Nell. She sat stiff in her chair, her cheeks ashen, looking directly across the table at her father.

"Sir?" said Gaff.

"You a young man and you able," he said. "You cain't expect to go on working another man's land in a cabin without a woman for the rest of your life." He had begun spooning clabber into his mouth again. There was a brittle silence over the table for a long minute. Then he looked up over his poised spoon and asked, "Can you?"

Sarah Nell and the old man watched Gaff across the table, and he, still holding the torn cigarette paper between his fingers, stared at the biscuit in his plate. Finally he pushed his chair back slowly and took off his hat. The band across his forehead where the hat had been was red and damp with sweat.

"They is some that has," said Gaff.

"Do you want to be one that has?" asked the old man, pushing the clabber bowl across to Gaff.

Gaff reached for the spoon and without lowering his eyes began to dip clabber.

"No," said Gaff.

"When you take Sarah Nell to Big Creek Church tonight, you ought to start looking," he said. "They's lots of girls just waiting."

Gaff stopped dipping.

"When I take her where?"

"I want you to drive her over there to the revival. The roads is bad with the rain."

"Tonight?" asked Gaff.

"She wants to go," said the old man.

Sarah Nell, her face set like a gray mask, leaned forward and with a steady hand ladled two spoons of syrup into Gaff's bowl.

"Clabber and syrup makes right good eatin," she said. "It's a wonder anything could look so bad and be so good."

A loud silence hung in the room. Gaff picked up his spoon, stirred the clabber, looked at Sarah Nell, then stirred again, his face as gray as hers. A drop of sweat broke from his forehead and trembled at the end of his nose. Only the old man had the color of life in his face.

"It *is* a wonder," said Gaff.

The old man moved his chair closer to the table, leaned on his elbows, and said, "Sarah Nell and me was talking on the way from town."

"You was, huh," said Gaff.

"Would you like another one of these biscuits, boy?" asked the old man.

"No sir, I ain't finished this un yet."

"We was talking about you and the doctor. Tell Gaff what the doctor said, Sarah Nell."

"About the doctor and *me*?" asked Gaff.

"Tell him, Sarah Nell."

"Doctor Threadly says Pa has to have his tongue taken off."

Gaff's mouth opened, worked over a word, then closed. His pink under-lip caught the light and trembled.

"His tongue?" he finally managed to say.

"That's the next thing," said Sarah Nell woodenly.

"The doctor says," said the old man, his mouth doing the best it could with a smile, "That if I don't have it taken off I'll die."

Gaff opened his mouth as though he would speak, but instead put a spoon of clabber into it.

"That's mighty good eatin once you get started," Sarah Nell said. Gaff raised his eyes to hers and she saw his throat work over the clabber.

"It's mighty good, thank you," said Gaff. "You going to have it taken off?"

"No, I ain't," said the old man.

"I'll have another one of them biscuits," said Gaff.

The old man looked past Gaff to the door, and his vision was distant, stretching past the porch, past the field and even the night, down to the forest of pines. "Since the first frost of November in this country, living on land I growed out of as a boy, I been a stranger. Not eating with anybody, not talking with anybody, and follered by a scent that'ed sicken a hog." His eyes suddenly snapped back, and Gaff met them steadily, sucking at a front tooth, and wiping his mouth with the back of his hand. "Now I'm supposed to fix it so I cain't even holler when I hurt."

"And Pa and me was just talking on the way this evening," said Sarah Nell, her face still ashen, but her eyes bright and moist.

"And I just wanted to set again..." said the old man, his voice trailing off, his eyes wandering to the door again. "...to set to the table again...."

"It was mighty good," said Gaff. "That syrup's got a good taste."

"That syrup's a tad too sharp, son," said the old man. "You biled it too long."

"You think so, huh," said Gaff, dabbing his finger on the rim of the syrup can and touching it to his tongue.

"Next year you cook it slower and not so long. It'll lose that tart."

"I'll do that," Gaff said. "I will."

"I smell myself," said the old man. "You'd think I couldn't smell it wouldn't you? To be able to smell it after all this time." He shook his head slowly, and pulled the clabber to his bowl again.

"We'd best be going, Miss Sarah Nell," said Gaff.

She went around the table to her father and kissed him on the scarred side of his face.

"Goodbye, Pa."

"Bye, Sarah Nell." He did not look at her.

When Gaff opened the door, the huge dog was sitting on the other side of the screen, his yellow eyes dull and unblinking. Gaff pushed back the screen and the dog walked through to the old man and lay at his feet. As they were going through the door the old man spoke again.

"Take the dog too," he said.

"Sir?" asked Gaff, already standing on the porch, but still holding the door open behind him.

"Take him out of here," said the old man.

Joe Gaff looked from the dog to Sarah Nell, who refused to meet his eyes, and then back to the dog.

"It ain't me that can make him leave you, sir," Gaff said.

The old man looked at the dog for a long, still moment and then raised his arm and pointed toward the door and the night.

"Go out of here. Git," said the old man.

The dog raised himself slowly and passed through the door between Gaff and Sarah. Outside, the wind was up again and it was raining. They left the dog standing by the car shed, tail and ears drooping, his body slicked black with rain. The car was already past the mule lot, halfway down the lane between the rows of pecan trees, before they heard the dog howl the first time, a long, moon-reaching wail breaking over the night.

Gaff turned to Sarah Nell as though he would speak, but did not. Instead, he pulled his hat lower over his eyes and guided the old car carefully through the mud out of the lane onto the big road.

"Pa always was a fool about clabber," Sarah Nell said, her wooded voice breaking over the last word.

Harry Crews (1935   )

Crews was born in Bacon County, Georgia. He has written many novels and essays. His memoir, A CHILDHOOD: The Biography of Place, was published in 1978. His short stories have not yet been collected in a single volume. "A Long Wail" was first published in THE GEORGIA REVIEW in 1964 and recently reprinted in NECESSARY FICTIONS: Selected Stories from The Georgia Review (1986).

"A Long Wail" was reprinted with the permission of Mr. Harry Crews.

Strong Horse Tea

Alice Walker

RANNIE TOOMER'S LITTLE BABY BOY Snooks was dying from double pneumonia and whooping cough. She sat away from him gazing into a low fire, her long crusty bottom lip hanging. She was not married. Was not pretty. Was not anybody much. And he was all she had.

"Lawd, why don't that doctor come on here?" she moaned, tears sliding from her sticky eyes. She hadn't washed since Snooks took sick five days before, and a long row of whitish snail tracks laced her ashen face.

"What you ought to try is one of the old home remedies," Sarah urged. She was an old neighboring lady who wore magic leaves around her neck sewed up in possum skin next to a dried lizard's foot. She knew how magic came about and could do magic herself, people said.

"We going to have us a doctor," Rannie Toomer said fiercely, walking over to shoo a fat winter fly from her child's forehead. "I don't believe in none of your swamp magic. The 'old home remedies' I took when I was a child come just short of killing me."

Snooks, under a pile of faded quilts, made a small oblong mound in the bed. His head was like a ball of black putty wedged between the thin covers and the dingy yellow pillow. His eyes were partly open as if he were peeping out of his hard wasted skull at the chilly room, and the forceful pulse of his breathing caused a faint rustling in the sheets near his mouth like the wind pushing damp papers in a shallow ditch. "What time you reckon he'll git here?" asked Sarah, not expecting an answer. She sat with her knees wide apart under three long skirts and a voluminous Mother Hubbard heavy with stains. From time to time she reached down to sweep her damp skirts away from the live coals. It was almost spring, but the winter cold still clung to her bones, and she had to almost sit in the fireplace to get warm. Her deep, sharp eyes had aged a moist hesitant blue that gave her a quick dull stare like a hawk. She gazed coolly at Rannie Toomer and rapped the hearth-stones with her stick.

"White mailman, white doctor," she chanted skeptically.

"They gotta come see 'bout this baby," Rannie Toomer said wistfully. "Who'd go and ignore a little sick baby like my Snooks?"

"Some folks we don't know well as he *thinks* we do might," the old lady replied. "What you want to give that boy of yours is one or two of the old home remedies, arrowsroot or sassyfrass and cloves, or sugar tit soaked in cat's blood."

"We don't need none of your witch's remedies!" said Rannie Toomer. "We going to git some of them shots that makes people well. Cures 'em of all they ails, cleans 'em out and makes 'em strong, all at the same time." She grasped her baby by his shrouded toes and began to gently twist, trying to knead life into him the same way she kneaded limberness into flour dough. She spoke upward from his feet as if he were an altar.

"Doctor'll be here soon, baby. I done sent the mailman." She left him reluctantly to go and stand by the window. She pressed her face against the glass, her flat nose more flattened as she peered out at the rain.

She had gone up to the mailbox in the rain that morning, hoping she hadn't missed the mailman's car. She had sat down on an old milk can near the box and turned her drooping face in the direction the mailman's car would come. She had no umbrella, and her feet shivered inside thin, clear plastic shoes that let in water and mud.

"Howde, Rannie Mae," the red-faced mailman said pleasantly, as he always did, when she stood by his car waiting to ask him something. Usually she wanted to ask what certain circulars meant that showed pretty pictures of things she needed. Did the circulars mean that somebody was coming around later and give her hats and suitcases and shoes and sweaters and rubbing alcohol and a heater for the house and a fur bonnet for her baby? Or, why did he always give her the pictures if she couldn't have what was in them? Or, what did the words say? . . . Especially the big word written in red: "S-A-L-E!"?

He would explain shortly to her that the only way she could get the goods pictured on the circulars was to buy them in town and that town stores did their advertising by sending out pictures of their goods. She would listen with her mouth hanging open until he finished. Then she would exclaim in a dull amazed way that *she* never had any money and he could ask anybody. *She* couldn't ever buy any of the things in the pictures—so why did the stores keep sending them to her?

He tried to explain to her that *everybody* got the circulars whether they had any money to buy with or not. That this was one of the laws of advertising, and he couldn't do anything about it. He was sure she never understood what he tried to teach her about advertising, for one day she asked him for any extra circulars he had, and when he asked her what she wanted them for—since she couldn't afford to buy any of the items advertised—she said she needed them to paper the inside of her house to keep out the wind.

Today he thought she looked more ignorant than usual as she stuck her dripping head inside his car. He recoiled from her breath and gave little attention to what she was saying about her sick baby as he mopped up the water she dripped on the plastic door handle of the car.

"Well, never *can* keep 'em dry; I mean, *warm* enough, in rainy weather like this here," he mumbled absently, stuffing a wad of circulars advertising hair dryers and cold creams into her hands. He wished she would stand back from his car so he could get going. But she clung to the side gabbing away about "Snooks" and "pneumonia" and "shots" and about how she wanted a *"real* doctor!"

To everything she said he nodded. "That right?" he injected sympathetically when she stopped for breath, and then he began to sneeze, for she was letting in wetness and damp, and he felt he was coming down with a cold. Black people as black as Rannie Toomer always made him uneasy, especially when they didn't smell good and when you could tell they didn't right away. Rannie Mae, leaning in over him out of the rain, smelled like a wet goat. Her dark dirty eyes clinging to his with such hungry desperation made him nervous.

"Well, ah, *mighty* sorry to hear 'bout the little fella," he said, groping for the window crank. "We'll see what we can do!" He gave her what he hoped was a big friendly smile. God! He *didn't want to hurt her feelings*; she did look so pitiful hanging there in the rain. Suddenly he had an idea.

"Whyn't you try some of old Aunt Sarah's home remedies?" he suggested brightly. He half believed along with everybody else in the county that the old blue-eyed black woman possessed magic. Magic that if it didn't work on whites probably would on blacks. But Rannie Toomer almost turned the car over shaking her head and body with an emphatic NO! She reached in a wet hand to grasp his shoulder.

"We wants us a doctor, a real doctor!" she screamed. She had begun to cry and drop her tears on him. "You git us a doctor from town!" she bellowed, shaking the solid shoulder that bulged under his new tweed coat.

"Like I say," he drawled patiently, although beginning to be furious with her, "we'll do what we can!" And he hurriedly rolled up the window and sped down the road, cringing from the thought that she had put her nasty black hands on him.

"Old home remedies! Old home remedies!" Rannie Toomer had cursed the words while she licked at the hot tears that ran down her face, the only warmth about her. She turned backwards to the trail that led to her house, trampling the wet circulars under her feet. Under the fence she went and was in a pasture surrounded by dozens of fat whitefolks' cows and an old gray horse and a mule. Cows and horses never seemed to have much trouble, she thought, as she hurried home.

Old Sarah dug steadily at the fire; the bones in her legs ached as if they were outside the flesh that enclosed them.

"White mailman, white doctor. White doctor, white mailman," she murmured from time to time, putting the poker down carefully and rubbing her shins.

"You young ones *will* turn to them," she said, "when it is *us* what got the power."

"The doctor's coming, Aunt Sarah. I know he is," Rannie Toomer said angrily.

It was less than an hour after she had talked to the mailman that she looked up expecting the doctor and saw old Sarah tramping through the grass on her walking stick. She couldn't pretend she wasn't home with the smoke from her fire climbing out the chimney, so she let her in, making her leave her bag of tricks on the porch.

Old woman old as that ought to forget trying the cure other people with her nigger magic. Ought to use some of it on herself! she thought. She would not let Sarah lay a finger on Snooks and warned her if she tried anything she would knock her over the head with her own cane.

"He coming, all right," Rannie Toomer said again firmly, looking with prayerful eyes out through the rain.

"Let me tell you, child," the old woman said almost gently, sipping the coffee Rannie Toomer had given her. "He *ain't.*"

She had not been allowed near the boy on the bed, and that had made her angry at first, but now she looked with pity at the young woman who was so afraid her child would die. She felt rejected but at the same time sadly *glad* that the young always grow up hoping. It *did* take a long time to finally realize that you could only depend on those who would come.

"But I done told you," Rannie Toomer was saying in exasperation, "I asked the mailman to bring a doctor for my Snooks!"

Cold wind was shooting all around her from the cracks in the window framing; faded circulars blew inward from the walls.

"He done fetched the doctor," the old woman said, softly stroking her coffee cup. "What you reckon brung me over here in this here flood? It wasn't no desire to see no rainbows, I can tell you."

Rannie Toomer paled.

"I's the doctor, child. That there mailman didn't git no further with that message of yours then the road in front of my house. Lucky he got

238

good lungs—deef as I is I had myself a time trying to make out *what* he was yelling."

Rannie began to cry, moaning.

Suddenly the breathing from the bed seemed to drown out the noise of the downpour outside. The baby's pulse seemed to make the whole house shake.

"Here!" she cried, snatching the baby up and handing him to Sarah. "Make him well! Oh, my lawd, make him well!"

"Let's not upset the little fella unnecessarylike," Sarah said, placing the baby back on the bed. Gently she began to examine him, all the while moaning and humming a thin pagan tune that pushed against the sound of the wind and rain with its own melancholy power. She stripped him of his clothes, poked at his fiberless baby ribs, blew against his chest. Along his tiny flat back she ran her soft old fingers. The child hung on in deep rasping sleep, and his small glazed eyes neither opened fully nor fully closed.

Rannie Toomer swayed over the bed watching the old woman touching the baby. She mourned the time she had wasted waiting for a doctor. Her feeling of guilt was a stone.

"I'll do anything you say do, Aunt Sarah," she cried, mopping at her nose with her dress. "Anything you say, just, please God, make him git better."

Old Sarah dressed the baby again and sat down in front of the fire. She stayed deep in thought for several minutes. Rannie Toomer gazed first into her silent face and then at the baby whose breathing seemed to have eased since Sarah picked him up.

"Do something, quick!" she urged Sarah, beginning to believe in her powers completely. "Do something that'll make him rise up and call his mama!"

"The child's dying," said the old woman bluntly, staking out beforehand some limitation to her skill. "But," she went on, "there might be something still we might try..."

"What?" asked Rannie Toomer from her knees. She knelt before the old woman's chair, wringing her hands and crying. She fastened herself to Sarah's chair. How could she have thought anyone else could help her Snooks, she wondered brokenly, when you couldn't even depend on them to come! She had been crazy to trust anyone but the withered old magician before her.

"What can I *do*?" she urged fiercely, blinded by her new faith, driven by the labored breathing from the bed.

"It going to take a strong stomach," said Sarah slowly. "It going to to take a mighty strong stomach, and most of you young peoples these days don't have 'em!"

"Snooks got a strong stomach," Rannie Toomer said, peering

anxiously into the serious old face.

"It ain't him that's got to have the strong stomach," Sarah said, glancing at the sobbing girl at her feet. "*You* the one got to have the strong stomach…he won't know *what* it is he's drinking."

Rannie Toomer began to tremble way down deep in her stomach. It sure was weak, she thought. Trembling like that. But what could she mean her Snooks to drink? Not cat's blood! and not any of the other messes she'd heard Sarah specialized in that would make anybody's stomach turn. What did she mean?

"What is it?" she whispered, bringing her head close to Sarah's knee. Sarah leaned down and put her toothless mouth to her ear.

"The only thing that can save this child now is some good strong horse tea!" she said, keeping her eyes turned toward the bed. "The *only* thing. And if you wants him out of that bed you better make tracks to git some!"

Rannie Toomer took up her wet coat and stepped across the porch to the pasture. The rain fell against her face with the force of small hailstones. She started walking in the direction of the trees where she could see the bulky lightish shapes of cows. Her thin plastic shoes were sucked at by the mud, but she pushed herself forward in a relentless search for the lone gray mare.

All the animals shifted ground and rolled big dark eyes at Rannie Toomer. She made as little noise as she could and leaned herself against a tree to wait.

Thunder rose from the side of the sky like tires of a big truck rumbling over rough dirt road. Then it stood a split second in the middle of the sky before it exploded like a giant firecracker, then rolled away again like an empty keg. Lightning streaked across the sky, setting the air white and charged.

Rannie Toomer stood dripping under her tree hoping not to be struck. She kept her eyes carefully on the behind of the gray mare, who, after nearly an hour had passed, began nonchalantly to spread her muddy knees.

At that moment Rannie Toomer realized that she had brought nothing to catch the precious tea in. Lightning struck something not far off and caused a cracking and groaning in the woods that frightened the animals away from their shelter. Rannie Toomer slipped down in the mud trying to take off one of her plastic shoes, and the gray mare, trickling some, broke for a clump of cedars yards away.

Rannie Toomer was close enough to the mare to catch the tea if she could keep up with her while she ran. So, alternately holding her breath and gasping for air, she started after her. Mud from her fall clung to her elbows and streaked her frizzy hair. Slipping and sliding in the mud she raced after the big mare, holding out, as if for alms, her plastic shoe.

In the house Sarah sat, her shawls and sweaters tight around her, rubbing her knees and muttering under her breath. She heard the thunder, saw the lightning that lit up the dingy room, and turned her waiting face to the bed. Hobbling over on stiff legs, she could hear no sound; the frail breathing had stopped with the thunder, not to come again.

Across the mud-washed pasture Rannie Toomer stumbled, holding out her plastic shoe for the gray mare to fill. In spurts and splashes mixed with rainwater she gathered her tea. In parting, the old mare snorted and threw up one big leg, knocking her back into the mud. She rose trembling and crying, holding the shoe, spilling none over the top but realizing a leak, a tiny crack, at her shoe's front. Quickly she stuck her mouth there over the crack, and, ankle deep in slippery mud of the pasture, and freezing in her shabby wet coat, she ran home to give the good and warm strong horse tea to her baby Snooks.

Alice Walker (1944–)

Walker was born in Eatonton, Georgia. She has written four novels, including THE COLOR PURPLE (1983), and several collections of essays and poetry. Her two collections of short stories are IN LOVE & TROUBLE: *Stories of Black Women* (1973) and YOU CAN'T KEEP A GOOD WOMAN DOWN (1981). "Strong Horse Tea" is taken from IN LOVE & TROUBLE.

The Best Teacher in Georgia

John McCluskey, Jr.

THE MUSING

As Dora FELL OFF THE BACK PORCH, next door Miss Mary Lou Hunter was turning the selector to a rerun of "The Rockford Files." In her front room Miss Mary settled down in her favorite sitting chair, a steaming cup of sassafras tea, sweetened with two teaspoons of honey, resting on a carefully folded square of newspaper. To make sure that she did not miss a word of her favorite afternoon show, the set was turned up loud, so Dora's first shout for help, an embarrassed yelp more than anything else, was drowned in the twangy guitar crescendo of the opening theme. Then Miss Mary blew into her tea, took two sips, and set her cup down. Scratching down an arm, she sat back and waited for the first chase scene.

Dora had tried to catch herself on her hands, then her elbows, but had failed. Her knees and chin were the three points that absorbed the impact of her fall. She was as surprised at the lack of pain as she was by the fall itself, surprised even that her glasses stayed on. The world had been spinning when she stepped to the back porch. There were plenty of pecans under the great tree and she wanted to bring them in for a pie. That spinning that she had now been so accustomed to for the past eight months started again as the back door slammed and she had stopped at the edge of the porch and, already falling, was reaching for the railing. She heard a *crack* before the ground rushed up fast. The ground was still spinning as she lay there even now, the faint smell of packed dirt in her nostrils.

She tried to get up, but could not. She could not feel her arms, though she could see them tensing. It was as if they had fallen asleep during some nightmare and she was armless. She remembered screams in such dreams and knew that the one she recalled from just seconds ago was her own.

Her weight was on her neck now and she slid forward and to one side quickly to relieve the pain. But her shawl tightened deeply across a shoulder. She struggled to lessen the strain, but could not. Finally, she managed to turn just enough so that she could free one end of it. She let out a sigh. Again, she could compare this to only a bad dream. Occasionally there would be one—whether someone was chasing her or she was shut up in a closet didn't matter. She would be suffocating and one part of her could tell the other that she was face down in the pillow and all she had to do was roll over. The feeling was so strange, because there would be the great will to breathe again and the easy urge to lie like that as sweet resignation washed over her. And she would turn, in some mighty effort, just enough to breathe fresh air, then search back quickly for the episode in her dream that made her realize that she was suffocating. She could never find it.

Bunny had brought the shawl home from a trip to Philadelphia two years ago. Bunny and her husband had spent the Christmas away, so the gift was not presented until New Year's Eve. That was the day before the coming of the deer. New Year's Day was unseasonably warm and from the thick woods over a mile away a small band of deer found Dora's backyard. Fawns were frolicking about the pecan tree by the time Dora came to the back window. They played close to the porch while two larger does kept to the edge of the yard, watchful. With potato chips or soda crackers in their hands a few of the kids like little Calvin, Thomasina's loud boy, tried to tiptoe up on one of the fawns. When they saw a big buck step out of the woods and start digging at the ground with one of his front legs—well, those children just backed on off and went up to the porch to watch the show like everybody else. The deer stayed out there for ten, twenty minutes and then, one by one, they were gone. Just like ice storms in that part of Georgia, they appeared as swift and silencing miracles and then, with no trace, they left. That was the morning of the day Bunny and her husband returned. She brought the shawl over after dinner. It was in a deep-red box hidden beneath the wrapping paper, and inside the blue and cream shawl rested on crinkly paper. Dora had been connecting the shawl to the deer to ice storms ever since.

She reached down suddenly. A gust of wind had started up the back of her legs and she felt the hem of her skirt rising, then the skirt ballooning up from behind. She quickly smoothed down her skirt. Don't want that Mr. Leroy to look down here and see me with my bloomers showing to the sky. Just like him, too, to look out of his window and stay up there grinning like a fool and trying to see what all he could see while I'm down here rolling around. I've caught him a dozen times riding that old piece of bicycle he got, riding past the porches and trying to look up some woman's dress. He bends down like he cocking his head to say "hello" but he got something else on his mind. That man's got to be ninety if he's a day and still carrying on all sorts of foolishness. He's the loudest one in church on Sunday mornings and he shouts "amen" loud enough to shake the rooftop when the preacher starts in talking about the lust in some men's hearts. Yes, he'd see all he could see first before he would get over here to help out, nasty thing. She tried to push up, but failed.

"Lord, I've got to get up from here," she heard herself say.

What else might be going on? She thought of how some young fool could break right in the front door while she was out here and steal the television set or those pretty brass lamps that she had bought her mother on her seventieth birthday. Her mother would be in the bedroom humming to herself and not hear or see a thing. Then Dora let her body go limp. As the sound of her heavy breathing faded, she could hear a car or two passing out front. Before too long there would be the four o'clock whistle from the paper mill. She could hear now, as plain as the ticking of a clock coming closer, the wooden heels of someone walking past the house. She wanted to scream but decided against it. And what would that whistling somebody with the loud heels find? Just an old woman without her hair piece who fell off her back porch and could not get up again. About as bad as Humpty-Dumpty with all the king's men. She saw knights in dull grey armor attempt to pull her up, fail in their grunting, then mount their glorious black horses, liveried in silver, and move slowly off in single file. She laughed drily. "Well, I'm not that bad off and I want everyone to know it."

She thought that if she stayed still for just a short while longer the ground would stop spinning and she could roll to one side, then sit up. Last spring she had fallen and she had had several dizzy spells since then, spells which made her sit up for minutes until her head cleared. The first time she was in the backyard where she had finished hanging out some sheets to dry. From here, she could see the spot where she fell, and she remembered how she caught herself on her hands and waited there on all fours, her knees sinking into the soft ground, until the world stopped. She didn't tell her mother about that time. Would her mother have understood? She who, until her own blindness, never knew a sick day or a knock-down illness in her life?

At some time in her late years her mother must have fallen. But now with her cane, the fingers of her free hand walking the rough plaster walls, she knew every dangerous step, every corner, every table in the house. And Dora, twenty years younger and fading already, it seemed, was given to dizzy spells that a smart-aleck doctor with a beard could not cure. Her mother had already outlived a husband and son and it looked like she would outlast the only one she had left.

She gained an elbow about the time Miss Mary whooped when

the private investigator, after hitting a lumbering goon on the chin, doubled up in pain, then blew across and kissed his aching knuckles. The giant merely blinked, rocked slightly on his heels, and chased Rockford off with a lead pipe. Miss Mary sipped again from her tea, then glanced to the window where the end of a branch was scraping. She could not hear it, however.

Still on one elbow, Dora concluded that her mother must be in the dim sitting room listening to the late afternoon symphony from a classical music station out of Atlanta. "The only colored woman in Spalding County, Georgia, to listen to the opera," she once boasted. But it was the news, the details of all events national and international, that kept her by the radio. She feared losing touch, feared not knowing the names of those who made the news. ("We as a people have got to get our heads out of the sand and realize there's a whole world out there. How come colored can't care about what's happening in India or Poland?")

Two squirrels skittered around the trunk of a burr oak in Mr. Leroy's yard. From somewhere a crow cawed and she could smell the smoke from someone's burning trash. At a two-year-old's height she could see the backyard. It was large enough for a child to run about, to feel small in. When she was growing up here, it always seemed that the yard was large enough for a dozen cows to graze in. The day she returned from Atlanta to live here she was shocked at the game her memory had played. It was still a large backyard dominated by one huge pecan tree at its center but three full-grown Herefords would have made it appear a pen.

Now she could only look. Just months earlier she had been hoeing in the garden which ran the length of the back fence. Now the green beans and most of the tomatoes had been picked. A few collards were left, but the sweet potatoes, somehow forgotten this year, might be a lost cause. Of course, as predictable as early November frost, there were the plentiful pecans. Each year, as an additional Christmas gift, she would send a large box of them to her daughter and her family in Milwaukee. The daughter would call on Christmas Day to thank her for the gifts, usually not mentioning the pecans. She called, too, after the arrival of flowery cards on Mother's Day and her birthday. Every two years the daughter with her family would visit and every other trip they would arrive in a new car. Dora would have appreciated a long letter on no special occasion and failed to convince herself that they were too busy adding on rooms, buying appliances, getting promotions on time. Had she as a mother failed to do something right when her daughter was six, or thirteen, or twenty? She wondered.

Adjusting her glasses, she tried to focus on the pecan tree now. During the late mornings of last August's brutal heat she would read in the shade of the great tree, its trunk cool along the length of her spine. Last summer she had stuck to poetry—Shakespeare's sonnets, the Brownings, and Countee Cullen. Six years before she retired she had been voted the best teacher in Georgia and she could recite Cullen poems with a voice pitched to the middle register of a flute: *These are no wind-blown rumors, soft say-sos/no garden-whispered hear-says, lightly heard...*

When she finished, her eyes often moist, the fifth-graders would look at one another in confusion. One or two might cover their mouths and roll their eyes, not knowing any better, and the silence would then beg for a snicker, a dry cough—anything to bring the room back to normal. How did she ever hope to successfully explain the weight behind the words she recited, the moons and suns those words created and softly landed upon? She hoped to merely provide them a form which their experiences would fill. In the all-white school where she taught during the last five years before her retirement they would giggle. Somehow she would expect it there, though. She imagined they took the sight and her words home with them to be brought up over dinner. ("Mama, we got the strange colored woman for a teacher and she can stare out the window and say poems by heart. And sometimes she seemed to be about ready to cry over them.") Aside from screams barely audible over guitars, they had no stories, no songs. It was even getting that way for the black children. She confessed to herself many times that she pitied the young with their anthems of screaming guitars and runaway saxophones. Many gave them noise for music, but few gave them a poem.

She was almost up now, but, leaning too far forward, slipped and fell to her other side with a groan. ("Mama, Mama, don't come now and learn I'm like this!") A door slammed; Mr. Leroy's dog barked twice. Her view was once again that of a toddler's. She listened to the beating of her heart. It was not racing. Her breathing was normal. The ground had stopped spinning. She was relieved by at least that much. She managed to turn over on her back, not caring how her dress and sweater would look when she finally did get up. She relaxed and looked up through the limbs of the tree to the sky. She had not lain on her back looking at the sky for nearly fifty years.

Though it was summer that time, she could not remember the heat. Her high school friend Alphonso had introduced her to George, who attended Morehouse and visited town that summer after his junior year. With Alphonso's fiancée, they had all bicycled out to a small lake for a picnic. Then they walked, the couples separating, and she and George found a hill all their own. After they shared their future plans, they relaxed in a silence. She closed her eyes and saw red against the insides of her eyelids. Clover was sweet and she smelled his cologne, a faint lemon it was, before he kissed her lightly. The next day they returned alone and kissed many times, she recalled now.

They made love quickly, awkwardly. Afterwards, briefly, she let the sunlight again paint the insides of her eyelids red. By the next summer he urged marriage, but she could not accept then. She would remember that hill, that red, those smells forever, but it had only been a few brief moments and she had imagined love to be a string of such moments, palpable, infinite in length.

Horace, however, was October, a vivid splash of color. She married him the year she found her first teaching job. It was a hard marriage. She grew to crave consistency. She fought for sameness, though it was the sudden peaks and valleys of emotions that raced her blood. He died fifteen years ago and she lived alone in Atlanta until she retired. Her daughter invited her to join her and her young family in Milwaukee. "Too cold," she had lied, not wanting to be a burden and, besides, her mother needed someone close by.

Perhaps it was the rush of those long ago moments, the slant of the afternoon light on this day, that had sent her to the back window before she decided that the fallen pecans were worth her trouble. Yes, perhaps that, before the porch started spinning. Rising on an elbow, she concluded once more that she would seek more moments, more vivid splashes of color. Just three days ago she had reserved a flight to New Orleans. She had planned the trip with Gladys, another retired teacher, but Gladys died suddenly in September. A local travel agency had made travel arrangements, reserved a seat at two plays, and was forwarding a listing of preferred restaurants with the ticket. ("You'll just love New Orleans, Mrs. Wright," said an agent over the phone, cool efficiency sugared by admiration. "We've got you a room in an elegant and quiet hotel on Royal. It's what we call a 'C and C,' clean and classy. All our clients just love the place. It's near everything in the Quarter. You're a mighty lucky lady.")

She and Horace had planned to visit New Orleans for two weeks around their fortieth anniversary. From the stories of clubwomen who had traveled there in groups or with their husbands, she knew all about the food, all about the balcony ironwork magically spun by slaves. This time of the year there would be no crowds and she would not be jostled on the sidewalks. But what if she had a spell there among strangers, collapsing on those ancient sidewalks before ancient cafés? She winced. Please hurry, ticket. With ticket and travel plans in hand, only then would she tell her mother. Another breeze swept up and terror was that sudden chill at the base of her neck.

AND FOND MEMORY

She was sitting upright now. She could hear her mother working her way through the kitchen. She shook her shawl out and placed it around her shoulders. She brought her legs together and smoothed down her skirt and apron. After a glance at Mr. Leroy's window, she found a few pecans nearby and dropped them in her lap one by one, as she might drop stones in a pond.

"Dora? Dora child, where you at? I been calling you for the past ten minutes and can't get word out of you."

"Out here, Mama. I'm out back."

"What you doing out there so long?" came her mother's voice.

"I'm just out here enjoying the weather."

Her mother pushed through the back door and came onto the porch. She tapped her cane against a chair, then against the wooden pillar that supported the railing. "You going to catch a cold out there. This fall weather can fool you."

She smiled. Over a long checkered dress her mother wore a faded brown sweater. She was a neat woman who dressed up and wore small gold earrings every day.

"I want to get supper started and I need you to slice a little of that ham off. Come on now. You ain't getting no younger and too much of this sitting around on the wet ground can give you arthritis. I know what I'm talking about."

"I'm on my way, Mama."

As her mother started to turn, the sleeve of her sweater caught a nail on the back post. In trying to pull away and misjudging her own strength, she pulled a hole in the sweater sleeve and, losing her balance, fell backward against, then through, the railing.

"Mama! Mama, the rail...!"

The old woman fell on her side, no scream, and her body made a dull sound when it landed, like that of a hundred-pound bag of seed.

"Mama, you all right?" She tried to inch forward on her elbows and stomach. "Mama, say something!"

Her mother was bleeding from the elbow and the forehead, a trickle of blood snaking between the eyebrows already. Her eyes wide—though her daughter felt the stare of such eyes long past fear— she looked to the sound of her daughter's voice as a child would. The blood, a thin crooked line, found the bridge of her nose.

"Oh, I'm all right. Just a scratch, child." She patted her own cheek. "Still...no, you're bleeding, Mama!" She was close now, close enough to touch her. Then with the hem of her skirt she wiped the blood from her mother's face, dabbed at the cut lip she had just noticed.

Her mother shook her head as if to push her away, the way an embarrassed child anticipates a rough kiss.

"Help me up, Dora."

"I can't."

"What do you mean 'you can't'?"

"I can't. Mama, I can't get up my own self."

Her mother bowed her head as if in prayer. "Dora, how long you been out here like this?"

"Fifteen, twenty minutes maybe. My arms and legs just went numb for a while..."

Her mother's soft shriek came as if she had been hit suddenly. Then her face tightened. Dora thought she was going to cry.

"Well, I'll be. How come you didn't call for me, Dora?"

"There wasn't any need. It's happened to me once before and I got right up, quicker than a cat. If it keeps happening, I better learn to pull up some kind of way."

"You better to see a doctor is what you 'better' do. Why, you could just drop down at the shopping center or at church or anywhere. Whatever it is, you better not play with it."

"I have seen a doctor. He just gave me some pills. He said if they didn't do any good to come back around Thanksgiving for some tests." She glanced off. By Thanksgiving she would have been to New Orleans. Maybe the trip would cure her. She had heard of spells that just went away mysteriously after coming on once or twice.

Her mother was silent for a moment, then spoke softly to no one in particular. "You ain't getting no younger. You can't all the time be hoping to pull yourself up." Then to her daughter: "Can you see anybody around? Let's call somebody over."

"Mama, just give me a minute. I'll have both of us up."

"Well, just one minute then. This cold ground cause arthritis sure as we sittin' here." She snorted, patted a thigh. "At least I ain't broke nothing. Women fallin' at my age break a hip the same way you break a toothpick. Remember Lila's girl, Hattie, slipped and fell on her steps that time and broke her hip in two places? That's been what—two, three years, ain't it? You ain't broke nothing, did you?"

"I better not break anything. Can you imagine me on crutches?"

"There's worse things than crutches," her mother said.

Then Dora chuckled. "We must look quite the pair. Two women plopped down in the backyard and can't even get up."

"It won't be funny an hour from now and we still sittin' here."

"Just another min...the front door locked? You sure everything's off the stove?" Dora suddenly imagined the house on fire, smoke billowing from the kitchen. Sirens before loud-talking, heavy-booted firemen intruding, crashing through the kitchen to find them in the backyard.

"Nothing's on the stove and I 'spect the front door is still fastened. I locked it right back after the mailman done handed me the mail." (The ticket! The ticket!)

Dora turned to her side, pushing, but her arms were numb,

250

muscleless. She sighed. She wanted to laugh. She wanted to cry.

"This telling me I'm getting old," Dora said.

"You got to use your common sense, Dora. You got to fall off the porch to find out you ain't thirty no more? Or even sixty?"

She looked at her mother's sightless eyes. They were hazel. Younger, Dora felt that when she looked directly at her mother the light eyes gave the impression of pools that you looked into. Her own eyes, dark brown and like most of her features, were those of her father. She fidgeted.

"Well, I don't like this. I don't like this feeling where you can't control what your body's going to do the next minute."

"What you gon' do about it? I don't like it either, but ain't nothing neither one of us can do about it. You gon' stop the clock?"

"I mean I'm scared, Mama. I been scared for a long time, but it took this to make it plain."

She brushed dirt from her mother's shoulders, then dabbed again at her forehead. The trickle of blood had slowed.

"Scared?" her mother asked. "I tell you what scared is. I'm talking after the change of life and after your teeth go bad and your hair thin. I do have to thank the good Lord my hair stayed thick as it was when I was fifty. But then your hearing go on you and you get tired of bothering folks all the time, asking them to repeat what they say. So you just shake your head at them and go ahead and say something to what you think they be saying. And you remember how it was early morning when you hear the birds just starting up, just before day-break? Well, you get so you can hardly make out the sounds. 'Bout the only thing you can catch is some big ole crow or Mr. Leroy's loud rooster. Then before you get used to not hearing as good as you used to, your smell give out on you. Oh, you can still make out cabbage all right, but what happened to cinnamon and thyme and just plain ole coffee? You see something that could be a rose or a apple, but unless it's right up against your nose, it might as well be plastic. Dora, you hear what I'm telling you?"

"I can hear you."

Her mother cleared her throat. "Then if all that ain't enough to make you scared and mad at the same time, you might get some real bad luck and get the cataracts on your eyes so bad that even after operations..."

"Mama, I know about what happened. You don't..."

"...listen good, now—after the operations you still can't see and over months you can't see nothing, not one blessed thing. You can tell light from dark, but you see things like they was ghosts or something and you know you'll be that way—even if you believe every jack-leg preacher between here and Nashville who say he got the cure for you—

251

know you'll be seeing ghosts for the rest of your life. And all the while your bones drying out and getting like…like chalk. Every little bump you pay for, every fall. You and me gon' feel this fall clear into next week."

Dora was shaking her head. She tried to see herself in ten years, fifteen, twenty. Wondered what her luck would be. Would she be able to see the morning light sparkling on heavy frost? Would she be able to see her amaryllis in bloom? Would she be able to do for herself alone? But her mother continued, reaching to pat her arm.

"Ain't no time to be scared, child. We just got to get on up from here before we have everybody laughing at us out here. They'll laugh first, then come running over here asking if they can help."

"They're not that bad."

"I tell you I know them, I know how they do."

She wanted to tell her mother that it was not just the embarrassment and confusion of a body failing, growing stranger. It was death, of course, that frightened her, that chilled her again that afternoon with terror. And when she finally brought herself to say it, she was alarmed at how still her mother became. A truck rumbled down the street out front.

"Don't be so scary, will you? You talk like you got one foot in the grave already. Plus, it ain't too late for a woman like you to have men to come calling."

Dora snickered. "Only eligible men 'way out here are not doing so well, in and out of the hospital every day. You talking about them calling and they can barely make it back and forth from the bedroom to the kitchen table to the bathroom…"

Her mother threw up her hands. "There you go again talking like you too good."

"I'm not too good. Don't you think I'd like to have a man to talk to, to have dinner with and dance with, all these years?"

"All I'm saying is that a woman like you—educated and who think about things—a woman like you need friends, educated friends. I know there ain't much here for you. Maybe for somebody like myself, when I was your age, there were one or two. You remember I used to see that Mr. Coates? Now he was a nice decent man to come courting and like me he just barely finished high school."

"Mama, college by itself doesn't mean a person's nice or decent or even educated."

Her mother talked on, low. Dora didn't know whether her mother heard her this time. Softening, she pitied her in that instant, pitied them both. After Horace's death, there had been a special friend once and, now, the sun flooding the yard with its dying light, she spoke of him. She had promised herself never to tell.

He had been five years younger and his wife was in poor health. Downtown Atlanta had only recently opened up for blacks and three nights a week they would meet at a small restaurant off Peachtree. They kept to the side streets, hand in hand. Once even they checked into a downtown hotel, avoiding the popular Paschal's Motel, as husband and wife. As excited as teenagers, they had been. But their affair lasted only three months. Except for her award, it was the most exciting time of her last fifteen years.

Her mother's face had registered curiosity when she first started. By the end of Dora's confession, however, her face revealed horror. Her head snapped once, as one shakes from a sudden chill or as if slapped from a trance.

"Shame on you, running around like some hot-blooded Jezebel! Rochelle Louise Fields didn't raise no child to run around with married men. Taking advantage of some sick woman that way and you a respectable schoolteacher and all. I bet you got plenty of secrets."

Dora's shoulders sagged under a heavy load. She saw herself in New Orleans alone on Rue Royal. The knocking of her shoes was the loudest noise in the world as she walked. She stepped into a puddle of light, scattering pigeons. There was a spring in her step as she moved on. The background music was not Dixieland, but Ella Fitzgerald's "A Tisket-A Tasket." Lilac was strong in the air, though it was autumn.

"I was lonely, Mama. He was, too. That was all it was." She dared not tell her that for six of those ten daring weeks it had been much, much more. Then as if some bright monarch butterfly skimming the tops of grass and grain, love had skipped away.

"You don't know how lonely I've been these last fifteen years. There have been times I've wanted to walk over to the woods and just scream like some crazy woman. You hear that clock ticking, cars passing out front with people on their way to…to something—work, a family, somebody to touch and talk to. And you know all you can do is sit or dress up to walk downtown or around the mall. Crowds make you feel even more lonely so you come back home and sit. Maybe you find a book every once in a while to take your mind off things. Even then you want to share it."

"That don't mean you take up with a married man," her mother said. "They're plenty of folks lonely—I can tell you a thing or two 'bout loneliness—but they ain't dabblin' in no other folkses' home business. And you don't have to talk about me on the sly, talking about what I didn't learn. I only got past high school. I know I never got the chance to go to college or nothing. My folks barely had enough to send one off and that was your uncle who just wasted his time and your grandpa's money…"

Dora clapped both hands to her ears, for she had heard many times the tale of the ungrateful son who had gone up to Fisk to be a doctor and had ignored his studies. He had been dismissed and worked in Nashville over a year before he found the nerve to tell the family what had happened. Meanwhile Rochelle had worked and bought second-hand books to know the worlds she thought only available to the formally educated. She learned manners from books of etiquette and from the languid gestures of young white women she served during lawn parties. Grew defensive, then rigid about what she learned in solitude. So when her brother returned to confess his failure, she wanted to throw a pot at him. She, not he, should have been the one to go to college. Later her carpenter husband would stand mute before her monologues on good manners.

How quickly we forget! Rochelle's own daughter took her own good fortune in stride. Why, even after she had been voted Teacher of the Year for the entire state and shifted to a formerly all-white school as something of a reward, Dora was not pleased. Dora's hands came down quickly when she heard.

"Mama, how many times I have to tell you that I made my way teaching among my own? I was happy at Phillis Wheatley. I didn't need white folks to tell me I was good. My students and other teachers and principal nominated me. That made me the proudest."

But her mother was convinced that such matter-of-factness before so astounding an achievement—she had been voted best out of the "colored" and the white!—was unnatural. Was vanity.

Dora now thought of the plaque, a gold-plated square on a walnut-stained shield, hanging on the front room wall where no one could miss it. Her mother had insisted that it be hung there. Dora thought of the telegram that she tore open with trembling hands and the long, flowery letter that followed. This, before the award ceremony and the plaque.

"Oh, Mama, remember how you came to Atlanta with Miss Mary and everybody? How I wore my best dress—it was the baby-blue one with the lace at the collar and sleeves, remember?—I put on so much rosewater I bet they could smell me clear to Macon. And, when that skinny man with the big belly announced my name, how I walked up— I don't know 'til this day how my legs carried me up there—and I had to practically tear the plaque away from him."

Her mother nodded and managed a smile. "He acted like you was taking gold." It was one of her mother's last sights. In a brief silence they sat. That night in an auditorium in downtown Atlanta had been one of the last genuinely happy moments they had shared. Now her mother cleared her throat.

"Dora, we ain't got all day. The past is dead and gone."

"Maybe." In two weeks, her ticket clutched against one side, she would board a gleaming silver jet with royal blue trim. Two stewardesses would flash smiles and point her to her seat. Her mother would be here in this house where she would be cared for by Miss Mary until Dora returned. By then she would understand why Dora needed the trip. By then all her questions would be exhausted.

She got to her knees and leaned on her mother. "Mama, just stay still. I need your shoulder here to help me up." Trying to put as little weight on the shoulder as she could, she pressed down and gained one foot, then the other.

"Glory," she sighed. "Mama, I'm up. I'll come from behind you and pull you up."

Slipping her arms inside her mother's, she pulled her up in one mighty effort. Then she brushed the dirt from both of them and led her mother to the porch.

"You smell good today, Mama."

"You saying I don't always smell good?"

"No, I'm just saying you smell special. It's that new Avon you ordered? You got somebody special to come calling?"

"Don't sass," her mother said.

Smiling, Dora did not look back as they opened the door. The pecans were still scattered behind. She would come back for them soon. Right now there was a supper to start.

Miss Mary turned off the set as the last of the theme song died out. She climbed upstairs to her bedroom and walked to the window. She heard the back door slam next door at the Fields's. Their backyard seemed to float up toward her. There was a spot just beyond the porch that was favored by the sun. Pecans had rained there. The yard looked like a meadow left shimmering after a morning mist had just lifted. She recalled that years ago a flock of pink flamingoes had played near that very same spot.

Or was it peacocks or rabbits or…deer?

John McCluskey, Jr. (1944-   )

McCluskey was born in Ohio of Georgia parents. He is the author of two novels, Look What They've Done to My Song (1974) and Mr. America's Last Season Blues (1983). "The Best Teacher in Georgia" was published in 1985 in The Southern Review.

"The Best Teacher in Georgia" was reprinted with the permission of Mr. John McCluskey, Jr.

Nobody's Fool

Mary Hood

FLOYD HEADED UP THE HILL to feed the dogs. They had been hoping for him, pacing the length of the near fence, for an hour. He was that much later than usual; it was his day to shave. A man with the shakes would be a fool to shave fast. When Floyd opened the door to the shed to get the food, Goldie padded down to the gate and poked her muzzle through the gap by the latch, sniffing, her blind eyes blue as the sky. Cinder, the puppy, tromped over the empty pans, dumping the water basin in his clumsy hunger. The bald patch on his hip was hairing over and he no longer limped. He looked as if he had been rolling in ashes. He always could find trouble.

"Now, listen," Floyd said, pleased as he always was by their boiling-over welcome. He staggered a little under the weight of the chow sack. It was hard to open. He tugged at the string, then took out his knife and cut it. He should have done what Ida said, put some food in a bucket and not carried the whole bag, but how could he, after she said it? The bag only weighed twenty-five pounds. That wasn't too much for a man. She was at work. She'd never know it if he didn't do what she said, and why should he? Just because she said?

"It'll weigh even less going back downhill," he told the dogs. They were busy eating. He stood in the open gate, watching them. They weren't doing anything but eat. They ate loud.

"All you think about's your belly," he said.

It was nice weather. Floyd liked spring. He thought he'd get the rake and sweep up those last oak leaves. Ida said for him not to get up on the ladder and do the gutters, but he could still rake. He'd rake.

Then—before he could say more than "Whoa"—the dogs got out, got past him, escaped, tore away across the yard as if they'd been planning it for weeks. Cinder was leading, Goldie at his heels. For a blind dog, Goldie was keeping up.

"Y'all don't," Floyd said.

But they did. Straight down across Ida's rye grass, under the cedar fence, and free, barking out of sight as if they were closing on a coon. Floyd listened for the squeal of brakes—nothing—so that was all right, they made it across the highway, heading for the woods behind the shopping plaza. He could imagine them pelting on like that for hours, till their dinner gave out and they circled back for supper.

"They'll be back before you get home," Floyd said aloud. He hoped so. He didn't want to hear from Ida about it. She'd say he couldn't even manage that, to leave it to her to do from now on.

"I was just trying to save you from walking up here in the mud and ruining your shoes," Floyd said.

He'd remember to mention that, if the subject came up. Let her think about *that* for a while. "The world ain't all me-me-me," he said.

He stooped to scrabble up the dog chow that had spilled from the sack while the dogs had his attention. He toed the rest over onto their pans and left the gate open.

"They'll be back," he said.

He started down to the house, the sack of chow in his arms like a baby. Ida had been a difficult child, sure of her ways and disapproving of everybody else's, from day one. Things had to be nice and they had to be all her way. Or she'd kick sand. Or do without. Or starve. She was proud. Nice about things, always wanting better. "Like her mama," he said.

Once Ida had gone without her lunch. Refused to eat it. Opened her brown sack at school and announced, "This isn't mine. Someone stole my lunch," in that flash and fury against all things wrong and second best that carried her through high school, chin high, and on past college too, to tell the world, for her living, how it was doing things wrong too. That day, she said, "My mama don't make black banana sandwiches." The teacher sent home a note. Floyd remembered it like yesterday. He laughed.

He set the chow sack against the shed door and sighed. It had been easier on the downhill. "A sight easier," he said. The pain in his shoulder eased in a minute, but he thought he would rest some more before he started raking. He sat on the patio and chewed. It was pouch tobacco, not his usual plug. Ida had bought it for him. She didn't approve, and didn't see any difference. Besides, Piggly Wiggly didn't carry Bull of the Woods, and Piggly Wiggly was where she got double coupons.

"No use in telling you," Floyd told her.

All day long he'd talk to her like that, till she came home from work. They'd eat in silence, or else she'd talk, talk, talk at him. It wasn't always quarreling, but it wore him out, so he'd go up to his room and listen to the radio till bedtime. Ida liked her TV in the evenings. She laughed along. Sometimes she talked on the phone at the same time.

It was ringing now.

Floyd spit into his soup can and had a sip of Coca-Cola before he answered.

"Hay-lo," he said. "This here's Floyd."

"I'm Bob, the computer," the voice said. Floyd listened. He didn't know Bob.

"Did you say computer?" Floyd asked.

The voice talked on without pause. It didn't matter if you were listening or not, Floyd thought. He hung up.

"Bad as you," he told Ida. He had better to do.

Ida said, "All you had to do was shut that gate."

"I was just trying to save you from some trouble," he said.

"Then why didn't you shut the gate?"

They were driving slowly along. All the yards they passed were empty. Everyone was at work, or indoors, watching TV. There was only one dog in sight—a Doberman.

Floyd said, "Those'll kill you soon as look at you."

Ida stopped the car and got out. The Doberman danced as he barked, his clipped ears, healing in their splints, white as horns.

"Somebody's bad news," Floyd said.

Ida got in and drove them on. They turned left. Her window was rolled down so she could whistle. She beat on the side of the car with her hand. Cinder and Goldie were nowhere to be seen.

"They'll come home when they get hungry," Floyd told her.

"You're the one who's hungry," Ida said. "That's why you want to give up looking." Whatever Floyd knew, she knew better.

Floyd took some tobacco and packed his cheek.

"And don't you spit from that window," Ida said. "I ran this car through the Bubble Wash this afternoon."

"I'd swaller it first," Floyd said.

They went past the shopping center. At the mud lane into the pines where the dirt bikers roared on weekends, Ida slowed.

"You reckon my babies got this far?" she said.

"I hope I'd have more sense," Floyd said. "Why do they dock them dogs like that? Ears and tail too. Didn't leave him more than a nub."

Ida said, turning onto the mud, "It's dry enough. We won't get stuck." She rocked them slowly along the ruts, trying not to splatter her clean car. Floyd sat up straight, his fist on the door handle. They ran over a piece of chrome from a junked car. There was a mattress sagging against a dinette chair. Ida edged past. Then they came to the scrap roofing and old tires, blocking the way.

"Trash is all they are who'd do a thing like that," Ida said. She had to saw the car, back and forth, back and forth, to get them turned around and headed back to the road. When she got to the highway, she blew out her breath and just sat there.

"Ain't nothing coming," Floyd said. "Either way."

"You-can-give-me-a-minute," Ida said, like she was counting out change, each coin clicking down to pay a righteous debt.

"Just trying to help," Floyd said, folding his hands.

"Help like yours I need like a hole in the ground," Ida said. "All you had to do was *shut that gate!*"

Floyd opened the door and got out. He had to spit. He worked on that.

She leaned across the seat and yelled, "You going to run off too?"

He swiveled around. "Better for both of us if I did."

"Wipe your chin," she said. She handed him a Kleenex. She was always right there with her Kleenex, her coasters, her spray wax, her dictionary, her Lysol, her vitamin tablets, her salt substitute.

He turned his back on her. "Ain't good for nothing no more," he said, just loud enough if she cared to deny it. He could set off, walking, if he knew which way was north. He could find friends. He checked the sun, held his hand forth, counting the hours between it and the horizon. He still wore his watch on his grandpa's chain, but it was broken.

"Get in this car, Daddy," she said, gunning it. Next thing she'd be blowing the horn.

"Maybe I'll walk," he said. "I've walked further'n that."

"*Right now, Mister*," Ida said.

"Many a day," Floyd said. But he was already trembling, like he'd gone miles. That lint cough, the one the mill had retired him for, bent him over, blind. He didn't even notice it anymore. He stood up, wiped his eyes, and eased back into the car.

"Pore as a snake," he said, catching his breath.

She just stared at him. "Why do you do this? Behave like a child? I've had students no worse than you. They don't waste *my* time, not a minute. I send them out."

She drove toward home, fast. The tire made a flap-flapping sound on the asphalt. Floyd heard it, but didn't mention it. Maybe they'd wreck.

She heard it too.

She slowed, eased over onto the shoulder, past the sign that said: BOILED P'NUT AHEAD FRESH HOT GOOD. Closed till summer.

"Well, check and *see*," she said. "Can't you even do that?"

Floyd got out and looked. There was a piece of board stuck to the right rear tire. The tire went on down to flat as soon as he had kicked the board loose. The long nails left holes like snakebite.

Ida got out and looked, too.

"I don't suppose anyone'll stop," she said. "Why should they?"

Floyd said, "I can fix it."

She didn't count on that, he could see. "I'll trouble you for them keys," he said.

When he got the trunk open and was fiddling with the jack—it had to fit in those holes in the bumper and he couldn't get it right—a truck pulled up behind them and a man in a camouflage jumpsuit offered to help.

It didn't take him long.

Floyd unbuttoned his front pocket and unwadded three bills from his snap purse. He handed them to the man. "Many thanks," he said. "If there's ever anything I can do for you some day..."

The man pushed the money back. He laughed. "Keep it, old-timer. Buy yourself some Red Man." He swung up into his truck and drove away.

Floyd stood there for a minute. Ida was already back in the car, washing her hands on a little towelette. Floyd flung the dollars into the sedge. He kicked at one of the bills that fluttered by.

Ida started the engine. "Daddy?"

When he shut his door, it hung up.

"*Slam* it!" Ida said. "Can you?"

Floyd said, "Don't worry about *me*."

They rode along not talking.

Just before they turned onto the street where Ida's house was, Floyd said, "If you was to need a transplant, I'd be who to ask. You can have anything I've got that'd do you any good."

Ida aimed the car up the drive, braked sharp, rammed the lever into park, then jerked out the keys. "I don't need anything presently," she said. She laughed.

Floyd just sat there, thinking. Ida went on into the house. She didn't look back out, or wonder.

The dogs came home on their own. Ida was out at the fence welcoming them, pouring red-eye gravy on their chow, talking to them like children past nine o'clock that night. Floyd watched from the kitchen door. He couldn't have gravy. Ida read where it was bad for his heart.

Floyd went to his room and packed.

He didn't know whether to tell her or just leave a note, but if he told her, she'd have something to say.

"Nothing I ain't heard," he decided.

He stayed in his room till she had left for work the next morning. As she left, she tapped on his door.

"Daddy? Daddy?"

When he didn't answer, she went on to school. He could hear her muttering, "Like a rock...whole place could burn down around him...thank Jesus he doesn't smoke..." She had to be at school by 7:30.

Floyd waited till her taillights were good and gone. Then he tied up the pillowcase with his extra overalls and Sunday shirt. Ida hated his overalls, hated the very sight and color of denim, but Floyd didn't mind it. He'd spent his life making it, so why should he mind? He was drawing seventy-five cents a day—"A *day*," Floyd said—at the sawmill when he got hired on at the cotton mill for three dollars a day. It made a difference in their life right from the first paycheck. Ida didn't know how to be grateful, that was what it was. Floyd had his Bible in the sack, too, and the photograph of all of them, that summer day at the river when he got himself baptized and stopped drinking for all time. A man could change for the better, Floyd knew. He liked to keep the evidence at hand. He put his knife in his pocket and counted what was left of his pension. He had enough.

He reached down his hat from the closet shelf, and put it on, by touch, from long experience. Floyd knew who he was. He could shave in the dark. His hat had that trademark billiard-rack block to the crown. Ida hated that hat. Said a sock cap, like babies wear, was warmer. She bought him one, and a muffler to match. Floyd left it in the box, saying, "Where's my mittens, Mama?" and wouldn't even wear it to feed the dogs.

Floyd dug out his pencil and licked it twice.

Now Ida, he wrote, *dont bother. I done it before and I no how to live. A man has to pull his own weight at least. I done fed the dogs. When I am settled I will let you no.*

Yore dad, Floyd.

He added at the bottom: *no usen calling me,*
it'll be long distance.
No usen hunting me.
I don't like it hear.
All you do is fuss.

In fairness, he marked that out so she'd read: *All we do is fuss.*

He set out, walking strong. If a man offered him a ride, he'd consider it. But he felt strong enough for miles, if no one did. When he saw just the right sapling he carved it down some and kept it in hand.

"To scare off varmints," Floyd said, nobody's fool. He read the papers.

He was meeting all the traffic on its way to town jobs. He wasn't going that way. Nobody even slowed. Some of them had on their headlights. The wisps of fog off the river blew into pieces as they drove through it. Even without the traffic, there was a wind. He stopped to put on his extra shirt. As he bent to retie the pillowsack—caught between his legs as if he were shoeing a horse—his hat blew off, skipping along, teasing him into chasing it with his stick.

Then the wind played a trick. Lifted the hat over the railing of the bridge and tossed it up, sailing it out on a curve, into the water below. Floyd watched it settle into its reflection, sinking slow. It was considerably oiled after years, randomly waterproofed by Wildroot. A little fishing skiff putted up to the rocks below the bridge and their mere trolling wake sent it under.

"Adios, hat," Floyd said.

He walked on across the bridge, then, bare-headed, clear-headed, undizzy. There was more to think about than a lost hat.

"I played here as a boy," he told the fisherman at the other end of the bridge. "Used to jump right off the mill into the deep over yonder."

The man looked where Floyd pointed.

The lake covered it now. And the fields he'd run. "Prettiest cotton," Floyd said. He saw the fisherman didn't remember.

"It's this new road," Floyd said, irritated. "It don't go where it used to, just to town and back. Look over *yonder*," he said. "That hill?"

The man looked again.

"Me and this old boy hauled Book Gravely up it with ropes and mules to be buried close by. Drownded himself in the mill. Nowhere else to swim, but you had to be strong against the tow. Dry summer."

The man said, "Drought, huh?" He was busy with his fishing. He took out a little red and white lure from his box and hooked it on his line. Floyd watched it swing out and down, and the ripples spread wide, from such a little thing.

"Grass growed in the riverbeds so cows could graze," Floyd said. "Only green left in the county." He got thirsty remembering. He wiped his face.

"Things was different then," Floyd said. "Book didn't have no kin and it being hot, we couldn't ship him. We did it as decent as we could."

"Back then, folks was different," the fisherman said. "Cared for each other, you know."

"It's so," Floyd said. He studied the man for likeness. "You from around here?"

"My mama was from over at Rose Creek."

"Maybe she knowed her," Floyd said.

"Who?"

"The lady who come on toward nightfall and laid weeds on Book's grave. We rolled a rock on it to mark it but nobody knowed who she was, never did."

"Weeds?" He was pulling in his fish, a little one, not worth keeping.

"Weeds was all he got, and a fieldstone, but that was more than he might've, considering."

"Mama never said nothing about that," the man said.

"We always wondered," Floyd said.

The man went back to his fishing. Floyd looked out at the lake.

"Nah, mama never said nothing about that," the fisherman said again.

Floyd checked his dead watch. It was a habit, marking time. He always had to be doing something useful, or he felt he was slacking. He said, "I could talk all day," and the man said, "Yeah, I know what you mean. I could fish for a living."

"Same thing," Floyd said. "Back to work, then, son." He took up his sack and headed on up the hill. He told the man, as he went on, "Take it easy on them crappie, son, save some for the rest of us."

Floyd struck off up the hill strong, past the Marina, not looking back. He had to rest his breath, though, at the top. He stood poking at the crumbly shale on the bank by Spain's old place, honeysuckled over now, boarded up.

"Dead now," Floyd said. "I knowed him good as a brother. His little sick wife. All them flowers he growed for her to look at."

Floyd blew his nose.

When the chicken truck stopped, Floyd told the man, "I won't say no," and got up in the cab. He had to leave his hickory stick behind. He glanced back, to memorize *where*, in case he got back by there. "I hope not," he said. They were rolling. The radio was on, and the heater. Floyd sank asleep almost at once.

The lady at welfare said Floyd *had* to tell her his name. He didn't see his way clear to do that. He said he'd manage, then, without her help. Could she recommend a rooming house? She wrote the directions on a scrap of paper and he took that—and his pillowcase—and stepped off toward town, steady as he could in case she was watching from the window. "I'm no hobo," Floyd said.

At the rooming house it turned out he had enough money for one week, if he ate lean. Floyd knew how to manage that, too.

He couldn't change his Social Security till the next week. The agent only came to the courthouse on Tuesdays. Even so, it meant the next check would go on to Ida's, too late to stop it now.

"If I was to die, mid-month, she'd have to pay it all back," Floyd said. He thought that through, how she'd look when she got the letter saying IMPORTANT and she read how she'd have to miss work to get it straightened out.

"Ida, she hates paperwork," Floyd said.

Every day he walked the streets, looking for work. He got a few little jobs—mainly handyman chores—mainly for widows who couldn't even change the light bulb in their ovens. Floyd had a little problem with that, too, till the man at Otasco told him to buy the heat-resistant bulb. That woman told him, when he came back with the right bulb and explained he wouldn't charge her for his mistake, "You're not too handy but you're sure a man."

He did better on raking. Hammermill had a lot of oaks.

"They bad to hold their leaves till spring," Floyd said, door to door. He had all the work like that he needed. He piled the leaves up and burned them if they didn't want them turned into their gardens. He didn't know anything about that ordinance against burning.

"I ain't from around here," he told the police. They didn't hold him. He wasn't a vagrant. He didn't have any money to pay a fine. They could see that. They didn't shame him into crying or telling Ida's name. He didn't even feel bad about it till he got to his room to rest. He lay on his cot, weak. He couldn't even go out the next day, to straighten out about Social Security. He kept a fever, and his cough was worse.

He thought Ida had found him. He thought Ida was spying on him. He told Mrs. Sloane, when she came around to get the rent, "Look." He showed her the markings, their code, the way they numbered his room when they came checking up. She laughed.

She said, "Ridiculous!" just like Ida.

"It's where the cash register tape got in some water," she told him. "The ink's left a stain on your table, that's all."

He knew by the way she laughed it off that she was one of them. He couldn't stay any longer. But he paid her what he could, so she'd think he was going to.

That night he took his Bible and extra clothes and left by the back door, while Mrs. Sloane and the others were in the front room, watching TV. He could hear them laughing.

It was twelve steps down to the back yard. Floyd took them in one. He landed hard on his arm. He crawled back up to the house and into bed before he called for help.

"I heared it snap," he told the doctor.

They didn't know to look for his things. They lay out in the rain all night. His Bible was ruined.

Floyd had paid Mrs. Sloane all the extra he had, and the hospital wanted more. If he gave them his real name for Medicare, he was as good as back with Ida again. They'd call her before the plaster dried.

He wasn't going to be handed back. He had legs.

Floyd walked out of the hospital. It was easy.

"They weren't expecting *that*," he said, getting clean away. He headed back by Mrs. Sloane's, and when she was talking to the milkman, he slipped around and got his things. He took the alleys and lanes, walking like he had business. He had his sleeve pulled down over the cast. He fit in. No one noticed. He staggered, bummed up from the fall, but he kept on going. He loosened up as he pressed on.

He could feel the heartbeat in his broken bone. He didn't dwell on it.

It wasn't raining now. That was a good thing. He sat on one of the benches in the park by the post office. He needed to think. He needed his tobacco. His head was clearer than it had been. Day was just getting going. The sparrows and starlings were awake, drifting down from the eaves and clock tower. From the courthouse roof the pigeons rose with a sound like worn-out cards being shuffled. Floyd watched them wheel. He always did like first light best. He felt young. Like he was on his way to school. Or to the mill. And none of the things that went wrong had yet come to him.

Then he thought, But they're behind me, at least, if they had to happen. The *pastness* was something. If he was young, it'd all be ahead, even if he didn't know to dread it. What was ahead now? He didn't know that, either. So it was like being young.

"If ignorance is peace," Floyd said, "I oughta be getting more out of it."

He felt for his Bible. It was swollen and damp, its pages sealed to each other around the photograph of his baptizing.

"Never mind," he said. He knew by heart what was in there. He knew what he had to do before sundown that very night. He stood. After he got moving, he was warmer. His feet woke. He picked up speed heading down the sidewalk toward the railroad. He didn't even feel hungry any more. At the depot he turned south.

It was Saturday. Plenty of traffic going both ways. He got a ride in the first mile that carried him as far as the river. After that, he rode, wind-whipped, with the sun in his eyes, in a plumber's truck that got him down to the four-way stop. There were three in the cab already. He didn't mind riding in back. "Take it easy," they told him.

"Or any way I can get it," Floyd said. He felt good. As if it were home he was nearing, not just Ida's. He walked up the drive fast.

Ida was still in her housecoat and slippers. She answered the door with half a biscuit in her hand. She just stood and stared, without swallowing. She looked hollowed out, like she could use that biscuit and some sleep too, Floyd thought. He saw, in that light, she looked way past grown, on the downhill side, like him.

"Daddy?" She reached for his hurt arm.

"I just have this one thing to say," Floyd said. "Let me say it."

She turned him loose.

"I think I made a mistake about that dog gate," he said. "That's what I think."

She kept staring.

"Next time I won't," he told her.

She still didn't say anything.

"What do *you* think?" he wondered. She had about gripped a hole all the way through the biscuit. She took another bite and leaned against the door.

"You still mad?" Why didn't she say something?

"Talk at me," he said.

If he could just get her started, it'd be all right again. He didn't have to listen.

"Ida," he said, priming the pump, "I throwed away my hat."

Mary Hood (1946   )

Hood was born in Brunswick, Georgia. She has published two collections of short stories, HOW FAR SHE WENT (1973) and AND VENUS IS BLUE (1986). "Nobody's Fool" is taken from AND VENUS IS BLUE.

Wintering

Greg Johnson

THE ALEXANDER BALDWINS never argue, but they are arguing now. Urgent whispers, rising up the stairway. Their three-story colonial is massive, beautifully restored (thick champagne colored carpet installed throughout, even in the bathrooms; double-paned windows; an expensive new central heating system that works inaudibly), and so solid that it retains all sounds, all passions. The Baldwins stand in the dining room, where they've just eaten lunch, or perhaps in the wide foyer with its teal-blue Persian rug, where Laura confronts Alex before he can escape out the front door.

The foyer, just at the base of the stairs. Where Alex has begun to shout.

"For heaven's sake," Laura hisses, "keep your voice down."

"You know he can't hear us—it's affected his hearing, the doctor said so."

"I remember very well what the doctor said. That's why I can't believe you're doing this."

"My God, you act like I'm throwing him out! He *wants* to go, you heard him yourself. It's December, Joey's expecting him. The routine is established, Laura."

"Routine, that's a hell of a word to use. And as for Joey—"

"Let's not get into *that*."

Silence. Alex has that way about him; a gift for deflecting you, for having the last word. I can remember him one evening thirty years ago, slamming his small fist on the dinner table, very precisely, then announcing that he *must* be excused, he *had* to continue work on his science project or how would he win first prize? His mother and I stayed silent, watching his erect little frame march defiantly from the table. Joey giggled in his hand.

Laura, cowed but still resourceful, now says in a wounded voice,

"How would *you* feel, being expected to leave at a time like this. We have so much room, Alex, and he's gotten to like the new doctor so well—"

"He has a doctor in Atlanta, remember? It's the weather, you know that. He always winters down there."

"But this winter is...different."

Alex pauses, considering. "Maybe so, but you know how he hates Chicago when the weather turns. And anyway the plans are made — he has his reservation, I called Joey and gave him very clear instructions—."

"Your plans, your instructions—is that all you think of?" Laura interrupts. Her whisper is thin, disgusted. "What about feelings? Your father's more than—than part of your damn schedule."

Alex, severely: "Speaking of which, you're making me late."

"And Joey is so inept, so irresponsible. What if something happens?"

"I'll be back by six," Alex says obstinately. "We'll drive him to the airport then."

"What if *you* had a child," Laura says, her voice cracking. "What if someone did this to *you*?"

The front door, opening. "But I don't have a child," he says sarcastically. "I only have you."

When the door slams, there is the sound of Laura's soft weeping. With a kind of malice, it seems, the house contains us all: our every sigh or whisper. I back away from the polished oak banister, thinking this.

Old men are permitted such thoughts.

Consciousness, anger, dread: do they diminish with advanced age, or do they retrench, slyly, for some final and invidious attack?

The first quarrel with Marguerite concerned, ostensibly, my contemptible dread of airplanes. Her father, one of the richest men in Georgia (farming and real estate interests, mostly, and a profitable dabbling late in life in the international oil business) and the first in his club to purchase, then learn to fly, his own airplane, had offered us a free ride to New York, the boys (then four and six) included, where he would wrap up a land-purchase deal and where I could meet a few of his stock market cronies. My fledgling career as a "broker" would be helped by such contacts, and there would be plenty of time for Marguerite and the boys to see the sights. My wife, who had led a typically sheltered Southern-debutante existence followed by two difficult pregnancies and two intense, protracted post-partum depressions, was elated about the trip. Not that she was concerned about my brokerage career, since the tacit assumption had always been that she, already possessed of an immense inheritance from her maternal grandfather and eventually to become even richer when her

own father died, would be my only client. Nor, oddly, did her enthusiasm come from her own need to get away, prodigious as that must
have been. Rather it was the six-year-old Alex, his alertness and
curiosity already showing themselves as serious, focused, and for-
ward-looking, who needed the stimulation of new sights and experiences, and she even insisted that Joey, though lethargic and fussy as
his brother was lively and precociously well-behaved, was old enough
to profit from the trip. When I had tried, the night before our departure,
to dissuade her by admitting the real reason I wanted to stay home—
my heartstopping fear of that flying machine, the nightmare of my
conscious wide-eyed self caught helpless within its tumbling, fiery
descent—Marguerite exploded. She was brushing her long hair, angrily. She hissed that I was a coward, and a poor example for my sons.
Behind her, I was a shadowy reflection in her gilt-edged mirror. We
argued for a while, but quickly the argument became a monologue, a
tirade—my wife's anger was disproportionate, wild, and I sensed that
during most of our seven-year marriage I had lived on time borrowed
against the Southern code of wifely submission and my own disincli-
nation to hamper Marguerite's quietly forceful style. Now, she'd had
enough; from that night forward, she abandoned her oblique manipu-
lations and daily proved that her power had always involved more than
money. We went on that trip, of course. While her father and his copilot
happily prevailed in the cockpit, she and Alex perched at the window
and exclaimed over rivers, mountain ranges, swiftly moving rags of
cloud. In the seats behind them a whimpering Joey huddled against
his father, whose bowels had turned to lead.

Since my wife's death of cancer, six years ago, flying has become
easier for me, and the biannual exercise in dread can even, at times,
seem instructive. For this evening it came to me that I didn't dread the
flight itself but rather my destination; and I knew that although my son
remained deliberately obtuse, his wife had seemed, somehow, to
understand.

Laura has always felt an instinctive sympathy for me, perhaps a
displacement of some unacknowledged pity for herself, and in defer-
ence to this I kept quiet during the ride to the airport. To trade upon
the "poignance" of the moment would have been distasteful, and
anyway I've never been a vindictive man. (Alex was correct, after all,
when he claimed that I wanted this trip; for I had told him so.) I sat
between them in the spacious front seat of their Continental, wearing
the benign, even slightly addled expression I've developed as a way of
reassuring Alex that I mean no trouble to him, that preternatural
docility has become a way of life. Not surprisingly, he chatted and
laughed during the long drive (the Alexander Baldwins live in Lake
Forest, more than an hour from O'Hare), talked about their plans to

visit Atlanta frequently this winter (plans that are talked about every year, and which never materialize), lavishly praised my new doctor in Atlanta, a young neurologist at Emory University Hospital (whom Alex has never met). As he talked, his cheeks seemed to glow. His suede-gloved fingers flexed on the steering wheel. My son's smell was as fresh, new, and leathery as the interior of his expensive car, and I felt embarrassed for my sour odor of old age, of illness, that must have been apparent to both Alex and Laura. To avoid such thoughts, and to insure that my silence wouldn't be misunderstood, I made feeble comments about the weather as we drove along: how surprisingly warm for December, how the low-slung, soupy clouds appeared to hold summer rain rather than malevolent bits of ice.

"Yeah, but it won't be long," Alex said comfortably. "They say it'll be a severe winter, much worse than last year's. You're lucky to be getting out."

I nodded. "Yes, and last year's was hardly mild. Even in Atlanta, it snowed three times."

"Really, did it? Three times?" Since boyhood, unusual facts had always pleased him. But again I feared being misinterpreted.

"It melted quickly, though. Usually the next day."

"That's good," said Alex.

Laura, who had stayed morose and self-absorbed thus far, said abruptly, "Where did you hear that?"

Alex looked over, irritated. "Hear what?"

"About this winter. Its being so severe."

He shrugged. "I don't know. The newspapers."

"Those predictions never amount to anything."

I wasn't watching him, but I could imagine his lips flattening against his teeth—a gesture that meant he'd had enough.

"Chicago winters," he said evenly, "are always severe."

This brought a few moments' silence. I had begun to feel unusually awkward, sitting there between them. The Alexander Baldwins, after all, are a very good-looking young couple. Alex has his mother's high, prominent forehead, her clear, imperious green eyes, her fine olive-dark complexion. Laura, dark-haired and demure, has the fault-less poise of upper-class Southern wives, cheeks and hands of an unearthly paleness, and unexpectedly full, sensuous lips. Next to them I'm a sack of bones, wispy yellowish hair and patchy skin where unexplained purplish marks, like bruises, come and go without warn-ing; my eyes are faintly bluish, watery. I didn't blame Alex for wanting to get rid of me, and I wished Laura would not protest. But the awkwardness came out of sharp, familiar longing that, during that silence, rose ungovernably in me: a longing to stay here, to spend the winter with these two healthy, well-dressed adults, safe inside their well-managed and well-insulated house.

Perhaps that was why I said, out of nowhere, "One thing your mother disliked about the South was the weather—she always loved the snow. She never felt happier, she once said, than when she could stand at the window and watch the snow falling."

Alex glanced aside, irritated yet curious. "Mother said that?"

"Oh, were you thinking of her too?" Laura broke out. She had, suddenly, the exuberance of nostalgia. Looking her way, I saw that her eyes were moist. "I do remember," she said, nodding, "how she used to talk about the snow. Whenever the two of you came for the holidays, she always hoped for a big snowfall on Christmas eve."

Alex picked up speed, though rain had begun to spatter the windshield. "I don't remember that," he muttered.

We stayed silent for the rest of the drive. I sat thinking how despicable it was, trying to use the specter of Marguerite on Alex. To the guilt I'd felt when overhearing their conversation was added the guilt I've always suffered, helplessly, at the spectacle of my own self-pity. Advanced age makes self-pity even harder to bear, because no one minds it. People pat your hand, they smile reassuringly. So I was grateful for the silence. Compared to this weight of guilt, my consciousness of dread or anger shrank to nothing. I could even imagine Joey's quick, furtive smile of greeting without a shiver of revulsion.

The point of no return. That is what we've reached, the flight attendant says with a wink, when I had only asked her for the time.

"Will the flight be late?" I ask now.

"What?" she exclaims in mock surprise. "Our flights are *never* late."

Sourly, I look away. Here in my first-class seat, mainly a salve to Alex's conscience but nonetheless welcome, I impersonate the old curmudgeon I should have long ago become. I order hot tea, then complain that it's too strong; I demand to change seats, wanting to escape a chain-smoking executive seated just behind me. The flight attendant, who pretends amusement at my high, whinnying voice and general irascibility, keeps glancing into my eyes as if to find a telltale twinkling there, but she finds nothing and eventually stops asking if there's anything I want. In the half hour before landing there is just enough time to remember how Marguerite, during our last flight to Chicago, pointed out that beneath my irritated behavior on airplanes lurked profound fear (which she no longer found contemptible, but "interesting") and to recall my own weak protestations that I'd conquered that phobia years ago. She had turned to look out the window, smiling. Even during her final illness she'd had that serenity and assurance about her, as though death were only another challenge for Marguerite Holloway Baldwin to confront with a nearly surreal grace and dignity. It strikes me, now, as unfair that Alex's memories of her should so often seem abstracted, as though she'd become a character in an old novel; he speaks of her with a polite, soldierly reverence but seldom with warmth or any sense of personal bereavement. Perhaps she is still with him, somehow, in a way she was never with me, so that there's no need for him to grieve.... This thought now causes my fingers to shake, in some blending of feebleness and terror, as I attempt to drink the cooled, black-looking tea that the flight attendant (stupidly? defiantly?) has placed again on the plastic fold-out tray before me. She appears just at the moment the airplane dips sharply, in it first gesture of descent, and the tea sloshes first onto my papery fingers, then onto the white, well-starched cuffs of my shirt.

"Oh, have we had a little accident?" she asks in the cooing, nanny's voice I've begun to inspire in the very youngest people.

"No, I've had an accident," I tell her.

She vanishes, then reappears with a cloth and some colorless cleaning solution. She wipes frantically at the cuffs, making little grunting noises with her head bowed as I sit stolid above her, scowling.

In a moment she straightens, eyes crinkled with regret. "Tea stains are tough—I've managed to get most of it, but still..."

I retract my arms like a pair of claws, hiding the soiled cuffs beneath the tray. "It's all right," I say gruffly, but then, noting that she seems genuinely depressed—she is responsible for my welfare, this perky twenty-year-old, and senses her failure—I add, irrelevantly, "If it weren't for my wife, I wouldn't be on this trip. She made me promise I'd always winter in the South, but somehow it never works out. This is only the first, I'm sure, of a string of mishaps."

She looks at me strangely. Her face, in that cruel transparency suffered by the young, passes through befuddlement to pensiveness to a slow, blushing delight whose source I cannot imagine. But of course she hasn't listened: she is only responding to the new, milder tone of my voice. In a moment, her impishness has returned in full force. She grins. She winks.

"Well, give her a message from me," she says. "Tell her not to let a handsome guy like you go flying off alone—he's liable to get into all sorts of trouble."

I don't respond. As the plane continues its descent, I recall the innumerable times Marguerite would remark upon my handsome, even formidable appearance.

Standing alone amid the crush of travellers, his shoulders hunched, Joey is hardly "formidable"; he looks defensive, as if fearing contamination. When he glimpses me, however, he springs forward like a wind-up toy, long-limbed, grinning, all gangling solicitude. He snatches the flight bag from my shoulder. He queries me about the flight, his breath reeking of gin.

Unlike Alex, my second son drinks to excess.

"It was fine," I tell him. "Excellent weather."

"Oh, that's a relief. I'd heard about this rainstorm, out in the midwest. So I wasn't sure…"

"You fly above the clouds."

Already walking along, father and son. He keeps lurching ahead with his long legs, then stopping while I catch up. He makes bantering conversation, he grins sheepishly. Tonight he has a rabbity, woebegone look, longish hair a bit tousled, nostrils pink and sore-looking. Anyone encountering him, I think uncharitably, might be the one to fear contamination, for his boyish, half-sickly grubbishness has never left him. When we reach baggage claim, he actually does turn aside in the middle of a sentence—he was narrating the story of this airport, the largest in the world, his excitement obviously genuine—for a long, raucous sneeze. When he turns back, his cocoa-brown eyes are glistening.

"Sorry, I have a cold. Whenever the seasons change, I get one. And then it stays for a week."

"You should take vitamins."

Guiltily, "I know."

We wait for the baggage, a prim and well-dressed elderly man with his son, a thirtyish slump-shouldered man/boy wearing Levi's, a khaki shirt, a fawn-colored suede jacket that has seen better days. Yet not an unhandsome man, my Joey. He has the Baldwin sturdy build and strong jaw, his mother's clear skin, high forehead, good bones. These advantages, however, are apparent only to the most sympathetic observer; what people notice are the pink nostrils, the slack posture, the ridges of dirt beneath his nails. Comparison with his brother is, and always was, inevitable. Even their mother remarked, when they were boys, that she felt she'd given birth to Jekyll and Hyde.

The carting of luggage, the maneuvering of Joey's rattling, malodorous car—only two years old but already despoiled—take up the next few minutes, but then we're on the interstate and an eerie tension arises between us. Joey shifts in his seat, fiddles with the rear-view. I sit looking at the shimmering skyline, limned by a crisp starry night.

"It was raining in Chicago," I tell him, conversationally. "And much warmer than here."

"Are you cold? I'm afraid this heater doesn't work." He fiddles desperately with some knobs on the dashboard, then curses.

"No, I'm all right. Keeps the blood moving."

"I meant to have that fixed, I'll do it tomorrow. You want this jacket? Here—" and he's already halfway out of it, letting the car swerve abruptly. A car in the other lane blares its horn.

"Keep the jacket, Joey. And watch the road," I tell him.

The jacket falls on the seat between us; Joey grabs the wheel and glances aside at the passing car. "Bastard," he mutters.

Patience. With this son I need patience, and fortitude, and a certain measure of abandon. If you ride with him, you know that your life could end momentarily. His mother often remarked, in a rueful tone, that the first funeral in the family would be Joey's—he was so vulnerable, so clumsy and helpless. The first day of spring training for his junior-high football team, he broke his collarbone. On his sixteenth birthday he received his driver's license and, from his mother, a new Thunderbird, and three weeks later was hospitalized with a head injury and countless minor lacerations, the car having become scrap metal. As a young man he was given an honorable discharge from the navy only three months after his impulsive enlistment; he never told us why, but there were predictable jokes that he had wrecked a battleship, or had been unsuccessfully offered to the Russians. Poor Joey. And yet he survived. Though his mother left him very well off, he has worked for the past several years as a magazine illustrator, a tame nine-to-five job that has occasioned no mishaps we're aware of. He does drink too much, and his marriage to a willful, discontented woman—a failed ballerina—has been quite tempestuous, not to mention a considerable embarrassment to the family, but as Alex remarked only last week, he does well simply to remain among the living. I try, as best I can, to share my eldest son's condescension—as though I too, the whole year round, could boast a thousand miles dividing me and Joey.

"So," I ask now, "how is Barbara doing?"

"She's all right," Joey says gloomily. "She's gotten this part-time dancing job. It makes her feel—validated."

"Well, good for her. We all need that."

"It's her word, not mine."

So they've had some argument, and this accounts for Joey's dour mood. I've begun to breathe easier when he half turns to me and says, imploringly: "I hate to ask this, but what did the doctor say?"

"The doctor? Which one?"

"The one in Chicago, Dad. They did some more tests last week—?"

"Right. It's not benign," I say quickly. "I wish you'd keep your eye on the road."

Unconsciously he has slowed to about forty, and on either side the traffic whizzes by. Obedient, as always, to the letter but not the spirit, he sits with his eyes trained vacantly ahead, all his earnest attention still on me. I seem to feel his body heat, radiating from his side of the car.

"We knew that already, Dad"—I feel a pang at his tone of weary

patience, like an adult dealing with a precocious, intricate obduracy—
"but I thought these new tests were meant to—to determine—"

Why should his faltering give me a surge of joy?

"They estimated anywhere from three months to a year," I say prosaically, "depending on what decision is made down here."

"But why would anyone choose a shorter—" but then, comprehending, he stops himself. Audibly, he takes a gulp of air. "This young guy at Emory, you know, he's had amazing success with these so-called hopeless cases. The even did a story on him on the six o'clock news."

"We didn't know that," I say idly.

A brief pause, as if stymied by the "we," but then: "And Alex seems impressed with him, just from talking with him on the phone. And the two doctors have been in touch, of course. Alex thinks—"

"All of Alex's opinions are well known to me."

I spoke more harshly than I intended, but decide to let it stand. Poor Joey, who's only trying to assume his part in all of this, glances quickly aside, hurt, then accelerates the car and, after a moment, sneezes. I sit erect and watchful. The skyline, once we've left the freeway, becomes an unassimilable surrounding of lighted towers, neon signs, slowed traffic. With a maximum of jolts and cursings Joey maneuvers us along Peachtree Street where, in the midtown section, Joey and Barbara live in their high-rise condominium. I find myself hoping that Barbara won't be home. The car's chill has, after all, begun to affect me, bringing a dull ache to the joints of my knees and hands. I imagine lowering myself, slowly, into a tub of lukewarm water, my glasses left beside the sink so that only in a blurred, wavering fashion can I contemplate my hollowed-out chest and abdomen, desiccated genitals, long thin bluish spindly legs. If I should feel a familiar throbbing near the base of my skull, then a slowly radiating darkness whose source is that spoiled part of me, that smallish clump of festering, rotted fruit, perhaps I'll sit in my twelve inches of colorless water and wait for the final dark wave and not even cry out for help.

We are stopped for the ticket at Joey's parking deck, and though my thoughts have exhausted me I say, irrelevantly, "I wonder if your mother could have intended this."

For reasons of his own, Joey doesn't answer.

Irrelevance. I am prone, lately, to sudden stray remarks, murmurings; though enunciated crisply enough, and ranging from the jocose to the vituperatively bitter, these are, I must assume, brushed quickly aside by my auditors as the mumblings of an old man's dream. My saying to Alex that Marguerite had loved snow and frigid weather. My offhand comment to the flight attendant about "my wife" and how she had planned out my winters to the end. The cryptic remark to Joey, which contained the implication that his mother had possessed a certain morally ambiguous omniscience, a prevision of the long, sterile aftermath stretching beyond her death, and even some notion that my summers and winters, arranged in this way, might keep her image perpetually clear and glittering before me. An implication that elicited, appropriately, a reproachful silence even from the tolerant Joey, whom I suspect of a sentimental, unflagging devotion to the memory of his mother.

His mother. My wife. Marguerite.

Several days pass, and then one afternoon I find myself at the door of my smallish middle bedroom, straining to hear an argument between Joey and Barbara that is taking place in the living room. The door is opened an inch, half an inch. Here the doors squeak; sounds carry cruelly through the small rooms; the children don't think to lower their voices. When Marguerite and I first walked through here, eight years ago, she remarked that the place didn't seem well-built—the floor creaked in places, she felt a draft coming from somewhere—but that nothing was well-built any more and at least it was new. It would suit Barbara and Joey for a few years, until they decided to make a normal life for themselves out in the suburbs. I can still see Marguerite's precise, sharp gestures, noting a wallpaper she liked or a door frame that seemed slightly crooked. Here, there. Pro and con. Finally she had pronounced herself satisfied, and naturally the children were very pleased with their wedding present—though unaware that years later Barbara would still be a failed ballerina and Joey stuck in a time frame where, as if a mediocre, mildly comical film were being endlessly replayed, he broke things and walked into walls and fell victim to small, vexing illnesses normally reserved for children. Since arriving, I've noticed with an old maid's disapproval how they've let their home fall into an alarming desuetude—the furniture ratty and stained, the carpet soiled, every shelf or knickknack blurred by dust, ashtrays heaped with Barbara's peach-colored cigarette butts. The kitchen sink is full of unwashed dishes. A stale, sickly-sweet odor, tinged with the faint smell of rot, hangs in the air like heavy, invisible gauze. No, Marguerite could not have intended this for me. I stand with my ear to the door's crack, straining.

"Let him do whatever he wants," Barbara says for the third or fourth time. "It's as simple as that, really."

"There's a difference, Barbara, between what he says he wants and what he *wants*."

My son, the psychologist. When I informed him, this morning over "breakfast"—two pieces of burnt toast, a cup of cloudy tea—that I really felt I must return to Chicago, he gave me what, for him, is a penetrating stare, his exhaustion-ringed eyes narrowing and his own cup quickly set down, sloshing tea into the saucer. "Have you been talking to Alex?" he asked and then, more darkly: "Or to Barbara?" "I called Alex last night," I replied, "and told him what the doctor said. He was reluctant, he made me repeat the doctor's words a dozen times, but finally he agreed. As for Barbara, how would I talk to her? She's never home." Joey had stared into his teacup, frowning mystically. He was already half an hour late for work, and had yet to shave or change out of an old pair of iridescent-orange overalls that he wears around the house like a second skin. "I don't know what you told Alex," he said finally, "but the doctor told *me* that you should stay here. The weather's warmer, and the facilities are better." My lips formed a smile as I flung a skeletal hand toward the breakfast-room windows: "This is your glorious weather?" I asked. It was drizzling steadily, the temperature in the low forties. "As for the doctor, I don't like him much. He's a know-it-all, and far too young. And anyway," suddenly intense, self-righteous, "an old man should be able to choose where he wants to die." That took the wind out of Joey's sails. Getting up from the table he said, whining, "I really don't want you to leave," but in my imagination I was already back inside that large, solid, well-lighted bedroom, the smiling moist-eyed Laura bringing me something on a tray.

For the first time since my arrival I've spent all of today indoors. No doctor's appointment, and thanks to the cold rain I missed the prescribed morning walk. Joey telephoned from work every couple of hours, but aside from this I've had relative peace. Barbara was gone the whole day, as usual, to dance lessons or to the stylish coffee shops where she meets her rowdy friends, other "artists" whose lives are as pointless and unproductive as her own. Yet I don't dislike her—she has a certain feistiness, a blindness to her own mediocrity—and have not resented her neglect. For much of the afternoon I sat in the overstuffed wingback in the living room, staring out at the bleak drizzling cityscape and dreaming myself northward, back into the home of "the Alexander Baldwins"—as they're known in the society pages—where I am often, between the regimented Alex and the sympathetic Laura, a bone of contention but am myself left in some white shadowless sphere of contentment, a soul's eternal, placid winter that forces troubling memories and internal frettings and even physical pain to recede, to diminish, to become attenuated and drained of color. Here, that peace is threatened every moment. Accidents happen. Unexpected things are said. I sometimes find myself hobbling around my bedroom, in circles, or mentally drafting long, plaintive letters to Marguerite, crammed with devotion and senseless pleading. Is it any wonder I should want to escape, despite Marguerite's own wishes? Even the pain has increased since I arrived, my spine and the back of my head throbbing in the dead of night.

So this afternoon's taste of peace was blissful, a prevision of days to come, and later, still straining to hear, I'm pleased even by the children's argument, the antiphonal and almost predictable back-and-forth of it, as if some monolithic pendulum were to swing between weakness and strength, anxiety and comfort.

Joey is saying, weakly and anxiously enough, "You don't even give a damn, you're just like Alex. Purely selfish, absorbed in your own routine."

Barbara snorts with laughter. "And what are *you* absorbed in?" I can picture the shake of her thin, rather equine head, its small ponytail swishing in punctuation. "The point is, he's not a child but an old man. He has the right to make his own decisions."

She speaks in her pragmatic, offhand way, as if she could simultaneously be doing other things—paying bills, knitting a sweater—and still comfortably win any argument with Joey. I can see him slouched in the wingback, pink-nostriled, staring morosely at the floor.

"You neglect him," he says pointlessly. "He might like it here if you'd be more attentive. I'll bet Laura doesn't leave him to make his own lunch."

"No, because Laura's a nonentity who doesn't have anything better to do. I've got a career, Joey, or anyway as much of one as you have. Why don't *you* stay home and take care of him."

Good for her. Joey is sighing, as he always does when he throws—literally—his hands up into the air. With weak sarcasm he says, "And I suppose Mother's wishes don't count for anything? Her saying that he should winter down here with us?"

Barbara exhales noisily; she must be smoking. "You're not conscious of it, I know," she says tolerantly, "but you speak of her as if she were a dictator, laying down the law for everyone else. The fact is that she's dead, he's alive. So I vote with him."

"Don't speak disrespectfully of Mother," Joey warns. But his voice is about to crack.

Barbara's manner can soften, very suddenly, once Joey is thoroughly vanquished; she is a graceful winner. I see her crossing to him, putting fingers in his tousled hair. She says, "Just try not to worry, you sweet dope, things will work themselves out. You're really a lot like him, in certain ways—I've noticed that through the years. And that's why you don't get along."

There is just enough time for Joey to say, in a strangled voice, "But this is the last winter, Barb, and if he goes back now—" before I manage, struggling, to get the door closed.

Marguerite, on her deathbed, had said in a clear bell-like voice, "You'll sell the house, of course. It would be pointless, your living here alone...." She gestured weakly, indicating not only the two dozen empty, high-ceilinged rooms but also the forty-odd years of our life together (the house had been, of course, a wedding present from Marguerite's father) and a future that, once she was gone, would be hopelessly diminished. Her hand was pale, ringless; it fluttered briefly in the air. "Yes, it would be impossible," I murmured, though she hadn't looked at me and didn't now.

What a difference the final illness makes!—her honey-colored hair had turned a limp iron-gray, her flesh had thinned cruelly along the bones of her face and hands, her lips were dry and sore-looking. Standing beside the bed in a dark suit, white-haired by then but still physically robust, I felt awkward in my good health, and suddenly very afraid of Marguerite. I could only repeat, "Impossible," and then Alex stepped forward to take command. I took a step back, relieved. I maintained the gravely attentive, deferential air of a family retainer, and while Alex talked with his mother in low, businesslike tones, Laura quietly took my hand. In the shadows beyond the floor of the bed stood Joey and Barbara, also holding hands; they both looked terrified.

"Don't worry, he can come live with us," Alex told his mother. "He doesn't have the—the ties to Atlanta that you have, so I'm sure that Chicago will suit him fine...."

Watching Marguerite, who was staring intently into Alex's eyes, I remembered how upset she had been when Alex, a graduate of the Emory business school, had accepted a position with a Northern firm; she had consoled herself by proclaiming his behavior rebellious, independent-minded, and characteristic of her family, which it was, and as a temporary aberration we would all laugh about someday, which it was not. She could never like the idea, of course, that Alex's life could take root so far from home, but because he prospered she accepted it, and he made partial amends by marrying a girl of impeccable Southern background. After his marriage, regular trips to Chicago became part of our yearly routine. We even invested in a shopping center and several residential developments there—"business interests" which I kept an eye on, whenever we came to town, while Alex and Marguerite visited. I'd never thought of Chicago as a future home, of course; but, my own family having long since died off, home for me had become wherever Marguerite was, and now that she was dying it seemed appropriate that she make any decisions about my future. While she and Alex talked I listened disinterestedly, as if they were discussing the fate of a stranger.

"But what about Joey," Marguerite protested, vaguely, "I don't want the family split apart...."

Alex patted her hand, all stoical patience. "It's been split apart for years, Mother, but we'll have Joey up regularly for visits. He can come whenever he wants."

My wife shook her head, frowning slightly and trying to lick her lips. Her tongue looked purplish and swollen.

"No, he'd never come, and anyway you'd forget to invite him...." She thought for a moment and then, her voice clear and bell-like again: "Your father could winter down here, where it's warmer, and then spend the rest of the year with you and Laura. That would work, wouldn't it?"

Alex said, "Or course it would," and unexpectedly, from across the room Barbara piped up, "We'd love to have him." Even Laura said, "It sounds like a lovely arrangement." Joey said nothing, but perhaps he hadn't heard: by then he had begun to weep, softly. I was standing there recalling how much he had cried as a baby.

Old men spend a great deal of time recalling things, after all, and our memories are selective: I'm hardly confident that Marguerite's deathbed scene was centered on my own fate, as I seem to be suggesting, or even that the problem generated much emotion from anyone concerned. The entire memory has been spurred by Joey's weeping—he is weeping now, as we sit pointed toward the airport but stalled in bumper-to-bumper five o'clock traffic—and the tears I remember were surely over the loss of his mother rather than the thought of my own future homelessness. Even now I sense the source of his grief as somehow apart from me, something my presence has crystallized for a brief painful moment. Perhaps it's the memory of his mother, once again; or the thought of his own wasted life.... But in an hour I'll be on that airplane, flying north: I try to think of that.

My Joey is drinking. As we inch forward, here on this crammed expressway, he takes regular swigs from the small metal flask he keeps in the glove compartment, and talks a great deal—whining, pleading, arguing with himself or with me—and now is weeping openly, unashamed. I sit staring forward, trying to ignore his jagged sobs, the sweetish stench of the liquor. Outside the sky is gray, the clouds low-hung and threatening, and the air is unusually warm. I try to pay attention to this weather, to the other cars, to watch for signs announcing the number of miles left between us and the airport....

Joey is saying, "It's always been the same, that's what gets me. It *never* changes. Even before Mother died, it was always what *Alex* wanted, what *Alex* thought.... Shit," he says, taking a long swig, "He had the wool pulled over *her* eyes, didn't he?" But he isn't asking me, of course; he's just asking. "...And he never was fair to you, even Barb noticed that. Always talking about the Holloway investments and the Holloway money, as if you hadn't earned some of that money yourself. You were a broker, you knew how to invest it. That's what counted."

At this I glance over, irritated. "You don't know what you're talking about."

But Joey is nodding to himself, not hearing. He began this drive with a plea for reason, insisting that I *must* stay in Atlanta, that my illness *could* be reversed with the very best treatment, and by now has become reasonless himself. He says wildly, "You see what has happened, don't you? You see what he did to us? He cut us off, made us into nothing, big clever Alex with his white strong teeth and his fancy brains and his charm, his charm. Even Mother fell for it."

"Quit blaming Alex for everything," I tell him. "He's just the type who likes to take charge, to keep everything moving along efficiently. Your mother was like that, too."

"Hah, he takes charge all right. He's like one of those computers he loves so much, spitting out the answers for everybody. Take it or leave it, that's what he says. I'm the Fascist and you people are the slaves, I'm the great white hope and you people out there, you little peons, you'd better just listen to me. That's what he says to himself."

"You're drunk," I tell him calmly. "Now look, that inside lane is starting to move."

"And the fucking hell of it is, everybody listens. Everybody bows and says Yes, Allah, anything you fucking say. Not just the family, I'll bet—everybody."

"Joey, don't make me late for the airport."

At this he straightens, begins trying to change to the faster lane. But still he mutters under his breath. He takes a drink from the flask. "God," he says, husky-voiced again, sentimental, "do I feel sorry for Mother. What she must have gone through, in those last years. Seeing how Alex had turned out."

"What, are you crazy? She adored Alex."

"No, she knew better." He jabs his finger into the air. "At some level, she knew better than that. I promise you."

He has changed lanes, but now the traffic is clogged again. "Joey, maybe we should exit and take a side street. We're in danger, really, of missing that airplane—"

"Everything would have been so different, without him. We would have had a normal family. Why should we be separated anyway?—why are we always driving to airports, always wrangling long-distance over when you'll visit or when you won't visit? It's not natural, it's not *good* for people to live like this.... This stupid plan, having you fly back and forth all the time—"

"Joey, that was your mother's plan."

"—it's not right somehow, its inhuman. You can say what you want, but I know Alex is behind your flying back like this—I know how he manipulates people, making them feel guilty. Even Mother, he even manipulated *her*."

"Listen, will you stop this talk? Will you pay attention to the driving? It should be obvious that I *want* to leave, I'm not feeling well and I need to go home. Even the doctor said so, he said I should be wherever I feel safest. Because they can't do anything, the doctors. They *can't*."

He looks over, blinking. "But—but this is your home—"

"No, this is not my home, this is crazy-land." It has begun at the base of my skull, that insidious throbbing. When this happens I weaken quickly, the blood rushing to the place of rot. And here is my son, thwarting me. Spouting these ridiculous lies. "It's true," I tell him, "that I often do things just to please Alex, just to keep the peace. But today, this is not one of them. In fact, he doesn't want me back, he wants me out of his hair, and I don't blame him. But today I'm being a selfish and stubborn old man, I'm going back where I belong. I don't belong here, and man, I'm going back where I belong. I don't belong here, and I never did. Your life is crazy, your house is a mess, I can't stand it there. After this past week, it's a wonder I'm not already dead."

"What—why are you—"

"Yes, *dead*. I'll get there soon enough, but at least I want some peace. I deserve that, don't I? Don't I deserve, at long last, to get what I want? Yes, it's true that Alex is somewhat manipulative, but you want to know where he learned it? Do you? From your bitch of a mother, that's who."

Joey, dead-pale, seems utterly stymied; he doesn't try to speak. Only a moment passes before we are jolted forward, my head slamming against the doorframe before I can raise an arm for protection. In his shock, Joey has relinquished control of the car and let it ram into the car ahead of us, which then hit the guard rail. Now both cars are stopped. Before it even began, it is over. We were driving only five miles an hour, no one is hurt seriously, we both sit for a moment in shocked silence. My head is throbbing. Spinning. I'm thinking that I must get out of here, there is somewhere I must go....

Finally Joey opens his mouth. "You take that back," he says childishly. "You didn't mean that." But he is weeping again; he doesn't count. "We have to stick together, you and I. They're so damn cold, so heartless, but we can't let them—can't let them kill us—"

I struggle to open the door, keeping my other hand cupped at the back of my skull. Must get out of here; must get away....

"My God," Joey cries, "what are you doing! The lane next to us is moving, you can't—" but I don't listen, I get the door open and stumble away from the car.

Outside, it has begun to rain. Enormous, tepid raindrops gently pelting me. I hear the blaring of horns, the sound of someone shouting from behind. But I must get away from here. Hobbling, clutching my head with one hand as I navigate toward the side of the expressway,

I struggle blindly forward, as if coaxed by some imagined wintry sphere in the far distance, out there, where Marguerite is waiting. Around me there are screechings, raised voices. So much noise and strife!—so much confusion! I move aimlessly through it all, a stumbling and contemptible old man. How fitting his destiny, this old man pathetically sick, dying, seeking to brush his knuckles against a stranger's car window in heavy traffic, begging for mercy, for shelter.... My head throbs wildly, even my eyesight seems to fail, yet before that moment of crashing, inevitable darkness I'm able to think, quite clearly, *Yes, she must have intended this for me—*

Greg Johnson (1953)

Johnson was born in Tyler, Texas, and has lived in Atlanta since 1976. He has published poetry, essays, two book-length critical studies, and two collections of short stories, DISTANT FRIENDS (1990) and A FRIENDLY DECEIT (1992). "Wintering" is taken from DISTANT FRIENDS.

"Wintering" was reprinted by permission of the Ontario Review Press. "Wintering" originally appeared in the VIRGINIA QUARTERLY REVIEW and was collected in DISTANT FRIENDS (Ontario Review Press, 1990).

About the Editor

BEN FORKNER is professor of English and American literature at the University of Angers in France. A graduate of Stetson University in Florida, he received his Ph.D. from The University of North Carolina at Chapel Hill. He has published essays on writers from Ireland and the American South and has edited several anthologies of short stories: MODERN IRISH SHORT STORIES, A NEW BOOK OF DUBLINERS, and LOUISIANA STORIES. With Patrick Samway, S.J., he has co-edited four anthologies of Southern literature: STORIES OF THE MODERN SOUTH, STORIES OF THE OLD SOUTH, A MODERN SOUTHERN READER (Peachtree), and A NEW READER OF THE OLD SOUTH (Peachtree).

CPSIA informatio
Printed in the US
241654LV